Angel Strings

ANGEL
STRINGS

A NOVEL BY GARY EBERLE

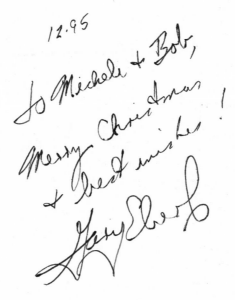

12.95

To Michele + Bob,
Merry Christmas
+ best wishes!
Gary Eberle

COFFEE HOUSE PRESS :: MINNEAPOLIS

Coffee House Press is a non-profit literary arts organization whose operations are supported, in part, by a grant provided by the Minnesota State Arts Board, through an appropriation by the Minnesota State Legislature, and by a grant from the National Endowment for the Arts. Additional support received this past year has been provided by the Lila Wallace-Reader's Digest Fund, the McKnight Foundation, the Lannan Foundation, the Jerome Foundation, Target Stores, Dayton's and Mervyn's by the Dayton Hudson Foundation, the General Mills Foundation, the St. Paul Companies, the Honeywell Foundation, the Star Tribune/Cowles Media Company, the Beverly J. and John A. Rollwagen Fund of the Minneapolis Foundation, the Prudential Foundation, a major grant from the Andrew W. Mellon Foundation, and through contributions from generous individuals.

Coffee House Press books are available to the trade through our primary distributor, Consortium Book Sales & Distribution, 1045 Westgate Drive, Saint Paul, MN 55114. For personal orders, catalogs or other information, write to:
Coffee House Press
27 North Fourth Street, Suite 400, Minneapolis, MN 55401

Library of Congress CIP data
Eberle, Gary.
    Angel strings : a novel / by Gary Eberle.
        p. cm.
    ISBN 1-56689-034-9 (pbk. : alk. paper)
1. eccentrics and eccentricities—United states—Fiction. 2. Men—Travel—United States—Fiction. 3. Musicians—United States—Fiction.   I. Title.
PS3555. B47A8 1995
813' .54—DC20

For Sue and Will

CHAPTER ONE

My father, the Amazing Raymond, was a magician, and when I was young I was his assistant. Everybody tells me how lucky I was to have had such an interesting childhood, but, believe me, it is not easy having a father whose idea of a good time is to blow your head off every night and twice on Wednesdays and Saturdays. On a regular basis, he would pierce my body with swords, saw me in half, guillotine my hands off, or kill me with arrows in the St. Sebastian illusion. The audiences thought this was truly amazing, but I can tell you from experience it is not half as interesting as you think.

Learning too much about the backstage aspects of magic tricks too early in life is not a good idea. It's like knowing how sausage is made and then being expected to enjoy eating it. I mean—and I am speaking from experience here—you don't want to know, too early, what really happens inside the arrowhead illusion or what goes on inside the box where you get sawed in two. It gives you the impression, right from the start, that everything in life is only a trick, a carefully crafted illusion. When you've been inside the trick since birth and you've seen the cheap wires and gears, and you've manipulated the silk threads and black velvet bags and mirrors, and you've learned how they all work, then it spoils you for later.

I grew up used to things not being what they seemed. My dad kept his illusions around the Airstream trailer we traveled in so he could pick them up and practice whenever he had a free moment. He was fairly good at sleight of hand, but he had to keep in constant practice. All day long he would roll half dollars and quarters smoothly from knuckle to knuckle, or palm things, or practice his drops. From the time I was in diapers, I was used to cards coming out of my ears and nose, flowers sprouting from my dad's shirt cuffs, lit cigarettes coming out of nowhere at odd moments. You'd think this would be a wonderful way to grow up, but after a while

I didn't even notice. In fact, sometimes it got downright irritating. I'd pick up a glass for a drink and the next thing I knew there would be a goldfish swimming in it. Or I'd grab an umbrella to step outside on a rainy day and it would turn into tattered silks and I'd stand there looking like a circus clown with a face full of rain. Sticks would turn into ropes. Ropes would turn into silks. I'd take a hankie from a drawer and end up with a string of thirty American flags. I'd try to play a game of cards with some friends and find out I had a Fox Lake deck with all Queens of Spades. I never even knew there was such a thing as a straight deck until I was in high school and we settled in Las Vegas where Dad got his semipermanent lounge act at the Lucky Lady. (Imagine a child having to learn about straight decks in Vegas!)

I shouldn't be blamed, therefore, for getting into my late twenties and not trusting people or things very much, or for being a little wary of life, or for believing, deep down inside of me somewhere, that this whole business of life, the universe and all was some kind of magic trick, a feat of *legerdemain* performed by a cosmic magician who, when you weren't looking, would steal your watch, clip your necktie, or rip up your last five dollar bill and leave pigeon shit in your tuxedo pockets.

This is all by way of saying that the night I met Violet Tansy for the first time, back in Porkville, Ohio, I was not expecting much. I assumed meeting her was just another cosmic trick, a gimmick that sooner or later would go off like a cigar load and leave me standing there stunned and blinking with a face full of ash. I certainly didn't think it would be any kind of magic, and I never suspected it would lead to magic of a kind that would make my dad's stage tricks, with their false bottoms and mirrored backs, seem downright trivial. And, as with the best of illusions, it happened when I wasn't even looking.

That night, I was picking and grinning at the Dew Dropp Inn just outside Porkville, Ohio, trying to earn enough money to get me to New York and put me up for a couple of days so I could audition for a rock group that was booked to front for Snidely Whiplash on a major tour. About six months before, I had separated from my wife Hazel back in Las Vegas because, as I told her one night when we'd come home from the Lucky Lady, I wanted to do something more with my life than what I was doing at that time, which was playing backup guitar in the house band of the Lucky Lady casino where we were into the tenth year of a show called "The Dead Superstar Review." Every night the corpses walked again—Judy, Marilyn, Elvis, Janis, Jimi, Liberace— and sang their songs or did the schtick that made them famous. The audiences loved it, but I was getting tired of all these nights of the living dead. I knew I was in bad shape when not even resurrection impressed me anymore. And then, one night, as I stood there playing rhythm guitar and listening to Earl Fleming, our Elvis impersonator, sing "My Way," something inside me snapped.

"I've got to go, Hazel," I said when we got back to our miniranch on the north side of town.

"Go where?" she said, coming into the living room with a Scotch on the rocks, which she held up to her forehead to beat the intense Nevada heat while we waited for the air conditioning to kick in.

"Out," I said, vaguely waving my hand toward the street and the horizon beyond that.

"Where to? It's kind of late, isn't it?" She sat down on the Herculon sofa and pulled off her false eyelashes and tossed them on the end table, where they lay like curled-up millipedes. (She was a blackjack dealer at the Lucky Lady and felt she got bigger tips if she looked glamorous.)

"I mean I'm going really *out*, Hazel. Out . . ." I had to think a moment but couldn't come up with any real destination, so I just pointed and sputtered, "There! Out there. Anywhere that isn't here." That was about as definite as I could get.

She wrinkled up her nose. "Right now?" she said, peeling off her panty hose and wadding them in a ball. She was used to my late night trips after shows. She tossed her stockings toward the hall bathroom and put her feet up on the coffee table. Her pale flabby calves hung there like fish bellies. "What for?"

"Because my life's going nowhere," I said, and even as I said it I knew I was about to go off on a riff of the sort I usually don't get into unless I've had a few drinks after the show with the Dead Superstars band. "Because I'm sick of doing what I'm doing. Because this town is driving me nuts. Because I think I'm too good a musician to be backing up dead Elvises every night." And so on until I had convinced myself that fame, fortune and immortality were all mine if only I would go and seek them. I got up and threw all my gear into the back of my van so I could hit the road and meet my destiny. By that time, Hazel got the idea this wasn't an ordinary trip, and she stood in the driveway in her bare feet screaming at the top of her lungs that I had gone totally nuts. As for me, I was so crazy by that point that I started singing back at her the words to "My Way," and the neighbors turned on their porch lights. I went up to Hazel, my wife, and looked her in the eye and, like a lawyer summing up his case, said, "I didn't realize it until tonight, Hazel, but this is what I want out of life: that some day after I'm dead, somebody like Earl Fleming will impersonate *me*. I'm tired of being a backup player. I want to be a headliner, I want to be a star, and I've got to do it *My Way*! That's what Earl was singing about tonight!" And with that, I roared out of the driveway and was halfway to Flagstaff before I knew I was headed east.

When I saw the sun coming up over the rim of the desert, I got that cool, reptilian feeling you always get when the light of day starts to illuminate the wreckage of the night before. But it was too late to turn around. I had set myself up, and if I went back to Hazel now she would have the upper hand on me for the rest of my life. I said stupid things that night, and between us we managed to dredge up every hard feeling and regret we had from seven years of marriage. By the time I finished my breakfast of cold watery eggs at Denny's in Flagstaff, I had convinced myself that what I was doing was the right thing. There was too much blood on the carpet for me to go back to Las Vegas for a while, and Hazel and I both needed time, I thought, to lick the wounds we'd inflicted. But even more, in the sober light of the desert dawn, I told myself I could make more of my life out here, on the road, than I had so far in Vegas. I didn't jump up there in the restaurant and start singing "My Way," but I told myself it was time to make my move to the Big Time. There was something huge out there waiting for me, something enormous. Deep down in my gut I could feel it calling me, and all I had to do was go out and find it. There was no turning back until I had become a living legend. My destiny was out there. Somewhere. Someplace. In America.

By the time I hit Porkville, Ohio, several months later, however, I had not made a whole lot of what you would call progress.

Porkville was about as close to nowhere as I had ever been, and I had been close lots of times when I was traveling with my dad in the early days. The only reason you might have ever heard of Porkville at all was because of their famous hams. And maybe you might also have read how the Porkville city council recently voted to take out the parking meters in downtown Porkville and replace them with hitching posts because there was a group of conservative Mennonites in the surrounding county who refused to pay taxes in any form or to hitch their buggies to anything that fed money into a government, and since the Mennonites raised the famous Amish hams that made Porkville what it was, and because the market for organically raised pig meat was growing, the city fathers bowed to religious freedom and took action. That was how Porkville became famous for two days a few months before I arrived for being the only town in America to *take out* parking meters and *put in* hitching posts. Someone from CBS *Sunday Morning* even showed up to make a two-minute story out of it. It was the first thing people mentioned to me when I arrived at the Dew Dropp Inn. Up on the wall, they had a couple of laminated newspaper stories about it right next to the deer heads. Like me, Porkville was verging on fame.

To tell the truth, I probably would have forgotten about Porkville and the Dew Dropp Inn altogether except that it was there I met Violet Tansy.

I had been traveling for several months, playing for drinks and change in forgettable places like the Dew Dropp. My dream of getting started with some stage work and meeting some big stars got me as far as Branson, Missouri, where I beat my head against the closed doors of theaters and clubs for several weeks before giving up and heading for Nashville where I had the same luck. Every street corner bar and studio in those towns had good guitar players spilling out of the windows.

After a couple more months of aimless traveling, I got desperate and a crazy idea came to me. I called Maurice, my dad's old agent, who still had an office in New York, but it wasn't Maurice who answered. Maurice had booked himself into a long-term engagement at a golf course on Sanibel Island, and the business had been taken over by his son Murray, who vaguely remembered me and my dad.

"Oh, yeah, you," he said, after I'd jogged his memory. "You're the kid who kept getting his head blown off. Great act. You still alive?"

"Sort of," I said. I explained my situation to Murray, and he sounded enthusiastic.

"Got just the thing, babes," he said. "Snidely Whiplash is about to go on tour and the rhythm guitarist in their opening act came down with some kind of STD that needs, like, immediate attention, man. I can get you an audition if you can get to New York within the next week—for old time's sake, huh? Your old man's act used to break me up."

"Is this for real?" I asked. "I got a chance to open for Snidely Whiplash?"

"It's for real, babes," said Murray, "provided you get here in time. The group's called Sclapped, don't ask me what it means, but they're getting hot. Their rhythm guitarist was a total fuck-up. I don't believe him, coming down with a disease when he's booked on the edge of the big time. Whatever happened to professionalism, eh? Here we are a month away from opening, we got stadiums booked in thirteen major venues in the continental U.S., and he gets himself a dose of superclap. Well, fuck him. He'll be the Stuart Sutcliffe of the decade. Who remembers him? He could have been the fifth Beatle. Sclapped is gonna be bigger than Snidely Whiplash someday. Can you pick things up fast?"

"Hey," I said, "I just spent ten years in Vegas learning new stuff by dead people every week. You name it, I can play it. I'll be there, man. Wow, opening for Snidely Whiplash."

"You'd have to jam pretty intense to get it together, but if you can cut the chops at the audition, the gig's yours. We're desperate, man."

"Snidely Whiplash!" I said. "Their *Headcrackers* video is topping the charts, isn't it?"

"Mega big time," said Murray, "And this new act that's fronting for them is only a step away. Think of it, man, thirteen cities, thirteen stadiums full of screaming fans, thousands of babes ripping their clothes off for you. What a life, eh?"

"Sounds like a good career move," I said.

"Career move?" said Murray, "This is more than a career move, man. This is fulfillment. What was it Freud said that every man wanted?"

"Uh, power, fame, riches and the love of beautiful women?"

"No, man. Sex, drugs and rock and roll! Ciao. See you in the Big Apple next week. In the meantime, you got my fax number, right? Keep your head on your shoulders, man. Get it? Get it?"

To tell the truth, I had never heard of Sclapped and I didn't much care for Snidely Whiplash's music, but the idea of playing to stadiums full of ravening fans every week for the next few months and maybe finally hitting it big had me high as a kite.

This was my last night in Porkville. I had been playing rhythm guitar for three nights with the Porkville Pony X-Press, whose regular axman, Larry, was on National Guard duty that week. From a three-night stand in a Porkville Bar to fronting for the hottest heavy rock act in America in only two weeks. Was show business great or what?

The Pony X-Press finished a set, and I had some time to kill before we went back on, so I grabbed a long neck beer from a waitress and stepped out into the parking lot for a breath of air that didn't have cigarette smoke or the sweat of farmhands in it. It was a hot, sticky summer night, but the wall of the Dew Dropp Inn felt cool against my back. Honky-tonk music from the juke box spilled out of the screen door, and inside some folks were doing the Texas two-step and line-dancing to "Achy Breaky Heart." I stood there watching bugs spatter themselves to death against the flickering neon sign of the Dew Dropp Inn and thought about how sweet the future suddenly looked. In the time I had been on the road, I had felt my old life slipping away, like the person I had been back in Vegas wasn't there anymore and the person I was going to be was out there somewhere waiting for me to find him. During that time I realized that my old life didn't fit me any-more, and even though I wasn't sure where I was going all those months, I had faith something important was about to happen to me. And now I knew what it was. I was about to shuck my old life the way a caterpillar sheds its chrysalis, and I was about to fly away into the superstar stratosphere on the coattails of Snidely Whiplash.

Even Hazel, whom I called every couple of weeks just to say hello and to lie to her about how close I was getting to hitting the big time, was fading in my mind. Now that I had been away from her for six months, I realized maybe we never really had a great relationship. We got married young after we met at the Lucky Lady. She'd drop in and catch pieces of the show during her breaks from the blackjack table, and we simply fell into going home together, and then that turned into getting married because it was the thing you did when you didn't know where else to go with a relationship. And since then things didn't get ugly, exactly, but we had just gone on automatic pilot the way couples do. We had the house, the car, and the van. We even had a dog one time. So we didn't question things. But since I'd left, I discovered that not having her around all the time was like not having a wart. You keep looking at the pale spot on your skin where it used to be, and you think about it, and you realize that it once was part of you, but it had been cut away, and you wonder how it's doing, but you don't want it back, not really. And then I thought about Murray and Snidely Whiplash and the life of the superstars, mega-bucks, and having it all. I thought maybe Hazel and I could patch it up once I bought the beach house in Malibu.

It was then that I noticed the dome light was on in my van, so I went over to check. Everything I owned was in the van except for what I left back at the house in Vegas, and I didn't want to get ripped off.

I opened the door and everything seemed all right, but then I noticed a girl hunched down on the floor in the back of the van, all curled up like she was trying to hide from something.

"What are you doing in here?" I asked.

"My name's Violet Tansy," she said, unfolding herself a little bit. She had a soft southern accent and her first name came out sounding like Vahlet.

"I didn't ask your name," I said.

"I need me a ride, if you don't mind," she said. "I can explain."

I took a flashlight out of the glove compartment and shined it on her. She winced in the light and held up her hand. She could have been a local town girl or farm girl who had been ditched by her boyfriend there at the Dew Dropp. She had straw-colored hair, sort of. I mean it was a bit blonde and a bit red and a bit brown here and there in patches. She had colored it so many times that it wasn't clear just what color it had started out as, though her eyebrows were dark, and I guessed that was close to her original hair color.

She looked like one of those lost mutts you see wandering the streets sometimes or like one of those small animals that shoot out of the woods and stand there, surprised to find themselves on the highway but too nervous to move and too scared to stay. They usually end up as road kill.

Even though it was as hot as the backside of a gila monster that night, she was wearing a tan leatherette jacket with Western trim on it. Appliquéd flowers and roses and vines spilled across the yoke and around her shoulders and down the front on either side. She had very light skin with a few pimples on her jawline, and her eyes looked scared in the flashlight. She was probably barely under twenty but she looked a few years older because she was so tired and drawn out. She could even have been considered pretty, I guess, in the way waitresses can look pretty if you're in the right mood.

On the other hand, she also could be the type of girl who was used to getting mixed up with the wrong kind of man, and now she was mixed up with me. I decided there was nothing I could do to help her, but I felt a little bad just throwing her out, so I looked around the van and realized there wasn't anything worth stealing in it after all, and, besides, in a few weeks I'd be traveling first class with Sclapped and Snidely Whiplash, so I said, "I don't know what kind of trouble you're in, but I'm going back in there to play my guitar some more, and when I come back out I'd like you to be gone, okay? I can't give you any ride."

She nodded and I went back into the Dew Dropp and played out my last set with the Porkville Pony X-Press. Since I was getting paid twenty-five bucks and all I could drink, I hung around and had a few rounds with the band and an old waitress who was called, for no reason I could figure out, Jugs. I impressed them all with my story of how I was about to go off to New York for a big-time audition and how if they kept their cable tuned to MTV they'd probably see me when my video with Sclapped came out, and pretty soon I was rehearsing my Grammy acceptance speech for them, and everybody applauded, and Jugs and the others asked for my autograph, and I signed their bar napkins, and someday, I thought, they'd tell people how I had once played there at the Dew Dropp Inn, and they'd hang newspaper stories about me and Sclapped right next to the ones about the famous hams and the Amish hitching posts. It was well after midnight, and I was pretty well oiled when they shut off the bug-spattered sign of the Dew Dropp Inn, and everybody roared off into the Ohio night. As for me, I had been so taken with my own story of fame that I had not bothered to go to the bathroom before Jugs locked up, so I went behind the building to relieve myself, and when I came back around my van was the only thing left in the parking lot. In a few weeks, I thought, the groupies will be waiting by stadium stage doors, and I enjoyed this moment of solitude before the tidal wave of fame overwhelmed me.

The Ohio night felt dark and sweet, and the crickets were whirring away loud and fast like a circus band. To tell the truth, I had drunk so much I had forgotten about the girl I found in my van earlier until I slid open the side door and discovered she was still there.

Before I could say anything, she started in on me, as if I had never left.

"You see, I need me a ride real bad, mister."

She looked scared and lost and would have reminded me of my kid sister if I'd had a kid sister to be reminded of.

I blew out some air and said, "All right, I guess I can take you home if you're willing to ride with me, but I don't want to get tangled up with any boyfriend or your father or anything like that. I've got a big audition in New York in a few days and the last thing I need tonight is to get my fingers broken or to get shot. You aren't married, are you?"

She shook her head and I got into the driver's seat and took a deep breath. The night air had a sobering effect.

"Well, then, where do you live?"

"Huntington," she said.

I blinked and shook my head. "West Virginia? That's way south from here, isn't it?"

She nodded, but she could probably tell from the look on my face that I wasn't inclined to take her that far.

"Don't worry," she said, "I'm not going back to Huntington. You see, I'm just coming from Norfolk."

"Virginia?" I calculated the distance in my head.

"Don't worry, I'm not going back there either," she said.

"Good," I said. Pause. "Well, just where would you like me to take you tonight?"

"San Diego," she mumbled.

"California?"

She nodded.

"You expect me to drive you to California?" I asked.

"Well, not all the way tonight," she said, "but I saw your plates and figured you were headed west."

"I'm not going west," I said. "I keep Nevada plates on my van because that's the nearest thing I have to a permanent address right now. As a matter of fact, I'm heading east, to New York."

"The thing is," she said, "I went to Norfolk a couple of days ago to see Billy but he wasn't there and I just *got* to get to San Diego by a week from Saturday."

"Who's Billy?"

"He's my boyfriend."

"I thought you said you didn't have a boyfriend."

"Well, not right here, you see. He's in San Diego, or he will be anyway by the time I get there."

"So you expect me to drop my life and take you to California?"

"Well," she said, "I was gonna ask before I climbed in the van, but you weren't around."

"There were lots of other cars out here tonight, lots of other places you could have ended up except inside my van. I'm sorry, but I can't take you west. I'm heading for New York, see. I've got an important audition up there. I'm a musician, see the guitar case?"

She seemed about ready to cry then and her voice was choked as she explained.

"Well, this guy he picked me up in a truck back on I-80 and brung me here to this place and he tried to mess around with me here in the parking lot, grabbing me and all, but I wouldn't let him . . ." She paused and bit her lip, as if trying to decide whether to add something or not. Then she mumbled, "Not with the baby, especially, I wouldn't."

"What did you say?"

"I said not with the baby."

"That's what I thought you said." I got out of the driver's seat—we had been carrying on this conversation through the rearview mirror—and I switched on the dome light and crawled into the back of the van. "You've got a baby with you? Where?"

"Right here," she said, nodding to the back of the van. There in the corner, inside a battered cardboard box that once was full of smaller boxes of Brillo pads, was a baby wrapped up in a dingy motel towel. She went back and got him and brought him back up to the front seat. The baby was smelly. He had on a gray cloth diaper that looked like it had been used and just rinsed out for a few days. The kid couldn't have been more than four months old, if that.

"This is my and Billy's baby boy, isn't he beautiful?" Violet said.

"Good God," I said, "What are you doing out here in the middle of nowhere with a baby in a Brillo box, or shouldn't I ask?"

I shouldn't have asked.

She looked me straight in the eyes for a moment, decided for some crazy reason she had to trust me, and then suddenly she let go with the whole story, weeping and wailing and crying and giggling and laughing all at the same time in one great flow. I must have opened up some sluice gate inside her and everything that had been dammed up came spilling out, as though nobody in the past two days had thought to ask her before why she was hitchhiking from Norfolk to San Diego with a baby in a cardboard box. Now that I think of it, maybe nobody had. Truckers who stop to pick up young girls by the roadside don't usually have babies on their minds.

"You see, it's all about my boyfriend, Billy," she said as she reached into a little bag strung around her neck and pulled out a wrinkled photo of a jug-eared kid in a navy uniform. She shoved the picture at me as if it would explain everything. I looked at it in the dim light from the dome bulb. It was a wallet-sized version of the official color service portrait, the picture they'd use in his hometown paper if he got killed in action. He looked as awkward as a boiled owl in front of the flag.

"That's Billy," she explained. "Billy's in the navy, see? He's a submariner. He wears this T-shirt that's got a skull and cross bones on it and it says 'Death from below' on the front in red letters that drip blood. But you shouldn't think he's violent or anything because he isn't. Doesn't his picture make him look like a hero? He's been out to sea eleven months now, and he doesn't know about the baby. But I heard in Norfolk his ship's going to be in San Diego next week, so I have to get there so he can marry me, but I didn't have any money or anything so I just took the baby and started out hitching. And we got this far but time's running out and you've got to help me, see, because this is a love cause and nothing can stand in the way of a true love cause, can it?"

I scratched my head and didn't know what to say. I couldn't tell if it was a true story or not. It was certainly stupid enough to be true, I suppose, but she might have been lying. As I said, after growing up with my dad the magician and then living for more than ten years in Las Vegas, it was hard for me to accept the idea that there were people out there who weren't on the con.

"Not that I don't believe you or anything," I said, "but how exactly did you end up in Porkville, Ohio, going from Norfolk to San Diego? It's not exactly in between."

"I dunno," she shrugged. "I think I got screwed up around Youngstown somewhere. I didn't have time to grab a map or anything. When I heard Billy was due in San Diego, I knew what I had to do—I headed west and trusted in the Lord." She looked at me earnestly for a moment, and then blurted out, "Hey, it isn't easy hauling a baby around in a box, you know! It doesn't make it any easier to get rides."

"I can imagine," I said.

And then the baby started in crying. "Waaa! WAAAA! WAAAA!" It didn't have any teeth yet, so when it cried there was nothing but two pink lines where his gums were.

Violet took off her jacket and lifted up her T-shirt. She was wearing a bundle of religious medals and lucky charms—rabbits' feet and four-leaf clovers and that sort of stuff—and she shoved the mess aside and stuck the baby's face up to one of her breasts. The baby worked the nipple like there wasn't going to be a tomorrow, and I thought that, in his case, maybe he was on to something. Violet made cooing noises for a while and stroked the baby's fuzzy head.

"Isn't he something?" she asked. "I am truly blessed, you know that?"

"What's your baby's name?" I asked.

"He doesn't have a name yet," she said as the kid made all sorts of sucking noises that filled the night. "That's what Billy and I have to decide when I get to San Diego. But we'll probably call him Billy after his daddy."

Violet looked down at the baby sucking at her breast and then she smiled for the very first time, and I could tell that underneath the road dirt and the ten different hair colors, she was a scared young kid, too young even to know how stupid it was to try to do what she was trying to do. She reminded me of women I'd seen down in the hills of Kentucky and Tennessee who are pretty when they're young but then one day—after five or six kids—their looks drop from them like the leaves from a ginkgo tree. By the time they're thirty they wake up old and nobody knows why. The fact that Violet already had a baby said something about where she was probably headed, and it wasn't San Diego. She sat there rocking the baby in her arms and humming softly to him, her eyes locked on his eyes the way that mothers do to let the child know that there is nothing else in the whole universe that matters.

"Can't you just take us somewhere that way?" she said, jerking her head to where she thought west was. "Then we'll be okay. If you could get us to Route 80—that's the turnpike, isn't it?—that would be okay, too. Can you do that, please, mister? Can you?"

It was hard to say no to her, sitting there feeding her little no-name baby, so I didn't say anything right away. After a few seconds the baby fell asleep, and I could see Violet was dead tired, too, so I finally said, "All right, here's the deal—you can sleep in the van tonight, one night only, but that's it. Tomorrow I'll take you to 1-80 and I'll drop you off there. You see, I've got to get to New York to see this guy about a very important gig. It's a once-in-a-lifetime thing, so I'll take you to the turnpike, but then you're on your own."

"That's all I can ask," she said softly. "The Lord'll provide."

"Uh-huh," I said, though I felt like a crumb.

*

There was a camping spot marked on the Ohio map a few miles from the Dew Dropp Inn. It was down at the end of a dirt road where a rickety wooden bridge crossed a slow-moving stream. There were other camp sites there, but no one else was using them that night. It was a hidden-away place beside the small river, but the closeness of the water didn't make it any cooler.

The effect of the drinks I'd had with the Pony X-Press had pretty well worn off and through the haze, the night felt as sticky and smelly as the inside of an old tennis shoe. The mosquitoes and crickets and tree frogs were buzzing so loud in the woods that it sounded like the inside of a lawnmower. Luckily I had fitted screen windows on my Ford van and I thought we might survive the night. My bed was a ratty piece of foam rubber I had bought and cut to fit the floor of the van.

The van was fine enough for me during the six months I had been on the road, but now that I had visions of a first-class tour bus in my mind, I noticed how shabby it really was. I wished I had covered up the speaker wires with duct tape or something, and I felt embarrassed about all the food wrappers lying around, but Violet Tansy wasn't complaining. In fact, she did not say a word all the way from the Dew Dropp.

The baby had fallen asleep in the box again and Violet's head kept bobbing as we drove to the campsite.

"We can sleep here for the night," I said as I started to unfold my sleeping bag on the floor of the van.

She stayed in the front seat, looking out the window with her arms crossed.

"I'd feel better about it if you were to sleep outside," she said, politely but firmly.

I stopped rolling out the bag.

"Pardon me?"

"I said I think it would be better if you were to sleep outside, us hardly not knowing each other and all."

"You want me to sleep outside?" I asked.

"I'd feel better about it," she said again.

"There are clouds of people-eating mosquitoes out there."

"I just don't think it would be right," she said, "not with the baby in here and all."

"I see."

"It seems to me that one of us has got to sleep outside," she said. "If Billy found out, there's no telling what he might think. And, besides, I got to be with the baby. You don't think I'm going to let my baby sleep outside with all them bugs and snakes and all, do you?"

"Why not?" I said. "You're taking him across the goddamned United States in a cardboard box!"

I waited for her to say something, but she didn't. She simply sat there and refused to move. And I refused to move, too. We sat that way for a long time until I got tired and went on rolling out my sleeping bag.

"You shouldn't do that," she said.

"Do what?" I asked.

"Take the Lord's name in vain," she said. "It isn't right."

"I'll say what I damned-well please," I said, too loud, though I stopped myself before I slipped a god in there.

"WAAA-WAAA-WAAA!"

"Now you've done it," Violet said. "Now you woke the baby up. I told you it wasn't a good idea for the two of us to be in here together at night. Shh-shh. Don't worry, the man won't hurt you, honey, he won't hurt you none."

I grabbed my bag and headed into the night.

"I don't need this, you know," I said. "I'm only doing this because in a couple of weeks I'm going to be sleeping on a giant king-sized overstuffed Sealy Posturepedic bed in a luxury suite somewhere. I'm going first cabin from here on out, hear me? That's why I can take maybe one night sleeping out here because I know it's the end for me. Never again will I have to do this. I'm this far from hitting the big time, hear? Just so you know who you're dealing with."

Actually, the ground wasn't that bad once I got used to it, and even the smell of the river scum and the odor from the nearby outhouse wasn't so sickening after a while. And the mosquitoes—well, they weren't any bigger than turkey buzzards, really, though about three in the morning I finally decided, in spite of the heat, that I had to build a small smoky fire to keep them down. Violet came out of the van when the fire was lit and sat there next to it. She hadn't been able to sleep either.

"I'm sorry," she said, "but this is how it's got to be. My baby's got to see his daddy in San Diego and I didn't have any other way to get there, mister. I know it isn't right, but . . ." Her soft voice hung there in the night.

It was easier to forgive her in the flickering firelight. She looked at me for a while and her eyes, full of tears, glinted in the camp fire. Then she looked straight up at the sky with her head tilted up all the way.

"The night's so full of stars it looks like spilled salt, doesn't it?" she asked. Her throat was white and soft and I realized she was probably right about us sleeping in the van together. Strange things can happen to people in the dark when they're alone and the crickets and the frogs are chirping and there's the smell of sweat in the air. I hadn't been alone with a woman since I'd left Hazel.

"I want to thank you for picking me and the baby up," she said.

"I've done smarter things," I mumbled to myself. Then I could see that hurt her, and she didn't need any more hurting. "You hungry?" I asked.

She bit her lip and nodded, as if she were ashamed of the fact, and I got two cans of warm Coke and some chips out of the van. It was all I had, but she lit into them like she hadn't had a meal in a while. When she was finished, she said, "We were real lucky to run into you tonight."

I grunted.

"Are you a spiritual person?" she asked.

"Not very," I admitted.

She reached inside her shirt and pulled out all her medals. She had tons of them. In addition to the rabbits' feet and the laminated four-leaf clovers, there were scapulars like Catholics used to wear and other kinds of medals, too, and even a set of army dog tags.

"I wear all these for luck," she said. "I put them all on before we left Norfolk because I knew we'd need luck and we've been lucky so far."

Yeah, I thought, if your idea of luck is eating stale chips and warm Coke out in the middle of a bug-infested swamp.

She fished one medal out of the clump and held it up for me to see. It looked like a cross with a couple of bumps on the end of each arm.

"I got this one from an ad in the *National Enquirer*," she said. "It's supposed to have big magic. The article said they gave one to a woman out in Nebraska who had cancer of the ovaries and it shrunk the cancer right up. It cost me seven dollars and fifty cents, but it's worth it. The article said this medal was brought to earth by Christians from the planet

Neptune because after Jesus left here he went to Neptune on his way to heaven and he saved them, too."

"Nice of him to do that since he was in the solar system anyway," I mumbled, rolling over to be closer to the smoke.

"He's everywhere really," she said.

The fire crackled away and sparks shot up towards the sky. An owl was hooting in one of the trees along the stream and once in a while there were animal sounds among the bushes.

"You'd better get some sleep," I said. "We're getting out of here early in the morning."

"Uh-huh," she said, but she didn't move. "You know what? I was hit by lightning once when I was little."

"That might explain a lot," I muttered, swatting at a mosquito whose mission in life seemed to be to kill itself by crawling into my mucous membranes.

"Getting hit by lightning makes a person special, if they live," Violet said. "It makes them lucky and their luck rubs off on other people, too. Maybe you'll get some luck, too, now that you and I have met up."

"What makes you think I need luck?" I asked, rolling back toward her. She shrugged.

"Everybody needs luck," she said.

"I don't. Not now."

"What's that supposed to mean?" she asked.

"A person makes his own luck. People who seem lucky have just had the smarts to make the right kinds of connections. It's about contacts and trying every option. If you're good, something will happen. It isn't luck, though. I have an audition in New York in a couple of days, and it's skill that's going to get me this gig, not luck."

"I'm lucky," Violet said.

"Yeah," I grunted and pulled further inside my sleeping bag to keep the mosquitoes off, even though I was sweating like crazy.

"I am," she insisted.

"Look, Violet, it's three o'clock in the morning, we're in the middle of Bugpatch, Ohio, and I need to drive to New York City tomorrow. If you're not going to go sleep in that van, I am."

"Some people get angry when they're around lucky people. They're just jealous."

"Violet," I said, "how can you call yourself lucky? You're hardly twenty years old, you've got a baby but no husband, and you're lost in the middle of North America someplace sitting ten miles from nowhere with somebody you don't know, and all you've got is that baby, and all he's got is an old cardboard box."

"That doesn't change things really," she said. "If you're lucky, everything will come out okay."

"I give up," I said. "Good night. You can sit by the fire all night if you want, but I don't want to hear any more about luck and all that. As far as I can tell, the only luck you've got is bad, and I hope it doesn't rub off on me because big things are happening in my life right now and I don't need to get them screwed up. Now I've got to get some sleep. Good night, amen, and that's all. I'd like some peace and quiet, please."

Violet sat there but didn't say anything more. After a while, I heard the baby cry and Violet went back into the van. A few seconds later, I heard her singing a lullaby to the baby. It was one I had learned when I was first learning to play guitar. James Taylor cut a version of it, too, a few years ago, but Violet's version was way older than his.

"Hush little baby, don't say a word,
Papa's gonna buy you a mockingbird."

She sang it pure and clear, with a voice that had the sound of West Virginia hickory smoke in it, and when she'd finished she made soft shushing sounds and then the night grew quiet again and there was nothing in the whole universe but the sound of the crickets and the hooting of an owl and the glittering of the stars far above me. The night seemed empty without her now and I got mad at myself for wanting her to come back out of the van and sit beside the fire again.

Something suddenly felt different. Something had changed. There are moments like that, moments when things happen that, after them, nothing is the same ever again, like one time when I was inside the arrowhead illusion someplace in Iowa.

My dad had put the big red box with doors on it over my head. The doors were open at first so everyone in the audience could see my face. Then Dad closed the doors, a black velvet bag dropped down over my head, and he started shoving arrows all around my head so that the box ended up looking like a scared porcupine. At the climax of the trick, Dad opened the doors, and it looked like my head was gone, thanks to the black velvet bag.

We'd done the trick a thousand times at shows and state fairs around the country and never had a hitch, but that day in Iowa, I made the mistake of thinking about what was going on.

It was hot and stuffy inside the black velvet bag and the arrows were sliding by my ears, my nose, my mouth, missing me by eighths of an inch. And I thought—what if Dad misses with an arrow? He's never missed before, but what if he misses today? I could end up blind or I could bleed to death in here. Would he stop the trick if I was bleeding? Or would the show go on while I was hemorrhaging inside the box?

Then, as I breathed my own breath inside the hot bag, I thought of something even worse. I don't know where the thought came from, but suddenly I got to wondering what would happen if, somehow, my dad actually *did* take my head off and make it disappear?

And all this time my dad's stupid patter was going non-stop as he shoved arrow after arrow through the box. And just like that I felt this rushing start in my head, like a black whirlpool, and the next thing I knew I was being sucked up into a big tube and for two minutes or so I did not know where I was. I was gone. My head had disappeared, and when Dad finally opened the box and showed people I wasn't dead or punctured with arrows, I was actually as surprised as they were to find myself still in one piece.

After that, everything was different. The whole world looked strange to me for a couple of weeks. Mom, Dad, everything and everybody had changed, and I felt dizzy and lost and confused for a long time.

"You thought what?" my dad asked when I couldn't take it anymore and confessed to him.

"Like what would happen one time if the magic really worked?" I said.

"What do you mean really worked?" he asked.

"I mean suppose my head did disappear?"

"Your head does disappear. Every night. It's a fool-proof illusion."

"No, Dad, I mean *really* disappear."

"You mean like *gone?*"

I nodded.

"Ha!" he snorted. "That would be some kind of trick, wouldn't it? Helluva thing. But listen, son . . . " And here he put a fatherly arm around my shoulder and said, "There's no such thing as real magic, not that kind. ESP, telepathy, levitation, spiritualism. I've seen it all and done most of it, and it's all gaffed, and anybody who believes in stuff like that ought to be out with the paying suckers in the audience, you understand?"

I understood. The paying customers, in professional performers' minds, are the enemy, a gullible herd of lower life forms that performers are separated from by the happy gulf of the footlights. You would no more want to be on the other side of that great divide than you would want to go to a leper colony and lick sores.

But my doubts wouldn't go away. I began to sense there were other worlds than the one we were living in and traveling through. You see, my mother had taken a Gideon Bible from a motel room someplace and she had been reading me stories from it as we drove from town to town. At night, after the shows, she'd tell me how Moses struck the rock and water poured forth, and how Joshua stopped the sun, how Daniel entered the lion's den, and how Shadrach, Meshach, and Abednego walked in the fiery furnace. These stories frightened me because they opened up the possibility that anything could happen at any time. These weren't simple things like the illusions Dad left around the Airstream. We were talking major magic, like strange visitations by creatures from different worlds, the sky opening and Jacob seeing angels climbing up and down on ladders, and the dead coming back to life. I had heard of horrible punishments inflicted on people for touching the ark of the covenant, and the deep voice of God calling on children like Samuel in the middle of the night and touching their lips with red-hot burning coals. It was too frightening even to think about.

But if what my dad said was true, then it was all a magic trick and something I already knew everything about. Moses' staff turning into a snake in the court of Pharaoh was a pretty simple illusion, and if Harry Houdini could escape from a milk can in the Detroit River, then Jesus could raise Lazarus from the dead with no problem at all. It was all done with wires and mirrors and clever machinery.

Since that time, I rarely thought about other kinds of magic again. As long as I looked at the world as a magic *trick*, then I was all right because I understood tricks. There is no stage illusion ever invented that can't be figured out eventually, and if you had the hope of figuring it out, then you could keep from getting too depressed or worried. From Moses to Robert-Houdin to Copperfield and Siegfried and Roy, it was all a question of wires and gears and black silk thread.

That way, for a very long time, I had stopped thinking about that other kind of magic, the kind that works without gimmicks, the kind you can't explain, the kind where your head really *can* disappear. Only now, in the few hours since I had picked up Violet Tansy, I could sense that the old crazy feelings were waiting in the wings, ready to take stage again.

I looked over at the van where she and the baby were sleeping, and I felt myself getting sucked up the long black tube once more, being transported to a different universe.

I tried to roll over and forget about it. Maybe it was just the night and being so far out in the country. I told myself I'd be rid of her tomorrow anyhow, and this was no long-term thing. I reassured myself by thinking that the next morning I'd do my good deed, drop her off at the nearest entrance to the Ohio turnpike and be done with her. She'd disappear into America, glide away down the long concrete tube of memory, and I'd be on my way to grab the brass ring. I wasn't about to get trapped. I was headed to New York, New York, the city so nice they named it twice. I had played the song often enough with the Dead Superstars and with pickup wedding bands to know that if you made it there you could make it anywhere, and I wasn't about to let my sweet self get tangled up in any coast-to-coast search for a no-name baby's father. Not me. Huh-uh, no sir, no way, no how, not when I was right on the edge of that Something Big I'd always dreamed about. And so, finally, about an hour before dawn, I fell asleep full of plans about how the future was going to be, but, as I was about to learn, when you're with a person like Violet Tansy, the future doesn't always come out the way you planned.

CHAPTER TWO

I took what I hoped was my last look at Violet Tansy as she stood at the side of the road, getting smaller in my rearview mirror. It was sunrise in Ohio. The grass was wet all around and it shined silver in the morning light, and I was heading out into the freshness of dawn, alone.

My plan was to pick up my toll ticket and pass beneath the green and white sign that said New York and be on my way to meet my destiny. Or so I thought.

My eyes kept flicking up to the mirror, and I kept seeing her there, her back to me, her big bag slung over her shoulder, that stupid box with the baby in it set down beside her on the edge of the highway, and even though I tried not to look, I couldn't help myself. I finally tried tipping the mirror up so I couldn't see out the back window even if I wanted to, but, of course, that didn't work either, and to tell the truth I think I could have forgotten about Violet altogether if it was just her involved. In my mind, Violet Tansy kept getting smaller, but, somehow, that battered box of hers with the baby in it kept getting bigger until it was finally about the size of a boxcar.

Something about that baby starting out its life on the edge of the road, cars racing by only a few feet from its head, helpless, hanging out there hoping for rides bothered me. It wouldn't let me rest. Maybe it reminded me too much of my own growing up.

Maybe I should have floored it, shot on to the eastbound highway and kept moving. After all, I had already left lots of people behind, Hazel was only the most recent, and over the years I had forced myself not to let it bother me much, not for long, anyway. I knew enough about leaving people and things to know I would forget Violet Tansy and her baby eventually.

At some point early in my life, I got used to people and places and things disappearing the way things disappeared in my dad's magic tricks. I taught myself never to look back. I found out it was the only way to avoid getting hurt. Or at least not to feel it much anymore, like when you learn to play guitar and your fingertips hurt at first and then they toughen up and callus over so you can play without pain.

But when I came to the toll booth, I made the mistake of readjusting my rearview mirror just in time to see some ugly guy in a beat-up black pickup slow down and swerve toward Violet and then swerve away again when he saw the baby in the box, and so there they were, all alone, still stuck by that strip of concrete in the middle of those Ohio cornfields.

I tried to step on the gas, but it wasn't any use. My foot froze. I couldn't leave them there.

"Toledo," I said when I'd backed up on the shoulder, and she came running up and flung open the door. "I'm actually headed east, you know, but Toledo's closer than Cleveland, so I'll take you there but not any further, and then I'll turn around. There's a bus station there in Toledo. The reason I'm not leaving you out here in the middle of nowhere is because I don't want you to blame me for your troubles or anything, you understand?"

She slid open the side door and set down the box with the baby in it between the seats and I kept on yammering.

"I'm only doing this because I remembered I was supposed to go up to Toledo anyway, to see a guy."

She nodded her head as she buckled herself into the passenger seat. I picked up a card at the toll booth. Soon we merged into the traffic stream and were moving toward Toledo full speed. If I dropped her there, I could turn right around and still be to New York by midnight.

"So who's this guy in Toledo?" she asked, twenty miles later.

"Some guy," I said.

She sat there quietly for a minute and I hoped she would let the subject drop, but she didn't. "There isn't any guy, is there?" she said.

"Just so you understand," I said.

"I understand," she said, looking out the windshield with a slight smile.

"Me and my baby thank you," she said.

"Yeah," I grunted.

"The Lord has provided. You are the instrument of our deliverance."

"Yeah, yeah, yeah, but only to Toledo."

*

We made Toledo by noon. I had about a hundred dollars cash tucked inside the sound hole of my guitar, which is where I kept my money, and I thought of buying her and the baby a bus ticket when we drove past the Greyhound station in the rundown section of the downtown. That would have moved her some distance west and left me free to go to New York for my audition, but, to tell the truth, I knew I didn't have enough money to pay for both a bus ticket and gas to New York. I decided I would have to come up with a plan.

In the meantime, I bought us lunch at McDonald's, and from the way Violet ate, I could tell it was her first hot meal in a while. I was witnessing a genuine Big Mac attack. She practically shoved fistfuls of fries into her mouth, but after a few minutes she began to color up nicely and the pasty white of her face got tinged with a little pink, though there were still dark circles under her eyes and she had two days of road grit in her hair. In any case, she looked better than she had since I picked her up the night before, or she picked me up, or whatever had happened back there at the Dew Dropp Inn.

When Violet was done eating the last crumb of her french fries and bun from her tray, she left me with the baby for a few minutes while she went to the bathroom. No sooner had she gone, of course, than the baby started to cry. And I don't mean he was quietly whimpering. He shrieked and screamed and gasped and spluttered so much the box started to wobble and nearly tumbled from the booth seat. Pretty soon, everybody in the place was staring at me and at the box like I was supposed to do something.

"He isn't mine," I said, grinning like an idiot. That didn't get much sympathy from the other customers, so I grabbed the edge of the box and started to rock it, which didn't do any good at all. The baby probably thought he was in an earthquake. His face was scrunched up as red as a tomato. He wailed so loud that the cups vibrated on the table. He had a gift, I thought; he could be an opera singer some day with lungs like those.

Not having had much experience in this line—Hazel said she didn't want babies until we were "ready," by which she meant never—I didn't know what to do, so I did what every beginner in the baby line does. I stuck my finger in the baby's belly button, wiggled it a little bit and said, "Googa-googa-goo." Of course it had the usual effect. The baby's eyes opened wide as cup lids for a couple of seconds and he actually stopped crying. I felt a brief surge of something like fatherly pride, but it only lasted a second, because I didn't realize the baby wasn't stopping because he was feeling good. He was terrified, only he had just emptied himself of air and needed to refill his lungs before he went cyanotic. He sucked in two lungs full and then let loose again with a high-pitched skirl even louder than before, and finally the manager came over to see if I was torturing the kid.

"I don't know what's the matter with him," I shouted over the roar. "He isn't mine or anything, honest."

"He's only hungry," said the manager. "Anybody can tell that."

I could see Violet emerging from the bathroom and heading our way. She had washed her face, combed her hair, and pinned her bangs back off her forehead with a pink barrette, like something a little girl would wear.

"I heard him all the way across the restaurant," she said. "Look!"

On her T-shirt were two dark spots at her nipples where the milk had started to run. "Isn't it amazing the way that happens?"

She picked the baby up, sat, and started to lift her T-shirt, but the manager made a noise, and we headed back to the van. The baby grabbed on to Violet's breast with both hands and fed like a hungry puppy there in the front seat, slurping and gurgling and making cooing noises all at once. Violet murmured gently to him all the time until at last the baby finished. His eyes closed halfway and his head rolled back like a drunk who's about to pass out, and two minutes later his head flopped over and he was sound asleep, as if he didn't have a care in the world. Violet laid him back down in the cardboard box.

I gave her some money, and she bought a box of diapers, and then we found a shady spot in a park where I pulled the van over. Violet looked real tired, so I told her to stretch herself out in the back of the van, and soon she fell asleep next to the baby on the foam rubber mattress. I could tell she'd be out for a long while.

I took my sleeping bag and guitar out beneath a tree in the park and spread the bag out like a blanket and lay there looking up through the leaves, trying to work out my next move.

One thing I learned from my father, the Amazing Raymond, was how to come into a town and get work quickly. You could go into music stores, magic shops, or places like that, and without much effort you could tap into the grapevine about where to pick up some extra change. My dad was usually booked by his agent, Maurice, who had an office in Manhattan and enjoyed sending Dad to small towns all over the Midwest and West—"Next week you're headed to Burnips, Michigan, baby. Now ain't that amazing?" Then he'd laugh and you could smell his cigar breath over a thousand miles of telephone line.

So Dad liked to pick up a little money on the side that Maurice didn't know about. It was his way of preserving his dignity in the face of the way Maurice constantly degraded him. Dad called the extra cash his retirement plan, though mostly he drank it away after the show.

Most cities have some kind of open mike contest somewhere any night of the week, and I figured Toledo would, too. Usually they give cash prizes, and usually it isn't much of a contest. After seven years with "The Dead Superstar Revue," I could pretty much walk into a place, figure out what style of music they'd pay money for, and do a reasonable job of imitating somebody famous to win the pot.

So I thought I could probably get a little more money that night, and maybe combining it with what I had stashed in my guitar I could buy Violet and her baby a one-way supersaver on the big gray dog to send her into the arms of her darling Billy and leave me with enough gas money to get on to that big audition with a clean conscience. That way I would know I hadn't simply left her in the middle of America on her own.

And then what? I lay on my back in the sun and played air guitar, pretending the light on my face was from a carbon-arc supertrouper. Then sixteen cities of music madness with Snidely Whiplash and Sclapped! Of course the fans would cry out for more and we'd double encore, and then leave the stadium with women throwing themselves at us every which way, and we'd have to hire body guards to keep them from

ripping us apart. And the press would be there, too,
flashbulbs bursting like fireworks all around us as we fought
our way to the limos, shoving back newspaper and TV
reporters clamoring for a few words. It was going to be the
American dream come true.

And then what? I thought. What if Sclapped turned out
to be a one-hit group? (Our first album, of course, would hit
the top of the Billboard charts and go platinum within a few
weeks.) Suppose we ended up like Freddy and the Dreamers
or Herman's Hermits or Dexy's Midnight Runners? You ride
the top for a while and then crash. What then? I shoved that
possibility right out of my mind. We were going to be bigger
than big, and someday, way in the future, I hoped, maybe
somebody would be impersonating us in the Dead Superstar
Review. I had played the gig often enough to know
necrophilia was a form of immortality.

I took my Martin guitar out of the case and tried to practice some rock riffs on it so I'd have my chops up when I hit
New York. I wished I'd had the presence of mind to stop at
the Lucky Lady on my way of out of Vegas to pick up my
Fender Stratocaster, but I didn't know I was going to be audi-
tioning for a heavy rock group, and I was too crazy that night
to think straight. I figured I could borrow a hard-bodied
electric guitar when I got to New York. I could do some
Eddie Van Halen, some "Stairway to Heaven," enough to
show them I could handle whatever they laid on me. Rock of
the sort Sclapped played was mostly wah-wah pedal anyway.
I was feeling very good indeed as I lay beneath that tree in
Toledo, Ohio. New York, New York was only about nine
hundred miles away. A few tanks of gas and I'd be there.

I looked up into the tree above me and remembered a
verse from the Gideon Bible my mother recited sometimes
when we had been on the road too many weeks and she was
weary of packing things in the trailer every day so they
wouldn't fall off the shelf as we drove to the next show town.

*"The foxes have their dens and the birds of the air have their
nests, but the son of Man has no place to lay his head."*

She didn't mean it to be a happy verse, but to me it
always was. Like me, Jesus was born on the road, and he had
to head to Egypt at an early age and had to keep on moving
until the end, town to town, crowd to crowd, with his roadies and groupies, and not even the grave could hold him
down long, if you believe what the story says, and looking
ahead I couldn't imagine ever wanting a place to call home
either. The future was a narrow strip of concrete heading over
the horizon. Traveling was the only world I had ever known.
The road was imprinted on my brain.

I was born moving and it didn't feel right to stop too
long. It made me dizzy and crazy, like I had been in Las
Vegas.

I got tired of rock riffs, so I retuned and started strumming a song that had come to me about a year before. It
was a tune played in an open-tuning D chord with lots of
harmonics and nice bass runs. It was strange how it came to
me. I woke up one morning out of a sound sleep and had
this tune running through my head. I must have had a
dream or something because I felt real groggy, almost half
drunk, and this melody was in my ears and it kept humming there. It sounded interesting, different from anything
I'd ever played before, so I grabbed a cassette recorder and
my Martin and headed for the bathroom so I could catch it
before it disappeared. I could feel it receding like dreams
slip away in the morning when your daytime brain takes
over. Why the bathroom? I didn't know, except the tune, as
I heard it my head, had an echo effect, as if I was hearing it
from the end of a long tunnel or something. After a few
minutes of fooling around, I realized the harmonics were
coming from an open-tuned D chord and pretty soon I had
the basics of it worked out and recorded a version of it on
the tape.

And I finished just in time, because Hazel came banging at the door. I had lost track of time and had been sitting in the bathroom for over an hour working out this song.

"Will you get out of there, please?" she yelled. "I've got to do my eyes."

"I'm working on something," I said. "I almost got it."

"Do you know what time it is? We've got to get to work pretty soon, you know. I haven't even started on my eyes."

Now that I think of it, Hazel spent forever on her eyes. It was one of those things in a marriage you don't really notice but that is driving you nuts beneath the surface, like a dripping water faucet. At first, I didn't remember her making such a big deal about her mascara, but I guess she gradually added more over the years until by the time I left her it took her two hours in the bathroom to do her eyes and when she came out she looked exactly like a raccoon. She said the guys at the blackjack tables tipped better if she looked "glamorous," that was her word, but I still thought she looked like a raccoon, though I didn't ever say so. Anyway, I quickly recorded one last version of the open-tuning thing that day and forgot about it. I penciled "open-tuning" on the cassette labels, then tossed it in a box and never got back to it.

Lately, though, somewhere between Branson and Porkville, I remembered it and had started picking it out again on my guitar. I woke up one morning and there it was again, floating through my head, and it wouldn't let me alone until I played it. And then—this struck me as very strange—ever since I had met Violet Tansy, the tune had been hovering somewhere around the back fringes of my mind, like an itch you're only half aware of, or like the smell of something you can't quite identify that clings to the back of your nostrils until you come up with the name for it. I remembered the whole tune, as if it was only yesterday I had written it, and as I traveled I improvised on it and added a few riffs high up on the neck, which allowed me to hit back and forth between the harmonics on the seventh and the twelfth frets, making little chiming sounds above the rhythm of the deep bass D. Between the low D and the highest harmonics, the song spanned almost the whole range of the instrument and had a kind of full-bodied warmth from the resonances of the open chord.

The guitar must have awakened Violet because she stepped out of the van. She looked fresher and somehow almost pretty as she stood there in the sunlight at the curb and stretched. She gave me a wave and walked over to where I sat beneath the tree with my guitar.

"The baby's still sleeping. He hasn't slept like this in days," she said. "That song you were playing was nice. Is that something you wrote?"

I nodded.

"What's it called?"

"It doesn't have a name," I said. "It's just some open-tuning thing."

"What's that?"

"It's when you tune your guitar to an open chord so you can do harmonics all up and down the neck. You touch it pretty well anywhere and it resonates, see?"

I hit a high D on the first string and then stopped it with my finger. The other D-tuned strings continued to vibrate.

"You touch one and the others sound," I explained. "It gives a richer tone."

"That's the way it is with me and Billy when we're together," she said. "We're tuned that way. Do you have anybody like that in your life?"

"Not really," I said.

"That's too bad."

*

We stopped at a Munchee Mart for supper. Violet was collecting game tokens for the Munchee Mart Dream House competition. Each token represented a door or a window or a roof, and if you got all thirty-two pieces to make the whole house, you would win.

"They'll build it anywhere in the continental United States," she said.

She was absolutely convinced she was going to win this dream house now that she was traveling coast-to-coast to find Billy. By stopping at Munchee Marts from Norfolk to San Diego, she could collect pieces from all over the country, and since in contests like this the pieces aren't evenly distributed in any geographic area, she thought her odds were increased.

I called a music store in Toledo and, sure enough, there was an open mike that night at a place called The Dead Zone. We got directions from the clerk at the Munchee Mart. ("You want to go there? Jesus, are you sure, man? Is your health insurance paid up?")

The Dead Zone turned out to be a sprawling converted bowling alley in the south end of Toledo. It looked like a tough place. First prize for the open mike contest was supposed to be a hundred dollars, but if I didn't win, I could at least have a few free beers and maybe get my nose pierced to prepare me for the Sclapped tour. (Hadn't Murray said twenty cities in thirty days, then to L.A. to do the video at the Playboy mansion?)

The parking lot was mostly crushed glass, and a rank of about a dozen chrome-and-black Harleys claimed the sidewalk nearest the front door. The lot and street were filled with high-testosterone cars, big bulging jacked-up American-made gas guzzlers with street slicks or fat tires and Yosemite Sam mud flaps on them that said, "Back off, Varmint!" or bumper stickers like "Kill 'em all and let God sort 'em out." The sound system inside The Dead Zone was set on max, and the walls bulged out with every beat of the industrial strength heavy metal jet-engine backwash that passed for music at the place. The attire was basic black, heavy on the leather and chains, and black T-shirts with AC-DC or Megadeth silkscreened on them in gold and those bright colors that glow under black lights. Now I really regretted leaving my Fender Stratocaster back in Vegas. After my years with the Dead Superstar Review, I figured I could walk into the Dead Zone and take the pot by picking out "Purple Haze" with my teeth. As it was, I thought I could simply plug my Martin acoustic pick-up direct into the Dead Zone's sound system and let it feed back for a while and the crowd would love it. If I was lucky, I might even get the prize money back to the van without getting mugged.

Violet insisted on coming in with me and, after thinking it over, I figured it was safer for her inside The Dead Zone than outside in the parking lot, though if the truth be told, your chances of getting raped, robbed, or beaten were probably about the same in either place. Luckily she had a black T-shirt Billy had given her before he shipped out. It had a death's head on it and a nuclear cloud with the legend, "Torpedoes of death, missiles of doom." I figured she would blend right in.

Violet brought the box with the baby in it, too, and I guessed it was the first time a baby had been in The Dead Zone because everybody stopped and looked. Some of them even looked hungry, so I told Violet to keep a tight grip on her cardboard box. The air was thick with burning hemp and, from the looks of the crowd around us, I thought I had wandered into a casting call for a caveman movie. The men had long hair, shoulder length, the uniform color of crankcase oil, and their women all seemed to have bought their jeans three sizes too small because rolls of fat hung out over their belt loops.

I signed in at the entrance for the open mike, and when we'd elbowed our way to a table, I ordered a beer and Violet

asked for a rum and Coke, which, for the Dead Zone bar-
tender, was a pretty complicated mixed drink.

"I'm with him," she said, when the waitress brought our
drinks back. "He's playin' his guitar here tonight."

"Only performers get free drinks," the waitress said, her
hand on the hip of her ripped jeans. She was not the sort of
woman you'd want to argue with, and I don't mean just
because of her Harley T-shirt and the rattlesnake tattoos
around her biceps. She weighed about two hundred pounds
and looked like she could bench press about half of the men
in the place simultaneously. I didn't want to start any brawls
with her, so I coughed up the money for Violet's drink and
ordered myself another beer.

"You shouldn't be drinking when you're nursing a baby,
should you?" I asked.

"It makes him sleep better," she shrugged. The baby was
beside her in the box. She had fed him a few minutes before
we went into the bar and now he lay there snoring in spite of
the sheet-metal works ambience of the place.

"He seems to sleep fine without it," I said.

Four local boys had the stage before me, and they were
shrieking and feedbacking their way through some Purple
Funk on cheap hardbody guitars, making up with wah-wah
what they lacked in talent. I didn't think I had to worry about
them walking away with what I thought of as my prize money.

Next came a pimply faced kid who introduced his first
song by saying, "Here's a song I wrote when I was in prison.
I was on this chain gang in Mississippi, see?"

Then he started into some horrible rendition of an old
blues number that Blind Lemon Jefferson recorded for
Folkways about a million years ago, and it was painfully
obvious this kid had never been outside Toledo in his whole
life, much less been on any chain gang down south. He
groaned and moaned and made all the right sounds, but it
just wasn't the blues.

The audience started hooting and an empty beer bottle hit the brick wall behind the stage and sent splinters of glass everywhere. Finally some big biker dude in leathers and chains slammed his fist down on his ringside table and shouted, "Get the fuck off the stage, motherfucker, your time's up!"

Silence reigned in The Dead Zone for five seconds as everybody waited to see what would happen. The biker, a gold tooth glinting from the half-smile beneath his big red beard, glared at the kid behind the mike like a pit bull looking at red meat.

"Hey, I got ten minutes on stage like everybody else," the kid said.

With that, the big biker stomped over and lifted him up by the scruff of his neck and tossed him off the stage right into the side brick wall of The Dead Zone, and everything returned to normal.

"Don't never let me catch you sayin' you was in prison when you wasn't in prison never, you hear me boy?" the biker said, jabbing the air with a grease-blackened finger. "And don't never come 'round here again on open mike night singin' like a nigger, 'cause only niggers have the right to sing the kind of music you're trying to sing and no white-ass lily-livered white boy can sing the blues no matter how many tattoos he's got, you dig that?"

The kid mumbled, "Yeah," as he slid down the wall.

"Who was that?" Violet asked as the biker sat back down at his table.

"He's one of the judges," a guy next to us said.

The next act, believe it or not, was a guitar-playing cowgirl in a silk shirt with a sequined cactus on the front. Each of the two arms of the saguaro cactus on the blouse reached up and ended on top of one of her breasts, so it looked like the cactus was feeling her up. She would be a tough act to follow, not because she was particularly good, but because she kept bending down in the direction of the biker-judge so he could peek right up her cacti.

When she sang, she was trying to sound like Wynonna Judd or something, but it sounded more like somebody was sawing a cat in half. The crowd didn't seem to mind, however, as long as she kept bending over. I figured I'd have a tough run for first prize until I noticed that the biker's woman was shooting knife-eyes at him every time he peeked up the girl's saguaro, so I knew she didn't have a chance. The guy may have been a tough judge, but he wasn't stupid.

I was due to follow her, but about five minutes into her act, I suddenly got afflicted by my old curse. It had gone away for a while in the years I played with the Dead Superstars, but now, of all times, it had come back. It was unmistakable. It used to drive my dad nuts. "What do you mean you have to go?" he'd ask me. "It's five minutes to show time, you can't pee now." We tried everything to get me over it, but I couldn't help it. Some show business people get flop sweat five minutes before curtain, some of them blank out, lose their memories, panic. Me, I had to pee. I had gotten over it during my years with the Dead Superstars because it got to be a routine like working at a gas station. But that night in The Dead Zone—maybe because I had been thinking all day about fronting for Snidely Whiplash with Sclapped—the curse struck again.

I set my guitar down beneath the table thinking it would be safer than trying to haul it through the press of beer bellies between me and the men's room. Over the years, I perfected the art of the quick pee. I had to learn it when we were working places where there might not be a john nearby, like at carnivals and state fairs. I used to have to sneak out behind the tent if it was a tent show and pee where the elephants were. Nobody would notice then.

When I got back to the table, I reached down to pick up my guitar, but all I came up with was a fist full of air. I bent over and looked beneath the table, but I couldn't see it. I got down on my hands and knees and felt the sticky floor among the peanut shells and wet bar napkins. Nothing. My guitar was gone, vanished, totally missing. I poked my head above the table.

"Where's my guitar?" I asked Violet.

The bar was packed with people, elbow to elbow, and she had trouble hearing me over the noise.

"What?" she asked.

"*Where's my guitar?*" I shouted over the cowgirl's screeching voice.

"Some guy just said he was going to tune it for you."

"What guy?"

"Him, over there," she said pointing to the front door toward which a skinny young guy in a sleeveless Kiss T-shirt was heading as fast as he could press himself through the crowd. I jumped on top of the table and shouted "STOP THAT SON OF A BITCH!" and what happened next was that absolute pandemonium broke out in The Dead Zone. There were so many sons of bitches in the place that nobody knew which son of a bitch I meant and so the bikers, sensing that something was beginning to rumble, rose to their feet all at once. Violet grabbed the baby and held tight.

"Who called me a sumbitch?" one of them shouted, and the next thing you know, the air was filled with flying knuckles, belt buckles, kung-fu sticks, Philippine butterfly knives, and everything else that you could grab, swing, or throw.

"I've gotta stop that guy," I shouted to Violet as I jumped off the table and ran through flying glass. Everybody in the place, almost, was kicking, punching, and heaving furniture, and I don't think that cowgirl ever did finish her song. Somebody slapped a quarter in the jukebox and the walls began to bounce to a heavy metal beat.

"Hey, wait for me!" Violet screamed. She picked up the cardboard box with the baby in it and elbowed her way toward the door. "Hey, wait for us!"

Meanwhile, the particular son of a bitch I was chasing had high-kicked it out the front door of The Dead Zone and was tearing down the sidewalk with my Martin D-35 held up over his head like a flag. I chased him for about half a block, but he had a stride like a kangaroo.

About a block from the bar he jumped into a waiting red pickup truck on the opposite side of the street. I raced back to my van. Violet was already inside, strapped in the passenger seat with her baby clutched in her arms.

"What you gonna do?" Violet asked.

"I'm gonna kill that son-of-a-bitch," I shouted as I peeled out and did a U-turn following him. "If I can catch him."

"Slow down," Violet said as I screeched out after him.

"Slow down hell, he's got my guitar!"

The guy was about a block ahead of me and I could hear his glass-packed mufflers roaring like jet blasts through the hot Toledo night. Violet closed her eyes and hung on tight as we ran a couple of red lights and shot across the Maumee River over a suspension bridge. It was the only time in my life I had prayed to see cops, but none were around. In a couple of minutes, the pickup led us out from the city into the flat farmlands around Toledo, tearing along the blacktop between endless rows of car-high corn. Pretty soon the sides of my van began to go whucka-whucka-whucka. I should have slowed down, but I wasn't about to lose my best guitar in order to save my old wreck of a van.

Somehow, I managed to push the gas pedal nearly through the floor and to pull up to within a hundred feet of him as we careened down a two-lane country road. The next thing I knew, things about the size of hand grenades came flying out of his side window. The first one hit my front bumper and I heard glass breaking. Then one hit in the middle of the road and burst like a star. A white foamy spray splashed up and glittered in the headlights.

"What's that?" Violet asked

"Beer bottles!" I shouted. "He's tossing beer bottles out the window!"

They came flying out the driver's side window one after another in a steady stream. Crash. Crash. Crash. He must have had a whole case sitting next to him on the seat. The bottles hit the concrete in front of my headlights and burst with dull pops. Some were already open when he threw them. I imagined him twisting off the cap and taking a drink before he snaked his arm out the driver's window and let loose. The bottles flew up, leaving white comet tails of foam, then they'd explode on the road in front of us. I had to swerve and twist every which way. It was like driving a slalom course through the broken glass, and every time I jerked the wheel Violet let out a little shriek and shouted "Look out!" or "Slow down!" but I wasn't about to do any such thing. I needed that guitar to practice for my audition with Sclapped.

Bottle after bottle shattered on the pavement in front of us, and the hot night began to smell of beer from the trail we were leaving behind.

After he'd tossed nearly a case of beer out at us, the guy had pulled away considerably. Another six pack, I thought, and he'd be gone, out of reach. I tried to push the van even faster, but it resisted. The fenders were flapping like bird wings, and though I made up some ground, the taillights of the pickup truck disappeared up a dirt road that ran off from the tarmac between the cornfields. I went right after him, eating the high plume of yellow dust his old truck threw up. My van got to hopping and skipping over the washboard road, and the whole underframe started to rattle like it was going to come off. I could taste the dirt from the road between my teeth and the headlights barely pierced the dark yellow dust in front of us.

"You're gonna wake up the baby!" Violet screamed.

"That doesn't help any, Violet!" I shouted back. "I'm gonna get that guitar even if it kills me!"

Just then my headlights picked up his two red rear reflectors and—miracle of miracles—he was sitting there, not moving. I gunned the engine, anxious to get hold of the skinny little guy's throat and separate him from a few teeth. And then a sign loomed up out of the dust. NARROW BRIDGE AHEAD.

I didn't see the sparkling line of broken glass the guy had laid across the dirt road about thirty feet in front of the bridge. I heard a loud bang, like a gunshot, and felt the van lurch to the right. The steering wheel bucked in my hands and we slid sideways for a few yards, almost toppling over the edge into the drainage ditch. We finally came to rest with the rear bumper against the bridge abutment. The front right tire was totally blown. I had driven straight into his trap.

"Fooled you, motherfucker," he shouted out his window, and I heard him strum the open strings of my guitar like a gorilla.

I flew out the driver's door and ran toward the narrow bridge toward where the pickup was parked. He waited until I'd sprinted almost up to his bumper and then he peeled out, showering my face with dust and stones before he disappeared into the thick night.

I stood there stupidly, gasping for breath, spitting dust out of my mouth, and wiping sweat and dirt and tears from my eyes. I shook my fist in the air and shouted, "Fuck you!" It wasn't real effective, I suppose, but I had to do something as I watched his taillights disappear into the cornfields. And then I realized that not only was my Martin D-35 gone, but so was all the money I had stashed in it that was going to pay for my gas to New York. I was busted, flat broke, not a penny to my name except for a little loose change in my jeans pocket.

When I got back to the van, Violet was sitting in the front passenger seat and the baby was sucking on her as usual.

"The baby woke up," she said.

"The baby woke up? The baby woke up!" I screamed, flinging open the door. I was going to throw them both out there on the country road, but I realized that wouldn't accomplish anything, so instead I climbed back into the driver's seat and beat my head against the steering wheel for a while. "I haven't had anything but trouble since I hooked up with you yesterday, Violet. Enough's enough! That was a twelve hundred dollar guitar. How could you let somebody take it away?"

"He said he was going to tune it for you."

"I can tune my own goddammed guitar!"

"Don't swear," she said. "Don't take the Lord's name in vain. I think it's His doing that we're together like this. It must be. Don't you think so? There's no such thing as an accident in this world, that's what I read someplace."

"Yeah, well, my meeting you was a bad accident, if you ask me." I laid my head against the steering wheel and stared at the dashboard.

After a minute or so when the only noise was my radiator clicking and the crickets out in the fields, Violet said softly, "The Lord must have his reasons for putting the two of us together, but He doesn't always write in straight lines."

Just then the baby started to cry again, and I had a sudden impulse to strangle them both, but instead, I said, "I got to change the tire."

"It was just a guitar," she said.

"It wasn't just a guitar," I told her. "It was a top-of-the-line Martin D-35 Dreadnought with a three-piece rosewood back and a custom-fitted, low-profile neck! I had a lot of miles on that guitar and now some damn hillbilly is off in the corn somewhere with it, probably whacking on it with no more knowing how to play it than a kid who picks it up for the first time. I feel like a man whose wife has run off with somebody else, do you understand?"

She didn't say anything back, only stared at me like I was crazy, which I probably was at that point.

"And not only that," I added. "I kept my money—what little I had of it—inside it. Now I've got . . ." I dug in my jeans ". . . about two bucks and some change. I'm busted and I've got to get to New York the way you've got to get to San Diego and without that guitar I haven't got any way to get cash."

"You kept your money in your guitar?" she said. "What'd you do that for?"

"So I wouldn't lose it, that's why!" I exploded. "I've lost my wallet a couple of times in my life. I even lost my pants once. But I didn't ever figure on losing my guitar—until I met up with you, that is."

Violet let things hang there for a minute, then mumbled, "Well, I'm sorry."

"Sorry doesn't bring it back."

I got out and changed the tire.

The night was hot and sticky and full of mosquitoes that kept stinging me as I tried to get the jack under the bumper. Luckily my spare had air in it—that was about the best you could say.

I changed the tire and kicked the glass off the road. I decided to drive on a little way to see if I could pick up the thief's tracks, but it was no use. There were so many traces of cars, trucks, tractors, and everything else up ahead that I'd never find him, and I wasn't about to spend the whole night wandering through cornfields.

"I'll pay," Violet said as we headed back to Toledo.

"How are you going to pay?" I asked. "You can't even buy a cheeseburger at the Munchee Mart. How can you pay for anything?"

"As soon as we get to San Diego, I'll have money. Billy has some back pay coming because he's been out at sea for eleven months now. As soon as we're married, you'll get your money."

"Violet," I said, "I don't know how to tell you this, but you aren't getting married and Billy isn't going to pay for that guitar. Get it through your head, none of this is going to happen, and if it does I don't intend to be around for it. You and I are done, finished, quit. I'll take you back into Toledo and drop you at the bus station, but that's it. No more. I've got to figure out a way to go east tomorrow, and you have to figure out your own way west. We're just back where we were yesterday—except I've lost my guitar and all my money."

"Could you take me to Detroit then?" she asked.

"What? No. Back to Toledo. That's it. End of the line. You and the baby have got to go your way and I've got to go mine. Forget Detroit."

"If you can get me to Detroit, I'll get you another guitar," she said.

I looked over at her. She was sitting there with that look of pie-eyed honesty on her face she always had, as if she really believed it herself.

"How are you going to do that?" I asked. "Win it at the Munchee Mart?"

"No," she said. "My Grandpa Tolliver lives in Detroit and he was a musician and he's got guitars and all kinds of stuff. He'd give you one of his guitars if I was to ask him."

I tried to explain to her again that what I lost wasn't just another guitar, it was a top-of-the-line Martin, the best guitar money could buy, bar none, and that was all there was to it. "If you could get me one of those, you could afford to fly to San Diego on a jet plane."

But she wouldn't let up.

"No," she said. "It's my fault because I didn't stop that guy and I got to make it up to you. Grandpa Tolliver will give you his best guitar and my aunt, who he lives with, will give you a little money maybe."

"Forget it," I said.

"Well, what else you going to do?"

She had me there. She had been with me long enough to know I was only scratching around hand to mouth as I traveled to New York, and I'd already told her I was down to my last two dollars. If she did have a grandfather in Detroit—which I doubted—and if he did have a guitar—which I wouldn't bet my life on—it would be a little better than nothing, which was what I had right then. The Martin and the money in it was my entire bank account, mortgage, and life insurance rolled into one. The only alternative was to go back to Vegas and gig with the Dead Superstars again.

"Where's your grandpa live?" I asked.

"In Detroit. He moved up there during the war with a lot of folks from Tennessee to work in the car factories. My mama was raised there."

"Detroit's a big city." I said. "Do you know the address where he lives?"

"Not exactly," she said, biting her lip. "I never been there myself but one time, when I was ten. My mother was raised there and she used to say that where he lived was like hell."

"Well, that narrows it down," I mumbled.

She turned to me and with the most sincere expression in the world said, "The Holy Spirit will guide us if we pray."

"Jesus," I said, throwing my head back and staring at the van ceiling.

"Him, too," she said.

"Yeah," I replied, shaking my head. "Or maybe we can look it up in a phone book, huh?"

"You just got to believe . . . Hey, I was gonna say you got to believe, John or Jack or something, and I realized I don't even know your name, and here we've been having all these adventures together. What is your name anyway?"

"Stupid," I said, grabbing my road atlas and trying to figure out how we could get from where we were to northbound I-75. "Just call me stupid. Stupid Stupid, it's my first name and my last name, too."

*

By the time we got to I-75, it was nearly midnight. The baby had fallen asleep again in the back and Violet nodded off beside me in the passenger seat. Her head bobbed back and forth a little as the van rocked, but that didn't seem to bother her. She was one of those people who could sleep anywhere no matter what had happened to them that day.

As for me, I wasn't worried about falling asleep at the wheel that night. I knew wondering about my Martin would keep me up, and if that wasn't enough to do it, I could keep alert by rehearsing in my mind exactly what I'd do to the guy who took it if I could ever get my hands on him. Killing him would be just for starters.

After a while, though, the drone of the tires got to me and cleared my head. Driving at night does that for me. Once in a while, back in Vegas, I'd light out into the desert and drive through all that flat nothingness until things felt good again. It seemed like the desert could absorb anything, or there was simply so much of it I could set out in any direction and eventually run out of energy, like a spent bullet, before I ran out of space. Now that I looked back on it, I realized I had been making a lot of those late-night desert runs in the few months before I snapped and drove away for what seemed like forever. Some nights after we closed the show, I walked out through the banks of slot machines and when I saw the late-night zombies pulling the cranks, I wondered if the dull look on their faces wasn't the same look I had on mine. I'd wonder if I wasn't turning into one of the living dead, too, playing the same gig every night for ten years, heading home to the same woman, my life going 'round and 'round like those whirling cherries and lemons, never quite matching up to a big score. And I'd want to get away from it all, so I'd drop Hazel off at home, get a tank full of gas and drive—anywhere, it didn't matter—and usually, after two or three hours moving across the flat dark of the desert, something inside me would turn around, and I'd be able to drive back home again and crash in bed until it was time to get up that night and go back to the Lucky Lady and pull the crank some more. The rhythm of the road was enough to soothe me, at least for a while.

One time, just before I left my life back in Las Vegas, I was cruising along as fast as I could, not caring where I was going as long as it was away. About three in the morning I lost the last of the radio stations, so I must have been way out in nowhere. There was nothing on the whole dial except a slight static. I almost switched the radio off, but instead I left it on and listened to the white noise, staring without blinking straight ahead of me at the dark wall on the other side of my headlights. I drove like that for over two hours without a thought in my whole mind, only the sound of the fuzz of the radio and the hum of the tires in my ears. In a sense, you could say I passed out for a while.

The next thing I knew it was a hundred and fifty miles later. The sun was coming up in my face, and I felt clean somehow. It was like I'd been picked up and set down again someplace new and I could go back to Hazel, to the Dead Superstars, to Dad, to all of it. For those two hours I had been a particle of dirt the wind blew off a clod in a field somewhere, flying away in every direction and no direction at once. Somewhere in that two hours or so, I blew past all the things and people I had known for the past seven years, and when I came out of it I was feeling good. The road is kind of a world unto itself and sometimes it feels good just to be moving.

Not everyone can understand that. My mom never could.

We lost her in Salt Lake City the year when I was fourteen. She couldn't take it on the road anymore, so she became a Mormon and dug in roots there. She said that traveling around the country in a trailer, even an Airstream, was no way to live.

They fought a lot, Mom and Dad, mostly when Dad had been drinking. They waited until they thought I was asleep, but I didn't sleep much when I knew they were building up to a fight. My stomach would get tight because I could feel it coming the way you can sometimes feel a tornado coming. The air gets all green and hollow and silent and you can't breathe.

They'd start out slow and quiet after I was in bed, but pretty soon it'd get louder and then, wham, slap, I'd hear the sound of skin hitting skin, a sharp crack, like nothing else in the world, and I'd pull my head under the covers. Pretty soon Dad would be hitting and throwing her so hard the trailer would rock, and in the morning she'd look haggard, but she wouldn't mention anything to me about it. Dad wouldn't say anything either.

Sometimes, after the fighting, there was a dead quiet, and if Dad wasn't too drunk, he would start up the car and drag the trailer out on to the road again and head for the next town where he was booked. It was as though he wanted to put distance between himself and the place where they'd had the fight, as if that would take care of the problem, as if you didn't carry your problems around with you like the smell of cigarettes on your clothes. It didn't work, of course, but it helped, and I'd be quiet in the back pretending to be asleep when he'd pull out on the road, though really I'd be shaking from all the beating that had gone on, but as we drove through the dark toward the next town, the sound of the road would hum in my ear beneath my pillow and that sound would make everything calm and perfect and okay after a while, and I'd fall asleep and forget.

So we went on like that until finally Mom fell off in Salt Lake City the way a suitcase might drop off a cartop carrier.

And so, as I drove north on 1-75 that night on the way to Violet's grandfather's, I felt the road start to work its magic on me again, and pretty soon I could almost forget there was a hole in the back of the van where my favorite guitar and all the money I had in the world used to be. The only thing that existed was the fifty or hundred yards in front of me where the headlights scooped a cone out of the dark. Other than that, there was nothing else, only me and the night and the sense of moving through a dark tunnel.

*

I pulled off at a Union 76 station on the southern outskirts of Detroit to get a little gas before we got into the city. I had been there often enough as a kid to know that there were parts of it where you wouldn't want to be alone in trouble because they were places where the weak were killed and eaten. Anytime we were within a hundred miles of Detroit, my dad would make a side trip and pull the trailer up in front of Grace Hospital.

"That's where Harry Houdini died, son," he'd say, his hand on my shoulder. "Harry Houdini, the greatest escape artist and illusionist in the business. Right there. You see, a guy snuck up on him and hit him in the stomach with a baseball bat after a show one Halloween, and let that be a lesson to you. Never let your guard down, son, or somebody will come up and sideswipe you good and you can't escape from the big black box of death, got that?" Dad was full of that sort of cheery advice, especially after he'd had a few shots to clear his sinuses.

Violet woke up and rubbed her eyes. She shook her head and her multicolored hair flew all over at once. She stretched like a cat does when it wakes up and said, "Where are we?"

"Near Detroit. We need gas."

And then I groaned when I remembered I only had two dollars and change.

"What's the matter?" she asked.

"Do you have any money at all? I've only got two bucks for gas. Everything else I had was in the guitar."

"I'm broke," she said. "Honest. I didn't think about money before I left."

"Well, maybe two bucks will get us to your grandfather's house," I said, getting out and heading for the self-serve pump.

"Hey, wait a minute," she said, jumping out of the passenger side and running around the van. "I know how I can get us some money."

"How?" I asked.

She pointed to a bright Day-Glo sign in the gas station window. "They've got instant lottery here in Michigan. You give me a dollar and I'll buy us a lucky ticket."

"Not this morning," I said, putting the nozzle into the tank. "It seems to me two dollars of real gas in the tank will take us a lot farther than your so-far non-existent luck."

"You've just got to believe," Violet said. "I told you I'm one of those lucky people."

She grabbed my hand and stopped the pump as it hit one dollar even.

"Look, you've got to spend money to make money, don't you?" she said. "Everybody always says that. Anyway, you got to cast your bread upon the water, like my momma always said. Now you loan me one dollar and I'll pay you right back when I win. I'm real lucky at this, you watch."

"All right," I said, a little irritated. "I've got one dollar in the tank right now. At about twenty miles to the gallon, that should almost get us to your grandfather's house, and I've had it with your lucky talk." I pulled the nozzle out of the tank. "Here." I handed her what was, for all practical purposes, my last dollar in the world.

She grabbed it in her hand and headed into the station with me right behind her.

"I want to buy an instant lottery ticket," she said to the clerk, a large woman whose orange and blue work smock made her look like a Union 76 advertising blimp. The clerk floated over to the cash drawer and took a stack of tickets out of the till. She slid the top one out from beneath the rubber band and tossed it on the counter.

"Unh-uh," Violet said, "Not that one. That one's not lucky."

"Well, which one do you want, then?" the clerk asked, rolling her eyes. "They all look the same to me."

"That's because you haven't got the second sight," said Violet, "the kind where you can see without your eyes. Take the rubber band off and let me pick."

"You twenty-one?" the clerk asked suspiciously.

"Yeah I'm twenty-one, of course I am," Violet said. She turned to me. "Right?"

I shrugged. The clerk took that as a yes, I guess, because it was too late at night or too early in the morning to care, and she slipped the rubber band off the packet of lottery tickets. Violet passed her fingers over the fanned-out tickets for a moment with her eyes closed like she was doing a card trick.

"I got things I could do, you know," said the clerk impatiently, though there weren't any other customers in the place. Off in the corner a six-inch black-and-white TV was playing an all-night monster movie, but she didn't seem to be watching it when we came in.

"Shh. I'm trying to find the luckiest one," Violet said, touching each ticket with the tip of her first finger. "I got it narrowed down now." The clerk rolled her eyes again and said hurry up and Violet finally took hold of one ticket and pulled it out of the pack to examine it. The clerk put the packet away and drifted over to a stool where she was reading a National Enquirer story about a woman who had herself surgically transformed into a mermaid and made her living catching fish with her teeth in a swimming pool at a hotel in the Florida Keys.

"Now I need a nickel," Violet said to me as she held the lucky ticket up in the air like it needed drying. "Or even a penny would do."

I dug in my jeans. "Sure. You got the rest of my money," I said, "why not my last nickel, too?"

"Just wait, you'll see," Violet said.

She set the card on the counter and rubbed the silvery film off the spots.

"Look here, it says Free Ticket," she said, waving it in front of my nose to make sure I saw it. "I made a match. See? I told you I was lucky."

"How much gas can you buy with a free ticket?" I asked the clerk. She hauled herself off the stool, not an easy thing for a woman her size, and got the tickets out again. Violet took her time picking another lucky one and rubbed the dots off it.

"Another free ticket!" she squealed. The clerk rolled her eyes again and fanned out the tickets one more time. Violet grabbed for another but pulled her hand back.

"Wait a minute," she said, and she reached inside her shirt and pulled out the funny little cross, the lucky one she claimed had come from the Christians on Neptune.

The clerk suddenly looked interested for the first time.

"Let me see that, would you?" she asked, reaching over the counter. Violet showed her the cross and the clerk asked, "Do those things really work? I read about them in the paper, all about how them spacemen came down to that woman and shrunk up her ovaries. I was thinking about getting one myself but seven-ninety-five seemed like a lot to spend. You had good luck with it?"

"Just watch," Violet said, picking out a ticket.

She read the numbers as she scraped off each dot with the foot of the magic cross. "Ten, five, fifteen, twelve . . ." Then she started jumping up and down, squealing and flapping the ticket in front of my nose again. "Yes! Fifteen! Another Fifteen! Look here! Look here! I won us fifteen dollars! See? I told you my lucky cross would do it. You just got to learn to believe."

"As far as I'm concerned, seein' is believin'," said the clerk as she handed Violet fifteen dollars from the till. "I'm gonna send for one of those crosses myself just as soon as I get off work."

I didn't say anything. What could I say, anyway? Without rubbing it in too much more, Violet gave me ten dollars and I was almost able fill up with it. Meanwhile, she ran across the parking lot to the all-night Munchee Mart and got two microwave cheeseburgers for breakfast and another MunchDoor ticket.

"You see what you get when you travel with a lucky person?" she said, coming back and handing me a micro-burger.

"So you got lucky once," I said.

"You wait," she said, tucking her Munchee Mart game ticket into her bag. "Pretty soon Billy and I'll have our dream house, too. And who knows what kind of luck you're going to have just for helping me out this way."

"We'll see," I mumbled.

CHAPTER THREE

As it turned out, Violet's grandfather did exist and he did live—if you want to call it living—in Detroit. We found his name, Ernest Tolliver, in the phone book, and with the help of the city map in my road atlas and two mailmen who were having breakfast at a Munchee Mart (Violet picked up another MunchDoor for her dream house, no purchase necessary), we got there a little before sun-up.

Grandpa Tolliver's house was tucked underneath an I-75 overpass down among the Ford factories in the area they call River Rouge. If you ask me, it was like being in one of the less pleasant neighborhoods of Dante's imagination.

It was still dark when we got down there, and all around us the huge shapes of factories and cracking towers loomed up into the night like prehistoric animals. The chimneys sent out billows of dark smoke, and from the refinery cracking towers giant yellow and blue flames burned off excess gas. The gas flares lit up the sky and turned everything orange, as though we were down in the devil's own living room.

The smell of sulfur and burning gas filled our noses, and everything was covered with red iron dust the color of dried blood. The dust billowed about, jarred loose by the banging of the trains that never stopped running through. Violet told me her mother said she had grown up in hell, and she wasn't far from the truth. It was about as close to hell as I've ever been.

The ground rumbled beneath us and the van almost lost its suspension in a couple of places where big chunks of the street were missing. It looked as though somebody had been dynamiting holes in the pavement. A rust-covered sign with three bullet holes in it said "Welcome to Detroit!"

It made me more eager than ever to drop off Violet Tansy as quickly as I could, get some cash and that old guitar from her grandfather, and leave for New York as soon as possible.

Of course, as I mentioned before, with Violet things don't ever turn out quite the way you planned.

We pulled up to the house Grandpa Tolliver lived in about the time dawn's early light came up and turned the scene to a dull, unpleasant gray. The house was covered with shredded asphalt shingles that over the years had picked up the red dust color of everything else down there near the Ford factories.

Violet's aunt, Verna Mae, opened the door after we knocked, but it took a while. There were about ten locks for her to click, slide and undo, and then her face peeked out from a crack no bigger than a rat hole. At first she acted like she didn't know who Violet was.

"I'm Violet, Rose's daughter," she said. "Maybe you don't remember me because I haven't been here but once and that was a long time ago. I remember you, though; you haven't changed at all."

Verna Mae didn't say anything. She opened the door a crack wider to check us out, and I got my first good look at her. Verna Mae was a skinny woman, thin as an insect, like a walking stick, so rail-like that I thought at first she must have TB or emphysema from living down there near the factories and refineries. But she wasn't only thin. She looked as brittle and stiff as the binding of a cheap Bible, with a pointy nose and cheek bones that stuck out at funny angles and eyes with red rims around them, like a lizard's eyes, that seemed to move independently of each other. Everything about her was nervous and wary, as if living too long in the devil's kitchen had made her distrustful of everyone and everything.

I didn't intend to stay there long enough for the same thing to happen to me. My plan was to get that guitar—if there was a guitar—and get back on the road to New York. In the meantime, I stood back, tried to smile, and let Violet do all the talking. Verna Mae kept the door only half open and held her foot wedged tight against the other side.

From inside the house I caught a whiff of a stench like stale cigars, mentholatum, and Lysol all mixed up together, as if the place hadn't been aired out in thirty years or more. It was a hot August morning outside, but the air coming from the inside of the house was even hotter, unbearably hot, and I wasn't so sure I wanted to go in.

"You say you're Rose's daughter?" Verna Mae asked.

"I got her picture here," Violet said digging in her bag. She pulled out a tattered snapshot of a thin woman in a white dress. The woman looked like Verna Mae, only more rounded out with softer features, the way Verna Mae might have looked if she hadn't been beaten hard over the years by the place she lived. Violet held the picture out to Verna Mae, who looked at it like it was a passport or something. "They say I got her nose," Violet said, and turned sideways for a minute.

Verna Mae didn't say anything to that. Instead, she sniffed twice and unchained the door.

"I guess you can come in," she said.

"I will in a minute," Violet replied, "but first I got to get something."

Violet had left the baby in the van since she thought it might be too much of a shock to Verna Mae to see both her and the baby at the same time. I guess she thought it would be better to ease into that complicated subject.

As Violet ran down to the van to get the box, Verna Mae undid the rest of the chains and let me through the door. I started to drip from the heat the minute I crossed the threshold. Beads of water popped out on my forehead like sweat on a watermelon, but I didn't dare reach up to wipe my face since I was afraid Verna Mae might have a shotgun handy. There was no sense making any fast moves.

Not knowing what else to do, I tried to make conversation while Violet was gone.

"Kind of warm in here, isn't it?" I asked.

I admit it wasn't real witty, but it was the best I could manage under the circumstances.

Verna Mae looked at me as if I were an idiot, and said, "If you don't keep your house sealed up around here, they'll come in and knock you on the head."

I nodded. So much for small talk. I wondered who, exactly, "they" were who went around breaking into houses with the express purpose of knocking people on the head, but I decided to keep mum. We stood there awkwardly in the silence with Verna Mae keeping a watch on me with her red-rimmed eyes in case I turned out to be a headknocker. If I could only get the old man's guitar and go, I thought, I could be in New York early the next morning, and if I could leave Violet Tansy with her relatives, such as they were, I could go to that audition with a clean conscience, knowing I had done about as much as any good Samaritan had to under the circumstances. People's families are their own business, and though this didn't look like much of a place for Violet and her baby, it was probably better for them than being homeless and on the road.

I looked out into the kitchen and could see three or four pots on the boil already. It was only seven o'clock in the morning, but the smell of steaming carrots filled the hot house. I wondered why anyone would want to boil carrots at seven in the morning on a hot August day, but after my previous attempt to open conversation with Verna Mae, I decided not to ask. Maybe she liked things well cooked.

After what seemed like about fourteen years, Violet finally trudged back up the steps with the box under her arm. She set the box on the floor and lifted the baby out. He started squawling right away, probably from the smell and the heat inside the place. I guess I half expected Verna Mae to soften up a bit when she saw the baby the way people do, but she didn't. The prospect of two more mouths to feed didn't overjoy her.

"Where'd you get that?" she asked sharply, jerking her finger at the baby.

"He's mine," said Violet.

Verna Mae grunted and shook her head.

Just then Grandpa Tolliver came stumbling in, feeling his way with his left hand a little in front of him. His corduroy slippers shuffled through the dust bunnies on the bare wood floor. In his right hand, he held a gnarled walking stick that thumped on the wooden floor like a peg leg. He had what looked like two pale blue marbles where his eyes ought to have been.

"Look, Grandpa Tolliver," Violet said. "This here's your great-grandson."

"Hand him here, girl," the old man said without even saying hello. He crooked his walking stick over his forearm, reached out and took the baby in his trembling hands and held him in one arm while his free hand felt all over the baby's face. The baby went on yowling at the top of his lungs and windmilling his arms around until one of his little hands lit on one of the old man's fingers. He grabbed it and shoved it into his mouth and started sucking on it.

"Hah!" the old man cackled. "He thinks my finger's a tit, now ain't that somethin'?"

Grandpa Tolliver's head was shaped like a pale white melon with a fringe of longish gray-yellow hair around it. The blind eyes in the middle of his face danced around like two blue butterflies, darting this way and that.

"You see," Violet said as her grandfather felt the baby over, "Billy and I were going to get married, only we didn't have time before his ship left Norfolk, but we're going to get married as soon as we get to San Diego."

"So his name's Billy?" Verna Mae asked, pointing at me. "You didn't say what his name was."

"Him? Billy?" Violet asked, with a little laugh I didn't much appreciate. "He's not Billy. He's only somebody taking me and the baby to San Diego. He says his name is Stupid."

"You can just call me Stu," I said, looking around the cluttered house for something resembling an old guitar case. The beads of sweat were rolling down my nose. I couldn't imagine what the house would feel like in the afternoon when the sun had been hitting it all day, but I hoped to be gone by then anyway. "And I'm not taking her anywhere but here. I don't think it's a good idea for her to be out there on the road, so I brought her here to be with you."

Verna Mae grunted. "I thought he might be the father," she said to Violet. "He looks the type who'd get a girl in this kind of situation."

I tried to maintain a steady grin, but I was sure it looked more like a grimace. I thought I had to be polite until I got the guitar in my hands because right then it was the only way I could see to getting the quick cash I needed to get to New York.

"My baby's daddy is a submariner in the U.S. Navy," Violet said proudly.

"Well, he sure torpedoed you, didn't he?" Verna Mae mumbled as she slithered away into the kitchen to stir the carrot mush. The old man lay his large hand over the baby's face again, staring up at the ceiling as he felt it.

"Yes," he said in an eerie, faraway voice, "I can tell that this baby's goin' to grow up to be something special someday."

"That's right," said Violet.

Grandpa Tolliver continued, his voice all trembly, "I prophesy great things for this boy. I may be blessed now in my old age. I have seen my children's children's children, Lord."

"Do you think maybe my baby'll be blessed with the sight like me and the rest of the family, Grandpa?" Violet asked.

The old man seemed to ponder this a bit and palmed the baby's head a little more, like he was feeling the bumps on it for a divine sign.

"This baby's got the Tolliver head, all right," he said, "and with a head like that 'most anything can happen. Like as not, he'll have the sight. It runs in the family."

"Sight, my eye," Verna Mae said, coming back in from the kitchen. "Most like, he'll grow up like his uncle Arzo, a drunk or in jail or both."

The three of them then fell into a huge cat fight over whether the boy was going to be the next president of the United States or a car thief and boozer, and so I took the opportunity to stumble through the heat to the bathroom and splash cold water on my face to keep from boiling over like an old radiator. Not that it helped much. The sweat and road grit washed off, but it made the heat in the house seem worse in the long run because it added to the humidity.

When I got back, they were still arguing over how the baby was going to turn out, and I suggested the only way to find out for sure was to wait around and see. That went over like a dustball, and I could tell they didn't want me horning in on their family argument. Not that I personally intended to wait around eighteen or twenty years and see what happened to the kid, mind you. In fact, I would have left right then if I could have got my hands on the guitar or at least some gas money for bringing Violet to her relations—not that they seemed to particularly appreciate her being there.

They kept on arguing—family stuff that I didn't know anything about, things that seemed to go back several generations—until finally I couldn't take the heat and the smell and the general pressure cooker feeling in the place anymore and excused myself. I pulled Violet aside for a moment while Verna Mae and Grandpa kept on hollering like bobcats in the background.

"Listen," I said, "I can see you and your relatives have got a lot of catching up to do, old family business and such, so I think I'll head out for a while and see if I can find a bottle of oxygen someplace. Meantime, could you check on that guitar?"

"What guitar?" she asked.

I tried to speak clearly and distinctly so she would understand.

"The guitar you promised me I could have if I brought you up here," I said. "The guitar to make up for the one stolen from me last night. Remember? The guitar I need to go to my audition in New York." I told her I'd be back in a few hours and that I hoped she could bring herself to ask her Grandpa about it. I tried to speak calmly but firmly, like somebody might speak to you if he was telling you he was going to kill your cat.

After that, I cruised around Detroit for a while until I finally found a quiet street where the likelihood of getting shot, slit, or murdered seemed pretty small, and I pulled over and tried to catch up on the sleep I'd missed the night before.

As I lay there in the heat, I thought about how Violet kept saying how *lucky* she was. Lucky in what? I wondered. She didn't have any money except for small change from the Munchee Mart. Was she lucky for her wholesome supportive family? Not that I could see. She didn't even have Billy. Anybody who knew anything knew she wasn't going to find him either, and even if she *did* find him, he wasn't going to do the noble thing and marry her and settle down and raise the kid. So how was she lucky and what was her luck made of? I suppose on one level she was lucky just to be alive with all the psycho killers out there on the road preying on the weak and wounded. But that didn't seem to be what Violet meant by luck.

It was something else, closer to faith than to anything, I guess, that made her believe, in spite of all the evidence to the contrary, that all would be well and everything would turn out for the best.

The fortunes of Las Vegas are built on the fact that most people believe in that kind of luck, of course. Most people are convinced deep down they will eventually get lucky. They believe this even as they send their lives down the slots a quarter or a dollar at a time. They never give up hope of finally getting touched by the golden finger of lady fortune. Hardly a day went by at the Lucky Lady but after the gig some old drunk would buy me a beer and tell me how lucky he was, not right then, you understand, but really deep down inside, he was truly lucky and all of this would become clear after the next crap shoot or the next hand of blackjack or the next turn of the roulette wheel. People never give up on luck and most of us keep plugging away getting nowhere as our lives continue to happen to us.

If I was really honest, I believed it, too, even though I knew the Lucky Lady pretty well after working in her casino for about ten years, even though I knew her for a tease, and even though I knew that for every poor soul she touched, a hundred or more ended up on the heap of empty change buckets. Like everyone else, I thought my case would be different, which was why I was going to take full advantage of this crack in the door that Murray had opened. I could feel the wheels of the cosmic slot machine turning and I was going to come up cherries as soon as I got to New York. I had luck on my side.

But, then, as I started to doze off in the van, I thought that maybe, just maybe, the kind of luck Violet was talking about might be different from the luck the people who junketed into Las Vegas had in mind. I didn't understand it, or her, at all, but as I drifted off to sleep, I had one of those funny little dreams you get sometimes when you're floating on that line between consciousness and sleep. In the dream, I saw Violet coming up the aisle of a wedding chapel in Las Vegas. She was dressed in a white bridal gown all covered with pearls, and the music playing was a strange and beautiful song totally unfamiliar to me until somebody reminded me that I had been the one who wrote it. And then I fell into a deep sleep and when I woke up a few hours later, I felt better than I had in days.

*

I slept in the van for longer than I intended and didn't get back to Violet's grandfather's house until supper time. My original plan was to grab the guitar and run, but Violet told me I had to eat supper first.

"It wouldn't hardly be right," she said, "sending you out hungry after all you've done."

Supper—or what passed for it—was the mushed up carrots that had been on the stove all day and something else that was white but had been cooked so long I couldn't tell what it was anymore.

We all sat around a rickety wooden table with a checked oilcloth covering on it. After the day's cooking and the after-noon heat, the house was as hot as a cheap room in Gila Bend. Little rivulets of condensed steam rolled down the walls and windows.

Verna Mae said grace. Her mouth was a tight hole the prayer had to escape from like puffs of steam.

"O Lord," she began after she'd set the smoking hot bowls of carrot mush and whatever else it was on the table in front of us. "You who took pity on the prodigal son who run off and left his father and spent his life sinning and whoring while the good child stayed home." Verna Mae looked up at her father at this and narrowed her eyes and tensed up her jaw, pausing only long enough to make her point. Then she cleared her throat and continued. "Bless this food, and especially them what provided it, so that through thy will righteousness may prevail, and may them journeyers and wayfarers"—here she looked at Violet and me—"that has no gratitude for such food as this be enlightened in your ways. Amen."

After that, Verna Mae seemed to be watching and passing judgment on every bite we took to make sure we were proper-ly grateful. Trying to eat in the steam-pressurized kitchen was like trying to eat with a rope drawn tight around your neck.

Nobody said a word for a long time. The sounds of chewing and the steady flup-flup of the still-bubbling stuff on the stove were punctuated by clinks of forks against china.

Finally, Grandpa Tolliver broke the silence.

"You been down to where they buried your mother lately?" he asked Violet. I saw Verna Mae stiffen up, and the little hole that was her mouth got even smaller. She set down her fork with a clack on the table, but Violet's grandfather didn't seem to pay any attention.

"Yes, sir," Violet said. "I took the baby down there a couple of weeks after he was born. I took some woodbine that was growing there and ate some of it so it'd get in my milk for the baby. Woodbine's big magic for a child."

Verna Mae pushed her chair back, making a scraping noise as she jumped up and pulled the lid off the still boiling carrot mush. A cloud of steam erupted from the mush and filled the already-hot kitchen. She lifted up a gob of the carrot mush in the spoon and turned it over. It made a sucking sound as it slid off the spoon and splatted back into the pot.

"That stuff Rosie did weren't hardly Christian, most of it," Verna Mae said.

Grandpa Tolliver laid his fork down. "She done a lot of good with her healing, Verna Mae."

"T'weren't Christian," Verna Mae said again.

They must have been picking up another old argument from where they'd left off on it. They probably had a lot of those lying around the house like unexploded hand grenades. Some families are like that. They can set something down that's red hot and pick it up weeks or even years later, and it's still burning. Most often, the argument isn't even about what the people arguing think it's about. One year, right after we were married, Hazel and I had a big argument over where to hang the Christmas wreath. She wanted it over the mantel, I wanted it in the front hall. We bickered about it for hours until finally we ended up hanging it outside on the garage door, just to get it out of the house, but the real question wasn't where we were going to hang the wreath. It was really about who was in charge.

In Verna Mae's case, I thought, it wasn't about theology, it was about forty years of resentment over being the child who had to give up her life to tend to her blind and aging father. She was a difficult woman to deal with, but I could sympathize with her.

"Well, what *is* Christian with you anyway, Verna Mae?" said Grandpa. "What besides hymn singing and washing everything in the house with Lysol every chance you get?"

"Cleanliness is next to Godliness," she said.

"That's only a theory that ain't been proved yet," snapped Grandpa Tolliver.

"Hmph."

He turned to me as if I were the jury in this argument. "A man can't smoke around here because it ain't Christian," snorted the old man, "can't drink because it ain't Christian, can't play good music 'cause it ain't Christian. I'd take my Rosie's way any day if I had the choice."

Verna Mae exploded now, her whole face scrunched up in anger and frustration. Finally the true point of the argument came out. "Rosie run off and I never did," Verna Mae said, sharp as a snake bite. "Who stayed here and took care of you all these years?"

Grandpa Tolliver wouldn't let up. How could he? If he let Verna Mae slip out of his grip, he'd be left blind and alone in that house in hell. They were locked together claw and tail like two battling scorpions.

"Who was it drove her off?" shouted Grandpa Tolliver, "You and your preachin', that's what."

"Rosie was a *witch*, everybody knows that. She toyed with devil's work with her spells and charms and herbals and all that, washing cats by the light of the moon and other stuff too unchristian to mention. The scripture says, *Thou shalt not suffer a witch to live.*"

He turned to me and Violet and tried to explain. "Violet's mother wasn't no witch. She was a healer. She had the power of Nature and knew every herb and what it could do and she could make simples and poultices and compounds for people who couldn't afford a doctor."

"And Rosie's burning in hell for it, right this minute," Verna Mae said bitterly, but with just a hint of triumph in her voice.

She got up from the table and quoted darkly: "*A generation of vipers; prepare to flee from the wrath to come, for the day is coming says the Lord.*" Then she ran out of the room crying. A few seconds later she came back into the kitchen, red-eyed but subdued. She had put on a black straw hat with a faded silk rose stuck on the front of it. The rose was half falling off. She had her Bible tucked under her arm and stood there for a second looking Violet in the eye.

"Your mother did things I never approved of," she said to Violet. "That's true. But it ain't fair everybody loved her when I was the one that stayed on here. It ain't fair."

Then she was off for the night, heading out the front door and down the steps.

"My momma was a healer," Violet said, after the echo of Verna Mae's footsteps died away. "She had powers and Verna Mae was always jealous. People came from miles around to get her herbs."

"That's all very interesting about your mother," I said to Violet, trying to change the subject. Time was moving on, and if I could get the guitar and drive all night, I could still be in New York the next day. "Listen, the dinner was great and your aunt really has a way with vegetables and I'm sorry I didn't get a chance to thank her, but I'm expected in New York City tomorrow, and if I could just get that guitar now, I could. . . ."

"Rose went back south when she was sixteen," said Grandpa Tolliver right over what I was saying. "This here was no place for a girl like her. She was part of the hills down there and when we took her out and come up here when she was eight, she near died from it. We sent her back home to live with kin, but it wasn't no use. You can get in trouble and die there just as good as anywhere else. Yes, she died anyway."

Not wanting to alienate the old man before I got my hands on a guitar, I tried to pretend I was interested in the conversation, but in my head, I was already on my way to the Big Apple. "Well, that's too bad and I'm very sorry she died," I said, "but life belongs to the living, doesn't it? By the way, Violet here said I could get . . ."

"Blame that on the man she married, that Lloyd Tansy," said Grandpa Tolliver angrily. "He was a handsome hell-raiser and she was young and didn't know no better. She thought she could change him, but she was wrong on that. He was only around long enough to beat up on her and get her pregnant every couple of years. And then he was on his way again, raisin' hell."

"Momma died givin' birth to a stillborn baby boy," Violet explained. "I was ten."

"Sorry to hear that," I said.

"She had the power," said Violet again.

"That's wonderful," I said, trying to figure out a way to derail this conversation and finally steer it around to the subject of guitars. Not that I didn't sympathize, but I had to wonder what good all Violet's mother's so-called "powers" did her if they didn't give her enough sense to stay out of trouble with a boozing hill boy that beat up on her. Maybe her life was so confusing to begin with that even ESP wasn't enough to help. From what I'd seen of Violet's family in the past couple of hours, fixing it up would be so complicated even extra psychic powers would be as hopeless as using a peashooter against a crazed elephant. I felt sorry for them, but this stuff about magical powers wasn't getting me any closer to replacing my lost Martin. My problem right then was getting some kind of guitar and heading to New York for the break of my life.

"Look, all this talk about powers and stuff is great," I said, "but you promised me when I brought you here that . . ."

"Violet's momma had powers even after she died," Grandpa Tolliver said. "You tell him, Violet."

I rolled my eyes and pushed the carrot mush away. I could see this conversation was going to happen at its own pace.

"They buried Momma down in a shady place in the hollow that was like a piece of Eden nobody'd touched since creation. Her grave was right beneath a big old tree that had been her favorite place. It was covered with moss and tangled vines, and once she'd been buried there, wildflowers grew everywhere around there, woodbine and myrtle, jack-in-the-pulpits and ladyslippers. An apple tree blossoms there early every year."

"That's really beautiful," I said, looking around the room for a guitar, "but . . ."

"The problem was the coffin wouldn't stay still," Grandpa Tolliver said.

That caught my attention.

"It's true," Violet said. "One year we went to her grave and found a big ol' bulge in the ground, like her coffin was just below the surface trying to fetch up. Then the next year there was a hollow there, as if she was gone visiting some-place else or maybe had rose up from the dead. And the year after, it was level as a pool table and all covered with moss. It's always cool in that spot, and birds and wildlife come. It's like they're attracted to Momma's soul."

"How interesting," I said. "By the way, does anybody ever come down there to your mother's grave and play guitar?"

"What?" asked Violet.

"Play guitar," I said, mimicking a couple of strums and chords.

"I suppose so," Violet said, missing the point. "You'd like it. It's a magical place. That's why I took my baby there. I washed him in some water caught in a hollow stone. Spirits are carried in water. I wanted him to be blessed with Momma's power."

"Yep," Grandpa Tolliver said. "And Violet was born with it, too. The power runs in our family. I don't know whether you noticed that about her or not."

"It hasn't been real obvious to me, so far," I admitted. "Listen, about that . . ."

"I won fifteen dollars in the instant lottery last night, Grandpa," Violet said.

"You see? It's a gift," said the old man. "I got it a bit myself, but not like Violet does, and she doesn't even have half of what her mother did."

"Listen," I finally said, looking at the clock. "I don't like to be direct about this, but Violet promised me you had some sort of guitar up here I could have for bringing her to you, and I hate to be rude, but I was wondering if I could get it and go because I've really really got to get to New York tomorrow for a big audition."

He turned his pale blue eyes on me and pointed at me with the end of his gnarled old walking stick. If he could have seen with those eyes they would have burned holes in me, but even though they were blind they locked on me and I felt like he was threatening me.

"You don't believe in the powers, boy?" he growled.

"My father was a magician," I explained, "and I learned not to trust anything. How would you like to grow up where every time you turned around somebody was pulling flowers out of your nose?"

The old man grunted roughly at that, then sniffed, like an old bulldog or something.

"Violet, there's some guitars in the closet in the living room. Get them and hand me down my fiddle. Let's go, Stupid."

Well now, I thought, as we all went into the living room, maybe the old guy does have the power of second sight. It only took him about all day to realize I didn't give a hoot about his family's psychic abilities. Maybe he finally realized, through ESP or something, that I wasn't thinking about much besides the guitar and how to get out of that hot house and on my way to New York City as fast as I could.

Violet went to a closet and got two battered guitar cases and set them down in front of me. Then she went to the mantel and took down an old dusty fiddle. It was so old that the varnish on it was black.

"I got two guitars there," said the old man. "One of 'em's good and one's not so good. Before I give you my good one, I got to hear how you play."

"Don't worry about that," I said, opening up the first case. "I can play about anything." The first guitar was in fairly good shape. It looked like it hadn't been played very much and my hopes went up for a minute. I tuned it and strummed a couple of chords. It didn't ring nearly as good as the Martin I'd lost back in Toledo. In fact it was a little cheap-sounding, but it was better than no guitar at all, and I figured even if I couldn't use it for the audition I could stop at a truck stop in Pennsylvania and sell it to some truck driver for forty bucks and use the money for gas to get me to New York, where I could borrow a good electric guitar and audition for Sclapped.

After I'd played a few licks on it, Grandpa Tolliver stopped me and said, "You ain't half bad, Stupid. Now try the other 'un."

I opened the second case. What a disaster. The guitar looked totally beat. It was an old no-name brand, probably from around the time of the Great Depression or before, and the finish on it was almost completely worn off, as though it had been sandblasted. This guitar had a lot of miles on it, and I figured from looking at it that I wouldn't be able to give it away, much less sell it for anything but firewood. But the old man urged me to try it, so I pulled it out of the case anyway.

The face of it had a crack running down it so big that you could see inside the sound box.

There was only one interesting thing about this guitar. A design had been drawn with colored ink pens all around the sound hole on the bare-grained wood. The drawing made it look like flowers were growing right out of the inside of the guitar, spilling out of the sound hole and covering the face of the instrument. The flowers were roses and honeysuckles and morning glories and other kinds of climbing flowers that grow on vines. The stems were drawn with green ink and the flowers themselves had been colored in with other pens so that there were red flowers and blue ones and green ones, too. I had never seen a guitar done up quite that way. It looked like the circle of the sound hole was a hole in the earth out of which all these plants just grew and grew and kept on growing. It was almost pretty, but I figured the guitar was so battered that, with the crack and all, I couldn't sell it. I picked it up to be polite to the old man, but I had already decided to take the other one.

I tuned the flowered guitar up. To my surprise, the strings held in spite of being rusty, and when I strummed the first chord my ears perked up. I could hardly believe the sound that poured out of that soundhole. The tone was ringing and deep and rich, the most incredible sound I'd ever heard out of a guitar. I played some runs up the neck, and the strings lay easy on the fretboard. It held the high notes long, and I could feel the low notes vibrate right through the back of the instrument and into my chest. It may have looked like kindling, but it was the best guitar I had ever played in my life. It was even better than my lost Martin, and I knew that any experienced guitar player in the world would pay over a thousand dollars for it. I could probably unload it in the Detroit area the next day and buy a plane ticket to New York, but I realized I might not want to. I wanted this guitar for myself.

I played some more. I had never heard notes from a guitar like the ones from Grandpa Tolliver's battered and flowery ax. Maybe the wood had gotten so seasoned over the years that the tone had grown richer and richer. The sound was pure silver and it rang out for a long time after my right hand hit the strings.

"Which one do you want?" the old man asked.

"This one," I said, so excited that I was almost slobbering. "I want this one."

"Well, you done picked the right one," he said, sticking the fiddle up under his chin. "Maybe you're not as stupid as you look." He held the fiddle there as natural as breathing, like it was a limb growing out of his body. He ran the bow over the strings once or twice, then said, with a sharp challenge in his voice, "Now let's see if you're good enough for me to want to give it to you. Play with me, boy."

And we started to play. We played songs I hadn't heard for years. First some familiar old-tyme fiddle stuff like the "Fourteenth of January" and "Soldier's Joy," pretty easy stuff, then some more complicated things I didn't know with strange chord changes in unusual places, modal tunes as ancient as the Appalachian hills. The old man was a good fiddler in spite of the arthritis that swelled his knuckles. In fact, he played like he didn't have any pain at all, though earlier he'd had difficulty just getting his fork to his mouth.

The fiddle bow gave off a little swirl of rosin with each stroke, and after a while we were pumping out some pretty good sounds. Violet held her little no-name baby on her knees and bounced him up and down like one of those clog dancer puppets they sell, and the baby was smiling. I couldn't blame him. I was smiling, too. It was hard not to smile the way that guitar played, and in my head I struggled whether to upgrade my ticket to New York to first class or to hang on to that old guitar forever, because I found myself falling in love with it.

I was dying to do something solo on it and really give it a workout all up and down the fretboard, and Grandpa Tolliver finally got tired and set the fiddle down.

I played for a few minutes unaccompanied, but if the truth be told, the old guitar was almost playing itself. I couldn't believe the old man would ever part with a guitar this good unless *he* was stupider than he looked, too. It sure was worth more than my old Martin, and I would have traded for it any day.

"That was right nice," old man Tolliver said after I'd played a while. He looked off into space for a minute, as if thinking on the matter. Then he said, "You know, there's only two things in life I like anymore at my age—one's fiddlin' and the other's whiskey, and I don't get enough of either of them while Verna Mae's around."

Now I happened to have an almost-full pint of Jack Daniels out in the van, stashed under the seat, so I ran straight out and brought it back in. I thought maybe if I liquored the old man up enough he'd part with the guitar more easily. I suddenly found myself wanting it more than I had ever wanted anything in my life.

"Oh, yes," he said as he took a deep soft sip of the whiskey. "That's worth waiting for."

While he was sipping, I laid a few licks on the old guitar. It played smooth and easy all the way up the neck. The fretboard was worn a little deep down by some of the frets, but otherwise it was in good shape for playing.

"How do you like it?" he asked.

"It's a fine instrument," I said, trying to conceal my enthusiasm. "Really fine." I couldn't believe he would actually give it to me.

"An angel drew them flowers on that guitar, didn't he, Grandpa?" Violet asked. "That's what you told me when I was little."

"He wasn't no angel," said the old man, leaning forward on his chair a little and taking another sip of the Black Jack.

"What was he then, a devil?" Violet asked.

"Wasn't no devil neither," said her grandfather. Then he stared off as if he could see something floating around up near the ceiling. I looked but there was nothing overhead but a thin cobweb dancing lightly in the draft. The old man got a tone in his voice that made me feel cold and I poured myself another shot of whiskey, too. "He was just something . . . different, that's all," he said and then let it drift off. By that time, I was almost used to Violet's family talking about spirits, so I didn't pay much attention.

I retuned the old guitar to an open-D tuning and started to play that little no-name open-tuning piece I'd written back in Vegas. The lowered D note on the sixth string sounded incredibly rich and deep and held the whole song together in a way even my old Martin hadn't done. The song had never sounded so good as it did on this guitar, and a weird thought flitted through my brain that it was as though the song had been waiting for this guitar, or vice versa.

No more had I thought that, though, than the old man's drinking hand stopped halfway to his mouth and I saw the glass of whiskey begin to shake. He set it back down on the side table so hard that some of the whiskey spilled out. His face turned white as a peeled turnip and he groped around with his hand for his cane.

"My stick!" he shouted suddenly. "Violet, give me my stick!"

"What's the matter, Grandpa?" Violet said.

"Ain't nothin' the matter," he snapped, though obviously something was. The song I was playing must have hit him someplace deep and hard, and he was so agitated I was afraid he was going to pick up his walking stick and hit me with it.

"Where'd you learn that song, boy?" he said, once he had the stick safe in his hand and was holding it between me and him.

"This?" I asked and played a couple more bars.

"That one," he said. "Who taught it to you?" His voice was high and excited. I idly played a few more bars, but he took his walking stick and shook it violently at me.

"Quit!" he shouted. "Quit that song now, damn you!"

So I quit and sat there with the guitar resting on my leg.

"What's the matter, Grandpa?" Violet asked. Even she seemed scared by her grandfather's sudden outburst.

"I seen things when I had eyes," he said mysteriously. "Wonderments, things nobody else's ever seen, you know what I mean?"

"What kind of things, Grandpa?"

"Just things," he snapped, making it clear he didn't want her to talk about it anymore.

Oh no, I thought, here we go again on another deep dive, and I felt the same sensation from the arrowhead illusion back in Iowa and from two nights before in the campground in Ohio with Violet, like I was being sucked up a tube once more. I knocked down a shot of whiskey and began to tune the guitar back to a standard tuning, hoping to return things to normal. As I hit the first notes, he turned to me and said, "I don't want to listen to that song no more, hear?" I didn't say anything right away, so he repeated, louder and more threatening, "You hear me, boy?"

"Yeah, I hear," I said, making sure not to hit any of the harmonics of the open tuning while I was tightening the strings. I felt all wired up, as though somebody had attached electrodes on my skin. It was eerie, like I was suddenly sitting in a cold spot. My arm hairs were all standing up like wires. I didn't know what else to do except to keep right on fooling around with chords on that flowery guitar, the way you do when you want to distract your mind from whatever is going on right then, and the old man sat and stared in my direction, blind as he was, and shook like a scared possum.

Finally, after a few minutes, Grandpa Tolliver managed to hoist the fiddle beneath his chin and started up a jig and then a reel in the key of D and I joined him on the guitar. Now he played like a man who's desperate to drive something out of his head. I could hardly keep up with him. He got to playing so fast I was afraid he'd have a stroke. His face turned red and his eyes squeezed shut, and he was so intense I began to think he was playing like his life depended on it.

Pretty soon, we were flying along so hard we didn't even hear Verna Mae coming up the front stairs, but suddenly the front door slammed open like it was cops breaking it down. The room was still so tense from all Grandpa Tolliver's weirdness about the open-tuning song that we all jumped at once and the old man took his fiddle away from his face.

"Oh, oh, the day of judgment is at hand!" groaned Grandpa Tolliver, who couldn't see it was only Verna Mae. He quick grabbed for the whiskey glass and threw back a shot like he thought it was the last time he'd ever taste whiskey in this life.

Verna Mae stood there, her red eyes cutting through us all like twin acetylene torches. She was so lit up with holy fire even I was scared. Nothing is more frightening than a Christian just come from church looking for damnation and the devil, and I guessed Verna Mae thought she had found them right in her own living room. All the vulnerability from earlier was gone.

Her lips quivered with rage as she stood there looking from the guitar to the whiskey bottle to the guitar and back again. She looked as though she was getting ready to blow us all down. She held her Bible over her head now in her fist like a thunderbolt. Her hat was cocked sideways on her head, and I'd have sworn that she was drunker than Grandpa Tolliver, but it wasn't liquor that got her that way; it was religion.

"Whiskey! Music!" she shouted. "That infernal guitar!"

The next thing we knew, Verna Mae swept into the room like an avenging angel and scooped the bottle of Jack Daniels off the table and heaved it clear across the room, out through the hall and into the kitchen, where it crashed in the sink.

"*Wine is a mocker, strong drink is raging,*" she screamed, "*and whosoever is deceived thereby is not wise.*"

With that, the baby woke up and started to shriek, and I could have cried too as the last of my Jack Daniels trickled down the drain through the broken glass.

Then Verna Mae came for the guitar I was holding and tried to rip it from my hands.

"Don't let her get that guitar," the old man pleaded, unable to see what was going on. "Don't even let her touch it; it'll explode for sure and we'll all be dead!"

We wrestled for a minute on the tacky, worn sofa until it became clear I wasn't going to give up the instrument, and Verna Mae stood up, her nostrils flared wide.

Grandpa Tolliver lifted his fiddle up in front of his face to protect himself, his two blind eyes darting around behind it like two blue pinballs. "Have mercy, Verna Mae," he pleaded. "Don't hit a poor old blind man! Somethin' truly wondrous has happened here tonight. This here man, this here traveler who brung us our Violet, he ain't no ordinary person, Verna Mae, he's a *sacred messenger!*"

I didn't know what the hell he meant, but at least it made Verna Mae stop hitting on us for a minute. Instead, she stood there glaring at us all until she finally let loose with some choice words about the lot of us being sinners and fornicators and drunkards and servants of the anti-Christ, and she began to sing a hymn right there in the living room. It was one of those Christian hymns in four-four time that sound like army marching tunes, not "Onward Christian Soldiers," but the same idea, and after a few measures everybody figured the safest thing to do was go to bed.

"G'night, Grandpa," Violet said as she headed for the little parlor where Verna Mae told her she and the baby were going to sleep.

"A starry messenger," the old man mumbled, leading himself out of the room with his stick.

Verna Mae went up last. "Starry, my eye," she muttered.

*

I was left in the living room alone. I didn't dare play the flowered guitar again, but before putting it away in its case I looked at the drawing on the sound board once more. The flowers almost looked alive and—maybe it was the effect of the whiskey on me—they seemed even brighter and more colorful than they had before, as if playing the old wreck had rejuvenated them somehow. I flipped the guitar on its face and turned it round and round, looking the whole thing over again. As far as I could tell, knowing what little I knew about guitar construction, there was no earthly reason to account for why the beat-up guitar sounded a thousand times better than the top-of-the-line Martin I'd lost back in Toledo, but it did, and that's the truth. I closed it in its case for the night, drank the little half-moon of whiskey left in my glass, and decided to lie down and rest for a minute before I left for New York, but I quickly fell asleep in spite of myself.

I slept deep for I don't know how long, but the next thing I knew, I was jerked wide awake again by something hard and stiff pressing down against my throat. It was pitch black in the house, and whatever it was that pressed against my windpipe so hard, I was seeing stars even before I opened my eyes.

"Now, you tell me about that song, boy!" a voice hissed. I could tell by the smell of stale whiskey that it was Grandpa Tolliver. His walking stick pressed down on my throat and his face was right next to my ear. His breath smelled of decaying teeth and the Black Jack we'd been drinking a few hours before. The house was as quiet as death with everyone asleep, and he had the advantage on me. I tried to push the stick away, but he held it tight. I could barely breathe.

"What song?" I squeaked.

"That song you was playing earlier tonight," he said. I managed to get him to ease up a bit on the stick before I spoke.

"The open-tuning thing?" I said. "I wrote it." I was gasping for air, still dizzy from being pulled out of sleep so fast.

The stick came down again hard.

"Don't tell me that," the old man snapped. He was talking in a whisper, but his voice was as sharp as a knife. Then, quite suddenly, as though something had suddenly occurred to him—some sort of terrifying possibility—he let up on the stick and I could feel him tremble. "My God," he said. "You ain't . . ."

"Ain't what?" I asked.

"Ain't *him*, are you?" His voice was quavering.

"Who?"

"Let me feel your face," the old man said.

"What?"

"Your face, your face!" His right hand reached out and played over my face, poking into my eye holes, feeling my nose, my ears. His hand was rough and smelly. He grunted as he felt around, then he jerked me up. "Now let me feel your back," he said.

"My back?"

"Your back, your back!"

I sat up, and his hand went around my shoulder and down to where my shoulder blades were. He felt there for a moment, then sighed, as if he was relieved or something.

"You ain't him," he said.

"I could've told you that," I said. "Him who?"

I shifted to a sitting position on the sofa and Grandpa Tolliver sat beside me.

"I seen things when I had me my eyes," he began.

"What sorts of things?" I asked, rubbing my throat where the stick had been. My Adam's apple felt bruised.

"Things you wouldn't hardly believe," he said. "That's why I had to feel your back, to make sure you weren't him."

"Who?" I asked.

"Who?" the old man said. "He was the one who drew them flowers on the guitar. It was fifty years ago."

"Well, who was he?"

"He could have been lots of things," Grandpa Tolliver mused. "At first we thought he was one of those wonderments there used to be more of in the old days. You was always hearing about things born on the farms, freaks of nature—like chickens hatched without feet and calves with two heads and all that. Most of them died pretty quick, but the boy, he lived somehow. Violet tells me you used to travel with the circus, is that right?"

"Sort of," I admitted.

"Well, then, you'd know what I'm talking about," Grandpa Tolliver said, and suddenly the air in the place began to get tight again, like I was being sucked up the old tube. The old man reached out and lay a hand on my thigh as if to make sure I was still there and wouldn't run away on him.

"There used to be more of what we called freaks," he said, "things like you wouldn't never believe. I was only a kid myself at the time and the man I worked for was named Bruno Gallante, you see. He used to travel with the Caribbean Turtle Boy, a human boy who had skin like a reptile and a hard shell on his back. He was famous in his time. You heard of him?"

I shook my head and guessed he heard it shake because he went on.

"Of course not," he said. "They killed the Turtle Boy long before your time and people forget or want to forget there ever were such things in this world. Some kids in Decorah, Iowa, dropped bricks on his back."

"I see," I said.

"This boy I'm talking about, the one who drew those flowers on the guitar, was just like me or you," Grandpa Tolliver said, "except he was born with enormous wings on his back. That's why I had to feel your back, to make sure."

I nodded and mumbled "uh-huh." I shook my head to see if I was awake. I was, but it certainly didn't feel like it.

"I'm telling you this because you should know," he went on, gripping my leg tighter. I could feel every muscle below where he grabbed me going cold from lack of blood. "You see, it was right after they killed the Turtle Boy, and Bruno Gallante and I used the insurance money to buy a Studebaker and drive up to where he lived, up north of Ames about a hundred miles. He wasn't hard to find; he was the only boy in those parts with wings. He was out in the barnyard when we come, tending to chores, just like any farm boy in those days, only out of his back grew these two giant wings, white as a swan's, and long and pointed."

"You mean like an angel?" I gulped.

"That's it exactly," Grandpa said. "Mr. Gallante said he could make the bird boy more famous even than the Caribbean Turtle Boy if he'd come along with us. Think of it: a human angel right there in Iowa. It happened in ancient times in Galilee, so why not here in America? Well, it was hard times then in the freak business, the tail end of the Depression and all. Mostly people only wanted to see machines, aeroplanes and automobiles, Lucky Lindy and Barney Oldfield and all that, but Mr. Gallante thought the winged boy would be enough to make them forget aeroplanes for a while and maybe we could make a few bucks besides."

From outside I could hear the muffled boom of railroad cars smashing against each other over in the Rouge. It sounded like thunder in the hot, sulfurous night. Grandpa Tolliver took a deep breath and proceeded to tell me how he and this Bruno Gallante toured with the Bird Boy here and there through Iowa and how he was barely starting to get famous when something weird happened.

"Yes," the old man whispered, looking up into an empty corner of the ceiling as if he could see it happening there. "It was one night near Alleman, Iowa, and we had just finished the exhibitions. After the show I rubbed the Bird Boy down with liniment and we went to bed like usual. Then I woke up in the middle of the night because I heard something, and I got up to look around. There was mumbles behind the tents, like somebody talking there, and I went around back. Well, you won't believe what I saw!"

His blind eyes were dancing around like crazy in his head now. I tried to pull away, but his grip got tighter on my leg until I had to bite my lips to keep from crying out.

"There was five of them back there with him!" Grandpa Tolliver said.

"Five what?" I asked.

"Five grown men with white wings growing out of their backs just like him! It was full moon and there they stood, their wings all aglow in the moonlight. They had come to claim him for one of their own! Then, all of a sudden, they saw me gaping at them. They turned and looked me right in the eyes and I felt this pain, like someone had struck me with a knife, and the next thing I knew I heard this flutter of wings. I had never heard anything like it, like a hundred flags flapping in the breeze, and as I watched they all took off, and the Bird Boy with 'em! *Good-bye, Ernest*, the bird boy called.

Good-bye, I've got to go. Thank you, Ernest, thank you. He was crying and his voice got farther and farther away. I ran after them, but it wasn't no use. I went to get Mr. Gallante, but by the time I got him up, the bird men were gone, and Bruno and I stood there looking up into the dark night. We could barely see them as they cut off across the face of the full moon like a flock of wild geese, and then they were gone forever. The next morning, I woke up blind!"

As he talked, he flapped his arms to imitate the bird men, and I managed to free my leg and slide away from him as far as I could. I was so dumbstruck, I couldn't say a word.

"There used to be them kind of wonderments all the time," Grandpa continued. "Where do you think they get them old pictures of angels with wings and stories like the one I heard one time about this guy who flew too close to the sun and his wings fell off and all that? I seen marvels in my own lifetime, but nobody believes 'em anymore. Why can't such things happen now?"

"Maybe it's not that kind of a world anymore," I said.

"Maybe," the old man replied, "but that song you was playin' tonight, that open-tuning thing? He wrote that."

"Who?" I asked.

"The Bird Boy!" the old man snapped, as if I were an idiot. "Who do you think I've been talking about all this time? He wrote that song fifty years ago and I remember it like it was yesterday."

"No, he didn't," I said. "I wrote it last year in my bathroom back in Las Vegas."

The old man laughed a little and shook his head as if he was dealing with a moron. "You just *think* you wrote it," he said.

"I did write it," I said, "just last year."

"I was struck blind, boy," the old man snapped, "but I wasn't struck stupid. The Bird Boy wrote that damned song, and I ain't heard it since before the night I saw him fly away with them angels, and so when you played it tonight I thought for a minute you was him and that you'd come back from the dead or from heaven or wherever you went with them others."

"I didn't go anywhere," I said.

"Not you, him, *him!*" the old man said.

"Oh," I said, still wondering whether I was awake or in the middle of some kind of bizarre dream.

"Anyway," Grandpa Tolliver continued, "the point is this—I've had lots of offers for that guitar over the years, people offerin' me more money than I had ever seen in one place at one time in my life, but I never took it, you hear, because I thought someday he'd come back and want his guitar again."

"His guitar?"

"He's the one who drawed them flowers on it. The minute he touched it, it sung like it sung tonight when you played it, so that's the nearest thing I've heard in fifty years to say who that guitar ought rightly to belong to, and I want you to take it and git."

"Git?"

"Out of here," the old man said.

"That's exactly what I've been trying to do all day long," I said.

"Well, then, take the guitar out of this place and play it somewhere again, that's what you got to do now."

"You're giving it to me?"

"Take it and go," he said. "Git. I'm gonna be dead soon and I don't want that guitar falling into the wrong hands. It's far too dangerous for that."

"Dangerous?"

"You'll find out what I mean," he said mysteriously as he got up and headed for the hallway with his walking stick. "You'll find out soon enough." As he was leaving the room, he turned and added, in a low voice, "By the way, boy, Verna

Mae keeps her money in a plastic bag in the sugar jar on top of the refrigerator. You can take it, too. I'm almost dead and after tonight I'm not going to fear her or nothing anymore. You take it all and get my granddaughter Violet out west so's she can marry her Billy, hear? There's things goin' on here don't none of us understand."

I nodded. "Yes, sir," I said. "Thank you, sir."

"You just remember who wrote that song, that's all, and it wasn't you."

"Yes, sir," I said.

And he was gone.

I had fallen asleep in my clothes and so didn't have to do anything complicated to get ready. Violet and the baby were supposed to be asleep in the parlor with the door closed, and Verna Mae was asleep in her room, probably with her Bible under her arm and an expression on her face to scare away the grim reaper, much less anybody who'd come in to knock her on the head.

I knocked—softly—on the parlor door, but there was no answer. My duty done, I decided I had given Violet enough free rides, and now that she was safely in the bosom of her family, such as it was, I could take the beautiful sounding guitar and a little money from the sugar jar and get myself to New York as soon as possible. I'd pick up some heavy leather gear and some makeup and head off for the twenty-city tour with Sclapped and Snidely Whiplash. I thought I could stop somewhere in Manhattan and get the old guitar drilled for a direct feed pickup and maybe even tour with it. What did the old man mean this guitar was dangerous? It was going to be my ticket to fame and fortune and maybe even the Rock-and-Roll Hall of Fame. When Earl Fleming or somebody like him went to impersonate me someday in the Dead Superstar Review, after I'd become a living legend first, of course, then they'd have to get themselves flowered guitars like this one.

As for Violet, if she wanted to get to California badly enough, she'd have to get help from her family. That's what families were for, weren't they? I had that guitar free and clear from the old man. He'd given me leave to take it.

So I snuck out into the kitchen and opened the sugar jar by the little light spilling in through the window from the street. It was exactly like the old man said. Inside I found a plastic bag with a roll of bills held together by a thick rubber band. I pulled it out, trying not to make a mess with the sugar, and stuffed the bag in my jeans pocket. I figured there wasn't more than fifty or seventy-five dollars there, but it would get me far enough away that I wouldn't have to think about Violet Tansy and her no-name baby ever again. Of course, I said to myself, once I make my first million dollars, I'll send the Tollivers a big check.

I rinsed the sugar from my hand and set the sugar jar back as near as I could to where I'd taken it from, knowing Verna Mae would probably have an eye for little details like that, and I didn't want her to know anything was gone until I had disappeared. I didn't need to be arrested by Detroit cops for taking what the old man said I could have.

I closed the front door of the house as quietly as I could and held the guitar case tightly under my arm. The night air felt cool and damp and free. Even the sound of the crashing trains over in the Ford factories sounded reassuring, as though I was coming back into reality after a night in the *Twilight Zone*.

My plan was to get in the van, start up the engine as quick and quiet as I could, and then drive off real slow with the lights out. I figured if I could get up the block without waking anybody up, then I could hit speed on the expressway and be on my way to New York long before Violet or anybody knew. As usual, I figured wrong. I eased into the van and clicked the door shut.

"I thought you'd try something like this," a voice said. "I told you I had the power."

I whirled around in my seat. Violet sat in the back, the baby sucking away at her breast and making gurgling noises that sounded like Niagara in the otherwise quiet night.

"Doesn't that baby do anything but eat?" I asked.

"Don't change the subject," she said, looking at Grandpa Tolliver's guitar case which I held in my hand. "You made a promise that if I got you a new guitar you'd get me and the baby to San Diego."

I searched my mind, trying to remember if I had ever made such a deal in those terms, but my brain was too fuzzed up to recall.

I was trapped like a rat. "Look," I said, "I lost my last guitar because of you and I figure this about evens us up. I've had enough of you and your loony family and your problems, Violet, and this old guitar isn't worth the gas money I already spent . . ."

"You spent?" she said. "Don't make me laugh. The gas in the tank right now was bought by me with the money I won in the instant lottery and you know it."

"Yeah, well, so what?" I said because I couldn't think of anything else to say at the moment. "The point is you aren't going anywhere, Violet, not with me, anyway. You need to see this from my point of view. I've got this once-in-a-lifetime chance to hit the big time, and I've got to get to New York sometime in the next twenty-four hours. If I leave right now and drive like a bat out of hell I'll make it, otherwise my future just went down the toilet. Now, I brought you all the way up here from Ohio and got you out of that mess, so you may as well get out here and stay with your family, such as they are. It's the best thing for you and it's the best thing for me, though I don't envy you staying with your aunt Verna Mae."

"Verna Mae's only jealous 'cause she ain't got powers like us and Momma."

"Will you stop that stuff and just get out?" I asked.

"I've got to get to San Diego so me and Billy can get married."

"Okay, but I'm not taking you," I said. "I have to get to New York the same way you've got to get to Billy, can't you understand that?"

She bit her lip real hard then, as if she was trying to remember something—or make something up real fast. Then she blurted out, "I'm sorry to tell you this, but you got to take us now, because now you're an accessory after the fact."

"A what?"

"An accessory. After the fact."

"To what?"

She paused. "To kidnapping," she said.

I blinked. "Kidnapping?"

I stared at her hard, but she didn't wince or look away even. She simply nodded.

"Because this isn't really my baby," she said. "I haven't told you this before because I was scared, but I stole him."

"You did not," I said.

"I did, too," she said, and she reached over the baby and rooted around in the bottom of the Brillo box. She pulled out a corner of the previous day's *Detroit News* that she must have taken from the house.

In a story datelined Norfolk, Virginia, the article said a four-month-old baby had been kidnapped from a park when its mother left it for a minute to go back to her car for something. The date of the kidnapping was about the time Violet told me she left Norfolk. The article said that the police, the FBI, and most of the known world were looking for the baby and whoever stole it.

"And if they catch us," she said, "I'll tell them you helped. What do you think of that?"

"Out," I said, "Get out of my van. Now."

But she didn't move. I thought about it for a minute—which wasn't easy to do, given my state of mind—and finally said, "You're lying anyway, aren't you? You've got to be this baby's mother because otherwise you wouldn't have any milk. Only mothers have milk. So there." I thought I had her.

She paused, looked sad for a minute, then swallowed hard and said through tears, "Well, if you have to know the truth, here it is: I done lost me and Billy's baby a couple of weeks ago. He was born premature and he died and I was all alone and didn't have nobody and I was confused, not having Billy or nobody, so I stole this baby just like it says here in this newspaper and that's why I got milk and if you don't want to go to jail you'd better get us out of here because if they find out it was me that took this baby, they'll come looking here first because these are my next of kin, except for my brother Arzo who's out West. So you and me and the baby and Grandpa Tolliver's guitar are going to San Diego, so let's go."

And so we went.

CHAPTER FOUR

By the time we got halfway to Kalamazoo, they were both asleep. I-94 west from Detroit was a mess of potholes, and the eighteen wheelers were pounding their way through them in convoys. My van shuddered with each hole and rocked back and forth every time a semi passed, but none of that seemed to bother Violet or the baby. They slept on like neither of them had a worry in the world.

That was good because it gave me time to think, and I needed time to consider all that had happened in the two days since Violet Tansy had crawled into my van.

For starters, I thought she was lying, but if I really believed that, then why was I looking in my rearview mirror for cops all the time? I didn't even notice myself doing it at first, but every couple of seconds my eyes would flick up, expecting to see flashers and sirens coming down on us from the darkness behind. And when a State Police car passed us one time in the night, my pulse beat like a tom-tom and my palms got all sweaty on the wheel.

And then I began to wonder what could happen if I had actually had the misfortune to fall in with someone who was telling me the truth. I mean, suppose Violet Tansy *did* steal the baby the way it said in the newspaper article? What then? I sure didn't want to go to jail for her. Even though I didn't know the legal ins and outs of kidnap law, I knew helping somebody steal a baby—which, technically, was what I was doing now that I knew about it—was probably a felony, and doing time in prison for it would have been even worse than still backing up the Dead Superstars.

I could have kicked myself for not leaving Violet in Detroit before she told me anything about stealing the baby. In fact, I should have left her back in Porkville and let some other poor pilgrim worry about her from then on because she was nothing but trouble, her and the baby, too. But then I realized it was way too late. I *was* tangled up in her life, *all* tangled up. Meeting up with Violet Tansy was like getting a snag in your fishing line. The more you fiddle with a bird's nest on your reel, the more snarled it gets until finally things get fouled up beyond all recovery. Sometimes the only way to deal with it is to cut the line and start over, and I knew I had to figure out a way to dump her and turn myself around to New York.

By the time we got near the Michigan-Indiana line on westbound I-94, we were running low on gas. I wanted to get some before we hit the Indiana toll road because they charge extortionary prices once they've got you on that not-so-free freeway.

It was still a couple of hours before dawn, but the air coming in the windows had the cool blue smell it gets right before the robins start to sing. Violet turned in her seat and moaned a little. She rubbed her eyes sleepily, turned to me, and mumbled, "I got to pee."

"There's an Arco station up at Michigan City that's open all night," I said. I had seen a billboard a couple of miles back and had decided to stop there for gas.

"Don't they have a Munchee Mart?" she asked groggily.

"Arco isn't good enough for you?"

"I want to get some more game pieces for my dream house," she mumbled.

Her head bobbed back down again once or twice before we got there but the bright fluorescent lights of the gas bay woke her up enough to crawl out of the van and run to get the key to the john. For the first time in my life I was glad women took longer than men in restrooms because I wanted to have a look in her big travel bag to see if I could tell how much of what she had been telling me was true.

As soon as she was in the toilet, I grabbed her over-the-shoulder bag and took a look.

The bag was stuffed with all kinds of junk, including the baby's Pampers. There was a tangle of lucky amulets and charms and things she must have got by mail order from places that advertise in *The National Enquirer*, and there was the newspaper story from Norfolk about the kidnapped baby she had showed me before.

I read the story again. The details fit all right. The stolen baby was a boy, four months old, and witnesses had seen a blonde-haired teenaged girl hanging around the park where the baby was stolen from. That was all there was, but it seemed to square with what Violet had told me. I usually feel good when I find out people have been telling me the truth, but this time my stomach went all queasy as if the trapdoor had just opened beneath the gallows.

She didn't have a driver's license—or any money—in her wallet, but an old high school identification card showed me her name *was* Violet Tansy and she had graduated from—or at least been in—high school in West Virginia the year before, which made her about nineteen or twenty. In the picture, her hair was longer and black. She looked much younger and more innocent than she did now, even though the picture couldn't have been over a year-and-a-half old. Kidnapping a kid and taking off on a cross-country chase could age you pretty fast, as I was finding out.

There wasn't much else in the bag but some clothes, some scraps of paper, and a couple of letters postmarked from Navy bases, probably from Billy. I didn't have time to read them, but it was good to know they were there, and I decided I might dig them out when I had more time.

I felt around some more in the bag, and toward the bottom—in amongst the grit and buttons and hairpins and stuff that always settle into the bottom of bags like silt in a lake—my hand hit something cold and hard. I pulled my hand back like I'd touched a snake, then I gingerly felt around the thing for a while, not wanting to admit that it was what it felt like. But it was, and I finally decided I had to pull it out and confirm what I already knew. I drew out a cold steel revolver, a thirty-eight special, with a carved wood handle, the sort of thing you could pick up at the corner store. It was what they sometimes call a *lady's gun*, not pretty but lethal just the same if you ended up on the wrong end of it. I whistled when I saw it, and the baby stirred in the box in the back of the van. For a minute I was afraid he was going to wake up and cry, but he only mumbled around a little and fell asleep again face down.

"Jesus, little no-name baby," I said. "What in the world is your momma doing carrying a gun?" Then I had a sick-making thought, "Unless she *isn't* really your momma after all, and I just had the rotten luck of running into somebody telling me the truth. I sure wish you could talk."

Violet came out of the bathroom right then, and I quickly shoved the gun back down to the bottom of the bag. By the time she returned the key to the Arco man and got back into the van, I was outside pumping gas. My brain was pumping, too. So suppose, I said to myself, the baby *is* stolen? The story Violet told me was ding-dong stupid enough to be true, and she didn't seem bright enough to make something like that up. So let's begin with this premise: you are about to carry a stolen baby across a state line. What follows? Stupid question.

The police follow. And the FBI. And the four branches of the armed service. In short, everyone in the country remotely connected with law enforcement would be following us. What then? I imagined my picture on *America's Most Wanted* and people in every small town and highway rest stop in America staring at me, chasing me with pitchforks and baseball bats like in one of those *Frankenstein* movies. I got so nervous thinking about it that I jerked the nozzle out and let about a nickel's worth of no-lead run on to my shoe before I had sense enough to turn off the pump.

As we pulled out of the Arco station and got back into the flow of predawn traffic, I asked myself if Violet Tansy was worth dying for. Was anything? When I was a kid, I read boy's adventure books in the Airstream as we tooled along the freeways. Everybody died pretty in them. I mean they always had time to finish their speeches and whenever anybody died it seemed to make sense. But dying in the real world wasn't like that. I checked the rearview again. No sirens, no flashers, but it was only a matter of time. Somebody told me once the FBI has sharpshooters that can put a bullet through your brain at two hundred yards. I remembered seeing *Bonnie and Clyde* on video one time and how their bodies fell out of their car full of holes, and I wondered if we'd end up the same.

I tried to push these sorts of thoughts out of my head, but I couldn't.

When I was a kid, I used to put myself to sleep at night sometimes by pretending I was dying. I'd imagine I was shot, and I'd talk to myself and choke out a death speech, a final few words timed so I'd fall asleep at the exact moment my speech ended. Especially on hot nights in the trailer when Mom and Dad had been arguing and the dog was bitching and I was tired, I'd lie there and die like they die in the movies, with a speech that rounded it out and made my life seem all worthwhile. Sometimes I'd do a great speech about how Mom and Dad shouldn't feel guilty because I was dying there, and then I'd sink off into the soft black bag of sleep, and next morning, I'd wake up and be fresh and alive again.

It's hard to say exactly when I stopped thinking death was like sleep, that you'd wake up from it again in the morning. I think it happened one time when Dad was traveling with a little circus.

This circus kid, Mario, who was about my age, was showing me something his father was teaching him to do on the slack wire. Mario was fourteen, a year older than me then, and his whole Italian family were wire-walkers, tumblers, and acrobats. He had thick curly black hair and he told me once he had felt up lots of girls behind the horse stalls. He took them back there and when the stallions' penises came out, he'd feel the girls up while they were watching. One day when he was learning to do flips on the slack wire, he called me over to watch him. He wasn't supposed to be working the wire without his father or one of his brothers there, but he did anyway, to show off. He was at home on the wire, and while he was warming up for his flips, bouncing up and down on the wire, he talked to me. The buckles and guys at the end were fixed tight, and the poles attached to the wire were flexing the right way with each jump. I always liked to watch Mario. His skin was the color of olives and his body was round and smooth where the muscles on his arms and shoulders were and everywhere else was taut as the canvas tents of the circus.

"I got somethin' to tell you," he said as he held out his arms and ran up the wire and then down it again to the middle. Any circus performer will tell you the slack wire is even more dangerous than the high tight wire, but Mario had grown up on it and was totally relaxed there. He grinned when he told me he had something to say, and I figured it was something about another girl and the horses, but when I asked him what, he simply waved his hand to say wait until he was done.

Then, changing the subject, he said, "Watch this. This is something my father's teaching me."

He took a few warm-up bounces to get in sync with the wire, and then he said, "Hup!" and up he went. He was wearing a black practice suit and he tucked himself into a ball and got all the way through a somersault in midair over the slack wire. He tucked his head all the way into his chest and then came out perfectly, straightening his neck and throwing back his chest a little, extending his arms. But then something went wrong. Instead of coming down like he was supposed to, Mario hit the wire off center. The wire threw him off to the ground in front of me. He landed on the side of his face, and the rest of his body piled up behind him. There was a loud crack like pool balls hitting when his face slammed the dirt. It was like the wire had slingshotted him straight down, and he didn't move. I ran up to him, but I could tell he was dead, just like that. His eyes were open and his cheek was pressed into the dirt and his lips were open, too. Then I saw a fly go into his mouth, maybe it smelled the death, and it landed on Mario's tongue and Mario didn't close his mouth, but he didn't open it either, and I never did find out what it was he wanted to tell me.

Ever since then I knew you wouldn't want to die for just anything. I worried about finishing things. Mario never finished his flip, and he never finished telling me what he wanted to say to me. So death was like that, I guess, a rude interruption, like hacking off a rope, whack, your life was over for no particular reason.

So I wondered if I would end up like Bonnie and Clyde because of Violet and her baby, shot full of holes, and never get my chance at that thirty-city tour with Sclapped, never see my face on the cover of *Spin* or *Rolling Stone*, never get that beach house in Malibu, and all because I was stupid enough to take this girl where she wanted to go. And would the flies crawl in and out of my mouth?

After I'd thought about this depressing stuff for a while, I reached for the radio and turned it on. I punched the search button, and it went from one station to another until finally it landed on one playing a solo guitar piece that sounded vaguely familiar.

The f.m. station was hardly coming in at all. Mostly I was hearing the sound of static bouncing off the ionosphere, but in there somewhere were snatches of a melody I found myself humming along to until I realized with a shock that it was *my* open-tuning song they were playing! The one I'd recorded in my bathroom the year before, the one Grandpa Tolliver got so upset about last night.

I turned up the sound and tried to fiddle with the tuning. How the hell did my song end up on the radio? Nobody knew about that tape but me. But there it was, me and my old Martin guitar hitting out the song in the D-tuning. It sounded very good, as though the tape had been remastered somehow, and I was impressed as heck with it, but then, after a few bars of my solo, an orchestra came in playing back-up, picking up the open-D chord and pulsing along with some odd Philip Glass-type synthesizer sounds. It was getting farther and farther from what I'd written, though the guitar part never faded out completely. Finally, the sound of voices chanting "ooommm" or "aaammmm" came in and made the whole thing go cosmic, like we were sitting stoned in a hot tub somewhere. It sounded as if a hundred and fifty people had collaborated on the recording. Funny, I thought, I don't remember anybody sitting there in the bathroom with me at the time I recorded it.

Violet had been sleeping, but she woke up and listened for a minute as we drove, then she turned to me and said, "Hey, isn't that the song you were playing last night on Grandpa's guitar?"

"Shh," I said. The song was almost over and the announcer came back on. He was a guy from San Francisco with velvet tonsils who announced on a show called *Music from the Depths of Space*. Hazel used to listen to it all the time back when she was into Zen. His voice came out of the speaker like thick gooey cream.

"You're listening to *Music from the Depths of Space*."

"Yeah," I said to the radio, "so wake up and tell me about my song."

"And that was 'Open Tuning.' By Zak Bendzi. And the Samsara Consort."

"I thought you said you wrote that song," Violet said.

"I *did* write it."

"Then your name's Zak Bendzi?" she asked.

"No," I said, "My name's Joe Findlay."

"Your name's *Joe Findlay?*"

"Yeah, I'm Joe Findlay," I replied.

"Well then," she asked, "who's Zak Bendzi?"

"That's what I'd like to know," I said, turning off the radio. "And how the hell did he get ahold of *my* song?"

I had to explain to Violet a little about myself and how I came to be there in Porkville the night she crawled into my van on her crazy adventure across the country with the stolen baby. I told her about my life in Las Vegas and how I left Hazel and then about my chance to get an audition in New York, and as we talked, the sunrise crept up on us from behind and overtook us as quick and secret as a cat, and a line of light crossed the landscape of Indiana cornfields.

We drove in silence for a while, and as we moved west on the Indiana Toll Road, I found that thoughts about who got hold of my open tuning song and how he stole it gradually got displaced by thoughts of food.

My skin was wet and clammy, and my eyeballs felt like two cold poached eggs laid on my face. I lit up a cigarette I found on the floor, but it tasted like salt, and I threw it out the window. My mouth was dry and my body craved caffeine. I checked the rearview mirror for cops even more than before. I didn't want to ask her about the gun right then because I figured it gave me some advantage to know something about her she didn't know I knew, but then I realized *my* fingerprints were now on the gun, too, and in my mind I could hear those prison doors slam with a cold and unforgiving clang, and I got to thinking about prison food, about last meals and that scene in *White Heat* where the inmates riot in the mess hall.

It was six-thirty in the morning, and I hadn't had a meal since the night before in Detroit. I was starving. I would have eaten anything right then, even though I was still burping up the memory of the orange-colored mush Verna Mae

served the night before. I wished I had got a cup of coffee at
the Arco station, even though it was probably as thick as
road tar.

We were already halfway to Illinois, and I realized we
could probably take a break, especially considering I wasn't
sure exactly where the hell we were going.

"You hungry?" I asked Violet.

"I could eat some," Violet admitted, and so we stopped
at one of those places they call "oases," as if I-80 was some
sort of long, four-lane desert.

The Indiana Road Commission back in the 1950s must
have thought that it would be cute to build rest stops right
over the turnpike because every fifty miles or so a restaurant
hangs right over the highway like an ugly concrete toad. The
food is usually pretty bad, but I was so hungry I figured it
wouldn't make any difference.

As we went down the cafeteria line, Violet piled four
cream-filled donuts, a big glass of orange juice, and a Sprite
on her tray. My breakfast was two scrambled eggs, toast, and
lots of coffee. I was tired enough that I felt sandy all over, and
this was the first real cooked meal I'd had in three days
besides Verna Mae's carrot mush, which didn't really count.
Luckily, Violet didn't ask where the money came from when
she saw me pull out the plastic bag full of bills I had gotten
from Verna Mae's sugar jar. I still hadn't taken the time to
count it, but I could see it was mostly ones and a few fives.

We ate without saying much, and I left Violet and the
baby for a few minutes to clean up.

There's an art to taking a complete bath in a highway rest
stop sink. First of all you've got to carry a little rubber disk
with you, like a jar opener or something, to plug the sink
with because usually the sinks in those places don't have
stoppers. Then you get the sink filled up with hot water and
dip your arms into it like a surgeon does and you let the
water run all the way up your arms. You get a rag and wash

under your arms and behind your neck with the liquid soap and then try to rinse it off. If you need to clean your private parts, you go into the stall because you don't want anybody coming in to think you're a pervert.

Shaving takes care of itself in the usual way.

By the time I got myself clean, I was feeling a little more hopeful we'd find a way out of this mess. I realized it was an hour later in New York City and I called Murray. Luckily he was in.

"Babe! What's happenin'?"

Okay, I thought, how much of this can I explain to him without him thinking I was insane?

"Uh, I've run into a bit of a snag on getting to New York right away, Murray," I said. "I was wondering if I could have a little more time."

"No change of plans or anything, I hope," he said. "Listen, man, I can't hold this slot open forever. I've got fourteen thousand hungry guitar pickers out there looking for work. You're still coming, aren't you?"

"Yeah, yeah," I said quickly. "I'll be there. No sweat."

"So where are you right now?"

"Uh, still in the Midwest," I said, not wanting to give away my location in case the police came asking questions.

"Like where? Last time I talked to you, you were like in Ohio or someplace, right?"

"Right."

"So now where are you?"

I cleared my throat nervously. "Heading toward Chicago."

"Oh," Murray said, sighing with relief, "That's all right. At least you're still heading this way then."

"Right," I said, grateful that Murray had a native New Yorker's sense of geography about anything off Manhattan Island.

"Listen, babe, what's your ETA here. I gotta know."

"Well, there's this girl, see."

"Shit," said Murray. "Bring her along. There's babes all over the place anyway."

"It's not that simple."

"You want this gig or not?"

"Of course I want it, man."

"Then ditch her."

"I've been trying to for the past five hundred miles. You see, I'm in kind of a situation, you understand."

"*Please deposit another fifty cents,*" said a nasal, computerized voice. Clang. Clang.

"Where'd you say you were?" Murray asked.

"Near Chicago," I said, "At a rest stop. I'm . . . I'm resting."

"Well get your buns out here, man. You can rest after the tour. And make sure you're looking good for the audition, too."

"Looking good?"

"Yeah, Sclapped is going full leather and chains for this gig. As long as you're in Chicago, see if you can find an s&m store and pick up some gear. If you make the audition, we can bill the tour so save the receipts. You ever worked a bull-whip?"

"Not at the same time I was playing guitar," I said.

"Geez, I thought you told me you were an experienced musician."

"I'm sure I can pick it up in no time," I said, groveling. "I really, really want this gig, Murray."

"*Please deposit . . .*" Clung. Clung.

I could hear Murray mumbling something to his secretary.

"Murray! Murray! Please don't hang up. I need this gig. I'll do anything, you hear? Anything."

"Anything? Fine. Then dump this chick that's giving you trouble and haul your heinie out here in the next forty-eight hours or it's over, hear?"

"I'll try," I said with as much conviction as I could muster at the time.

"Don't try, *do*, babes." He was starting to hang up.

"One more thing, Murray," I said, desperate to keep him on the line, thinking the longer I held his attention the better chance he'd remember me. "I heard this song on the radio this morning and I was wondering if you knew anything about it."

"Well, hurry up, I've got a call waiting."

"Please deposit . . ." Clung. Clung.

"It's called 'Open Tuning' and . . ."

" 'Open Tuning'? What kind of a title is that? You know what Sclapped's title for its maiden album is? *Born Without a Brain.* Now *that's* a title. So what's this 'Open Tuning,' metal?"

"No, I heard it on a New Age show. The reason I ask is . . ."

"New Age?" he said. He squealed the way a teenage girl might squeal if she stepped barefoot into a bucket of raw oysters. "Eeeeeeeew."

"Well, anyway . . ."

"I got to ring off, babe. Don't forget the leather. New Age? Give me a break. No money in it compared to heavy metal and rubber suits. Don't forget the chains, either, and get a dog collar. Ciao."

When I got back to the table, Violet's eyes were glued on the TV screen. CNN *Headline News* was running a blurb on the Norfolk kidnapped baby and Violet looked ashy white. Beneath us, trucks and cars rocketed out from under the floor of the floating restaurant and disappeared toward the horizon. The story only lasted for a few seconds, but it was the kind of news item likely to get legs and attract more attention as time went on. I thought back to Baby Jessica in the well and the O.J. Simpson car chase in L.A., and I wondered how long it would be until the news helicopters started hovering over us.

Violet turned to me with tears in her eyes.

"Joe, I've done stupid things in my time, but this is the stupidest thing I've ever done, and I'm scared to death.

Where are we, anyway? I ain't never been this far away from home before. I didn't think it was gonna be like this when I left Norfolk. It's so . . . so *big* out here and here I am in the middle of it all trying to get to Billy and I don't know what to do and I'm scared to death."

And before I had the good sense to say "good-bye," I had slid into the booth beside her and put my arm around her shoulder and, like a fool, I was saying, "It'll be all right." Of course, I didn't know if it was going to be all right or not, but it's the thing you say when everything falls apart around your feet and you don't know what else to do.

I loaned her my rubber sink stopper and told her to get herself cleaned up, and I held the baby while she was gone. We watched the trucks and cars fly out from beneath us and get smaller as they headed out across that land in northern Indiana that's as flat as God's ironing board. Out beyond us in the distance was Illinois and Iowa and two thousand more miles of continent to hide in.

When Violet came back, I made her eat some ham and eggs. If she was breast-feeding a baby and running away from the law, she needed more than pop and cream-filled donuts. I took a refill on the cafeteria's thick, tarry coffee while on CNN they reflashed the headline on the kidnapped baby. The ratings were good and the story was picking up momentum.

On the far side of the cafeteria two Indiana state troopers, Smokey the Bear hats and all, were eating breakfast. Even though they hadn't looked at us, the coffee went cold in my mouth and a voice in my head said, "This is what prison coffee tastes like, Joe," and suddenly I had a vision of myself strumming a guitar behind the bars of some Hoosier penitentiary for the next twenty years. The song I was playing was "Open Tuning."

*

We drove as far as Davenport that day and camped out on the banks of the Mississippi. The following morning, we hit the road again after dawn.

I first noticed the blue Ford Escort behind us just past Quad Cities. From the looks I was able to get of it in the rearview, I guessed right away it was an undercover cop car. We were being surveilled.

The Escort was the color of a robin's egg but with a dull finish, nearly rusted out along the rocker panels. It was the sort of car the police would confiscate and then, when nobody bothered to pick it up because it was such a broken-down piece of junk, they'd use it for undercover work. The reason I first noticed it, really, was because the front bumper was hanging off a little to one side, as if the car had been used as a battering ram. The whole thing was held together with Bondo and bungee cords.

Every time I looked up in the rearview, there it was—that same blue car. After about twenty miles of this, I was sure we were being followed. Is this what it has come to, I asked myself? After five hundred miles with Violet Tansy, was my life about to end in a blaze of Iowa gunfire? Watching that blue Ford playing cutesy with us, I was sure of it, and I kept my eyes open for the marked cop cars I knew would come.

The Escort just hung there, keeping his distance, cool. Trucks pulled into the space between us now and then, but every time one pulled out, there he'd be. Probably he thought we didn't notice him. There was no need for him to get close if he was following us. The roads in the Midwest stretch out for hundreds of miles in front of you, leaving no place to hide. Exits are fifty or a hundred miles apart. Midwestern roads aren't like the roads in the East, where towns came first and the roads followed. Out east, it'd be easy to lose somebody.

The roads go every which way and what they say in Boston is true, sometimes you can't get there from here.

But out in the Midwest and West, the roads were cut straight as arrows across the prairie, and the people and towns followed. Your only hope was to keep on going in a straight line and outdistance whoever or whatever was behind you and either wear them out or move so far ahead of them they'd finally give up.

Perhaps I was being too paranoid, I thought. Spending two whole days and three nights with Violet Tansy had cut me off a little from reality, so to speak. I tried a little game with the blue car. I'd slow down a bit and then speed up in order to see what he would do. Every time I slowed, it seemed like he did too, and when I sped up he kept about the same distance behind us.

It could have been mere coincidence, of course. It's like that as you head west on the concrete river of the Interstate. You see the same faces and cars day after day to Denver because the only reason almost anybody's out there at all is because they're trying to beat their way through empty space and get somewhere worth getting to. But every time I looked it was there again, the blue Escort, and I started getting crazy. Since he'd followed us across the state line from Illinois to Iowa, I thought the driver must be FBI. I saw images of those sharpshooters they had on the old FBI TV show, guys who can shoot a fly's gonads out at a hundred yards. They were up there already, I knew, waiting for us on some overpass somewhere in the middle of Iowa, ready to bury two bullets deep in our brain pans.

I finally pulled into a rest stop somewhere near Iowa City to see what would happen. I was relieved when I saw him pass on down the road and disappear into the cornfields. I even laughed at myself for letting Violet's craziness get to me.

But then, along about Williamsburg, a few miles after that rest stop, there he was again, right behind us a quarter mile, keeping the same distance. I speeded up, I slowed down, but he seemed to stay there, always a quarter mile or so behind.

"What's the matter with you?" Violet finally asked, turning around and looking out the back window. "You keep looking out the rearview mirror like the devil himself was back there."

"Maybe he is," I said. "I haven't gotten a good look at who's driving yet. Are you sure you told me the truth about that baby and you?"

She looked out the side window at the passing rows of green and gold corn glittering in the morning sun.

"You're calling me a liar," she said.

"I'm not calling you anything," I said, "but there's somebody back there in an old blue Ford and it seems like he's following us."

She turned around and looked through the rear window of the van again.

"There's nobody back there," she said.

I looked up in the rearview and she was right. Nothing. No blue Ford, anyway. Just a gray ribbon of highway laid through the green hills. Those FBI boys were as good as their reputation, I thought. He disappeared into thin air right in the middle of all that Iowa corn, a slicker trick than my father the magician could ever have pulled off.

"He'll be back," I said. "Just you wait."

And, of course, he did reappear.

We pulled off the interstate somewhere in greater Des Moines and had lunch at a Munchee Mart in a strip mall. Violet got more doors for her dream house, but she said she already had about a hundred doors and what she really needed was a Jacuzzi and a swimming pool to finish the set. After a Big Gulp and a micro Munchburger, we picked up some more Pampers for the baby, and as we pulled out of the parking lot of the Munchee Mart, the old blue Ford pulled in.

The driver pretended he wasn't looking at us. He was cool. He acted as if we weren't even here, as though he hadn't even been following us for the past two hundred and some miles, and I got my first good look at him. He was a clean-cut guy about twenty-seven or twenty-eight, junior agent, I thought, with eyes as blue and cold as Munchee Mart popsicles. He had short reddish hair and pale raw skin. FBI, for sure, I thought, as he got out of his car and went into the Munchee Mart.

I decided the best thing was to try to put as much distance between him and us as I could, so I raced out of the parking lot, and when I hit I-80 I floored it until the sides of the van started going whucka-whucka-whucka again, which meant I had reached maximum velocity. We drove due west through the Iowa corn for two hours with no sight of the blue Escort, but I knew as long as we were on I-80, young Ephraim Zimbalist would keep on coming, calling in his location every hundred miles or so until they could get the sharpshooters up on the bridges. What we had to do was find someplace to hide that was so out of the way, so unimaginable, that even the FBI wouldn't have any idea of where to look for us. Luckily that's about when we ran into Pete Fagan.

After two hours of pounding west on I-80, my van started to cough and wheeze. I smelled the familiar smell of wet burning rubber and knew that I'd blown a hose somewhere in the cooling system. I was able to coax us to the next exit and pulled into a Munchee Mart parking lot to let the engine cool down.

Violet took the baby into the Munchee Mart, and I popped the hood on the van and waited for the steam to die away. I dug a roll of duct tape out of the back of the van. I never travel anywhere without duct tape. Half of America is held together with the stuff. I don't know anybody who actually uses it for ducts, but everybody's got something held together with it, whether it's a muffler on their car or an old axe handle or electrical system. I talked one time to a guy who'd flown bush planes up in Alaska, and he told me one time he practically held a wing on with the stuff. Anyway, my van was half duct tape already, and I had my head down inside the engine compartment trying to stick the loose hose back on with duct tape when Violet came back.

I didn't even know she was there until somebody poked me in the back and said, in a loud voice, "Greetings, fellow earthling!"

I jumped up and nearly sheared off part of my scalp on the open hood. I turned around and there stood a guy holding an Army surplus duffel bag who looked exactly like a gnome with an excess of pituitary hormone. I was staring at a six foot tall dwarf!

"Pete Fagan," the guy said, holding out a hand that was the size of a honey-baked ham. "They call me the Pagan." The moment I saw him, I figured him for an ear-masher, and I was right. He never let up talking from the moment he hooked up with us.

"I was in the Munchee Mart there blasting aliens on the video game when I saw your woman come in."

"My woman?"

"Her." He nodded towards Violet. "She's your woman, right?" The way he said *woman* made it sound like I had won her in a meat-eating contest. "She told me you were traveling together, going west, and she said you'd give me a ride. I'm only going as far as exit 64."

"Sorry," I said, turning myself back in to the engine to finish wrapping that hose. "I have enough hitchhikers as it is."

"He's only goin' a few miles," said Violet.

"I said we've got enough hitchhikers," I repeated.

"You're so selfish," Violet said. "All you ever think of is yourself."

I let the duct tape roll hang there on the hose for a minute and stood up.

"I don't do hitchhikers anymore," I said. "I picked you up a few days ago and I haven't had anything but trouble since. I will never pick up another hitchhiker again as long as I live."

"But he's wearin' the cross," Violet said.

I looked at Fagan's chest. He was wearing one of those black strap T-shirts with a scoop neck, and, sure enough, in amongst the gray chest hairs was a cross like the one Violet used when she won the instant lottery back in Michigan, the one that she got from *The National Enquirer* that had come from the planet Neptune.

"So, are you a believer, too?" Fagan asked me. His eyes twinkled, and I couldn't tell if he was putting me on or not. He had a big smile across his face, but I didn't trust him for a minute. He looked like a fat and degenerate Santa Claus. His face and ears were flushed bright red as if he was half-drunk all the time—which I later found out he was—and his gingery-gray hair was curly around his big head except for the top, where he was bald and it glowed pink from sunburn. His mouth was like a slash in a watermelon, with his bright red lips and tongue appearing in a bush of ginger-colored beard that was streaked with gray. I guessed he was fifty years old, a leftover hippy. His big beer belly shoved its way out from beneath his black T-shirt like the rear end of a curious animal.

"I don't believe in anything in particular," I said.

"Your woman strikes me as the spiritual type."

"She isn't my woman," I said.

"I'm Billy's woman," she said.

"Who's Billy?" Fagan asked.

"He's a sailor, in the submarine corps."

"Ah, a servant of the great sea father Neptune, eh?" Fagan said.

"No, he's in the U.S. Navy," Violet said. "This is just Joe Findlay, and he's takin' me to San Diego."

"We're not going to San Diego," I said angrily.

"Whoa, hey, listen, man," Fagan said. "I don't want to be the cause of any bad vibes between you and your woman . . ."

"She isn't my woman," I said.

". . . so I'll just go."

"That's fine with me," I said, poking my upper body back into the engine compartment and wrapping one more loop of duct tape around the hose. I yanked on it until it seemed it would stick long enough for us to get to a Wal-Mart and buy a regular clamp and a new section of hose. I stood up, but Fagan the Pagan hadn't moved.

"Listen, you and your woman got a place to camp tonight?" he asked. "'Cause I'm going to the convention and I can get you in there for free."

"What convention?" I asked.

"The Midwest Pagan Convention," he said. He pointed to a button on his T-shirt. It said, *I'm off to see the wizzard.* "The Midwest Pagan Conference is holding its annual camp out down near Wiota. There'll be pagans from all over—Ohio, Indiana, Illinois, Mo-Kan-Ne."

"Mo-Kan-Ne?" I asked.

"Missouri, Kansas and Nebraska went together," he explained, "because there wasn't enough pagans in any one of them to make up a state organization. They got witches and stuff, but not as many as in states where they have big cities."

I turned to Violet.

"Do you just talk to anybody you meet?" I said.

I was about to tell Fagan the Pagan to fly to his convention if he believed in witchcraft and all that when I looked up the road to the freeway exit and saw the damned blue Ford and the young FBI agent with the Aryan blue eyes. He was stopped at the end of the ramp waiting for some trucks to pass, and his turn signal told me he was heading right for the Munchee Mart.

"Jesus," I said. "Get in the van."

"Huh?" said Violet.

"I said get in the van. Now! Move."

"What about . . . ?"

"Him, too, just get in. Fast."

I started up the engine and revved it enough to know the tape was holding, and then I slammed the hood down and peeled out of the Munchee Mart parking lot as the blue Ford pulled in. The red-haired agent was cool as ice again, a master of surveillance. He didn't even look at us, but I saw him get out of his car and head for the Coke cooler. Damn, he was smooth, you had to give him credit for that. We pulled on to westbound I-80 again and merged with the flow.

"This is really great of you two to take me to the convention," Fagan said. "You'll like it, lots of mellow people there. I'm right now on my way from a Native American sweat lodge ritual in Indiana and I'm working my way to California to study some more with Swami Jody. Ever hear of him?"

I shook my head. I was busy checking the rearview for the blue Ford. So far as I could tell he hadn't pulled back on to the freeway. Yet.

Meanwhile Fagan ran on and on. His voice had a triphammer effect to it, wham, wham, wham, so you could hardly get a word in edgewise.

"Yeah, Swami Jody says it's all here, right now, you know what I mean? Like this is all there ever was and if you can't be happy here where you are, you could never be happy anywhere."

"Sounds like a deep guy," I said. "Where'd you say you wanted to get off?"

"Exit 64, a little past Anita. Jody lives in a ranch house in Chula Vista, outside San Diego. He says all the aluminum siding in southern California draws in good vibrations. He says that's why things were so peaceful during the 1950s. All those aluminum siding jobs in new subdivisions drew in nothing but peaceful rays. It was kind of a religion, and Eisenhower was like the high priest of the whole thing."

"Well, that sounds great," I said, watching the mile markers count their way down until we could dump this weirdo. "But what's happened since? Seems to me like all that aluminum siding is still out there, but things keep getting worse."

"The siding got old, see, and Swami Jody says it lost its power, you know."

"So Swami Jody will do a realuminizing job for you to get the vibes back up?"

"That's the idea," Fagan said. He stared out the window for a while, and I thought we'd have a moment's peace, but it wasn't long before he started in again.

"Look at all that corn, man," he said, watching the rows of it whiz by. "As you go by you can look down the individual rows and if you stare at it the right way, it kind of hypnotizes you, you know?"

"It hasn't put you to sleep yet," I said, checking the rearview again.

"Corn, man," he said, ignoring me. "All this fuckin' corn is like a zen garden, isn't it? You know they rake the sand in zen gardens into neat rows like this, only this is, like, miles and miles and miles of narrow, perfectly parallel little lines. The state of Iowa is like one huge zen garden, man. You could get a big satori out here. Yeah, Iowa's a mellow, tuned-in place. They're like way ahead of us here, man." His head nodded up and down for a minute like one of those cheap toy dogs you buy for the back of your car in Tijuana, then he pulled his Army surplus duffel bag up on to his lap and unzipped it. He rooted around in it for a moment and came up with a small plastic packet of white powder.

"You guys want some unicorn dust?" he asked.

My eyes flew to the rearview.

"What is that stuff?" I asked.

"Unicorn powder, man. You sniff a line of it or put it in your drink, and pretty soon you're seeing unicorns." He opened up the packet and poured a bit into his palm.

"Put that stuff away now," I said. The blue Ford was nowhere in sight. With any luck, I thought, I'll be able to drop this weirdo and his load of drugs before they catch us and then the FBI could only get me for being an accessory to a kidnapping.

"Oh, sure," Fagan said, licking the stuff off his palm and resealing the bag, "I understand, the woman and kid and all. You guys are like into family stuff, right? Hey, I'm cutting back myself. I had a close brush with the law back in Ohio. I mean there I was following my bliss, you know, like trying to cleanse my third eye of negative thoughts when this cop pulls me over—this was a few years ago—and says, 'What are you smokin', buddy?' Luckily I'd eaten or toked all the evidence before he came up, but I was screwed up for days."

"And you're not screwed up anymore?" I asked.

"Not since they put the plate in my head," he said. Then he put his finger up in the air to shush anything I might have said. "Hold it, hold it," he said, "I've got an incoming." He put his hand over his forehead and closed his eyes. He looked real intense for a minute, then opened his eyes. "It's okay," he said, "message received."

"You receive messages like that often?"

"Pretty regular," Fagan said. "It's better than a cellular phone. I wish I could get call waiting, though, because you never can tell when a really important one is going to arrive and you don't want to be preoccupied with something minor. I'm kind of psychic, in case you haven't noticed. Once I received a telepathic message from a friend in California three days before he sent it, man. To tell the truth, it's kind of a nuisance sometimes. I'd shut the system down, but I got to keep the lines open for the M Squad."

"M Squad?" No blue Ford in the rearview. My mind calculated the possible combined sentence for kidnapping and transporting drugs across state lines. If I could serve the sentences simultaneously, I'd probably only be 108 when I got out. Maybe I could play with the Lawrence Welk orchestra.

"The M Squad's short for the Meditation Squad," Fagan went on. "We're a nationwide network. We're like a metaphysical SWAT team. We go around doing guerilla meditation."

"Guerilla meditation?"

"Right. We're modeled on Greenpeace, you know? Suppose something really out of karma's going on. We send in a team to meditate there. Remember Three Mile Island? It almost blew. You read the reports and you'll see no one could figure out why it didn't go nuclear and destroy most of Pennsylvania. We were there, that's why. We ringed the place in a predawn raid and chanted *Aum*. We pretty much saved the whole world one time or other the past twenty years or more."

"Gee, thanks," I said.

"Nothing to be proud of," said Fagan.

"So if you're so great, how come nobody's ever heard of you?"

"We like to keep a low profile," he said. "We keep our shields up, do our job, and fade back into the cosmic flow. We almost blew our cover a few years ago during the Harmonic Convergence, though. Hey, you remember what you were doing during the Harmonic Convergence?"

"When was it exactly?" I asked.

"Back in '87."

"Yeah, I was playing backup for Elvis," I said.

"Elvis?" said Fagan, "But, hey, wasn't Elvis like dead by then?"

"Yeah."

"Wow, you must be one tuned-in dude, man! Anyway, we thought things got a little out of hand. You see, these ancient Mayan calendars predicted the world was going to end back then . . ."

"Yeah, but it didn't, did it?"

"That's my whole point, man," Fagan said. "The M Squad had to go above ground for a while. We got about two hundred thousand people meditating at spiritual points around the world, places of heavy-duty karmic convergence like the pyramids, the Acropolis, Malibu, Central Park. We were everywhere, coast-to-coast, ocean-to-ocean, in one moment of global harmony. Made the cover of *Newsweek*. And hey, it worked, man. All that harmonic converging held the earth together."

"Of course there's still a few cracks here and there," I added.

"Nothing the P-Net can't handle," Fagan said.

"P-Net?"

"Pagan Network, man, that's where we're going. It's the pagan energy that's holding the whole thing together, see?"

"But things are a mess," I said. "All you have to do is turn on the radio to hear the whole world's going to hell."

"Yeah," said Fagan. "But think how bad things would be if we weren't around, man."

I had no answer for him on that one. I looked in the rearview again and saw something coming over one of the rolls in the horizon. It could have been the blue Ford. Fagan opened up his duffle bag.

"No more unicorn powder!" I shouted.

He pulled out a cassette tape.

"Hey, you mind if I play this?" he asked.

"What is it?"

"Some really mellow stuff, man. A friend of mine gave it to me. Back in the sweat lodge I was doing some third-eye meditation with it, Ram Dass stuff, you know, and like I saw the face of God while I was listening to this song. You'll love it."

I didn't get my hopes up, but I figured if he went into some sort of trance it would at least keep his mouth shut until we could dump him and his bag of unicorn dust at the Wiota exit.

He popped the cassette into my tape player and pretty soon out came the sound of me playing my guitar. It was "Open Tuning" again!

"Where'd you get that tape?" I said.

"You heard it before?" Fagan asked.

"Heard it?" I said, "I wrote it."

"I thought it was some other guy," Fagan said.

"Zak Bendzi?" I asked.

"Yeah," Fagan said. "He must be some real evolved dude, eh?"

Once again, the song began with me playing in the bathroom, just that simple open-tuning melody with the other five strings as a drone underneath, then along about a minute into it the synthesizer kicked in and the next thing you know, the tune was in la-la land with a mushy string track and voices going "ooommmmm" and "aaaaaaaahm," like they were supposed to be angels or something. It sounded like cosmic elevator music.

I popped the cassette out of the player and looked at the label. It was a bootleg copy Fagan's friend had made, so it didn't have any production information on it. I couldn't figure out who Zak Bendzi could be or how he could have stolen my song. I put the cassette back in and we were once again floating toward Jupiter with the Samsara Consort.

"Where did your friend buy this tape?" I asked Fagan.

"I don't know," he said. "You can get them anywhere. They're in all the stores. This is one hot tune on the cool circuit, if you know what I mean." Fagan had put his hands, palms up, on his knees and closed his eyes. His head was tilted up toward the roof of the car and he was humming along. Before he passed out of reality altogether, he mumbled, "They'll be selling them at the festival if you want one, man, they've got a music booth."

*

Before we left the freeway at the Wiota exit, I checked my rearview one last time. No blue Ford. We were safe, for the time being.

We picked up a couple of cases of Budweiser at a party store in Wiota, and Fagan directed me through the cornfields to a private campground located on the banks of a little drain named Troublesome Creek. If you don't believe the name of the place, you can look it up on a map of Iowa. It's a bit west of Wiota about six or eight miles south of I-80, far enough, I hoped, to shake the blue Ford off my tail.

The campground looked pretty much like a regular campground as we drove up to it. There was a patch of trees along Troublesome Creek and a bunch of Winnebagos and pop-ups and tents set up here and there in camping spaces. Coleman stoves and laundry hanging on the lines made it look like it was an ordinary gathering of campers.

There were indications, though, that these folks weren't members of the Good Sam Club. A sign at the gate said "Welcome Pagans," and if you looked closely, you could see the clothes hanging on the wash lines were long vestmentlike things, Druid outfits and togas, and everywhere people were wearing five-pointed stars called pentacles and crosses with knobs on the ends like Violet and Fagan wore. Bumper stickers on the cars read "I brake for unicorns" and "Have You Hugged a Witch Today?" Over in the corner Druids had set up a magic circle and upended some stones to make a mini-Stonehenge.

All in all, it was a bizarre group. Both the men and the women, most of them, were tattooed, but not with bikers' tattoos. These peoples' tattoos were of pentacles and mystic daggers, unicorns and wizards, Rosicrucian stuff you see advertised in the backs of fantasy comic books. The smell of balsam and sandalwood incense mixed with the smoke from their campfires.

Down in Troublesome Creek a fat lady was skinny-dip-
ping. Her toga lay on the bank and she had a daisy chain
woven through her hair. Some farm kids had wandered into
the campground and were standing there laughing at her.
"I am Mother Nature," she said in a huffy tone. "I am the
earth goddess. You don't laugh at Mother Nature. I'll wither
your father's corn, I will, you little . . ."

Meanwhile, Fagan was hanging out the window saying
hello to everybody we passed. Some greeted him with the
kind of mystic hand signs Mr. Spock gives on *Star Trek*.
Others bowed deeply as if they were Japanese monks or
something. Some simply belched and grinned.

The way people welcomed him, you'd have thought he
was the king of all Pagans. Everybody in the place seemed to
know him, and they had even reserved a camping spot for
him where they directed me to pull in.

He tumbled out of the passenger side of the van and
stretched his arms up in the air. "Greetings, pagans!" he
shouted. "Fagan has arrived bearing gifts!" Cheers came up
from all over the campground. He slid open the side door,
hauled out a case of Bud, and ripped it open.

"Yo, druid fluid!" he shouted. "Got it right here." He
started tossing beer cans to other pagans who were nearby or
who came up clutching wads of bills in their hands and looking hopeful.

"Is this great or what, man?" Fagan said to me, popping
the top on a Bud. The foam sprayed out and he took a deep
drink. Some of it rolled down his gingery beard and he
wiped his fat arm across his lips and gestured at the entire
campground full of pagans, witches, sorcerers, and wizards.
"You used to just find this stuff in California, man, but now
it's all over. Look, you got your Wiccans, you got your
Egyptians, your ancient Greeks, your Atlantans, your plain
old generic pagan nature worshippers, everything. Right here
in Iowa, man. Is this America or what?"

He yanked his duffel bag out of the front seat and plopped it on the ground beside the van. He pulled out a Peruvian poncho and started spreading out little packets of unicorn powder and plastic baggies full of what looked like marijuana but which he had labeled sweet grass. He also had a bunch of little bottles—about the size of expensive perfume bottles—full of liquid of some kind.

"Get your love potions here," he said loud enough that you could hear him several campsites away. "Get your herbal essences, see the face of God tonight at the campfire, step right up, pagans. Emotion potions? We got 'em right here. Step right up, you pagans and witches. Ten percent discount for card-carrying members of the Midwest Pagan Conference."

Pretty soon people started drifting up to buy unicorn powder, aphrodisiacs ("Guaranteed," said Fagan, with a lewd wink, "to erect your Maypole") and special "herbal preparations," and to make a long story short, our van soon became a little pagan social center with people hanging around drinking my beer and talking about how they used to live next door to each other in previous lifetimes.

"Do you remember that time we got burned at the stake?" one guy asked Fagan, as though they were discussing an old football game they had played one time. "Man that was hot."

"Yeah," said Fagan, "when was that, 1347? '48?"

"Naw," said the other guy, "that was the plague year. I was in London then. 1602 was when we were burned at the stake together."

"Oh, that's right," said Fagan. "I was a witch then. I was a witch in almost all my previous lifetimes. That's why I get them confused sometimes. How about you, Joe? Were you ever burned at the stake?"

"Not to my recollection," I said, watching all the beer I'd paid for going down the gullets of Fagan and his pagan friends.

"Maybe we can do a past-life regression this afternoon, eh?" said Fagan. "You never know who you are until you journey back and find out who you were. But hey, what am I telling you? You used to play for Elvis after Elvis was dead, right?"

All this time, Violet and the baby were sitting around the beer cooler, too, taking it all in. She seemed a little more at home with it than I did, which made sense with all her talk about her mother's powers.

"Isn't this interesting?" she asked. "All these people searching after something bigger than themselves?" She was holding the baby on her lap, and he sat there playing with the lucky charms and scapulars and stuff Violet had hung around her neck, and his eyes went from Fagan to the witches who walked by, to who knows what all. "I've got a feelin' we met before," she said to Fagan.

"It could be," said Fagan, "Maybe we did meet before. Maybe in Atlantis."

"Maybe you and me and Billy was neighbors in Atlantis," she said to Fagan.

"I doubt it," he said, popping the tab on another Bud. "I was a ritual prostitute in that lifetime. I wouldn't have met you then, not if you were a profane woman. But maybe Billy came to see me at the temple once or twice for the great ritual."

"He wouldn't never!" Violet said, blushing. "Not in any lifetime or I'd break his neck!"

The conversation went on this way for quite a while, and we had some baloney sandwiches for lunch, and little by little the pagans drifted off to take naps or call up spirits in their magic circles or snort their unicorn powder or whatever, and Violet told Fagan the story of how she was trying to get to San Diego before the next Saturday, which was when Billy's sub would be in from its cruise, and she was going to go meet him and they were going to get married and all that.

"Hmmm," said Fagan, stroking his long beard. "Does Billy know you're coming?"

"No," she said. "He doesn't even know about the baby, really. He's been at sea so long. They go down for an awful long time."

"Well," said Fagan, still pulling at his beard and suddenly looking fatherly. "You don't just spring that on a man, you see, Violet? He may not be prepared, spiritually, to accept fatherhood. Maybe you should break it to him gradual-like. I'd hate to see you get hurt after you gave me your hospitality and all."

Violet suddenly looked worried. I guess she had always thought jug-eared Billy was going to do back flips when she showed up unannounced in San Diego carrying a stolen baby and toting him off to a sort of shotgun wedding.

"But how can I get ahold of him?" she asked, "They don't get mail at sea. And I can't call him neither."

Fagan continued stroking his beard and pursing his lips for a minute then said, "I've got it!"

"What?" asked Violet.

"Astral projection."

"Astral projection?"

"Yeah, we'll project your astral body down to Billy's submarine. Then you can plant the idea in his head that he'll meet you in San Diego and marry you."

The way Fagan described it, astral projection sounded no more difficult than making a long-distance call with MCI. He explained we all had astral bodies right beneath the surface of our real bodies and if we wanted, we could peel off from our physical bodies and let the astral body go wherever it wanted. He told us he'd already been to the moon several times—which I could believe—and to the lost city of Atlantis and even to Baltimore once. He'd gotten so good at it, he said, he could now even bilocate and split his astral body in half, so one half could be on Jupiter and the other half in the bleachers of a Tigers' game.

I sat there listening and tried to drink as much of my beer as I could before the pagans finished it off, while Violet got more enthused about this astral projection idea.

"Can I take the baby and show Billy, too?" she asked.

Fagan considered it for a moment but then said it was too risky. "A baby's astral body isn't strong enough yet," he said. "Besides, babies being what they are, they're already everywhere at once, if you know what I mean."

Violet nodded and handed me the baby.

"Now you stay with Joe," she said, "while I go visit Billy. I'm going to tell him all about you and how we're going to meet him in San Diego."

"I'll be getting ready," said Fagan, lifting himself up from the log he'd been sitting on and staggering towards the van. Violet started to follow him.

"Hey," I said, "what if your baby gets hungry while you're in there out of your body?"

"Oh, we won't be gone long," Fagan said. "Violet said he's in the Pacific Ocean somewhere, probably about five hundred feet down. All we have to do is locate him. We'll be back in about half an hour." He lurched into the van and lay back on the foam rubber mattress like a beached killer whale.

"Don't let him give you anything," I told Violet, holding her back for a second. "No unicorn powder or angel dust or anything, and, whatever you do, don't let him touch you— you know what I mean."

"This is purely spiritual," she said. "You got a dirty mind, Joe Findlay."

Violet went into the van and slid the side door closed. The next thing I know, a humming sound started coming out of the van, Fagan and Violet chanting "ammmmm" or "ooooommmm," almost like the voices on the tape of "Open Tuning." It reminded me that Fagan had said they'd probably have a booth at the pagan conference selling tapes, so since it didn't look like anything more was going to happen at the van, I took the baby and went for a walk around Troublesome Creek campsite.

The pagans had themselves pretty well organized. In a lot of ways the paganfest reminded me of a Presbyterian church picnic except with more colorful outfits. They had a sales area where they had set up card tables to sell things like chakra balancing kits ($29.95), chromotherapy color healing wheels, Tibetan bells, Viking rune rubbings, solar energizers, and some stuff called "Mantra Patch" that came in a glue tube.

I picked up a program and saw that they were having workshops all afternoon. "How to Use a Blue Candle to Improve Your Love Imaging Power" and "The Kabbalah: Mystic Key to Lotto Millions." The one called "Massaging Your Third Eye" sounded interesting, but I had missed it already. Besides, I was looking for my record, and it didn't take me long to find the table where a guy in a sleeveless black Druid gown was selling meditation tapes.

"Andreas Wollenweider, right?" he said, adjusting his white headdress as I walked up to the card table. It was spread out with tapes, CD's, and little bottles of gem elixirs.

"No, Joe Findlay," I said.

"No, I mean you're an Andreas Wollenweider fan, right? See, I try to guess what people want before they come up. It's a hobby of mine. I've got ESP."

"No," I said, shifting the baby to my other hip so I could browse through the tapes and CD's easier, "I don't want Andreas Wollenweider. I've never even heard of him."

"Never heard of him?" said the Druid. "Never heard of the, like, literal archangel of New Age harp music? Well, then I was right."

"What do you mean, right?"

"You really want Andreas Wollenweider's new tape, only you don't know it yet. Only $13.95—or are you a pagan? We give discounts."

"No," I said, "I'm not a pagan, and what I'm looking for
is something called 'Open Tuning.' "

"By Zak Bendzi?"

"No, by Joe Findlay," I said.

"But I thought you said you were Joe Findlay."

"I am Joe Findlay," I said.

"But 'Open Tuning' is by Zak Bendzi. It's on Bosky Dell
records. Monster hit, man. I can hardly keep it in stock."

I didn't see it on the table.

"You're out, eh?"

"Like I said, I can't hardly keep it in stock. I got lots of
Andreas Wollenweider, though."

"You don't have any 'Open Tuning?' "

"The only copy I've got is my personal one."

"How much?"

"With pagan discount or not?"

"I'm not a pagan."

"Fifteen bucks."

"Fifteen bucks?"

"It's my last tape, man. I was going to do meditation
to it tonight. Without it I might not be able to get
attuned."

"Ten," I said.

"Thirteen," said the Druid.

"Does it have liner notes?"

"Good as new."

"Twelve," I said.

"Sold."

He crawled into his pickup cab and got the tape out of
the glove box. After trying to sell me some gem elixirs—
made from New England stones, the most powerful ones, he
explained, because once upon a time New England was connected to the lost continent of Atlantis—I gave him his
money and the Druid did a thanksgiving-for-selling-some-
thing ritual in which he jumped up and down with a big

gnarled stick in his hand chanting the name of some pagan god that sounded like "Crumb-crumb-crumb."

I set the baby down beneath a tree beside Troublesome Creek and pulled the liner out of the cassette box. There was no picture of Zak Bendzi on it. Instead, there was a soft focus photograph of the silhouette of a man with wings growing out of his back hanging suspended in blue space. The body of the winged creature was surrounded by a white-light aura and the title "Open Tuning" was written in a sort of Hindu writing as if it was in Sanskrit or something.

I quickly flipped it over to see the production credits. "Open Tuning" by Zak Bendzi and the Samsara Consort, it said. There was no mention of me anywhere on it.

I was totally confused. How in the world could this Zak Bendzi—whoever he was—get ahold of my song? Then I looked at the liner a little closer, and down at the bottom, in teeny-tiny print no bigger than fruit fly droppings, it said "Produced by Hazel Findlay."

Hazel! I should have known. My own wife stole my song and gave it to this Zak Bendzi character, and now it was turning into a monster hit and they were making tons of money! With my song!

I resisted the temptation to throw the liner, tape, case, and all into Troublesome Creek and instead started to devise ways to kill her. Shooting her would be too sudden. Strangling would be too kind. I finally decided I would kill her by making her listen to what Zak Bendzi had done to my song until she died of boredom or went crazy, whichever came first. I was interrupted in this pleasant pursuit by Mother Nature, the fat lady who'd been nude bathing in the creek when we arrived. She stood before me looking very put out, as though I had done something personally to insult her. Her arms were crossed over her white toga and her forehead had thunder clouds on it.

"That baby," she said, pointing down at Violet's child lying on the ground beneath the tree, "is not wearing cloth diapers."

"So what?" I asked.

I shouldn't have asked. Mother Nature proceeded to lecture me on the hazards of disposable diapers. I tried to shut her up by saying it wasn't my baby, but that didn't cut much ice with Ma N, so finally I picked the kid up and headed out of range back to the van.

Violet was just stepping out. She was glowing like one of those old pictures of saints you see on holy cards in old Catholic churches. She looked like she had just had the most incredible rush of her life.

"I saw him!" she said, smiling, blissed out. "I saw him." She took the baby in her arms and gave it a big hug.

"Saw who?" I asked.

"Billy. I went down into his submarine and saw him sleeping in his bunk, kind of like a hanging cot in the submarine. He had my picture hanging right on the bulkhead."

"Swell," I said. I wasn't paying attention, thinking, as I was, about Hazel and how she could have gotten hold of my tape of "Open Tuning." And who the hell was Zak Bendzi anyway?

Meanwhile, Violet rattled on and Fagan stepped out of the van squinting in the sunlight. He looked like he was just waking up, and I figured he'd fallen asleep during the astral projection.

"Isn't that wonderful?" asked Violet.

"Yeah, great," I said. "So what'd you say to him?"

"Nothing."

That caught my attention.

"You left your body and went eight thousand miles under the Pacific ocean to see this guy and you didn't say anything to him?"

"Fagan said not to."

Fagan waddled his way over the beer cooler and pulled a Bud from under the melting ice.

"Neither she nor Billy's evolved enough spiritually to interact between forms," he said, lifting the flip top. He took a long drink and held the cold can up to his forehead. "I always like to pop a cold one after an astral pro," he explained. He drank again. "It was a good trip, totally omni-cosmic, though the pressure down there bothered my ears some. I've never been that deep in the ocean before, except when Atlantis sunk, of course, but I was dead by then anyway." He finished the beer in one swallow and tossed the empty can in the general direction of the garbage bag. He belched and reached for another. "Yeah, your little girly here did right good, considering it was her first trip."

"I got the power," Violet said. "I got it from my mother."

"Well, it shows," Fagan said. "If you had a little more experience, you could have entered his dreaming while he was sleeping there the bunk. Me, I was fifteen years old when I first left my body. I tried to ignore it at first, thought everybody could do it, but after a while I got good at it. Entering Billy's dreaming would have been easy for me, but it's definitely not for a beginner. You'd need more training. I mean you were out-of-body to start with, so if you'd have entered his head and he happened to be some-place else at the time—well, the trip back could've got pretty complicated."

"Yeah," I said, grabbing one of my beers to protect it from Fagan. "You might have got rerouted through O'Hare."

Fagan looked at me and shook his head as if he was talk-ing to a child. "Boy, for a guy who claims to have written such cosmic music, you're not really very evolved spiritually, are you?"

"For a guy who's drinking someone else's beer, you're cop-ping quite an attitude," I said, angry more at Hazel than at Fagan at that point.

"Whoa, hey," Fagan said, quickly finishing off the beer he held in his paw, "am I sensing hostile vibes here or what?" He looked down at the cassette I held in my hand. "I see you got 'Open Tuning,' man, maybe you should listen to what you say you wrote and get peaceful, huh?"

I ignored that comment and things hung there awkwardly for a couple of seconds.

"Hey, listen," Fagan finally said, stretching and yawning as if he was finally just waking up—or just coming back to earth—"I heard the Luciferians are going to be slaughtering a goat tonight. I think I'll go see if I can find out where. Ciao, earthlings."

And with that, he staggered off. He stopped for a minute by a tree, unzipped his cut-off jeans, and began to pee.

"Hey!" somebody shouted from across the campground, "Hey, that's a sacred oak tree, buddy!"

Fagan turned and belched. "Sorry."

*

Evening at the paganfest was not your typical Iowa night out. The half moon hung in the sky like a slice of white melon. Campfires crackled. The smell of hamburgers and hot dogs grilling wafted over the Troublesome Creek campground, and everywhere pagans were putting on their vestments for the night's rituals. The Babylonians were practicing their chants to the sun god Shamash, the Druids were drawing their magic circles on the ground, and the witches were spitting in the four directions to ward off evil spirits.

Violet had spent the afternoon chirping like a bird. She really believed she had left her body and gone out somewhere deep in the Pacific Ocean and seen Billy. Who could prove she was wrong? She described the inside of the submarine and the place where he slept. She even thought she saw her own picture hanging above Billy's bunk. Everybody believed it, and pretty soon she became like a celebrity in the pagan camp because Fagan had taken her on a deep dive.

As for me, I was skeptical. If Billy was a normal sailor, then the picture he would have hanging above his bunk for darn sure wouldn't have been of Violet Tansy.

She and the baby made the rounds of the tables, trading herbal cures and witchcraft stuff her mother had given her. She fit right in, though she never did any of the rituals or anything. Violet's magic seemed to be a more natural sort of thing that didn't need costumes or funny languages. She simply carried it around with her, like a smell.

The sun sets late in that part of the time zone, so it was getting on to about nine-thirty before the serious ritual started happening around campfires. The ancient Greeks in their togas were sucking fumes and doing something Delphic, they said. The Egyptians were down by Troublesome Creek pretending it was the holy Nile, and here and there different groups were chanting, singing, and generally looking intense. I grabbed a beer and wandered from circle to circle. The whole shebang was going to end with a Great Chant around midnight.

That afternoon, the beer supply had run a little low thanks to Fagan and his friends, so I volunteered to go back into Wiota for more. This time, though, I took up a collection, and even Fagan donated some of the cash he had collected from selling his unicorn powder.

The party store in Wiota was a rundown shack of a place with wooden floors and the usual collection of dirty maga-zines, Jiffy pop popcorn, and Eagle Brand snacks. At least it wasn't a Munchee Mart. In the corner behind the counter, the clerk had a TV set going. It was an old black-and-white with a grainy picture, and the rabbit ears on top had tinfoil wrapped around them to improve the reception. She was tuned in to an afternoon tabloid news program called *Inside Track*. It was kind of like *The National Enquirer* for folks who couldn't read. I had been on it one time myself when they did a special feature on the Dead Superstar Revue in Vegas.

Anyway, the signal coming out of Des Moines was a little weak by the time it got to Wiota, but the program caught my eye right away because they were interviewing the girl in Norfolk who'd had her baby stolen, the one Violet showed me the article about, the baby that Violet claimed she herself had stolen. I was so shook up when I heard them talking about it that I almost forgot about the beer I'd come for.

The mother was no more than Violet's age, and she was weeping and crying on camera. Weeping and crying was what *Inside Track* specialized in, and sometimes you had to really pay attention to figure out what the real story was about because from one end of the show to the other there was nothing but mothers and wives and men and women of all kinds crying their guts out on the tube, and that's what made *Inside Track* the number-one late afternoon news pro-gram—if you want to call it news—in America.

I tried to be cool about getting the beer without letting on that my heart was racing like it was about to beat right out of my rib cage and fly out the door and head west real fast.

The chief of the Norfolk police came on the air, looking tough as a pit bull.

"We'll get him," the chief said. "You can bet your life on that. We'll nail his [bleep]."

The clerk, a big fat woman in fluorescent pink toreador stretch pants and a tank top with her bra straps falling out, was talking back to the TV.

"String the bastard up when you catch him," she said as I nervously brought the beer to the counter. "Castration wouldn't be good enough for him. Cut his balls off him and he wouldn't do that no more."

"How do you know it's a he?" I blurted out before I could think.

"Huh?" she said, turning slowly around. There wasn't much room behind the counter, and she had trouble manoeuvering herself between the candy rack and the register. Her beady eyes looked like two raisins pushed into the dough ball of her face. They narrowed and turned rat-like.

"Have you got any suspects?" the TV reporter was asking.

"We've got a few leads we're following," the chief of police said vaguely.

Did he say following? I dropped my wallet, and my license and a few dollar bills scattered around the floor.

"The FBI has been called in, too," the chief said.

The Escort!

"What did you mean it might not be a him?" the clerk asked after I gathered up my money and stuff.

I fumbled for a minute on that one. My lips spluttered and misfired.

"Well, er, I mean why would a guy steal a baby, for cripes' sake, huh? A man'll steal your money or shoot or rob you, that's guy stuff. No man I know'd steal a baby, for cripes' sake. What would he do with it once he'd got it? It's got to be a woman, don't you think?" and I threw some money on the counter, grabbed the cases of Bud, and headed for the door. Luckily, by that time *Inside Track* had gone on to a story about midget lesbian Anglican priests, but I still backed out of the parking lot carefully and made a point to drive away so the clerk couldn't see my license plates.

By the time I got back to Troublesome Creek, everybody was asking Fagan about something called the Saucer Ritual.

Fagan, cheery as ever, smiled and waved and said, "Later, baby, after the Great Circle. Come by the van."

I asked Fagan about the Saucer Ritual, too, mainly because if he was going to put some weird chemicals into a saucer and explode them or something, I wanted to know about it so my van didn't get blown up in the process. But Fagan wouldn't tell me any more than he told the others.

Finally I asked a passing high priest about this famous Saucer Ritual, but he only said, "You've never heard of it? It's Fagan's specialty, man. He's famous for it."

"What is it, exactly?"

"Just be there, man."

"I'll be there, all right," I said, "He said he was doing it at my van."

I finally found Violet about half an hour after the rituals began. She was standing outside a Wicca circle watching some women burn herbs. I told her about the TV show I had seen, about how this Baby Jeffery—that's what they were calling him—was being looked for all over the country. It would only be a matter of time before he showed up on the milk cartons at the Munchee Mart and shouldn't she think about turning herself in?

"I can't," she said, "I really can't." She wasn't looking at me. She was avoiding my eyes altogether, staring at the campfire into which the witches were throwing dried grass. I tried to turn her toward me to see what was in her eyes, but she wouldn't come 'round.

"I've simply got to get Billy to marry me," she said. "Didn't you ever love somebody so much you'd risk everything you ever had for them, didn't you, huh?"

I decided not to answer that one, and I asked her again about the baby and whether what she was telling me was the truth about it or not.

"After Billy and I get married, we'll take the baby back," she said.

"And everything'll be all right, is that what you think?" I turned her around now for real. "Listen, Violet, you've got the FBI following us, did you know that? The Norfolk chief of police said that the Federal Bureau of Investigation was on this case. Don't you know what that means? Didn't you ever see that TV program? They always, I mean always, get who they're looking for, Violet, and they're looking for you!"

One of the pagans in front of us turned around and went, "Shhh!" as if we were in church or something. I guess we were wrecking their magic circle.

Violet didn't say anything. She only held the baby closer to her and started to cry, so I left her there and wandered back to my van. I had seen about enough of bunches of people hanging around in bathrobes doing voodoo.

Cool and damp air came out of Troublesome Creek pretty fast after dark, so I built a fire next to the van. Once the fire was crackling, I opened a beer and took the old guitar Grandpa Tolliver gave me out of its case. I hadn't played it since the day before, but it held its tuning pretty well. I figured I could get a new set of strings for it in Denver, but even with the old strings on it, it still sung. I played a little blues, and it played nice and easy high up on the neck. There was no bow in it at all, and the strings lay close to the fret board but didn't buzz a bit.

I looked down at its face in the flickering orange light of the campfire. I couldn't be sure, but it looked as though there were actually more flowers coming out of the sound hole now than before, and the colors—even in the firelight—were more intense somehow, as if the flowers were alive. It was hard to tell for sure if there really were more flowers because the thing was already so flowery when I got it, but it looked different, like it was changing.

Of course, I didn't believe for a minute old man Tolliver's story about that Bird Boy or whatever he was coming down and playing that guitar all those years ago and painting those flowers on it, but even without that part of the story, the guitar was the best instrument I had ever played. The sound spilling out of its soundhole was like liquid silver, and I found myself able to do things on it that I had only dreamed about on my old Martin.

I got to playing so hard and deep I didn't even notice when the area around my van filled up with pagans who came over for the saucer ritual. When I finally noticed, most of them looked pretty wiped out from their dancing and singing all night, and it wasn't long before there wasn't much beer left in the cooler. I quickly grabbed myself a can before they had all disappeared.

"Cool guitar," a witch said. "Where'd you get it?"

"I got it from an old man who said he got it from an angel," I said, popping the top on a Bud.

"Cool," said the witch. "I met a guy who said he was an angel once, but he only gave me chlamydia. Play some more."

I was about to retune and do "Open Tuning"—my way, not Zak Bendzi's—when Fagan arrived. He stuck his arm up to the elbow into the beer chest, rooted around for a minute, and came out with two cans. Lifting one up in each hand over his head, he shouted, "Fellow pagans, it is time for the Great Saucer Ritual."

The people shouted, "So mote it be!"

"Let us then get ourselves into the proper frame of mind," Fagan said, popping the tabs on both cans of beer. "We need balance, we need connectedness, we need at-one-ment with the universe."

The firelight glinted in his eyes and he started scanning the sky like a weatherman.

"Perfect conditions," he muttered, raising up his arms as if he was going to give the world a big bear hug. Then, louder, "Give me some rhythm, somebody, who's got a drum?"

One of the American Indians—a guy I'd met earlier who was really a Polish electrician from Cleveland—pulled out a tom-tom and started a slow four beat. Pretty soon people began beating along, on logs, sticks, beer cans, anything they had handy, until everything was dancing along like that scene in Woodstock where people go wild, jumping up and down and singing in the rain. Then somebody starting chanting, holding one note as long as she could without breathing, and lots of other people joined her. The whole thing swelled up into the night, and after about ten minutes Fagan closed his eyes and began to sway back and forth, moaning and groaning as if he was in a deep trance. Still holding his arms out, he angled back his head and pointed his beard at the sky, turning back and forth in three-quarter circles as he went "Hmmmmmmmmm-Hmmmmmmmmm-Hmm-mmmm."

"Isn't he great?" someone whispered in my ear.

"Yeah," I said, "but what the hell's he doing?"

"Calling the saucers, man."

Somebody shushed us.

"Hmmmmmmmmm-Hmmmmmmmmm-Hmm-mmmmmm!"

Everybody began to hum along with him and all the pagans' eyes went to the sky, looking from horizon to horizon. I looked up myself, but I couldn't see anything except the sparks from the campfire going up into the dark like red birds, and, above them, hanging in the sky above the Iowa farm-land, a zillion stars.

"Hmmmmmmmmm-Hmmmmmmmmm-Hmm-mmmmmm!"

Fagan kept turning, the beer cans sweating in his hands.

"Hmmmmmmm-Hmmmmmmmm-Hmmmm-mmmm!"

I didn't know what the hell was going on, but I picked up the humming anyway and strummed out a chord on the strings of my guitar so I could be part of the party.

"Hmmmmmmmm-Hmmmmmmmm-Hmmmmmmm!"

Finally the rhythm of the ritual built to a pitch and beads of sweat were streaming down everybody's face. Fagan had his eyes squeezed shut and the skin between his eyebrows was bunched up so intensely you'd think he had a walnut up there, the way his muscles were straining.

Then, all of a sudden, a skinny guy in a long red gown jumped up from the middle of the circle, moved into the light of the campfire and shouted "Look! Look!" He was pointing his gnarled druid staff into the air.

The drumming and the humming stopped at once, and all of a sudden there wasn't a sound in the air except the scritch of crickets down by Troublesome Creek. Everybody sucked in their breath and looked up in the sky because there, about a quarter mile up, we could see blinking red lights making their way over the Iowa corn.

"They've come!" the red pagan whispered breathlessly. "The saucers have come! Praise the lord god Crumm."

Fagan dropped his arms to his sides and blinked up at the moving lights in the heavens. The beer cans he held in his hands turned upside down. He was so slack-jaw, open-mouthed amazed he didn't even notice he was watering his feet with beer.

"Holy shit," he whispered, "you mean we actually did it?"

*

It turned out to be only an airplane, of course, and everybody seemed disappointed, though if you think about it, an airplane is pretty miraculous in its own way. There it is, like something out of mythology, a long shining aluminum tube with wings weighing fifteen tons, crammed full of people eating Eagle snacks, roaring twenty thousand feet above the ground.

But that didn't seem to satisfy the pagans. All day long they had primed themselves for miracles, chanting like Egyptians and ancient Greeks, drawing magic druidic circles on the ground, and carving mystic staffs from oak branches they found in the forest. As far as I could tell, however, no real miracles happened that day, and they had laid their last hopes on the saucer ritual.

A lot of people today seem to expect miracles to come from outer space. I guess they expect there will be some kind of superior beings on board UFOs who will come down from heaven and solve all our problems here on Earth. Maybe they expect ETs to do what no god ever did—save us from ourselves.

Personally, I don't think it's likely to happen. Aliens, if they really exist at all, will probably be life forms pretty much like us. If they ever do land on earth, they'll do what humans would do: look around a while, decide there's nothing of importance here, and then turn the whole planet into a time-share condo development of some kind. Earth would become nothing more than a sort of interstellar resort planet. Spaceships would come in regularly like the cruise ships that dock at St. Thomas, and we earthlings, even the most intelligent ones, would be turned into natives diving for coins. As somebody who lived in Las Vegas for about fifteen years, I know what it's like. Oh, you could turn a pretty good business on package tours—seven planets in six days, that sort of thing, bring in a shipload of aliens on a junket, throw in a few complimentary house chips and a couple of tix to the Wayne Newton show to get them started, and turn over some big interplanetary dollars. Maybe they'd even like the Dead Superstar Revue, who knows? In my opinion, the space people aren't likely to bring miracles any more than jet planes. It's not that kind of world anymore.

Somehow the noise of jet engines and the smell of diesel fuel are not the stuff out of which miracles are made. What if Ezekiel had looked up and seen just an airplane instead of wheels within wheels? What if he had taken a helicopter instead of a chariot of fire? Would it have been miracle enough? Would Jesus rising up into heaven have been as wonderful if he had gone by transporter beam? Of course not. We expect more from miracles than contrails and ozone depletion.

So after they saw that it was only an airplane above Troublesome Creek, the pagans felt let down. The air went right out of their mantras. Fagan, standing in the middle of the enchanted ring, sighed and said, "It's not going to happen tonight, guys. There must be somebody here contaminating the vibes, somebody who doesn't believe."

Now maybe I was being overly sensitive, but it seemed as though the disappointed Druids looked in my direction at that point, and I started feeling a bit worried, because the next stage to getting what they wanted might be human sacrifice, so I gently picked up my guitar and played something, diddling around, you know, to keep them from focusing on me so much. I mean it wasn't my fault they thought a 727 was a mother ship from Alpha Centuri, was it?

After a few bars, Fagan shrugged and rubbed his belly.

"There's a sky-clad ritual going on over at Babylon," he said, and he and a few others drifted off. *Sky-clad* meant naked, and the thought of seeing Fagan dancing naked around a campfire didn't entice more than a handful of people. The rest of the ones from the saucer ritual sat there around the campfire listening to me play. Since nobody objected, I started playing a little louder. I was in an open tuning, but I didn't play "Open Tuning." I'd had enough of that song. I played some other stuff I had written for that particular mode where I used the fourth and fifth strings for the melody and modified the chords to fit the new tuning.

The music from the rose-covered guitar filled the night around the campfire and I got lifted someplace else, as often happens when you start to improvise that way. You get this feeling you're neither here nor there, and you don't know what time it is or what place it is or even who you are anymore. You have this music flowing through you, like you were a pipe or something, and the music was water coming from some spring and going through you and coming through your fingers and then spilling out the hole in your guitar. So, as I played, all my problems went away. The paganfest, Hazel, "Open Tuning," Violet Tansy and her baby—all of those things melted into one another and sank out of sight for a while. It was a good feeling.

The people sitting around the campfire must have felt it, too, because couples snuggled closer together and people scratched the backs of one another's necks and made little moans and groans. Then, two by two, they drifted off into the darkness of the campgrounds, and when I finished playing I was there all alone—or so I thought, anyway.

I sat hunched over the guitar the way you do when you've played yourself out and you're feeling spent and real mellow about things. I stared into the fire and listened to it crackle, not thinking of anything in particular. Here and there around the campground some rituals still went on, but they didn't bother me. Most of the pagans were already asleep. The fire popped once or twice and flocks of red sparks flew up into the night. Over by the creek, crickets filed away and a tree frog in the willow kept croaking like somebody scraping a thimble over a washboard. A whippoorwill in a nearby tree started up its monotonous call.

And then a voice came out of the darkness. "That was lovely."

I jerked my head up. Across the campfire, on the edge of the circle of orange light, I saw two eyes glinting at me from the shadows. A woman got up and walked across the magic circle towards me. She was not your typical pagan.

She was about forty years old, dressed in a white cotton jumpsuit from head to toe. A brightly colored scarf was tied through her shoulder-length black hair as a headband. She was as tall and cool as a gin and tonic served in a frosted hurricane glass. I had noticed her earlier in the day walking around with a minicassette recorder and a 35 mm camera.

"I'm Sylvia Atherton-Barnes," she said. She said it "Sylvia Atherton-hyphen-Barnes," and it took me a while to sort all those syllables out. She came over to where I sat and held out her hand. She had incredibly long, thin fingers, and her hand was cool and dry. She looked like the type of person who never sweats, no matter how hot it gets. She sat down on the log next to me.

"I enjoyed your music," she said.

"Thanks," I said. "Only please don't tell me you saw God or anything while I played it, all right?"

She laughed. "All right."

She looked out of place at the pagan fest. For starters, she didn't have any tattoos, at least not as far as I could see, but she also had a kind of quick-eyed intelligence about her. She wasn't as intense as the pagans were, either, but seemed to keep a cool distance between herself and what was going on.

"You're not a pagan, are you?" I asked.

One of her gold hoop earrings caught the firelight and sparkled.

"No," she said, "I'm a writer. I'm covering the paganfest for a magazine."

"Not *Better Homes and Gardens*," I guessed.

"No." She smiled. "Actually, I'm doing it for *Asymptote*. I guess you could say it's kind of an *HG* for people in Jungian therapy, which, I suppose, is a kind of interior redecoration."

"Oh," I said, already out of my depth with her.

"What a beautiful old guitar," she said. "Do you mind if I touch it?" She reached out the fingers of her right hand and rubbed the flowers. I looked at the sound board. Was it just my imagination, or were there one or two more flowers than when I'd started playing it earlier that evening? I made a mental note to sit down and actually count the number of buds on the thing because it seemed every time I looked at it, it was different, which was impossible, I knew, but still the darned thing didn't look the same as it had when I had picked it up from Grandpa Tolliver's place two days before.

"Have you had it long?" she asked.

"Not too long," I said. "The old man I got it from said he got it from an angel."

"So you're a pagan, too?" she asked. "You believe in angels?"

"Me, I don't believe in anything much, I guess." I shrugged, touching a chord on the guitar. The sound rang pure as silver.

"Those songs you were playing reminded me of 'Open Tuning,' " she said. "Have you heard it?"

I groaned.

"What's the matter?"

"I wrote 'Open Tuning,' " I said. "At least that's me playing on the opening part of it."

I explained how I made a tape in the bathroom the year before, right before I left Hazel, and that I didn't know how in the world the CD and tape had come out but that my name wasn't connected with it in any way. I told her a little bit about how I left Hazel, too, just to let her know I hadn't any connection with anybody right then, not even Violet Tansy, who was hanging around the campground somewhere with her baby.

"How fascinating," Sylvia said, "So you think your wife somehow bootlegged your tape and then had it, what shall I say, enhanced?"

I shrugged. I didn't know anything about it, having only heard the thing for the first time two nights before while we were running scared from Detroit. I told her I intended to find out about it as soon as I could.

"And so your wife is Hazel Findlay?"

I nodded.

"Curiouser and curiouser," she mumbled.

"Why's that?" I asked.

"Do you mind if I tape this?" she asked.

"Last time I taped something, it got turned into an album without my knowing it," I said.

"Sorry," said Sylvia, pulling out a microcassette recorder. "I mean tape this conversation."

I asked her what for.

"You probably aren't aware of this," she said, "but Hazel Findlay has become something of a New Age guru over the past few months."

"First I've heard of it," I said. "What do you mean?"

Sylvia explained that there was a booming industry out there in America selling spiritual enlightenment. This pagan-fest was only an offshoot of the whole thing. Everywhere, it seemed, people were looking for a quick fix on heaven. Tapes, books, talk shows, big revival-style meetings and conferences, all kinds of stuff. There were men's groups with wild-eyed poets leading middle-aged white liberals on shaman journeys, professional drummers helping people tune in to the rhythms of the cosmos, folks out West who were rearranging rocks in national parks to form Indian medicine wheels, and house-wives from Milwaukee and Kankakee who were experiment-ing with ancient goddess religions. It wasn't really crank stuff anymore, she explained, it was moving into mainline Protestant churches, even. You could go into Episcopal and Methodist chapels almost anywhere in America and find people doing yoga, chanting mantras, reading ancient mysti-cal texts and basically buying anything in sight that promised them an enlightenment they weren't getting from their Sunday sermons. It was a metaphysical salad bar out there, Sylvia said, with people taking a little Zen, a little Hinduism, a little witchcraft, whatever suited them.

"And I've run across Hazel Findlay's name more than once in the past month," Sylvia said.

It seems that what Sylvia did for this *Asymptote* magazine was to keep tabs on pieces of what was called the New Age movement. She was like a restaurant reviewer, trying to help people separate the good mantras from the bad and the fake gurus from the real ones. She used a rating system with one-to-four little Buddha heads behind the good ones and a big X for the bad ones. According to her, tons of stuff poured out every week and people latched on to gurus and channelers and gave them thousands of dollars for teaching them how to say "Ommmmmm."

"It's a bit like the sixties all over again," she said, "but we're more sophisticated about it this time around. Everything's plugged in on the Internet. And there's more money in it, too. My job is to go from place to place, like this paganfest, and rate what's going on. In this business it's hard to separate out the real from the fake, you know."

"I've noticed," I said. "But what about Hazel?"

"She's been on the New Age talk show circuit for the past couple of months promoting 'Open Tuning' and this Zak Bendzi character. I haven't been able to get a fix on whether she's legitimate or not," Sylvia said.

I laughed. "I can tell you that right now," I said.

"If, as you say, she stole your song, plagiarized it, then that's one big strike against her."

"And you could sink her if you published that in your magazine?"

Sylvia nodded.

"Let's talk," I said.

*

For the next I don't know how long, I told Sylvia the story of my life, the whole thing, starting with growing up in the Airstream and ending with the long miniseries that was my crazy cross country flight with Violet Tansy. By the time we'd finished, the campfire was about burned out and Sylvia said, "How about coming back to my tent for a nightcap? There's something serious going on here, Joe, and I'm not quite sure you're aware of it."

"What do you mean?" There was something about Sylvia that led me to trust her, and I could see she was a lot more informed about these things than I was, and, to tell the truth, I had to talk to someone about all this or I'd go nuts.

She stared into the fire for a moment. The orange light was reflected in the dark irises of her eyes.

"From what you've told me, there are too many synchronicities occurring for all these events to be merely unrelated accidents. You know what a synchronicity is, Joe?"

I shook my head.

"Sometimes things happen, little meaningful coincidences that, taken individually, seem fairly insignificant, but taken together they form a pattern. Right now, you seem to be the point of convergence for about three or four different but possibly interlinked fates. Some kind of destiny is shaping up right now and you're in the middle of it, for better or worse."

"Fate?" I said. "I thought you said you weren't one of these pagans."

"Fate is simply the name we give to things that happen to us outside our conscious control. You don't have to be a pagan to understand not everything turns out the way you plan it."

"You can say that again," I said, thinking back on the past few days.

"Sometimes we choose our fates and sometimes they choose us. You've been launched on some kind of adventure here, Joe. The question is, are you ready for it?"

Before I could say anything, she added, "You may well be, even if you aren't aware of it. Somebody wise once wrote that we always get the journey we're ready for. Let's go back to my tent and maybe I can help you clarify things."

She told me to bring the guitar, and she led me back to her tent—a big top-of-the-line North Face dome—on the far side of the campground. Beside it was parked a $50,000 Range Rover.

"Writing must be a pretty good gig," I said.

She laughed as she opened the flap of the tent. "I got the money with the hyphen in my name," she said. "The

Atherton was canned food, the Barnes was aerospace. Daddy set up a trust fund and I've been living off it, studying in Zurich when I get the time. The writing is just something I do to help out in these confusing times. Come on in."

I went in, and it was like entering one of those weird illusions at the carnival where you think you're going into what looks like a small wooden box and you suddenly find yourself in a huge fun house a thousand miles from the place you just left. This tent was like no place you've ever been. I expected the usual stuff—Coleman lantern on the floor, sleeping bag spread out and all that, but this Sylvia Atherton-Barnes camped out in style.

The whole inside of the tent was white, and the place seemed much bigger inside than it looked like it could be from the outside. White mosquito netting of fine fabric hung looped from the roof of the tent and a big white bean bag chair sat in one corner. On a small white table, there was a lantern, which Sylvia lit. Her sleeping bag—a deep red mummy bag opened and spread on the floor—was the only spot of color in the place. In the corner was a bronze Chinese dragon and out of its mouth spilled some sweet-smelling incense. Sylvia opened a white ice chest and pulled out a brandy bottle and two cold and frosty mugs, half metal and half glass, like crystal that had been set into pewter stands. They looked antique and very expensive. She pulled the cork from the bottle and poured something into the glasses that was gold and amber in the lantern light.

She handed it to me and we chinked the glasses together. The drink tasted sweet, familiar, and yet strange at the same time.

"What is this stuff?" I asked.

"Mead," she said. "The ancient Anglo-Saxons used to drink it. Hereabouts they call it druid fluid."

"I thought you said you didn't go in for neopagan stuff."

"I didn't say that, exactly," Sylvia said. "I only said you had to separate the good from the bad. This is part of the good. Drink up."

She lowered herself cross-legged to a cushion on the floor of the tent and set her drink beside her. In the soft light, sitting that way with her palms up on her knees, she looked like an Oriental statue.

"Maybe I should explain more about what I do and why I do it," she said softly. "You see, up until about ten years ago, I was nothing more than a spoiled rich girl. I'd grown up with the best of everything money could buy. My life was organized around the perma-tan zone, baking on some of the most expensive beaches in the world. I was married then. When we wanted snow, we flew in my husband's private jet to wherever the powder was finest. I had everything and thought nothing."

She picked up her glass and took another sip of mead.

"And then I had the good fortune to almost get killed."

"Good fortune?"

"We were skiing up above Steamboat," she explained. "We had helicoptered up to the summit. It was one of those places where they drop you right off the helicopter runners onto the peak, and you start to drop through the thin air, rocketing down towards the earth. I'd done it maybe a half a dozen times before in my life. It was the only way I could get a rush anymore. I was bored, you see. I was thirty years old and the only way I could feel alive was to be dropped out of a helicopter ten thousand feet above the earth."

She said, "There is a passage in Dostoyevsky that predicts someday people will become so bored with how easy modern inventions have made life that they'll stick golden needles into themselves in order to get some kind of sensation or feeling at all. That's where I was then in my life. Dostoyevsky was right. I was seeking thrills and I got them.

"I slid off the chopper and in the first moments I was blinded by the snow from the prop-wash. Then I burst out of it and it was like flying because the slope was so steep. I could look straight out and see nothing but sky. Then something happened. I think I got disoriented by all the white and lost track of the slope. I hit what I thought was a pocket of fluff and the next thing I knew I was falling, as if somebody had pulled the plank out from beneath me. It was all white and silent and I never experienced a moment when the whiteness stopped until I woke up in a hospital in Denver a full week later."

"Sounds terrible," I said.

"No, that's the amazing thing, you see. It wasn't terrible at all. It was calm, suspended, and when I fell, I fell through worlds upon worlds. Each time I hit what I thought was bottom, I crashed through. It was as though these worlds were separated only by layers of soft snow. And I fell down and down like in a dream for a whole week until I finally landed in that hospital bed. I opened my eyes and the room was white and the nurses were in white, too, and the only spot of color in the whole world was a bunch of closed red tulips in a white vase. I was in traction and couldn't turn my head, could barely talk or eat, and—this is hard to explain—I went inside those tulips and, as they opened, I opened. Petal by petal, my insides underwent an expansion until I knew things could never go back to the way they were. The trapdoor had opened beneath me and I saw things I could only dimly grasp the meaning of."

This was strange stuff, but as I listened, I realized Sylvia was making a lot more sense than Fagan and the pagans. She wasn't talking about doing witchcraft to win the Lotto or learning magic spells to cure warts. She was talking about something that had changed her down to the root. It had taken her three years to pull herself back together. She practically had to relearn how to walk. And all the time she was hauling herself along the parallel bars or learning to move with canes, she was putting herself back together on the inside as well, and in the end, she said, she came out such a different person that all her old friends dropped off one by one. Her husband accommodated her for a few years, but then he dropped off, too. But she found other people with similar experiences and similar interests, and they formed a loosely organized network she called the Watchers and Seekers. I said it reminded me a bit of Fagan's P-Net, but she said it was much more sophisticated than that.

"Something's happening in history right now, Joe," she said. "Something we can't fully explain. I was dropped off that mountain for a reason. The world's turning over like a lake in springtime. Things long sunken are coming back to the surface, but we have to recognize them when we see them. My friends and I are part of that process. I think you are, too. Now, I'd like you to play 'Open Tuning.' I want you to play it the way you wrote it. Could you, please? It might help us get to where we need to be if we're going to understand what's going on here."

I took another drink of the mead and sat down and started to play, softly, the song I actually wrote, which is not what Zak Bendzi—whoever he was—had turned it into. I was a little drunk and very tired, I admit that, but as I played, the song sounded more beautiful to me than it ever had before, and—I hate to admit this—it started to do to me what Fagan said it did to him. It opened something up inside me, a place I didn't know existed before, a place filled with light.

Sylvia must have felt it, too, because her hand moved up my back and then came to rest on my neck. She began to massage a spot right at the cross where my shoulders and neck met. Her long cool fingers kept rubbing in a small circle right there, and I closed my eyes and let the smell of incense fill my nostrils as I played.

"Just relax," she said, "and let the journey take you."

We could have been a thousand miles from the paganfest then. It felt like we were floating on top of one of those big fluffy clouds that sail above the Iowa cornfields like giant sail-boats, lying back on that big white deck drinking mead and letting the world float away below us.

"What's in this stuff?" I asked as I finished "Open Tuning" and took another sip of mead to wet my lips.

"I mixed in some unicorn powder from Fagan," she said.

"Oh no," I muttered, and then I found myself drifting off on that white cloud into a place somewhere between sleep and being awake.

"Let the journey take you, Joe," she repeated calmly.

I floated away and then suddenly I heard the sound of big wings hovering right over the tent like a great bird of prey had swooshed through the trees of the pagan campground and come to rest right above us. The great bird hung there for a while, then the wingbeats stopped, and a moment later there was a light thump next to the tent, like somebody's feet hitting the ground, as if an Indian wearing moccasins had just jumped out of a tree. I was terrified and tried to move, but I couldn't. Sylvia had gently tipped me backward and I lay flat on my back on her red mummy bag. My body was heavy, as though all my muscles had been turned to bread dough, and I could only manage to lie there, flattened out on the earth, waiting.

Then I heard a long zipping sound and the dome opened around us. Something separated the top of the tent from the bottom cloth, and the whole dome lifted up. I saw we were lying on a great flat plain, all white and covered with snow. Sylvia was now lying beside me, on her back, her arms out-stretched beside her, only she had turned pure white, too, as though she was made of marble or cool alabaster. And then the tent top simply disappeared and I saw that the sky above us was also white. Everything was the talcum powder white of dove's wings. Then I saw a tall young man, very beautiful, wearing a white robe, coming toward me. He was barefoot and he had great big wings growing out of his back!

I realized this was none other than the Bird Boy Grandpa Tolliver told me about back in Detroit. This was him, the very one who disappeared so many years before and now, I thought, he had come back to Iowa looking for his guitar! I wanted to jump up and run away but I couldn't move. I was tied to the ground with thousands of invisible strings, and as I watched, the angel or whatever he was walked to the guitar and leaned down over it. Then he turned and looked at me and nodded, as if he approved of something that was happening.

He reached back and pulled out one of his long white flight feathers and dipped it in some colored ink that had suddenly materialized, and he started drawing more flowers on Grandpa Tolliver's guitar with that feather. His hand moved surely, like he was an accomplished artist, and the flowers glowed again as if they were alive.

I wanted to shout out, but I couldn't. My mouth was stuffed full of cotton, and all I could do was moan and stare, like in a dream.

When he was finished drawing, the Bird Boy sat down on a white cube and began to play his guitar, and I saw the strings turn to air, and the flowers on the face came alive and out of the sound hole animals started flowing—first doves, then sparrows, then chickadees, goldfinches, cardinals, birds of all different sorts. They perched for a second on the edge of the sound hole, then flew away. Don't ask me how they got past the strings, because it was as though the strings weren't there anymore.

Then bigger things started coming out of the sound hole. They started out real skinny, just a bit of brown or gray feather or fur or skin poking through, then they'd get bigger and bigger, squeezing themselves out of the hole. Rabbits and possums, two raccoons, a beaver, three eagles and a great blue heron, lizards and snakes and all sorts of other things big and little flew out of the guitar as the Bird Boy played it, beasts of the air and the sea and the land, lions and elephants and fish, whales and dolphins until, last of all, a man and a woman, naked and beautiful. The man and woman came out together, side by side, and started to fly, without wings, in the air above me. They circled twice over my body and then flew away, arm in arm.

The angel—or Bird Boy or whatever he was—set down the guitar and came over to me, his eyes deep blue and beautiful, and he put his hand on my forehead. When he saw I was asleep—for I was asleep by then, or in a dream, lying there beside Sylvia, also dressed in white—he leaned over and kissed me on the forehead the way you might do a little child. I felt all warm and good inside, as though I was glowing with a sort of cool light. I knew I had never felt that way before in my entire life.

Then he disappeared. I heard the sound of wings but I couldn't see anything, and I wanted more than anything to see the Bird Boy again, but he was gone. I tried to call out but I had to force out every word through cotton soaked in molasses. "Come back! Come back!" I tried to say. "Who are you?"

Things went into nightmare mode. First there was laughter, like the witch's laughter from the *Wizard of Oz*, and it bounced off the sky, which was no longer white but was pitched over like darkest night. A voice came out of that Bible-black sky from where the Bird Boy had disappeared and it said, "I'm Zak Bendzi, Joe. It's me. It's me!"

Next my father appeared, only he wasn't wearing his usual sequined magician's tuxedo. This time he was dressed in wizard robes like something the pagans might have worn, and he was grinning and showing me a bunch of magic para-phernalia. He said, "You get the act when I'm done, Joey, it's all yours. You get the act when I'm done," and I knew he meant when he was dead, so I said, "No! No! No!" I was inside the arrowhead illusion again, sliding down the long hole.

I woke up all of a sudden, though I wasn't sure I was really awake. It was like coming out of dark room and finding yourself in another room, then another, until finally it felt like my body had slammed against the earth, and I realized I was back in the tent, staring at the top of the dome. My eyes burned as though I'd held them open for hours without blinking. My nose was dried from the incense smoke and my mouth was slimy from the mead and unicorn powder. A pounding headache raged through my head and my skin felt like it was covered with half-hardened Jell-O.

I inhaled deep. The air smelled cool and blue. I opened my ears. Off in the distance I could hear a dog barking. I blinked my eyes and opened them again. There was gray light coming through the walls of Sylvia's tent. It was dawn. I had been somewhere else for hours. There was nothing stirring in the pagan camp. I stretched and shook my head, clearing it of the last of the dream. Sylvia still sat there in her meditation posture, only her eyes were open now and focused on me.

"Welcome back, Joe," she said simply. "Did you have a good flight?"

"I'm not sure," I said, warily looking around the tent. "Was what happened real or not?"

"The deep brain doesn't make those kind of trivial distinctions," she said. "Perhaps you could say it was as real as it needed to be."

"Oh," I said, "Now what?"

"You'll have to wait and see."

"That's all?"

"That's all."

The angel's guitar lay in the corner. As far as I could tell, it didn't look any different than it had the night before. I picked it up uneasily and decided to head back to my van and do my morning stuff before Violet and the baby woke up. I had sweated heavily during the night and needed a change of clothes and wanted to hit the showers so I could clear my head.

As softly as I could, I unzipped the door flap of Sylvia's tent and warily stepped out into the dawn, still unsure of my footing. Everything was quiet in the Troublesome Creek campground. I was reassured by the normalcy of it all. Thin lines of blue smoke came up from what was left of the ritual bonfires. Pagan vestments lay strewn on the ground here and there. It was turning daylight and, I thought, I was back on planet Earth.

Then, as I was about to step away from Sylvia's tent into the pagan dawn, I noticed something lying at my feet. A long white feather lay there in the sand, amidst the prints of large bare feet. It was like no feather from any bird I had ever seen. There was colored ink on the tip of its quill, and as I bent over to pick it up, the feather disappeared.

And, after that, things began to get rather strange.

CHAPTER FIVE

By noon, we had said good-bye to Sylvia and the pagans and were blazing down I-80 again, heading for the vast unending blankness of Nebraska. It seemed like the best thing to do under the circumstances.

Fagan was asleep in the back of the van, naked as a gigantic plucked chicken. He had come back from the Babylonian sky-clad ritual while I was seeing angels in Sylvia's tent and heaved himself into my van and passed out. The rest of the pagans broke camp early and were mostly moved out by noon, but Fagan slept on like he was in a coma or something. The way he had mixed beer, other booze, marijuana, and unicorn powder, he might have been brain dead from all we could tell. We tried shouting, shaking, and dowsing him, but it didn't do any good. He was too big to move, so in the end we threw his duffel bag in the back of the van and headed out with him lying there like a stuffed trophy.

Violet and the baby had spent the night with some witches from Indiana. It was a gentle coven of Wiccans, and they had spent the evening drinking herbal teas and trading white magic spells. One of them did an aura reading on Violet and told her everything between her and Billy would work out fine, so Violet was grinning in the passenger seat all the way through the rest of Iowa.

As for Sylvia, by the time I'd showered and got back to her tent, she was loading her things into the Range Rover. She made me promise to stop by her place in Denver if I ever got there. She said she wanted to talk to me more about my rose-covered guitar and the song "Open Tuning." I helped her load her folded-up dome tent into the back of her Range Rover. It was amazingly light and compact for a tent that so much had happened in the night before.

The radio news was full of stories about the lost baby from Norfolk. The story of Baby Jeffery—that was what they called him—had taken grip of America's forebrains, and you couldn't turn anywhere on the dial without hearing the crying mother, the growling chief of police, and reports from the FBI Leads were developing, said the newsmen. Police were not at liberty to discuss, we can't comment on that at this time, and on and on and on.

I scanned the rearview constantly for sight of the blue Escort, and I told Violet to keep the baby down, but she didn't seem worried.

"The witches told me it would all work out," she said. "They did a special wicca-way blessing on me and him last night and gave me this." She reached into her T-shirt and pulled out a pentacle on a chain. "I also got a secret weapon," she said. "Fagan sold me this." She held up a little plastic packet of white powder.

"Cocaine isn't going to help you at this point," I said. "Throw that stuff out."

"It's not cocaine," she said, "It's unicorn powder. It's a true love powder. Fagan says all I have to do is put it in Billy's drink and he'll be dying to marry me."

I shook my head and drove. There was no way to convince her of how hopeless all this was.

About halfway between Omaha and Lincoln, which we reached in the early afternoon, Fagan rolled and snorted in the back of the van.

"Whoa," he said as he came around. "Hold on tight, earthlings, we're in motion!" He gripped the foam rubber of the old mattress for a minute until he figured out he was in a van, then he sat up. He didn't seem to notice he was naked because he just crawled up to the front of the van and squinted out into the sunlight.

"Corn!" he said, rubbing his eyes and squatting like a big dog between the seats. "We must be somewhere in the Midwest, right?"

"Nebraska," Violet said. "Isn't it pretty?"

"Yeah," said Fagan, nodding his head up and down, over and over, like he was still stoned. "Corn, man, the Zen of corn, can you dig it? You got any coffee?"

Now that he was awake, sort of, I was trying to figure out a way to get him out of the van. Not only was his weight cutting down on fuel mileage, but I didn't want his bagful of unicorn powder used as evidence against me in case the FBI took us alive. There was an outside chance I might not get life in prison if I could convince them Violet forced me at gunpoint to take her and the baby west, but if they caught me with a character like Fagan along, I probably wouldn't see the sunshine ever again.

"The Aztecs were right," Fagan was saying to Violet. "Corn is like God."

"It's just corn, for cripes' sake," I said.

Fagan hit the side of his head, like he just remembered something. "Right! Right!" he said. "I should know that. Sure, corn is just corn. Like the Zen thing—at first mountains are mountains, then they aren't mountains anymore for a while, then when you finally reach satori they're just mountains again. Geez, you got good Zen, man." A green sign flashed by. Lincoln, twenty-five miles.

"Shit, we're past Omaha already?" Fagan asked.

I nodded.

"Stop the van, man, stop the van!"

"I'll pull over at the next rest stop," I said. "Can you hold it?"

"It's not that, I'm supposed to fly out of Omaha. I've got to get to San Diego to work with Swami Jody."

"We're going to San Diego," Violet said. "Whyn't you ride with us?"

"Don't count your chickens before they hatch," I said to her, looking in the rearview. "You aren't there yet."

"Stop the van," Fagan said. "I'm not gonna *drive* across this friggin' country. What do you think I am, crazy?"

"You got a ticket?" I asked.

"Who needs a ticket?" he said, raising his arms like wings. "I said I was gonna fly. I didn't say I was gonna take a plane."

"Jesus," I sighed.

Fagan poked me in the ribs so hard the van nearly swerved into the other lane.

"Hey, only kidding, man," he said. "I made enough money selling unicorn powder to the pagans that I can buy a friggin' airplane ticket, cash money, at the Omaha airport. Stop the van."

I pulled the van over to the shoulder and Fagan grabbed his duffel and started to climb out the side slider door. He had one foot on the road before I stopped him.

"Hey, Fagan," I said.

"Yeah?"

"Have you forgot something?"

"Like what?"

"Like you're naked."

"So?" he asked, climbing out the rest of the way. "I'm going sky-clad, clothed with the sun. If Nebraska can't deal with that, so mote it be. Ciao, earthlings." And with that he slid the door closed and off we drove.

The last I saw of Fagan he was hauling his sky-clad body across the median strip toward the eastbound lane. A few minutes later, I saw a Nebraska State Police car, flashers going and sirens wailing, heading toward the spot where we'd dropped him off. So mote it be.

Every few minutes I turned on the radio and scanned the news. There were no new developments in the Baby Jeffery case, but that didn't seem to stop the newscasters and talk show hosts from jumping all over the story. They had interviews with his baby sitter, his second cousins, with sociologists and psychologists and criminologists of all kinds. The chief of police said he was in contact with the FBI almost constantly and it was only a matter of hours before the suspects were apprehended. My hands got sweaty on the wheel. Still no blue Escort behind us, but he might have changed cars to throw us off, make us feel everything was okay, get us feeling comfortable and then, somewhere in the middle of nowhere, when we least expected it, the bullets would come through the windows and we'd be dead. I punched the seek button on my radio. Baby Jeffery, Baby Jeffery, Baby Jeffery, Hazel Findlay, Baby Jeffery . . . Hazel Findlay? Whoops!

I dialed back. What the hell was my wife doing on the radio in the middle of Nebraska?

"Actually," she was saying, "the song has been called an ecofeminist parable, Miles."

"The Way of the Mother Earth . . ."

"Exactly."

"So the song functions both at the microcosmic and the macrocosmic levels?"

"That's right," Hazel said. "Zak is terribly concerned about our global environment."

"It shows in his music," Miles said.

Miles was Miles Kindley, host of *New Connections*, a New Age talk show that aired out of San Francisco. It was put out by the same people who produced *Music from the Depths of the Space*, where I'd first heard "Open Tuning" two nights before. Miles Kindley was so New Age that sometimes I wasn't sure if he was awake. Now he and Hazel were pumping "Open Tuning" and Zak Bendzi live on the airwaves coast to coast as if it had been Zak and not me who had written the song.

"Zak is very much in touch with his anima," Hazel was saying.

"The anima being Jung's term for the inner feminine in the male," Miles Kindley kindly put in.

"That's right," said Hazel as if she had known that all along and hadn't quickly primed herself on it before the show, "His shakti or inner feminine emanation is very close to the surface, as many people who've listened carefully to 'Open Tuning' have remarked."

"But he's a reclusive genius?"

"Terribly shy," said Hazel. "He scores a zero on the Myers-Briggs extraversion scales, but he says it doesn't matter because music is his soul, and that's what shines forth in his works like 'Open Tuning.' "

He ought to be shy, I thought. The friggin' thief! He stole my song and was making more money off it than I had ever dreamed of. He could afford to be shy and let Hazel shill for him like this.

The more I listened the madder I got until, without noticing it, I had speeded up the van and the sides were flapping again. Whucka-whucka-whucka. I eased off the gas so the noise from the sides wouldn't interfere with the radio. I marveled at the way Hazel was able to include the album title in every sentence without mentioning me once.

"We're live on air and taking calls," said Miles, giving an 800 number. I would have killed for a phone right then to set the record straight, but we were in the middle of Nebraska fifty miles from the nearest phone, and by the time I got to one, the show would be off the air.

"The whole album is suffused with the energy of the Mystic Mother," said Hazel.

By then I was shouting at the radio and banging the dashboard with my fist.

"I know who the 'mother' is," I yelled. "Hazel, how could you do this to me?"

Violet, who had been dozing off in the passenger seat, woke up and asked who was on the radio that I was so mad at.

"My wife," I said.

Violet listened for a minute while Hazel went on and on about how Zak Bendzi was part of the new wave of mystic consciousness, the vehicle for macrocosmic rhythms and harmonies.

"She sounds real intelligent," said Violet. I groaned.

Next a caller from somewhere in California said he had done some kind of interstellar communication while he was listening to "Open Tuning" in a sensory deprivation tank—which seemed a little unnecessary to me, seeing as how what Zak Bendzi had done to my song was make it seem like being in a sensory deprivation tank to begin with.

"We're taking calls," said Miles Kindley. "And we'll be back right after station identification."

I was feeling totally helpless, and then a guy in a BMW pulled alongside us and I saw he was talking on a cellular phone! Whatever cellnet he was on must have had a huge footprint, and I was sure I could reach Miles if I could only get my hand on that phone.

I stepped on the gas. The sides of the van went whucka-whucka-whucka, but I managed to stay even with him. I honked my horn and blinked my lights, but he had his air conditioner on and didn't see or hear me. I stayed abreast of him and lay on the horn some more until, finally, he looked over.

"Phone! I need the phone!" I shouted out the window and mimed talking on the phone, but the guy just shook his head like I was some species of weirdo or something.

"We've got a caller from Denver," Miles was saying.

"Yeah, listen," the caller said. "I was reading in this morning's *Denver Register* that some guy named Joe Findlay claims he wrote 'Open Tuning.' It was in the Names and Faces section, right next to a story about Madonna's secret breast implant surgery."

I could hear Hazel suck in air over the radio. It only took her a second to get her composure back, though. Sylvia, I thought, must have faxed the story in to the paper.

"An outright lie," Hazel said, cold as ice. "That would be typical of him to start a story like that."

"Who is Joe Findlay?" asked Miles.

"My husband," Hazel said. "A lower, less evolved lifeform you couldn't find. He left me in a typical male fit of testosterone poisoning last winter and I haven't seen him since. I would expect him to perpetrate a lie like that to try to steal a little of the reflected genius of Zak Bendzi."

That did it. She was getting personal now. The guy in the BMW was still on the phone and still ignoring us. Hazel was running me down from one end of the country to the other and Miles was egging her on.

"So he was your typical white male Anglo-Saxon dominant sexist pig, eh?" said Miles.

"He was totally undeveloped in terms of higher consciousness," she said. "Thoroughly phallocentric."

I looked up in the rearview and, as if I didn't have enough problems right then, the friggin' blue Escort and the FBI agent from hell reappeared! And he was talking on *his* car phone, too, probably getting authorization from headquarters to pull out the firearms. Somewhere up ahead in Nebraska, I could feel it in my bones, a team of FBI sharpshooters was loading hollow tip bullets into their long-range rifles, getting ready to blow my brains out for the sake of Baby Jeffery.

Meanwhile, on *New Connections*, a listener from North Carolina called in to say I sounded exactly like her first husband.

That did it. Before the FBI got me, I was going to get into this conversation or die trying.

"Get out your gun," I shouted at Violet.

"What?" she said.

"The gun, I know you've got a gun in the bottom of your bag, get it out. Now!"

She protested, but I yelled at her again. I didn't have time for fooling around. *New Connections* was going off the air in a few minutes and I wanted to get my licks in before the FBI put an end to my short miserable existence.

Violet handed me her gun. I pulled up right beside the guy in the BMW and shook it out the window so he could see it glinting in the sunlight.

"Pull over now!" I shouted clearly enough that he could read my lips. I even nudged my van over the line and tried to force him off the road.

He turned toward us, took one sneering look at my van, its sides rocking with the speed, and said, so I could read *his* lips, "Fuck you." With a gentle nudge on his accelerator he shot away from us like we were standing still and left me eating his expensive German diesel exhaust. In two seconds he was out of gun range. By the time I could have pulled the trigger he was halfway to Colorado.

I looked back in the rearview and the guy in the blue Escort was closing the distance. By now he had probably seen the gun, and I scanned the vast prairie skies for the attack choppers. My only chance was to take him on right then and there before the sharpshooters could get us in their sights. And then I remembered that when you're arrested you always get one phone call. Yeah, I said to myself, everybody's entitled to one phone call, and I was going to make mine to *New Connections* with the FBI agent's own cellular phone.

I slowed down the van until the Escort pulled alongside. Cool as ever, the young agent didn't even look at us. He just kept driving and talking on his cellnet as if he was only another pilgrim on the westbound highway of life, but I knew better. I checked out the front seat. No shotgun lying there as far as I could see, and he wasn't wearing a jacket, so he couldn't have a shoulder holster with a deadly German Ruger under his armpit. I decided it was time for desperate measures. As the blue Escort came window-to-window with us, I stuck out the gun, aimed it in his general direction, and shouted, "Pull over, pull over now!" I waved with the gun toward the right shoulder of I-80, and he got the message.

He pulled over. I could hardly believe it. I had actually caught one of the FBI's best off guard! Either that, I thought, or it was a trap. A cold vise clamped down on my heart. I felt a sharp pain in my chest where the bullets would enter in. I prayed that ratty Escort wasn't really one of those James Bond cars with missiles that fly out of the tailpipe. I let the car slide in front of us, being careful to watch that the agent kept his hands on the wheel and the car phone so he couldn't grab for his weapon. I scanned the blue sky again. No attack choppers so far.

Of course this was a stupid thing to do. He was probably explaining the situation and giving our location to the command center right then on the car phone, but I didn't care— I would at least get one last blast at Hazel on coast-to-coast radio before the *federales* took me out in a blaze of gunfire.

The blue Escort rolled to a stop on the shoulder and I pulled right in front of him. As I jumped from the van, my knees were shaking and my insides turned into lumps of cold macaroni. I realized I may have only a few moments of life left. There was nothing to lose. I decided to grovel. I didn't want to get my brains blown out before I got a chance to use the car phone, so I threw my gun into the grass beside the highway and raised my arms. Reaching for the sky, I headed towards the blue Ford shouting, "One phone call! That's all I want. I give up, but I want one phone call!"

I squeezed my eyes shut and threw myself on the Escort's hood. By this time I could feel the bullets coming at me. I knew the FBI had a million ways to kill you, and I started whining like a puppy, "Don't shoot me, please, Mr. Agent, don't shoot me, it was her, it was Violet made me take her and the baby along." The snot was coming out of my nose and running onto the hood of the blue Ford. "Just let me use your phone to make one phone call, please, mister, please."

"You want to use my phone?" the guy asked, his voice cold and pointed as an icicle.

"Yes, that's all, then I'll go quietly," I whimpered.

"Well, hang on," he said, "I'm talking to an agent . . ."

"I know," I said. "I know you're talking to an agent, please tell him not to kill me, please, all I want is a phone call."

By this time Violet and the baby came up the shoulder, too, and stood there looking stupidly at me. I thought of using her as a human shield, but instead I lay there snivelling on the hot hood of the blue Ford.

"Keep down, Violet," I said, cradling my head in my arms. "Keep down and they may not get you. Save yourself. You're young enough that you'll still be able to have a life when you get out of prison."

The guy got out of the car and handed me the phone receiver. My fingers were so cold and numb, I could hardly hold it right.

"Oh, thank you," I said, punching the *New Connections* 800 number through my tears, "this is so good of you."

The phone rang twice before I heard the tender-as-filet-mignon voice of Miles Kindley.

"This is *New Connections* and you're connected," he said suavely.

"Yeah," I said, wiping away my tears, "well, this is Joe Findlay, and I don't like what you've been saying about me."

"Joe?" snapped Hazel.

"Yeah," I said. "It's me."

"I don't believe it."

"Don't pretend you don't recognize my voice," I said. "It's only been six months. This is my last call, Hazel."

I could hear my and Hazel's voices echoing weirdly in my head. At first I thought it was one of those hallucinations dying people have, you know, where they see dead loved ones and go down the tunnel of light and everything gets echo-y and all, but then I realized the guy in the blue Escort was listening to *New Connections*, too, and there was a three-second delay between what I was saying and it coming out of his radio. I didn't have time to think it was a little bit weird that an FBI agent on the tail of a couple of kidnappers would be listening to *New Connections*.

"I don't see any socially redeeming purpose to this phone call," Hazel said.

"Don't worry," I said, scanning the Nebraska sky. (Where were those Apache warships?) "This is the last time you'll hear from me." I studied the FBI agent's face. He looked cool as Mt. Rushmore. Amazing, I thought, how such a vicious killer could have the face of a choir boy.

"That's encouraging," she said, "Miles, can we . . ."

"Hang on a minute. Hang on just a danged minute," I said, trying to fit everything in at once. "That guy who said he read in the paper this morning that I wrote that song 'Open Tuning' was right, only I didn't call it 'Open Tuning.' I was gonna call it 'The Talking Fish Head Blues,' but that doesn't matter because the point is you stole that song from me, Hazel. I don't know how you did it, but you did it, and that's me playing the song, and I never got a word of credit on the jacket notes and not a penny from anybody, and I want everybody out there listening, all you New Agers, to know, now hear this, Hazel Findlay and Zak Bendzi—whoever the hell he is—are thieves. I, Joe Findlay, wrote 'Open Tuning'!"

"You didn't write it," Hazel said, matter-of-factly, trying to bluff her way through. I could tell she was nervous. You don't live with somebody seven years and not know when you've got them cornered like a rat. "Besides, what if you did?"

"Hah!"

"But what *is* authorship?" oozed Miles. "The Dhammapadda would say you must not cling to the fruits of your action."

"You keep out of this," I shouted at Miles. I could hear the echo of my voice, time-delayed three seconds, coming out of the blue Ford's dashboard.

"Miles is right," Hazel said. "Once something is written, it becomes part of the cosmic web."

"Who told you that?" I shouted. "Your lawyer? It's my damned song."

"Hey, Joe," said Violet, putting her head into the Escort, "you're on the radio, did you know that?"

"Yeah, I know I'm on the radio," I said, and three seconds later my voice came out of the radio saying exactly that.

"Can we talk about this off the air, Joseph?" Hazel asked.

I knew I had her now. She never called me Joseph unless I had her roped, tied, and facedown in the mud. I glanced at the FBI agent. He was looking at his watch.

"Hey," he said. "Do you have any idea how much cellnet charges a minute?"

"This is my last call," I said.

"Good," said Hazel.

I eyed the agent nervously. "I mean I may not have another chance."

"Miles," Hazel said. "Can we go off air?"

"You hold on, Miles," I said.

"I really am sensing some bad vibes here," said Miles. "We have a call waiting from New Jersey."

"You leave me on the air!" I screamed. "I'm going to expose Hazel and this Zak Bendzi guy for the fakes they are right here on national radio, you hear me? For once in my life, I'm going to do something right before I die."

"Joseph, this is personal business," said Hazel.

"There's nothing you and I have to say to each other that can't be shared with four million other people," I said.

"You're a pig, Joe Findlay." Hazel said, "You were a pig when I met you, you were a pig when you left me, and you're still a pig. Hang up on him, Miles."

"I'm afraid we're going to have to go to another caller," said Miles. "Joseph, you sound as though you're in deep anger and denial. This conversation may be impinging on our listeners' comfort zones."

"You changed my song!" I shouted.

"We didn't change anything," Hazel said. "We merely purged it of its crypto-phallocentricism."

"You said it was an ecofeminist parable," Miles chimed in.

"That's right," said Hazel. "Do we have another caller?"

"We do have a caller waiting in Parsippany, New Jersey," said Miles.

"You hang on right there," I said, putting as much threat into my voice as possible. I didn't want to hang up now. I had four million people listening. The FBI sharpshooters and Nebraska's state police SWAT team had me in their crosshairs, but they wouldn't kill me on the air.

"We do have to move on," Miles was saying. "We've only got a few minutes . . ."

"I've got Baby Jeffery!" I shouted, like a moron.

"What?"

"I've got Baby Jeffery," I shouted again, "I'm the one, me, I got him, and we're in the middle of Nebraska."

Violet stood up out of the car window looking like a scared raccoon. "Shhh. Don't be saying that. You shouldn't ought to say that on the radio."

I looked at her like I would look at a fool. I gestured toward the FBI agent who'd been following us for the past thousand miles.

"They know," I said. "They know already. The game is over, Violet. Do you hear me? It's all over."

Suddenly the *New Connections* line went dead.

"We have a caller in Parsippany," I heard Miles say over the radio. "Hello, Parsippany, you're new connected."

A whiny, nasal woman's voice came out of the radio. "Well," Parsippany said, "I personally think this conversation is typical of the sort of narcissistic male behavior that takes credit for everything women do. The examples are legion . . . " and blah, blah, blah. As it turns out, she had done her PhD in Women's Studies at some big university and had proved Shakespeare's plays were really written by his sister and blah, blah, blah, and before sixty seconds were out, America had forgotten everything I said—except the part about Baby Jeffery.

It was finished, all over. I gave the handset back to young Ephraim Zimbalist, taking what I thought was my last free breath. A few days before, I had been a sane, fairly rational person. All that seemed like ancient history. I held out my wrists for the cuffs.

"I'm yours," I said.

"Huh?" the agent said.

"Do with me as you will," I said. "Read me my rights, I'm guilty. I agreed one phone call and then we'd call it quits. Just don't shoot me in the face. I want my father to be able to recognize me."

The red-haired guy squinted at me in the Nebraska sunlight. Trucks rolled past at seventy miles per hour on their way to God knows where. Sand blew in our faces. The car rocked in the tailwash from the semis. The sky was clear blue as far as I could see.

"I don't know what the hell you're talking about," the guy said.

I looked him square in the eye and asked him to repeat what he had just said. He did. He said he didn't have any idea what I was talking about. He didn't blink. What a genius, I thought, he's brilliant. He is cooler than James Bond, playing dumb like this until reinforcements show up. I decided I wouldn't let him get away with it. I wanted to surrender and be done with Violet, done with all of it.

"You mean to tell me you haven't been following us since right past Chicago?" I asked.

"Well," the guy said, "now you mention it, I do recall seeing that old van of yours all over, but that happens out here. There's this family from Cincinnati I keep running into at every rest stop, too. I don't know, maybe it *is* sort of strange we keep seeing each other, now that you mention it, but I noticed you go to Munchee Mart a lot, so that could explain it."

"Explain what?"

"Wait a minute," said Violet, coming around the car and looking more closely at the red-haired guy. "Hey, don't I recognize you?"

The guy blushed a little and said, "Maybe," but he wasn't letting on where she might have seen him before.

"I got it now," she said. "I knew I recognized your voice. I know you from TV commercials. You're Munchee Mart Marty, aren't you?" She didn't say it like a question. She had him nailed, and the guy blushed and nodded.

"Yeah," he said. "That's me. I signed a new contract a few weeks ago and I'm working my way out to L.A. doing promotional stuff along the way. In fact, I was just talking to my agent when you came up to use the phone. We're working on a feature film idea."

My head was spinning again. Things were racing by me faster than the semis in the outside lane.

"You mean you haven't been following us all this time?" I asked.

"No," he said. "I've been working my way from town to town doing promotional spots at Munchee Marts, you know, blowing up a few balloons, patting some kids on the head, that kind of shit. I'm headed for a gig right now at the Munchee Mart in Grand Island. You might want to pop in and catch my act."

He went around to the trunk and popped it open. Inside was a box with a turquoise and yellow clown suit and an orange fright wig—Munchee Mart's corporate colors. He propped up a mirror, opened up a makeup box, and started putting on his white face.

"Matter of fact, I better get ready now," he said, smearing his clown white over his forehead and onto his cheeks. "Letting you use the phone will make me late."

"Wait a minute," I said. "You mean you're not FBI or state police or anything?"

"What would give you that idea?" he asked, painting a giant red smile around his mouth. "Oh, yeah, well, I played a cop once on LAPD, but it was only a bit part. I got shot before the first commercial break. I'm surprised you remember."

He slipped on his clown suit. It was a loose-fitting thing that went right on over his clothes.

I went up and grabbed him by his pom-poms.

"You mean you're just an actor?" I shouted.

"Hey, not *just* an actor, man," he said. "I've got my MFA from U. Cal at La Jolla . . ."

"I've been chased for five hundred miles by a *clown?*" I shouted, tightening my grip on his costume.

Munchee Mart Marty looked over at Violet.

"Hey, what's with this guy? Is he a psycho or something? I read about these heartland psychopaths, man, but I thought they were only in slasher movies."

"You're a *clown?*"

"Not an ordinary clown, I'm Munchee Mart Marty."

I shoved him up against the car.

"YOU'RE A CLOWN?"

"Hey, I tried being a legitimate actor, you should have seen my Othello at the Goodman in Chicago. It knocked the critics' socks off. I've done Beckett and Ionesco, too, but a guy's gotta make a living, right? Munchee Mart made me an offer I couldn't refuse."

I shook him so hard his rubber nose almost fell off.

"Don't you understand?" I shrieked. "Because of you I just confessed to kidnapping Baby Jeffery on national radio!

I'm going to spend my life in a federal penitentiary because of some Ronald McDonald Bozo clown."

"No, no," Marty said. "Ronald McDonald and Bozo are different clowns. People often get us confused . . ."

I cocked back my fist to punch him in the nose.

Marty winced. "Hey, you can't hit me," he whimpered. "I'm a registered trademark of the Munchee Mart corporation."

By the time I turned him loose, he was shaking and so nervous that he sat down on the edge of the opened up trunk of his old blue Ford.

"If you're so famous, how come you're driving this piece of junk?" I asked.

"I've got a Jag waiting for me in L.A., man." he said, "This was my New York car. Hey, you got to be an idiot to keep a good car in New York. It'd be stripped faster than a thirty dollar hooker. I thought if I could get one more drive across the country in this clunker, I could drive it off the Santa Monica pier when I get to L.A."

Why shouldn't I kill him? I wondered. There's a gun in the ditch about fifty feet away and nothing but corn for a thousand miles in any direction. Who would ever know? Just then, the top-of-the-hour news blared out of the radio in Munchee Mart Marty's Munchee mobile.

"New developments in the Baby Jeffery case," the newscaster said in a *March of Time* voice. "Unconfirmed reports say the kidnappers of the Norfolk baby have taken the child to Nebraska, authorities have a suspect, but the FBI refuses to comment. In other news . . ."

There was no other news, not that I heard, anyway. I forgot about Munchee Mart Marty and staggered back to the van. I called to Violet to come on, but she had to get Munchee Mart Marty's autograph first. While she was getting it, I walked down the highway and got the gun out of the ditch. I put the muzzle up to my temple and thought seriously of pulling the trigger. At the time, it seemed the easiest way to get away from Violet Tansy and all the weird stuff that had been happening for the past six days since we met. And I would have pulled the trigger, too, except plain old morbid curiosity made me want to hang around and see how this *Looney Tune* story would end up. I mean, traveling with Violet was stranger even than touring with my dad, the Amazing Raymond. At least with him you could sometimes predict what was going to happen next.

Meanwhile, Munchee Mart Marty, in full clown costume, pulled into the traffic flow on I-80 and disappeared over the horizon. Violet changed the baby's diaper in the back of the van and as she was doing that, I stood there looking off into Nebraska with the gun in my hand. I would have fired the thing into the wheat fields—just to do something about the stupid situation I found myself in—except I was afraid it might backfire and blow my guitar hand off. Besides, I thought, we might need the bullets.

Back in the van I angrily punched the seek button on the radio. As we started to roll west, every station in Nebraska was running the update on the Baby Jeffery story. The Nebraska State Police had been notified that somebody named Joe Findlay had confessed to having Baby Jeffery in their very own state. It would take them a minute or two to get my license number and vehicle description from the Nevada Department of Transportation, but pretty soon they'd have me. I was starting to feel like road kill.

*

We passed Grand Island and made it as far as Kearney before we needed gas. The van had a range of only two hundred and some odd miles before it ran out of gas, and in a straight-ahead state like Nebraska it drank fuel pretty quickly. We passed on the chance to see Munchee Mart Marty do his stuff at the Grand Island Munchee Mart, but at Kearney we pulled off and while I filled the tank, Violet took the baby and headed in for a Super Gulp and another ticket for her dream house.

Violet left a trail of Munchee Mart cups and wrappers wherever she went, so while the tank was filling I cleaned up. I took the opportunity to rearrange some stuff in the back of the van and took my guitar case and everything out, set it on the pavement, and put it back in again in some kind of order.

It wasn't until I went in to pay that I realized I had been robbed. I reached in my jeans pocket for the plastic bag and found there were only three dollars left. Violet held the baby by the register as she flipped through the tabloid newspapers. She was reading an article about an eleven-year-old girl who had Bigfoot's baby, and I asked her if she knew where my money went.

"Well," she confessed, "when you were in the showers this morning at the campground, I borrowed a little to pay for that unicorn powder I bought from Fagan."

I groaned and banged my head against the Frito rack.

"Well, I needed the love potion," she explained.

I groaned again. I owed twenty-one-fifty for the fill up and the Super Gulp and I only had three dollars in my pocket.

"You got plastic?" the clerk said.

"No, I haven't got plastic," I said.

"Well, then we got a problem, don't we, buddy?" he said. He was a big hairy guy with a black mustache who looked like he spent his free time leading peasant revolts in some South American country. "Now you can pay and go, or we can sit here and play gin rummy while we wait for the sheriff's department to come over and say hi. Which'll it be?"

"No, no cops," I said quickly. "I'll figure something out."

I thought briefly of going out to the van and getting the gun and robbing the place. Why not? The police in Nebraska were already after me. At the time it seemed like a logical proposition and it would only add a few more years to my already lengthy sentence. In fact, I was about to head for the gun when I felt someone tugging at me.

"Have you hit a pothole on life's highway, brother?" a voice behind me said.

I turned around. There was nobody there. Well, I mean I *thought* there was nobody there. I felt another tug at my pants leg. I looked down and I saw a midget in a white suit standing there behind me in line holding a Super Gulp and a couple of Slim Jims.

"How's that?" I said.

"I said, have you just run off one of life's curves, friend?" the midget replied. He held out his tiny hand and said, "Allow me to introduce myself, I'm the Reverend Lenny Laird, the Lord's Littlest Laborer."

I shook his hand, it was tiny, like a dog's paw. I couldn't help feeling that I had seen Lenny Laird before, but I couldn't place him. You'd think I'd remember a midget in a white suit, but in my current state of mind I was losing track of the details.

"I couldn't help but notice you had a guitar case out there on the tarmac, brother," he said. "You wouldn't happen to be a musician, would you?"

I said I was, and he said he had a proposition for me.

"Talk," I said.

"First let me pay your gas bill, son," he said, and he whipped out a wad of bills, reached up to the counter, and laid a fifty dollar bill in front of the clerk. The cashier rang it up and gave him change, and we went outside to the parking lot.

Beside the Munchee Mart a big Winnebago was parked. It was a top-of-the-line cruising whale with all the goodies, and he led me, Violet, and the baby into it. In the driver's seat was a tall woman who looked like one of those Viking warrior types you see in comic books, big breasted with a head of hair like spun straw, and legs that were about six feet long. All she needed was a spear and helmet and a couple of hubcaps for her chest and she could have played a Valkyrie. She was polishing her fingernails and Lenny introduced her as Sasha. She didn't say anything, but she probably wasn't hired to make conversation anyway.

"Do you know how many miles of interstate there are in the u.s. of a.?" he asked me when we had all got comfortable around the table in the camper. Before I could answer, he told me. "There's over thirty-five thousand miles of restricted-access highway across the length and breadth of this great country of ours, brother, and I have determined to bring the Lord's message to the lonesome travelers on life's thruway. Come to me all you who labor and I shall give you rest stops, relief from the fast lane."

I waited for him to get to the point. Like most preacher types, he was used to speaking for an hour or so at a time, so he warmed into his subject gradually. As he talked I watched him and tried to remember where in the world I had seen him before. The way he waved his little paddle-like hands and pointed at me with his finger, I knew I had seen him somewhere, but I couldn't place him.

But then he started talking about how he had once wrestled with sin and the devil and had whipped them both, and it finally clicked. It was in Vegas, at a permanent Wrestlemania place they had off the Strip. Little Lenny Laird, the Lord's Littlest Laborer used to be a midget wrestler on the Big Time circuit. As I recalled, he used to wrestle under the name of Mighty Mo Michaels, the Mini-Mite Mauler. His specialty was launching himself from the bottom rope right into his opponent's groin. He called it the human slingshot. His manager would pull the rope out and fire him headfirst into the gonads of whoever he was wrestling against. Funny, you'd think I would have remembered earlier, but then I didn't recognize him without his cape and mask—and who would have thought he'd have had a conversion experience and ended up in the religion business?

"The point of all this is this, friend: I'm in a bit of a jam, you see. I had a keyboard player with my traveling revival and it turned out he wasn't really Christian."

"He tried to hit on me," Sasha explained from the front seat. She blew on her nails and looked out into the parking lot of the Munchee Mart.

"Anyway," Lenny said, "the point is this—we got a revival coming up tonight in North Platte, you see, and I need somebody to fill in. You play keyboard or just guitar?"

"I play keyboard some," I said. "How much does this gig pay?"

"Well, I done bought you gas," the midget said.

"That might get us to North Platte," I said.

"This is music for the Lord, brother," he said.

"We need to get farther than North Platte," I said.

"I like you, friend," said the reverend, "so I'm sure we could come to terms. Twenty-five dollars."

"That's sounds pretty good," said Violet.

"Let me handle this, Violet," I said. I turned back to the Reverend Lenny. We were in a desperate situation. The more cash we could get in one place, the more inconspicuous we could be. From the looks of the Winnebago—wet bar and wall-to-wall shag—I'd say he had a pretty prosperous act going. He had intimated his road crew was up ahead in North Platte, and I figured his advance publicity was pretty good. He had a pretty good marketing angle, too, him being a midget and all, and the Nebraska Christians at North Platte would probably eat it up. After a little negotiation, we finally agreed on terms, and Violet and I got out and headed for the van. I was to get a percentage of that evening's love offering, and, with any luck, we'd get enough money to be able to make it through to Denver if we drove all night after the revival. I figured the Nebraska state police would never come looking for us at a tent meeting, and if we drove at night we might be able to slide through into the Rocky Mountains. As Sasha put the big Winnebago into gear, we followed them out on to the highway. On the cover of the back spare tire of the camper was written, "Remember: God Allows U-Turns."

*

In a cut-down field on the southern edge of North Platte, in what used to be Don's Used Car Lot, the Reverend Lenny's roadies had set up a cavernous green and yellow circus tent. The smell of hot canvas baking under the late afternoon sun took me back to the days when I was travelling with my dad and the circus, only instead of a ring in the middle of a bunch of bleachers, Lenny's tent was set up more or less like a church, with rows and rows of folding chairs and a wide aisle down the middle leading up to an altar area made of folding risers. Above the risers was an American flag and an old rugged cross, two potted plants, and red velvet drapes to serve as a backdrop. Right up front in the middle was a special pulpit custom-made for Lenny Laird with three steps leading up to the microphone.

Lenny's advance men had plastered North Platte with flyers. There wasn't a telephone pole, parking lot, or laundromat bulletin board without Lenny's picture on it.

APPEARING TONITE ONLY AT OLD DON'S USED CAR LOT, THE WORLD'S SMALLEST PREACHER PREACHING JESUS CRUCIFIED, DIED AND RESURRECTED! COME SEE HIM, HE IS REALLY SHORT!

Sasha sat outside the tent at a card table selling Lenny's videos, including *Walking Tall with God*, *Tall Love* and *Tall in the Spirit of the Lord*.

The musicians, a skinny drummer who used to play with a country-western band, an electric bass player, and I sat off to the side of the risers up front, where we could see both the congregation and Lenny.

Violet and I had grabbed some supper at the local Munchee Mart, where she picked up more doors for her dream house. She seemed discouraged. If she could only get the swimming pool, she would have her dream house finished, but she had to get it fast, because the contest only lasted through August and we were quickly burning up the days.

The sun set about nine-thirty and as the big orange ball was going down behind the grain elevators of North Platte, people started pulling into Don's old used car lot. Lenny's advance men had worked the rest stops east and west of North Platte and had also plastered car windshields at the motels along the I-80 strip. There were licenses from all over the country coming in for salvation that night. Plenty of Nebraska plates appeared too, and by showtime we had a pretty good cross-section of America sitting in the sweltering heat, fanning themselves with their programs.

With all the things to do in North Platte—Adventure Golf, Video Palace, Show-biz Pizza Parlor, Splashworld Fun Park—I was surprised so many people turned out to hear Lenny preach, but then, how many times do you get to see a midget preacher?

Violet and the baby sat in the back. She said she had been saved about six times already, but it never really took.

The music was not difficult. Mostly it was holy marching music in four-four time that seems to get Christians all stirred up to do the Lord's work. The electronic keyboard they had me play had all sorts of fancy settings on it, but the guitar player told me the guy before me played straight-ahead piano or organ on it, and since I hadn't played keys in a while I stayed right with it and kept it simple. The left-hand chords were easy enough, and all you had to do was pound the rhythm out to keep the crowd swaying together. The only thing I was a little bit worried about was the meditation. The bass player told me the keyboardist always played that on the organ stops, and I didn't feel good enough about my keyboard playing to handle it.

I finally decided to forget doing the meditation on the keyboard and to bring in that guitar that Violet's grandfather had given me instead. I figured I could fake out a version of "A Closer Walk with Thee" on it while they were passing the collection plate.

Lenny's show was professionally paced, slick as anything I'd seen in Vegas, even if it wasn't on so grand a scale. It started off with some rousing hymns everybody knew, slow ones at first, then building to a fever pitch with the drums flying and banging all over the place and the electric guitar strumming out salvation. As night fell outside the tent, the stage lights came up and what with the singing and the heat and all, the people swayed back and forth and waved their programs in time to the music. Then there was an overture, very rhythmic, that vamped the way you do in a Vegas act when the headliner is about to come on. The drums and cymbals built up a fever of anticipation and the stage lights went down, and a big supertrouper spotlight came up and laid a hot blue-white circle on the curtains in back of the stage. When we got the cue from the stage manager, we let loose with Little Lenny Laird's theme song, "Standing on the Shoulders of the Lord."

After the first chorus of "Shoulders," the curtains parted and out came Little Lenny Laird, all dressed in white. Everything on him was white. His suit, his vest, his shirt, his tie, his little tiny shoes, and his socks burned bright in the light of the supertrouper. Only his hair—wet-combed back to give him an extra inch of height—was black, that and the cover of the Bible he carried.

The crowd went wild, singing at the tops of their lungs and waving their arms and shouting hallelujahs as Lenny took stage.

The little guy beamed, his eyes glinting with the glittery brightness you see on preachers when they're really psyched up and ready to roll. You could see those eyes from across the tent and they shone like glass. He seemed like a white glistening cloud as he floated up the three steps of the pulpit and shoved his little fists up in the air.

"Amen, hallelujah, and praise the Lord!" he shouted into the microphone.

The crowd shouted out Amen.

"I know what you're all thinkin'," Lenny said. "You're thinking, boy, he's short! Ain't you? Ain't you?"

The crowd didn't know whether to laugh or be ashamed.

"Well, let me tell you somethin'," Lenny went on, "I may be short, but my legs reach all the way to the ground, brothers and sisters, the same ground the Lord Jesus himself walked on. Let me hear somebody say Amen."

The crowd said Amen.

I had to admit Lenny had some good material. He'd obviously been working it on the road for quite a while. He built up a rhythm from the place where the music had taken the crowd, and pretty soon he pumped the audience so full of fear of the Lord and the devil that he had them in the palm of his hand.

"I know many of you out there are travelers," he said. "I saw those license plates in the parking lot from Ohio, Michigan, Illinois, Indiana, Missouri, Nevada, Colorado, New York, even one from California, praise the Lord."

Praise the Lords erupted from all around the crowd as he mentioned their home states. The congregation waved like

wheat in the field, leaning into the rhythm Lenny was building. It was a hot night, and they all fanned themselves with
their programs. The faster he talked, the faster they fanned,
like they were trying to blow away the fires of hell itself.

"Yes, you're all out there traveling from one coast of
America to the other. Out here traveling on the great highway that follows the Platte River, the river our pioneer ancestors journeyed beside on their great trek westward only one
hundred years ago in their covered wagons. Those people,
brothers and sisters, do you know how they went west? Do
you know how our very own grandfathers and grandmothers
crossed these trackless prairies just one hundred years ago?"

He paused for dramatic effect, then let loose with the
answer.

"They walked, friends. That's right, they walked. Hallelujah.
They didn't have fancy cars with air conditioners. They didn't
have Winnebagos or Pace Arrows to get them through, no, sir.
They went by shank's mare. It was a hard and gruesome journey,
brothers and sisters. Starvation, snow storms, plagues of
locusts—Indians!—you name it and those ancestors of ours,
walking to the promised land along the South Platte River, they
suffered it. And do you know how they got through, friends? Do
you know what sustained them in their hardships?"

Pause, the fans whipped the air and made the sound of
fluttering wings. Men, women, children sweated and rocked
back and forth.

"Tell us," somebody said in a desperate voice. "Tell us."

"I'll tell you," said Lenny Laird. "In every covered wagon,
in every saddlebag that traveled west across this land there
were two things, friends, two things to protect them, two
things only that stood between them and destruction. Do
you know what the first one was?"

"What was it? Tell us."

"The first was their guns to protect them from the evils
of this world . . ."

"Amen, Amen."

". . . and the second was the holy word of God, the Holy B for Bible, praise the Lord, the Holy Bible, to protect them from the evils of the next. They kept that good book, brothers and sisters, right beside their Remingtons, and that's how this great country of ours got built. Let me hear somebody say Amen!"

"Amen!"

"And tonight, you travelers, you folks from all over this great country God loves so much, this America of ours, when you go back to your hotel room tonight, I'll bet you there's a good book, the only book, right there in a drawer or on a nightstand. And why is it there? I'll tell you why it's there. Because the way is still treacherous, friends. The devil is out there putting up detour signs all over the highway, four-way stops and traffic diversions to keep you, yes, you, from getting on the highway to heaven! That devil don't want you to merge into God's four-lane thruway to paradise. But don't you *yield* to that devil, brothers and sisters. You say to that devil, 'I'm passing you, Satan, get thee behind me and eat my dust, you devil you!' You say 'I'm putting my soul into overdrive! I'm on my way to that eternal rest stop promised me by the Lord Jesus Christ!'"

Lenny picked up the rhythm and really laid into them now. Hallelujahs shot up like Fourth of July fireworks from all around the tent.

"Do you know the way to heaven, brothers and sisters? Do you? You won't find it in no road atlas. You'll find it right here." He waved the Bible up in the air. "This is your roadmap. This is the only Rand McNally you'll ever need. And Jesus don't care if you're tall or short, he'll be your Triple A tour guide anyway. If, on the highway of life, your lane ends in a quarter mile, you call on Jesus. You men out there, when you see some woman with soft shoulders and dangerous curves, you just steer your way to Jesus."

"Amen," said the wives.

"Jesus wants to see Men Working," Lenny went on. "There's No Parking on the highway to salvation, friends, No Standing. Every lane's a passing lane on this road, yes it is, yes it is, let me hear somebody say hallelujah! There's no speed limit on the highway to heaven, you go there just as fast as you can! Let's all praise, puh-raise Je-sus!"

And they did. They went nuts. People were on their feet crying and heading up the aisle, tumbling all over themselves to testify. The band launched into a quick-paced hymn that scanned like something by John Philip Sousa, and people shoved each other out of the way to get touched on the head by the Reverend Lenny Laird. I looked up one time and saw even Violet coming down that aisle, tears streaming down her face, carrying Baby Jeffery in her arms. Everybody was filled with the power of the Lord.

After a quarter hour of this, wherein more than a few people fell twitching on the floor, it was time for the meditation. By now Lenny was sweating and he had taken off his white coat and loosened his white tie. He unbuttoned the top button of his shirt. In a hoarse voice, calmer now, toned down, he finally made his pitch to the people, now mostly back in their seats. Calling them all his friends, he explained how his ministry needed their help. As they listened to the meditation, could they give, just a little, whatever they could afford, could they reach into their pockets so others might be reached as they had been reached?

I leaned down and grabbed the old guitar and adjusted a mike up to the sound hole as the bass player whispered to me that it was time for the meditation. I started to play something inspirational from the hymnal in front of me, a tune called "Strolling Through the Vineyard with Thee," but as I played, a weird thing happened. The guitar wouldn't stay in tune. It kept falling out, as if the strings were stretching or something. At first I thought it might be the heat, so I stopped and tried to retune, but, try as I might, I couldn't get it. Then I noticed something truly bizarre. The guitar was actually retuning itself! I pulled my hands back real quick. Maybe Verna Mae had been right about it. Maybe the thing *was* possessed and wouldn't play Christian hymns. As I watched, the tuning pegs turned *on their own* and when I strummed it, they had put themselves into an open-D tuning! I was dumbfounded, but I did what I thought I had to do. I segued as best I could into "Open Tuning" and played it instead of "Strolling Through the Vineyard with Thee."

Pretty soon people closed their eyes and began to sway back and forth along to it, and some even began humming the "ommmm" part. I couldn't believe it. There they were, a bunch of Christians in the middle of Don's old used car lot, sitting there with their eyes closed, humming away like a bunch of Buddhist monks! They already knew the song! Could it be that a bunch of born-again Christians also listened to *Music from the Depths of Space*? Or had the song gone crossover? Or were they just getting into it so much that they began spontaneously to hum along?

It was like they were hypnotized by it, and as the wicker collection baskets went around and up and down the rows of seats, I saw people digging deep in their pockets and purses and dumping in wads of money, scads of it, without even counting. One woman, with a big blissful smile on her face, opened up her purse and dumped the whole thing, Kleenex wads and paper clips and all, right into the collection basket.

The Reverend Lenny's road crew kept emptying the overflowing baskets into sacks, and by the time the baskets were through passing around, the crowd was pretty well wrung dry. I didn't know what to make of it. I didn't know if it was the guitar or the song or what was causing it to happen, I only knew I was glad Lenny agreed to let me work on commission. The money we'd collect would easily get us well into Colorado and beyond, if the cops didn't catch us first.

When the song was done, I let the last open chord ring itself out. People sat for a moment smiling blissfully until the last sounds of "Open Tuning" died away. Nobody said anything for what seemed like a long while, then, slowly, they began to blink and come back around.

The Reverend Lenny stood up front and looked a bit dazed himself, but I think he was more knocked out by the amount of money than by the song because he kept staring and blinking at the baskets and the sacks of money the way the apostles must have stood around and stared when Jesus pulled those thousands of loaves and fishes out of his hat.

"Thank you, friends, thank you," said Lenny, overwhelmed. "The Lord has been generous tonight. Hallelujah. Thank you, Jesus, thank you, Jesus." He wrapped his arms around the bags of money and prayed.

People were shaking their heads now, and some of the men began patting their wallet pockets rather uneasily. The woman who'd dumped her purse into the offering basket began to look around the floor as if she'd lost something. They were like people who were remembering the morning after what they'd done the night before, and they didn't looked too pleased with themselves about it. Lenny called for a quick closing hymn and everybody shuffled out of the tent looking pretty confused.

Afterwards, back in the Winnebago, Sasha and Lenny counted out the money they'd taken in. Not counting the hairpins and key rings and buttons and other stuff that ended up in the offering basket, Lenny had taken in about three thousand five hundred dollars.

"How'd you like to sign on and travel with us regular, Joe?" Lenny said, handing me my commission. "I don't know what that song was you played during the meditation, boy, but a few more nights like this and I could finally afford to buy that satellite uplink I've been after. Once I get on TV, I can bring the Lord's message of salvation to millions more. How'd you like to stay on and help me with this good work, son?"

I pocketed my money and said no thanks. Now that it was nighttime in Nebraska, I wanted to slide right through and make it to Denver as quickly as I could without the Nebraska state police seeing us. I loaded Violet and the baby into the van and got ready to head west.

"Hey, what did you say the name of that song was again?" Lenny asked as we drove into the night.

" 'Open Tuning,' " I shouted back, "and I'm the one who wrote it."

*

Two hours out of North Platte, we turned south at Julesburg where I-80 meets I-76 heading toward Denver. Near Ogallala, Violet started counting. Every once in a while a number would spill out of her mouth.

"One-twenty-six," she'd say, then a while later, "one-fifteen."

"What are you doing?" I asked.

She turned toward me and said, "I'm counting down the miles until we get to Billy."

The mile markers along I-80 count down to the border, but when we veered south on I-76, the mile markers jumped back up again to one-eighty-something, so Violet felt for a while there like we were going backward. Still, she seemed optimistic.

"We're almost to Denver," she said to the baby, holding him in her lap so he could see the green-and-white mile markers flash by us into the dark. "Then it's just over the mountains and we're going to be in San Diego."

"I've got news for you, Violet," I said. "San Diego isn't just over the mountains. When we get to Denver we've only got about halfway to where you think you're going. You can look on the road atlas if you want to."

She picked the Rand McNally up off the floor and looked at the map.

"You mean I've been on the road about eight days, six of them with you, and that's all the farther we've got?" she asked. She sighed and her shoulders sunk. "I never knew the country was this *big*."

Another mile marker flashed by, but this time she didn't count.

"Well, we'll get there," she said, hugging the baby tight and rubbing her cheek gently against its head. "Everything will work out fine." The baby was sleeping and the two of them looked almost helpless sitting there lit up only by the light coming off the dashboard. Outside it was totally black, and we were so far out into the plains there was hardly any traffic at all now, nothing but some trucks pulling all-nighters who passed us from time to time and left us rocking in their tailwash.

"Are you sure you want to go on with this, Violet?" I asked.

"I've got to go on," she said. "I've got to get to Billy."

"So what do you think Billy's going to do if you get there?" I said.

She looked ahead into the night, way out in front of the headlights. As far as I could tell, she was trying to look all the way out over the mountains, all the way back into the ocean where his submarine was.

"I planted the suggestion in his head the other day when I astrally projected," she said. Her voice was sure of itself, as though she had no doubts about what had happened. "He'll be expecting us. He'll be waiting for us, with open arms. You'll see. It'll work out."

I sighed. "Violet . . ." But then I gave up because I didn't know what I could tell her at that point. She was bound and determined that she and Billy were going to get married in San Diego and he was going to be overjoyed to see her show up with a kidnapped baby in her arms. She just knew it was going to happen exactly the way she said.

And all of that, of course, was supposing we weren't going to get shot and killed by the police somewhere for kidnapping Baby Jeffery. Frankly, I didn't see how we were going to escape. The Nebraska radio stations were going insane over the local angle on the Baby Jeffery story. Ever since I had confessed on *New Connections* that we had Baby Jeffery in Nebraska, there wasn't a station on the A.M. or F.M. band that hadn't put out a description of Joe Findlay. I guessed by now that Hazel had been contacted by Nebraska authorities and had given them everything about me, including my birthmarks and moles. I even went so far as to break out the light above the back license plate so nobody could read the number in the dark, which I had seen Humphrey Bogart do in a movie one time.

"Joseph Raymond Findlay, an itinerant musician who yesterday claimed to have been the composer of the smash New Age hit 'Open Tuning,' is being sought by Nebraska state police for questioning in the Baby Jeffery case."

They were painting me as a psychopath, a whacko who called in to talk shows to make claims that weren't true. Well, I did write "Open Tuning," only I didn't call it that, and I did have Baby Jeffery in the van with me. It would probably suit Hazel fine if I was to go up in a blaze of gunsmoke because then she wouldn't have to share the royalties from "Open Tuning" with me, but I was determined that I was going to survive.

As for Violet, she sat there dandling Baby Jeffery on her knee as if she didn't have a care in the world. I couldn't believe she was so far gone into her own head as to not know how things worked out in reality. On the other hand, I thought, what do I know about reality anymore? In the past few days with her I'd had more strange things happen to me than ever in my life, the most recent of which was that guitar retuning itself during the revival meeting and the way people had dumped their money into the offering baskets while I played.

And, speaking of that guitar, it seemed to be getting more flowers on it all the time. I still hadn't had the time to sit down and actually count them, but when I put it back in the case after the revival, it seemed there were more flowers on it than ever, thousands of them. The guitar also played sweeter every day. Holding it was like holding something alive, as if it had a life and mind of its own. I swear I could have let go of it during the meditation and it would have played all by itself.

I didn't know what it all meant. Sylvia had said something about fate and about destinies converging, but I still couldn't see a pattern to all this.

Underneath the van, I felt the land beginning to rise in the long slow climb to the Rockies. It starts gradually, like the thin edge of a wedge, in Nebraska and continues through eastern Colorado in such a slow ascent from the flat scrubland you hardly notice that you're a mile high until you hit Denver.

That's what traveling with Violet had been like the past six days—little by little I had been lifting off, getting separated from wherever and whoever I'd been back in Porkville when I'd met her less than a week before. I thought I had been pretty much at sea level back then, more or less connected to the way things work on planet Earth, but once in a while in the past few days I'd felt like things were floating, cut loose somehow, as though something was happening all around me that I didn't have any control over.

The way I felt was kind of like when you hit a harmonic on the twelfth fret of the first string of a guitar and the strings you *didn't* hit also get to vibrating in sympathy, even though you didn't touch them. It was that kind of feeling I had now, as if things I didn't understand and didn't start were suddenly resonating all around me. I didn't like the feeling, either, not one little bit. Sylvia had called them synchronicities, but that word didn't begin to explain the uneasy feeling I had inside my gut.

So what could I do about it? Nothing. Sylvia had said I needed to go meet my fate and I guess that's exactly what I was doing, at sixty-five miles an hour, heading west. I drove on grim-faced, watching the mile markers count their way down to Colorado.

Because we were climbing uphill, we were getting lousy mileage, so I had to pull over for gas again near the Nebraska border. I could feel the gray dawn about to crack behind us on the eastern horizon. I wanted to gas up before it got light so we'd have less chance of being recognized. I pulled into an all-night Munchee Mart. In the window was a life-size color cardboard cutout of Munchee Mart Marty in his clown costume. His right arm was motorized and he waved and waved and waved. Hi, c'mon in and have a Super Gulp.

I pumped the gas and went in to pay. Violet had fallen asleep, so I left her in the van. I bought a Denver paper because Miles Kindley had said on the radio the day before that my name was in the Names and Faces section. I quickly flipped open the paper and saw the item. It said that a musician named Joe Findlay claimed to be the real composer of "Open Tuning" and that Hazel Findlay, his wife and the real producer of the recording, had denied it. Meanwhile, on page one, buried down in the bottom of the Baby Jeffery story, I was mentioned again as the caller on a national radio show who had confessed to the kidnapping. Authorities were declining comment, only saying they were following a number of leads, one of which, I knew, was me.

I picked up some micro ham and cheese sandwiches and two Cokes for breakfast and was hoping the clerk wouldn't pay too much attention to my van. It was right then that a Nebraska State Police car slid into the parking lot and nosed itself up to the plate gas window of the Munchee Mart. The cop who was driving it looked as lean and mean as an attack Doberman. This wasn't any Midwest potbellied goofball cop like you see in the movies. As he got out of patrol car, I slid behind the potato chip rack in the back of the Munchee Mart, trembling, prepared to meet my doom. I never thought I would die clutching a bag of barbecue chips.

The guy swaggered through the double glass doors and stopped to adjust his gunbelt. He was tall, thin, rawboned—six feet of killing machine, ready to fulfill his prime function. His uniform pants were creased like knife blades and his leather holster bulged and creaked. Yellow spots swam in front of my eyes and somewhere in the back of my head I heard Tex Ritter singing "Do Not Forsake Me, Oh My Darling."

I crouched behind the chip rack and prayed. I prayed he was only coming in for donuts and that he wouldn't check the plates on my van. I prayed nothing stupid would happen, but, of course, it did.

"Morning, Lula-Mae," said the cop, tossing a pack of powdered donuts on the counter.

"Mornin', Ray," said the clerk. She was behind the counter, her back turned to him, switching on a small TV set that sat on a stool. It was time for *A.M. AMerica*, America's favorite morning news show.

"At the top of the news this hour, a major new development in the Baby Jeffery case," the anchor said.

The lady anchor of *A.M. AMerica* had a chirpy little voice no matter what kind of disaster she was announcing, but that morning, to me, it sounded like the chains of handcuffs tinkling. As I listened, my heart pounded and I heard a screaming noise in my ears as I crouched down on the linoleum behind the chip rack. I hoped the bullet would enter my brain and kill me quickly. I held my breath, waiting for her to announce my name, but she only said, "Right after this."

They cut away to a commercial for a decaf coffee that was supposed to calm your nerves. I wished I had a gallon of it right then.

"You boys catch that demented psycho yet, Ray?" the clerk asked the cop during the commercial.

"That one that called in to the radio?" Ray replied. "Not yet, but we'll nail his ass."

My sweat was falling on the floor in hard drops like BB's. I bit my tongue and squeezed my eyes shut, waiting, waiting for the sound of doom.

"Probably an escapee of some kind," said the clerk.

"From the nuthouse, most likely," said Ray, pouring some black coffee into a styrofoam cup. "Only thing to do with 'em is put 'em down like foaming dogs."

I heard cellophane crinkling and peeked around the corner of the chip rack. Ray had opened the donuts and stood there with one in his left hand and his coffee in his right. I felt a little better because I figured he couldn't go for his gun too quickly that way. I told myself I might have time to throw myself at his feet and whimper for mercy.

The news came back on.

"A dramatic new development in the Baby Jeffery case," the anchor said. "For the story we go to Norfolk and our on-the-scene reporter Brad Blowdry."

My head was pounding. I knew they were going to have my picture on the screen. The local affiliate in Vegas probably headed right out to the house and Hazel no doubt gave them a picture from the family album. Did they have capital punishment in Nebraska? I wondered. It didn't matter. I could feel the razor shaving a hole in my scalp for the electric chair. The rope circled around my neck. I could feel the lethal injection flowing through my veins. My legs shaking, I stood up. It was time to turn myself in. If I could catch the cop while he was biting into his donut, he might not drill me through the head first thing. I would plead for clemency. I would plead insanity. I came around the front of the chip rack with my arms in the air.

"I . . ."

The cop turned and stared at me. His eyes were gun-metal blue.

Then Brad Blowdry said, "BABY JEFFERY, OBJECT OF A NATIONWIDE SEARCH IS HOME, YES, HE'S BACK HOME AGAIN IN NORFOLK. IN FACT, HE NEVER LEFT."

I dropped my arms and said, "Aaaaaaaaaaaaaaaaaaaaaaaaaaaaaa?" After a while the sound stopped on its own and I stood there with my mouth open staring at the TV. I almost had to reach up with my hand and hinge my mouth shut again.

"Something the matter there, bud?" the cop asked.

Brad Blowdry continued his silver-tonsiled March-of-Time delivery: "YES, BABY JEFFERY IS HOME AGAIN WITH HIS MOTHER AND, TO ALL APPREARANCES, IS HAPPY, SAFE, AND HEALTHY ONCE MORE. Police have arrested one Deborah Anne Smith, a high school dropout from Norfolk, who said she took Baby Jeffery because, in her words, she 'just wanted a baby like everyone else.' "

I pointed at the TV like a zombie and said, "Habababababa-bababa," or something equally intelligent as the news showed a girl about Violet's age and size being taken into a court-room in Norfolk for arraignment. She confessed to stealing Baby Jeffery from the park and had turned herself in because, she said, she got tired of feeding him all the time. Next the camera cut to the real Baby Jeffery and his mother. Reporters were crawling all over her wanting to know how she felt. Baby Jeffery's mother was idiotically happy, of course, and drooled and cried and slobbered all over him while her agent did the talking for her. Baby Jeffery was home, and they had sold the rights for the movie-of-the-week to a major studio for half a million dollars.

I couldn't believe it. *Baby Jeffery was home?* I wanted the clerk to rewind the tape and play it again, but then I realized this wasn't a video. It was news and it was live, happening right then, and most importantly for me, it meant the baby in the van was not Baby Jeffery, and I was not an accessory after the fact. I was innocent. I was free. I was on my way back to New York for the Sclapped audition!

Meanwhile, the cop eyed me suspiciously because by that time I managed to find my tongue again and was shaking all over as I put my gas money down on the counter, babbling, "They found Baby Jeffery! Look, look, they found Baby Jeffery, isn't that great? Isn't that wonderful?"

"Yeah," said the clerk. "That's real nice. I'll bet his mama's happy."

"I'm happy, too," I said, grinning like an idiot.

"Well, Ray," the clerk said, turning to the cop, "I guess you won't have to be lookin' for that psycho weirdo after all."

"Never thought I would," said Ray. "Every time something happens, there's always sick people out there who call in and confess. After a while in the police business you get a sense of who's real and who's crazy. I knew that guy who'd called the radio show the other day was a kook from the start. Forget him."

I nearly hugged the cop and kissed him on the cheek.

"Yes, forget him," I said, tears coming down my cheek. "Forget all about him."

The cop furrowed his brow. Did he make a move for his gun?

"I'm sorry," I said, falling back. "But this just makes me feel so . . . *good* that Baby Jeffery is home."

"You okay to drive, buddy?" he said.

"Oh, yeah," I said, clearing my throat and trying to pull myself together. I wiped my eyes. "I'm not drunk. I've just been up all night for the past few days, that's all. I'm going on to the next rest stop and get myself some sleep and then I'm going straight through to New York, right after . . ."

"Right after what?" the cop asked.

"Never mind," I said, leaving the store.

Right after I kill Violet Tansy, I thought as I headed for the van.

*

Of course, I didn't kill her, although we had what in diplomatic circles is known as a frank and open discussion about her and Billy and Baby Jeffery, and when it was all done—about a hundred miles toward Denver later—I guess I could see how a young girl in her position would get desperate enough to tell a lie that big.

We hit Denver about noon, and we both agreed it was the end of the line for us. I had enough money from Lenny Laird's revival to buy her and the baby a one-way, no-return bus ticket to San Diego on the Greyhound, and we stopped at a shopping mall in Aurora and bought a plastic laundry basket for her to put the baby in because after eight hundred and some miles from Porkville that Brillo box was pretty beat. I made sure she had enough Pampers and supplies for the baby and even gave her a few dollars for food along the way. This seemed better to me than dumping her on the road somewhere in Colorado and letting her work out the rest herself. You get attached to somebody after being with them for a week, even if they do make your skin itch every time you think of them.

"It's been quite a week," I said when I left her at the bus station, "but this is the end, Violet."

"I'm sorry I lied to you," she said.

"I guess you were desperate," I said, giving her the benefit of the doubt, "but that doesn't make it right."

"I just saw that picture story in the paper about Baby Jeffery, and it seemed like a way to make you take me somewhere. This is a true-love cause and God'll understand."

I realized there was no point in arguing because it was the last time I was going to see her. Besides, I felt like a fool for letting her make me believe the Baby Jeffery stuff in the first place. And so we said good-bye at the Denver Greyhound station, no hugs, no kisses, not even a handshake, only a brief and mumbled "So long." After eight hundred miles and seven days of craziness, Violet Tansy and her baby were leaving on the big gray dog. Violet said she'd sit in the waiting room until her bus left.

When I left the station I felt about a hundred and ten pounds lighter. It was four o'clock in New York, so I could still phone Murray.

"Babe! Where are you, man?"

"Denver."

"Denver? Isn't that like way out West? What are you doing out there? Last time you called you were in Chicago, right?"

"It's hard to explain," I said. "Is that Sclapped gig still open?"

Murray mumbled a bit to himself then said, "I don't know why I'm doing this, but I'm holding an audition slot open for you tomorrow. Can you be out here tomorrow? They got an airport in Denver, right? I mean you don't have to take the stagecoach, right?"

"I'll be there," I said, "even if I have to crawl."

I quickly called the Denver airport. There were plenty of flights to New York, but because I was booking late, they were all expensive. I was fifty dollars short of the ticket price, thanks to buying the Greyhound ride for Violet. Of course, there was no way I could drive to New York by morning, even if I hadn't been totally sandbagged by my week with Violet. It was then I found Sylvia Atherton-Barnes' business card in my shirt pocket. If she had enough money for a Range Rover, I thought, surely she would loan me fifty dollars for a plane ticket to my dreams. I would ask for a loan, and as soon as I got my first paycheck from the world tour, I'd pay her back.

Sylvia, being a freelancer, worked out of her home. *Home* was an apartment in a high-rise apartment building that shot up thirty stories, all mirrored glass on the outside. I parked the van, grabbed the guitar, and psyched myself up to ask for the money. I was feeling good for the first time in seven days, in spite of the fact that I was broke and dead tired. I was a mile high in Denver and free once again. New York City, fame, fortune, and pop star immortality were only fifty dollars away.

But as I was about to pick up the intercom phone at Sylvia's apartment building, I felt a tap on my shoulder.

"Joe Findlay?"

I turned and saw a skinny guy in a black T-shirt and jeans. He had an oriental charm hung around his neck from a leather thong. I had never seen him before, but the first sight of him reminded me of a lizard. His bright pink tongue kept sliding in and out of his mouth. It was a pointy little thing, like a gila monster's tongue. His black hair was slicked back with styling mousse, and he handed me a card.

"Lester Thoroughgood of the Thoroughgood Personal Surveillance Agency," he said. His card listed a Las Vegas address and phone numbers.

"Are you a cop?" I asked.

He laughed. Heh-heh-heh. He had a little lizard laugh that escaped between his pointed teeth.

"No, not a cop," he said.

"Private eye?" I asked.

"Sort of."

I could see this Lester, whoever he was, was not the talkative type. He reminded me of Joe Friday, only without the old *Dragnet* warmth. He stared at me for a minute with his ice cube eyes and then said, "I've been following you for the past nine hundred miles or so. I picked you up right after Chicago."

"You what?" I asked.

"I've been following you," he said, "in that." He pointed over to his car. The thing looked like a fire department emergency vehicle. It was a big, bright red Buick with flashing chrome that he said he'd rented at O'Hare.

"You've been following me in that thing and I didn't see you?" I asked.

He nodded tersely. "It wasn't easy."

"You've been following me in a bright red bulging Buick and I didn't see you for nine hundred miles?"

Where? I thought. How? I had checked my rearview mirror every five minutes. I had seen Munchee Mart Marty's nondescript blue Ford everywhere, so how the hell had I missed a fire engine red car?

"Pretty good, eh?" said Lester. "But don't feel bad. You're not the first one to be caught by Lester Thoroughgood. You see, I've perfected the art of being invisible."

"Okay," I said. "You're nuts. I've had nothing but nuts for the past seven days, so what's one more? So what's your story? You can turn invisible, right?"

"Right," he said. "I've been right behind you the past five days, but you never saw me. Watch this. Close your eyes and count to three."

I did. When I opened my eyes he was nowhere. The street we were on was fairly busy with people all around walking back and forth, but there was no place to hide really. No trash barrels or big pillars or anything. I looked around his car. He was no place. I reached up and scratched my head. Then I felt a tap on my shoulder again. I turned and there he was.

"See?" he said. "Don't feel bad, though, I wrote the book on invisibility." He pulled a thin paperback out of his back pocket. *Zen and the Art of Personal Surveillance.* "Only ten bucks. It's also available on video for $19.95. I take VISA."

"So what's the point?" I asked. "They found Baby Jeffery."

"Baby Jeffery's got nothing to do with this," he said. "Your father hired me."

"Dad?"

"He's a little worried about you, not having heard from you for six months. It seems your wife Hazel . . ."

"Hazel again!" I said.

"Ah, then you're aware of her success with 'Open Tuning.' "

"It's my damned song," I said.

"Your father would like to talk to you," Lester said. "But he didn't know where to find you."

"How did you know where to look?" I asked. "I haven't been in the same place two nights in a row in months."

"I know. You keep a pretty fast pace. I've been drinking so much coffee the past couple of days, I think my bladder's gonna die. When do you sleep, anyway? Thank God for that paganfest or I'd never have gotten any rest."

"You were there, too?"

He nodded. "I disguised myself as a slave of Osiris. Actually, I had a pretty good time until they tried to dismember me."

"How the hell did you even know where to look for me?" I asked.

"It wasn't that difficult," he said. "The Law Enforcement Information Network coughed up your license plate on my home computer. Seems you knocked over a sugar jar in Detroit. Big-time hood, eh?"

Verna Mae! I thought. She turned me in.

"Not to worry," said Lester. "Detroit cops got more to worry about than one old lady's sugar jar. I called her and asked what she knew and from what she said about you going to San Diego, I simply figured out when you'd hit Chicago. The rest was easy."

"You mean you tailed me all the way from . . ."

"I prefer the word *surveilled*," he said. "Yeah. The only part I couldn't figure out is why you beat up that clown back there in Nebraska."

"So what's the message?" I asked.

"Call your dad," he said.

"That's all?" I asked, "He sent you on a two thousand mile chase to tell me to call him?"

Lester shrugged. "Must be important," he said. "You'd better call quick." He looked at his watch. "Wow, look at the time. I've got to disappear."

And he did.

*

By the time I got to Sylvia's apartment, thirty stories above Denver, my head was still spinning. Like the inside of her tent, the apartment was mostly white, and off in the distance through the plate glass window walls I could see the snow-capped tops of the Front Range of the Rocky Mountains. Everything about Sylvia's place was white and cool and clear, but between getting rid of Violet Tansy and meeting Lester Thoroughgood, I myself was feeling pretty confused.

"You look beat," Sylvia said as I set my guitar case down on the white living room rug. I thought I'd bring the guitar up because she seemed interested in it back at the pagan fest. If I told her more about it, she might be more willing to loan me the money I needed.

"I am beat," I said. "You wouldn't believe what I've been through in the past few days."

"I'd love to hear," she said, "but you look like you could use some rest first."

I looked at a mirror she had in her entrance hallway and she was right. My eyes had huge dark circles under them from not sleeping for a week. My hair stood up in spikes of dirt and sweat, and I had an Emmet Kelly beard. My clothes were streaked with road dust and grit, and now that I was indoors I also noticed that I smelled like a not very clean goat. All in all, I looked like a poster child for Insomniacs Anonymous.

"Must be the altitude," I mumbled.

"You need to keep your fluids up," she said. "Would you like some soda water and shiatsu?"

"Sure," I said, "I had some once in a bar in Reno and it wasn't half bad."

She laughed. "No, no. Shiatsu isn't a drink. Mikoko is here to do me. She comes once a week. Follow me."

Sylvia was wearing a thick terrycloth bathrobe and had a towel around her neck. Her hair was pulled off to the side to expose her neck. Like her tent, her apartment seemed larger than it could have been from the outside, as if I had walked into a sprawling ranch house. The hallway led by some large and bright modern art and then we went into a workout room with a Stairmaster and an exercise bike and a massage table, beside which stood Mikoko, a middle-aged Japanese woman in a blue flowered kimono. Mikoko told me to take off my clothes down to my shorts and get up on the table. I was a little bit embarrassed when I took off my shoes and realized my feet smelled like month-old French cheese. Mikoko politely suggested I take a quick shower, which I was more than happy to do.

After the shower Mikoko massaged the balls of my feet with her fingertips, and Sylvia told me that there are thousands of acupressure points on the human body like little relaxation buttons. After seven days and nights of driving from Porkville to Denver and all the craziness in between, it didn't take long for Mikoko to turn me into spaghetti.

"Where are the girl and the baby you were traveling with?" Sylvia asked.

"Gone," I explained. "They should be leaving Denver right about now on their way to San Diego. Thank God."

"Why do you say that?" Sylvia asked, looking worried.

"This has been the nuttiest week of my life," I said, and as Mikoko worked her way up my body to my head, I filled Sylvia in on all that happened to me since I'd found Violet and her baby in my van outside the Dew Dropp Inn, ending with what happened since we left the paganfest. By that time, Mikoko was massaging a point at the crown of my head and my whole body felt limp.

"And you let a woman like that just slip away?" Sylvia asked.

"What do you mean?"

"I mean this Violet is loaded with some kind of *mana* for you, Joe. Don't you see? Before you met Violet, nothing of any significance had happened to you, but since you met her—pow—your life's been upside down."

"What's so good about that?" I asked. "I almost missed a monster career opportunity because of her. If I can get to New York by tomorrow, I might be able to save it."

I told her more about Murray and Sclapped and was about to mention how badly I needed fifty dollars to buy the plane ticket when she cut me off.

"Never mind that," she said. "That's only fame and fortune. Tell me more about what you saw that night in my tent."

So I told her more details about the dream or vision or whatever it was I'd had in her tent when I'd drunk the mead and unicorn powder. Sylvia told Mikoko to go, and then she left me there on the massage table while she went into another room. She came back a minute later with a large book. The book had a tattered green cloth cover with a goldleafed title on the spine that I couldn't read because her hand was over part of it. I sat up. She set the book on the massage table and opened it. It was full of pictures of angels.

"What did he look like?" she asked.

"Look like?" I said.

"What was he wearing for starters?"

"Well, it was like a white nightgown," I said.

"Did he have an aureole or a gloriole?" she asked.

"A what?"

"A halo," she said. "Any light phenomena around him?"

"Say, don't tell me you believe in this stuff, too," I said.

"Joe, for whatever reason, you've been granted some kind of vision. For the past week, you've been at the nexus of various paranormal phenomena, and it all seems to center around Violet, the baby, and that guitar. Now the old man said an angel gave it to him, and then you had this dream vision of an angel in my tent. Sometimes angels appear in different guises. In the Hebrew scriptures, the Book of Tobit, for example, they're sometimes indistinguishable from humans. Other times, as in Revelations, they appear in an apocalyptic manner. Raphael, Gabriel, Michael—the *-el* at the ends of their names comes from Elohim, one of the Hebrew names for God. Angels are manifestations of divine power. Something significant is happening here, Joe, something bigger than you or your own life, and if we can pin down what your angel looked like, we may have a better clue to both his identity and his mission."

"Mission?"

"These phenomena are happening for a reason we can't explain. Your reality is becoming dreamlike . . ."

"That's for sure."

". . . and whenever that happens, you can bet something bigger than yourself, bigger than any of us is going to happen. It's part of that pattern I told you about back at the paganfest. Now, see if you can find him in here."

I flipped through the pages. The book was some sort of field guide to angels. The beings in it were of all kinds, done in black and white illustrations, mostly, but there was one section of color prints. There were angels with four wings, some with six wings, and some were nothing but wings. Some had wings with eyes on them or wings in the shape of wheels and wings of fire. Some had bat wings. Those were the fallen angels, Sylvia explained. Some wore long gowns and some had skintight suits on while others wore clothes of many colors.

I flipped through the book but didn't find any picture that looked exactly like what I had seen in her tent. My angel looked exactly like an Iowa farm boy, I told Sylvia.

"Except he had wings and a long white gown," she said.

"Yeah, except for that," I said. "What in the heck do you think is going on here?"

"It's impossible to say until it happens," Sylvia said. "The important thing is to be aware something is happening. That way you don't miss your chance."

"To do what?"

"That's not clear. People see these sorts of things occasionally. They're epiphenomena, these sightings, now here, now gone. They don't happen with enough regularity to be statistically significant, and you can't make them happen in a lab, so the scientific community ignores them, but that doesn't mean they're not there. People have seen creatures like the one you saw for thousands of years, Joe. We don't know what they are, but every once in a while, usually when we think we finally have our lives all neatly ordered and everything seems clear, they appear—almost as if to remind us there's more going on in this world than we think, that all of our plans and all of our strategies really come to nothing, that maybe there's a hidden hand directing this whole business."

"What do you mean?" I asked. "Like God or something?"

"God may be an actor in this drama, too," she said. "We'll just have to wait and see."

"You mean I'm not going crazy?" I said.

"Not necessarily."

"Good," I said, falling back on the massage table relieved. "I've been hanging around with so many whacko people in the past week that I was afraid it was starting to rub off."

"Now tell me once again exactly what's happened this week," Sylvia said, getting out her tape recorder. "You may have left out some significant details. In cases like this, everything counts."

I told her once again as best I could about everything, about Grandpa Tolliver's story of the Bird Boy of Iowa, about the guitar retuning itself, about the flowers seeming to grow out of the sound hole, about the dream I had at the pagan-fest, and I told her about the white feather I'd seen in front of her tent. We went into the living room, and I took out the guitar and showed it to her. I told her how it changed from day to day since I'd picked it up from Grandpa Tolliver the week before, getting brighter as we came west. Only now it looked duller somehow, as if it was losing some of its luster. Sylvia took all this down, and I asked her what she was going to do with it.

"I'm collecting people's experiences for a book," she said. "You'd be surprised how many people have stories similar to yours. It was me, by the way, who planted that story in the *Register*. After we talked at the pagan camp, I wanted to put an item into the flow to see what Hazel would say. I was quite impressed with your performance on *New Connections* yesterday. I think in Hazel we've got a hundred per cent opportunist, somebody trying to cash in on the current interest in New Age phenomena, but she may not be conscious of all that's going on either in this case. She may only think she is. Somehow you are at the convergence point, Joe."

"Why do you think all this stuff is happening to *me*?"

"Who can tell? We're merely space-time events," she said. "Here one minute and gone the next. I realized that years ago when I fell off the mountain. Our lives come and go so quickly in the cosmic flow that the universe hardly notices we're here, and yet sometimes one or another person is chosen as a conduit or vehicle for a divine message."

"Yeah, but why *me*?" I asked.

Sylvia shrugged and smiled as if she were a bit embarrassed. "How shall I say this so you won't be insulted? You see, Joe, sometimes the gods pick a sort of, what shall I say, empty vessel, a *tabula rasa* or blank slate, a cipher, you see. That way they can work through him more easily."

"Oh," I said.

"You have a right to be confused," Sylvia said.

She told me to go sit in her hot tub and relax while she called a friend of hers who knew more about this sort of thing than she did. What was going on called for someone with more experience and knowledge about paranormal phenomena, someone, she said, who regularly walked in the realm of the spirit.

I slid into the hot tub and relaxed in the warm herb-scented water and stared out over Colorado. Thanks to the shiatsu, it felt like somebody had stolen my bones, like when the meat falls off a boiled chicken, that's how relaxed I was. The hot tub room had a glass wall overlooking the mountains in the distance, and it seemed as if I was hanging there in space, three hundred feet above Denver with a clear unobstructed view of Colorado as far as I could see. So much weird stuff was happening that all I could manage was to lie there like a sack of Jell-O, and pretty soon I drifted off into a half sleep. My brain rode on the surface film of a still pond, hanging between two places like one of those long-legged water spiders that dimple the water. I couldn't move. All I could do was stare, feeling floaty, and then I saw a small white dot break off the mountains and start coming toward me.

It got bigger and bigger, and at first I thought it was an eagle, but it kept getting larger until very quickly it had flown right up to the window of Sylvia's apartment. It was the angel! His wings were as white as the snow on the range of the Rockies in the background, and I was so terrified I couldn't move.

The Bird Boy rode a thermal in the updraft of the building, hanging there trying to say something to me, something urgent I couldn't hear because of the glass. I couldn't read his lips either.

I tried to call out to Sylvia, but my tongue was stuck.

He rapped on the window and pointed down toward the street thirty floors below. He gestured wildly out over the city of Denver. It made no sense at all.

I groaned and tried to move, but my body was frozen in place. Finally, the angel reached around, took one of his long flight feathers, and yanked it out. It must have hurt because he winced. Little drops of blood flowed from the spot where he pulled it out, and he dipped the tip of the quill into the blood and wrote something right there on the window glass. I couldn't make out the message right away because the letters were written backward but finally I managed to turn my eyes to the large mirror in the hot tub room, and there I read the Bird Boy's bloody telegram: "VIOLET NEEDS YOU!"

Sylvia came back into the room.

"Feeling relaxed?" she asked.

I turned around and looked up at her and managed to raise my arm up out of the hot tub to point to the window, but when I looked back, the Bird Boy was gone and there was no writing on the window at all.

And then I passed out. Or something.

*

Somewhere in there I must have crawled out of the tub and slithered my way into the bedroom because when I woke up I was lying on Sylvia's immense white bed and looking out over Denver and the mountains in the background. It was late afternoon and the sunlight slanted down golden into the room as Sylvia came in and sat on the edge of the bed.

"Oh, man," I groaned as I came around. "I had the weirdest dream about the Bird Boy again. He was right there outside the window."

"It may not have been a dream, Joe. Tell me about it, every detail."

I told her as best I could what had happened.

"But what did the message VIOLET NEEDS YOU! mean?" I asked.

"It probably meant exactly what it said," Sylvia said seriously.

The intercom from the street door rang shrilly. Sylvia picked up the extension by the bed, said, "I'll buzz you in," and then punched in a couple of numbers.

"That was Rahu," she said.

"Rahu?"

"Rahutatanhok Pandibhabhantur," she said. "He's a brilliant Tibetan bardo master, and he's come to help you."

She explained that Rahu had been part of the Dalai Lama's entourage when the Dalai Lama did his world tour a few years ago but that he had got separated from the rest of the group when they changed planes at Indianapolis, and he had been wandering the country ever since.

When Sylvia opened the door, Rahutatanhok Pandibhabhantur came in. He looked like a Tibetan fireplug, with a bald head and a purple robe that hung off one shoulder. He reminded me of one of those laughing Buddhas you see in Chinese restaurants except he was wearing tinted glasses and an L. L. Bean backpack. He put both palms together and made a deep bow and came up saying, "I am here."

He spoke with a weird, hesitant accent, as if he had to think about every word before he said it. His voice was breathy and sounded about eighty-nine years old, though looking at him I would say he was only fifty or so. It was hard to tell because he was so short and fat for starters, but also because he laughed like a three-year-old at everything. This was the man who was going to help me?

Sylvia and Rahu disappeared into the study to discuss my case, and I used the chance to call my dad in Vegas. I didn't get hold of him, but I did get his answering machine, and instead of his usual message, he said, "I'm not here to answer the phone right now, but if this is Joey, please please *please* get home as fast as you can, son. I got to talk to you about something *big* that's happening."

His voice sounded desperate, and it wasn't like the Amazing Raymond to get flustered at anything. That bothered me, and it added to the confusion I was already feeling about the dream or vision or whatever it was of the Bird Boy writing on the window that I was supposed to help Violet. But how was I supposed to help her? If everything went according to plan, she was already on a bus heading to San Diego and there was no way I could catch up with her.

Rahu and Sylvia returned from the study. He gave me a deep bow and said, "We go now, yes?"

"What?"

"We think you and Rahu need to take a ride," Sylvia said.

"Where to?" I asked.

"Wherever dharma take us," he said.

"Who's dharma?" I asked.

He bowed again and said, "Today you are dharma, and you take me, yes?"

"Where?" I asked.

"Where you go?"

I scratched my head. "I don't know where I'm going," I said. "I thought I was going to New York, but it seems like my dad's in some kind of trouble in Las Vegas. I'm totally lost."

"Good," said Rahu, "then we are ready to begin." He bowed deeply again and when he stood, his eyes lit up and he said, "But first we will get french fries!"

"Good-bye, Joe," Sylvia said. "And, remember, pay attention."

*

I was in no condition to go looking for anybody. Between the shiatsu and the hot tub and the vision of the angel, my bones had turned to rubber, and I was so strung out from not sleeping for a week that I felt like my brain had turned into banana pudding. Luckily Rahu could drive—sort of. He slammed the transmission of my old van into gear and with me as navigator, we set out for the last place I had seen Violet, the bus station. I really would have preferred to sleep at Sylvia's for a while first, but Sylvia wouldn't let me so long as I hadn't yet done what the angel wrote on the window. Besides, Rahu insisted that the moment was ripe for movement. He had consulted *The Book of the Dead*—he asked me if I had read it, but I said I was waiting for the video—so I had no choice.

Rahu made a turn into a McDonalds' drive-thru for french fries. Luckily he did not want to eat at a Munchee Mart. This french fry obsession of his was a little complicated. Being a vegetarian Buddhist monk, he had to watch his diet, but he also discovered he loved french fries when he was chosen to accompany the Dalai Lama and a movie star on their North American tour. Somebody fed him fries once at a reception and he ate them, not knowing they were cooked in beef tallow. By the time he found out, it was too late. He was hooked, but he couldn't let the other monks see him eating them, so he got into the habit of sneaking away from the group whenever he could. Apparently Rahu got separated from the Dalai Lama's entourage when he wandered off at the Indianapolis airport to scarf some fries on the sly. It was something he felt guilty about because he knew that some animals had to die for him to eat potatoes, but he was hooked on fries. By the time he found his way back to the concourse, the Dalai Lama's group had already boarded and were taxiing on the runway to take off for Cleveland. Since then he had been trying to catch up with them, but they were jetting around the world so fast he was always a city or two behind them. Luckily, he had since found out that McDonalds now cooked their french fries in vegetable oil instead of beef tallow, so he could have McFries guilt-free. But he was still having trouble reconnecting with the Dalai Lama. I could see why. His sense of direction left something to be desired.

"We go this way, yes?" he asked, turning wildly out of the drive-thru, then down one street and then another, eating fries from the bag on his lap until we found ourselves on Colfax Avenue.

I tried to convince him it was nowhere near where we wanted to go, but he insisted he knew exactly where we were going. It was already early evening, and the hookers along Colfax were out and getting warmed up for the evening's work.

"Where the hell are we going?" I asked as we drove what seemed to me to be the wrong way.

"This is way dharma leads us, Joseph," Rahu said. "We must relax now, yes? You like some french fries?"

Ahead, in front of the Blue Bird theater, I noticed a ruckus going on. A couple of police wagons were out front, and cops were rounding up the street girls and shoving them into the back of the vans. As we flashed by, I noticed one of the girls was carrying a laundry basket with a baby in it.

"Stop!" I shouted. We had found Violet.

Rahu's sandaled foot slammed on the brake, and we screeched to a halt right in the middle of the traffic lane. We couldn't back up because of traffic, so we circled the block, but by the time we got back, the police vans were just taking off. I got Rahu out of the driver's seat and followed the vans to the precinct house, where I found Violet in a long line of streetwalkers sitting on a bench in the squad room. I deliberately left Rahu out in the van, thinking this was one part of America maybe a Tibetan holy man didn't need to see, and I was right. The room was a smelly swirl of activity, people running all around the place shouting, sleazy types leaning up against the walls smoking cigarettes, drunks sleeping it off in the corners, and Violet and her baby.

"What the hell are you doing here?" I said.

"You her pimp?" a cop said.

"No," I said. "We're, that is, we *were* traveling companions, I'd guess you'd say."

Violet's eyes were dry, but I could tell she had been crying for a long time because there were dusty tear tracks going down her cheeks.

"I got lost," she said.

"Lost? All you had to do was wait in the bus station until the bus left for San Diego. What happened?"

She sniffed back and looked ashamed of herself.

"I was never in Denver before," she said, "and when we were driving in it looked kind of interesting, so I decided to take a little walk around before the bus left. I got lost and couldn't find the station, and so I walked around a while and then this guy pulled up and asked me did I want a ride and so I got in and the next thing I knew, he was asking me strange questions about was I a party girl and I said 'I like a good time as much as the next girl,' and then he arrested me and the baby too."

"Jesus," I said.

We waited while the girls were processed until Violet's turn came. I tried to explain to the cop behind the desk that she wasn't a hooker, she was only a naive country girl, but that didn't seem to cut any ice with him.

"Where you from?" he asked me.

I pulled out my Nevada license and told him how Violet and I had met back in Porkville. I made it seem like we were boyfriend and girlfriend and that we had a fight when we got to Denver. I didn't even try to tell the truth, knowing the truth was so goofy the cop would never believe us. I certainly didn't want to mention the part about the Bird Boy and his message written in blood on Sylvia's window.

The cop was pretty weary by the time I got through the whole improvised story. Some of the girls behind us were kicking up a stink because they wanted to get booked and hit the streets again, so the cop finally said, "You got somebody can vouch for her?"

"Like who?" I asked.

"Anybody, like a clergyman or something?"

"Yeah," I said, "as a matter of fact, I do. Hang on a minute," and I went out to the van and brought in Rahu. I think it's safe to say that the Denver precinct house had never seen anything like a Tibetan bardo master before, unless they had arrested some Hare Krishnas for panhandling. One of the girls along the bench said, "Nice threads, man," when she saw his purple robe. Rahu went right up to the desk and did a deep palms-up bow in front of the sergeant.

"What's this?" the cop asked me, looking over Rahu's gown and sandaled feet.

"He's a lama," I said.

"Don't kid me, buddy," the cop said. "Llamas are furry animals that live in the Alpacas or something."

"No," I said, "a lama's a priest."

"Catholic?"

"Sort of," I said.

"All right," said the cop, stretching his writing hand out over the blotter. "Name?"

Rahu let loose with a flurry of weird sounds, the only ones of which I got were Rahutatanhok Pandibhabhantur because at least I had heard that much before.

The cop wrote down, "Wahoo Patterboard," scratched it out, and asked Rahu to repeat his name. Rahu let fly with it again, the whole Tibetan alphabet. The cop wrote down "Rocketship," crossed that out, and wrote "Radio Shack," then finally gave up.

"You say he's a lama, eh?" said the cop.

I nodded.

"All right, get out of here," he said.

Rahu smiled, put both hands close together, and bowed again.

"Thank you, thank you very very much," he said, bowing up and down like a Texas oil rig and exiting backward through the squad room.

I took Violet by the arm and led her toward the door, but she pulled away.

"Wait a minute," she said, marching back to the table where the sergeant sat. She set the laundry basket with the baby in it on the desk and said, "What about my unicorn powder?"

"Your what?" the cop asked.

"I had a little bag full of unicorn powder I bought from this guy," Violet said. "It was supposed to make Billy fall in love with me, and when they arrested me they took it away."

I grabbed her by the arm, told the cop she was mentally unstable, and promised to get her out of town in fifteen minutes, but she wouldn't leave without her unicorn powder.

"Get out of here," said the cop. "We don't want to have to book you on minor narcotics charges."

"I want my unicorn powder," she said.

"All right," said the cop to me. "I believe you, she is crazy, now get her out of here," but Violet refused to move. She mashed her fists into her hips and stood there.

"Unicorn powder very valuable stuff," said Rahu, coming up behind us again.

The cop looked at us as if we were all insane and then rolled his eyes. "All right," he said, picking up the phone. "You asked for it, girlie, but if the preliminary lab tests show dope, you're all gonna have to be booked."

The sergeant dialed the lab and told us to wait a minute. I wanted to run out right then, get in the van and disappear.

I'm sure the guy would have let us go just to be done with us, but she wouldn't leave. As Violet was getting nearer and nearer to San Diego, it seemed she was getting more worried about what Billy would do when she showed up. She was piling up the lucky charms, spells, and aphrodisiacs as a backup. We sat there and watched the parade of hookers and dope addicts shuffle up to the desk until finally a guy in a white lab coat came out of a back room carrying Violet's packet of unicorn powder. He stopped and talked to the cop at the desk.

The sergeant called us up. His lips were pursed.

"Tell them what you told me," he said to the lab technician.

"It's not cocaine or heroin," he said. "It appears to be, well, some sort of powdered animal horn."

"That's right," said Violet, taking the plastic bag back from his fingers. "It's unicorn powder to make Billy fall in love with me."

The lab guy shrugged. "I thought at first it might be rhino horn, but I compared it with some stuff they picked up in Chinatown a couple of months ago and it didn't match. Whatever it is, it doesn't appear on the illegal substance list and it doesn't appear to come from any endangered species that we know of."

"Begging to differ," said Rahu bowing again, "but sacred unicorn is most endangered species."

"What?" snapped the sergeant.

"He said *unicorn*," I said.

"This here's unicorn powder," said Violet like she was talking to an idiot, "I told you that."

The cop growled in a pretty good imitation of a pit bull.

"Get the hell out of here, all of you. Now!" he snapped. He pointed toward the door with his pen. Rahu bowed and we left, Violet and baby in tow.

*

"All right," I said when we were back in the van, "Here's the plan. First, we head back to Sylvia's . . . " I was thinking like a madman. My mind raced along like it was on speed or something. I looked at my watch and realized it might still be possible to get out to Stapleton Airport and catch a red-eye flight to New York in time for the Sclapped audition. I had the guitar, I had my clothes, I had my chops, and I was ready. I figured if I raced into the audition straight from LaGuardia, the combination of fatigue, adrenalin, road dirt, and jet lag would make me look like I belonged in Sclapped. Everything I'd been through would actually have been to my advantage.

Since Rahu could drive, I would give him the van and he could take Violet to San Diego. Once he was in Southern California, he could get a job in a fast-food joint and wait until the Dalai Lama's entourage showed up again in Beverly Hills. Then he could rejoin them and head back to bardo land and be happy. The only part that wasn't taken care of by this plan was my dad's weird phone message, but I could call him from New York in the morning and, if I had to, he could send me money to fly out to Vegas after the audition. This plan provided for all the loose ends. It fulfilled the angel's summons, it took care of Violet and Rahu, it got rid of the van, and it still allowed me to become a rock and roll legend in my own time. It was too good be true, I thought. And I was right.

Sylvia gave me the money I needed, but I spent a fruitless half hour trying to wheedle a ticket out of the clerk at the desk of the last airline flying out of Denver before morning. The terminal was nearly deserted, with only a few maintenance people picking cigarette butts off the cold terrazzo floor.

"The flight is booked, sir, complete. Every seat is taken."

"Haven't you got anything?" I asked. "Can't you fly me out in the baggage compartment?"

She tapped on her computer terminal for a few seconds, watched the display screen flash some numbers. For a moment I felt a surge of hope, then she shook her head.

"Sorry, sir, there's nothing we can do."

I raced down to the departure gate. A motley assortment of business people sat there half awake, waiting to board the flight, *my* flight to New York. I ran from seat to seat like a madman.

"Would you take a bump?" I asked feverishly. They all shook their heads or refused to look up from their laptops.

"Won't *anybody* here take a bump?" I finally screamed to the near-empty terminal. "Please, please, please! I've been trying to get to New York for over a week now and I have to be there tomorrow—I mean, today, by noon. My God, look at the time, it's almost sunrise over Manhattan. Please! I'm begging you."

My voice echoed off the cold walls.

When all else fails, I thought, head west. There were flights every hour out of Vegas's MacCarran Airport. I could get to my dad's, find out what the problem was with him, call Murray, beg and plead, and catch the first flight to New York. Maybe, I thought in my crazed condition, I could even audition by phone. Why not? People were teleconferencing and video-conferencing. I wasn't licked yet, I told myself, as I piled into the van where Rahu and Violet were waiting just in case. I got behind the wheel, and we left Denver in our dust.

We crossed the Rockies in the pitch dark and slid downhill into the deepest hours of the night. I drove the first shift until I could hardly see anymore and then turned the wheel over to Rahu who, I figured, couldn't do too much damage driving in a straight line on the interstate. Violet sat in the back with the baby and fed him when he cried. She talked about how excited she was that we were back together again until I couldn't take it anymore.

Well, I thought, I had done what the Bird Boy wrote on the window. I had helped Violet. Now what?

"Don't worry, Joe," Violet said. "Everything'll work out the way it's supposed to, you'll see."

Rahu drove like a crazy man, rocking the wheel back and forth and pressing the gas pedal to the floor so hard that I was afraid his foot was going to go right through the firewall. Every once in a while, since we were riding the downslope, we'd actually get some speed going and the sides of the van would start to flutter like wings. The first time it happened, Rahu broke into a big smile and his eyes lit up with a childlike light. "It is like great bird," he said, beaming. "Flappa-flappa-flappa! We are fly-y-y-y-ing!" And then he broke into a high-pitched, insane laugh. "Aha-ha-ha-ha!" I thought the engine was about to have an internal hemorrhage the way Rahu was driving, but I was so tired I didn't care. Somewhere near the Utah border, I fell asleep in the front seat.

Along about three in the morning, we were somewhere in Utah and Rahu's screaming woke me up. He had rolled down the window and was shouting at the top of his lungs out into the darkness.

"Hallo! Hallo! Hallo!" he screamed, taking one hand off the wheel to wave out the window. We were still going as fast as the van could carry us, and we were swerving over the center line of the highway now and then.

Violet woke up, too, and sat looking out the window into the dark, squinting to try to see what Rahu was looking at.

"Most beautiful night-flying birds you have in your country," he said. "Hallo! Hallo!"

Then we saw him, just outside the halo of the headlights' glow. The angel was back and he was flying with us!

He flashed into the headlights' beam, his white wings brilliant, and cut right in front of the van like a swallow or a meadowlark will sometimes do when you drive along a country road. He was keeping pace with us even though we were doing well over sixty by then. He circled the van and glided alongside us through the dark. Sometimes he'd fall behind a little and then fly over us, then he'd disappear into the night, angling off on his wings, and then come back again. He stayed with us about fifteen miles. And, weirdest thing of all, he was smiling.

"I told you everything would be okay," Violet said.

CHAPTER SIX

I had no idea what time it was when we finally dragged ourselves across the Las Vegas city limits. There aren't many clocks in Las Vegas because the owners of the casinos don't want you thinking about unimportant things like time while you're feeding coins into the slot machines. It was day. I could tell that much as we rolled down the Strip, but the specifics of it beyond that were a little fuzzy.

Why shouldn't they have been? In the week or so since I had picked up Violet, I had crossed three times zones, tried to call down UFOs with a bunch of pagans, got hooked up with a midget preacher, almost got shot, killed, and arrested, had picked up a Tibetan lama, and seen a Bird Boy flying sixty miles an hour through the desert. After all that, it wasn't surprising that I didn't know if it was Monday or Tuesday or Friday or next month even, much less what time of day it was. I figured it was pretty good that I even noticed I was still connected to Planet Earth by gravity. All I knew for sure was that I wanted to get to my dad's house, find out what was going on, change, and call Murray to grovel for an audition slot that night or the next day.

"This is the most exciting, elegant place I have ever been," Violet said. She held her baby up so he could overdose on all the stimulation spilling off the fronts of the casinos along the Strip. "Look at the cowboy," she said, pointing the baby's face at Vegas Vic, the famous neon cowpoke on the front of the Pioneer Casino, who waves his arm back and forth to the tourists day and night. "I seen him on TV, but I never dreamed he would be so tall. Isn't this wonderful, Rahu?"

For his part, Rahu wasn't saying anything. He was too busy trying to keep his eyeballs from flying out of his head. I would guess when he was growing up in the Buddhist monastery back in Tibet he had never even hallucinated things like the stuff he was seeing out the windshield of my van. If french fries were still a big deal for him, then Las Vegas must have put his dharma circuits on overload.

He finally managed to say, "Please to tell me, Joseph, what means 'topless pizza lunch'?"

It's a bit of a challenge to explain Las Vegas to those who've never been there. First of all, you've got to understand it's surrounded by Nevada. After all life is blasted away from the earth, most of the world will look like Nevada. It's no accident they did nuclear testing there in the 1950s; they figured nobody would notice.

And the city of Las Vegas is plunked down in the middle of that nothingness, a town of three hundred and fifty thousand human souls and probably twice that many lizards and scorpions crawling in off the desert. Maybe the people who started Las Vegas thought it would be so much fun that it needed to be surrounded by a couple of hundred miles of empty sand in every direction just to keep all the good times from spilling out and doing damage elsewhere. Las Vegas is all about fun, if, that is, your idea of fun is standing in the middle of twelve thousand drunken chain-smoking zombies screaming, "C'mon, baby, hum-baby, come, come, come!" while kissing a pair of dice.

I suppose, though, that if Las Vegas didn't exist, somebody would have to come along and invent it. It serves as a sort of safety valve where all of America's tightly wound heartlanders can let off a little steam. It's nothing to see a bunch of Methodists flying in from Indiana for a weekend to do things they don't even talk about back in Terre Haute. They step off of one of the four hundred and fifty flights coming into McCarran every day, blink once or twice in the desert light, shout "whoopee!" and let all their inhibitions go to hell. They figure nobody back in the corn belt would believe them anyway, so they get caught up in the spirit of the town, get sloppy drunk, wear silly hats, go to the shows, see a little nudity, and gamble their life savings away. After that, full of remorse, they wind themselves tight again and head back home for a couple of years.

Maybe it's the neon that does it to them.

There are fifty miles of it in a five-block area around the Strip and an additional two million light bulbs to make the place glow with a surreal light. It all adds up to a pretty over-whelming kind of scene for folks whose usual idea of a wild time is to go down to the Western Auto store on a Saturday night to get spare parts for their refrigerator.

Of course, Las Vegas is more than mere gambling. There's also the great tradition of entertainment: Wayne Newton, Elvis, Sammy, Frank, Liberace, Bobby Barosini's orangutans, Pavarotti, Sophie Tucker, Lena, Bette, Jimmy Durante, Bugsy Siegel, Spike Jones, the Mills Brothers, Vic Damone, and a famous guy back in the fifties whose whole act was eating light bulbs. It doesn't matter that half of these performers are dead, they keep getting booked anyhow. And if you get bored with dead singers, you can always go down to the Mirage and watch the artificial volcano erupt or find some dancing chimps someplace.

And there's also the Amazing Raymond, my dad, the reason we were there in the first place. Well, all right, Dad's no Siegfried and Roy, but in his time he was good enough to entertain the Texas Armadillo Association—motto: "To promote, protect, and preserve the heritage of the armadillo"—every year when they came to town. They even gave him one of their armadillo hats one year and made him an honorary member. He didn't have floating elephants and disappearing pythons, but he always man-aged to do a good show and over the years had managed to keep the Armadillos happy.

My dad lived in a subdivision north of the city. It was a typical American suburb, built around strip malls and super-markets and such.

Those who don't know Vegas very well never think about where all the performers and dealers and waitresses live. They probably figure they live off under the rocks with the scorpions out in the desert. All the tourists see and care about is the glitter on the surface, and they might be surprised to see just how dull the rest of Las Vegas is, because backstage, back where all the workers live, Las Vegas is pretty much like any other city in America except for the slot machines in the laundromats.

By the time we pulled into the driveway of Dad's ranch house, Violet had decided she and Billy were going to come up to Vegas and get married in the little wedding chapel with pink angels painted on the plywood façade she had seen amongst the neon storefronts somewhere.

Dad ran out of the house as soon as he saw the van pull into the drive, and he started talking even before I could explain why we were there.

"Joey, Joey, Joey!" he said, rushing up to the door. "Thank God, Joey, you've come in the nick of time."

I turned the engine off. It had reignition problems after all the hard driving, and it went pocketa-pocketa-pocketa, whuff-whuff-whuff, until it finally wheezed itself out like a guy dying of lung cancer.

Dad was wearing Bermuda shorts and an unbuttoned tomato-red shirt, and he was wringing his hands as if he were real concerned about something. My dad is not a tall guy, and without his magician's tux on, he looked like a hard-boiled egg on two sticks. He was older and more worried than I remembered when I'd left only a few months before. He used to have to frost his goatee and temples to make him look more like a magician, but in the past few years his hair, what he had left of it on top, had all gone silver on its own. It was the first time I had noticed my dad was getting older.

I was stiff all over and felt about a hundred years old as I crawled out of the van and hit the hot cement. Dad hugged me, and I introduced Violet and Rahu with just their names. Dad didn't seem too curious about them as he hustled me into the house. I was surprised to find Hazel there, too.

"Thank God you've come, Joe," she said, rushing up to me and grabbing me briefly by the hands. She looked worried and tense, too, and I quickly ran through my mind to think of who could've died to make them both seem so relieved to see me.

Hazel had changed. She didn't look older like Dad—I hadn't been gone that long—but she had upgraded her appearance somehow and now appeared trendy in a way she never had before, as if she had suddenly come into a bunch of money. Her formerly shoulder-length hair was cut stylish and severe, like something you might see in one of those expensive women's magazines where the models all pout in front of the Eiffel Tower. Beneath her white rhinestone-studded blouse she was wearing NFL-sized shoulder pads.

"I didn't think you, of all people, would be glad to see me," I said to Hazel. "Not after that radio show last week. We have a lot of talking to do."

"Joey," Dad said. "Try to say something nice, please. This is no way to treat your wife, not at a time like this."

I looked at the shoulder pads again. They stood out like wings and made Hazel seem four feet wide. She had shorts and sandals on and seemed to have lost about ten pounds.

"All right," I said. "You're looking very aerodynamic. Now what's this all about, Dad? Your phone message sounded desperate."

"Zak has locked himself in the bathroom," Hazel said.

"Zak?" I asked. "As in Zak Bendzi? The guy who pirated my song?"

"Not pirated."

"He won't come out for anything," Dad explained. "He's been in there since last night."

Hazel went over to the bathroom door, knocked softly, and then said, as if she were talking to a child, "It's all right, Zak, you can come out now."

There was a snuffling sound on the other side, as if somebody was all hunched down on the floor in the corner trying to hide from something that terrified him. Then, a little tiny voice, almost like a mouse would have if a mouse could talk, said, "Is that him?"

Hazel hesitated a moment, put her palm on the door like she was trying to pet him through it. "No," she said. "It's Joe."

"Your husband?" Zak said, suddenly terrified. "The one who talked so crazy on the radio show the other day?"

"Yes," said Hazel, "him." More whimpering behind the door, the sound of somebody retching, or trying to retch into the bucket. "But he won't hurt you, Zak."

"It was *her* idea," Zak whined. "She made me do it. Kill *her.*"

"Will somebody tell me what this is all about?" I asked.

"It's about this, Joey," Dad said, handing me that morning's *Variety.*

There was a story in it by Sylvia—she had connections everywhere, it seemed—about me and Zak Bendzi. She was sure that I had written "Open Tuning," and she was hinting that New Age musician Zak Bendzi had committed the age-old crime of plagiarism, and I should be getting some of the huge royalties due me for composing the song in the first place. Not only that, but she had painted me as some kind of genius, talking about the rose-covered guitar and saying I had visions of angels and all that. She even called me a "new Orpheus," whoever he was. (I never heard of the guy personally, but I figured he was dead like Elvis or else she wouldn't have called me the new one.) Anyway, I guess Zak combined that with the way I had talked on the radio show a couple of days before and figured I was coming to get him. But that wasn't all, as I soon found out.

"The problem is that all of a sudden Zak Bendzi is real controversial hot stuff," said Hazel. "We've had feeler calls from Oprah, Phil, even Letterman. So far none of them has booked except Miles Kindley. It seems your little fit on the air the other day shot his ratings through the roof. People are used to Miles' show being about as exciting as Valium, so when you and I argued about 'Open Tuning' on the air the other day, people actually came out of their alpha state, and now they're clamoring to have the reclusive Zak Bendzi come on the show to defend himself. Zak is scheduled to go on air live tomorrow with Miles Kindley in a *New Connections* special broadcast from L.A., and now he's literally freaking out."

"You can't make me go," squealed Zak from behind the bathroom door. "I'm not going, you hear me?"

"The idea that Zak Bendzi might have plagiarized the song blew Miles's mind," Hazel explained, "He can't believe that anybody who wrote anything so spiritual as 'Open Tuning' could have stolen it. Now he wants Zak to come on *New Connections* and defend himself live on tomorrow's show."

More sounds of retching in the bathroom.

"So what's the problem?" I asked.

"Stagefright, Joey," Dad whispered so Zak couldn't hear.

"Worse than stage fright," whispered Hazel, pulling me aside into the living room where Zak couldn't hear us. "You see, well, Zak isn't show people, he's, well, kind of shy."

The way she said "shy," I knew she really meant this guy was terrified out of his gourd to deal with more than two human beings at the same time, much less to go on a national live radio call-in show. Hazel told me Zak had been a night clerk at the local Munchee Mart up until she convinced him to do the work on "Open Tuning." In fact, he was living with Hazel. Not as in *living with*, of course. He was much too shy for that, but after I left Hazel had rented our guest room for a little extra help on the monthly payment.

"So I still don't get it," I said. "Why doesn't this Zak guy just go on the air and tell the truth?"

"Are you crazy?" Hazel snorted. "Zak would absolutely collapse."

Dad came into the living room then.

"She got him out," he said, looking immensely relieved.

"Who?"

"That girl you brought with you, that Violet," he said. "She just went up to the door, knocked a couple of times, and introduced herself. She said she had to use the can, and he opened the door. It's amazing. Who is this girl anyway, Joey? She some kind of angel or what?"

The reclusive Zak Bendzi, the one the whole New Age movement—and a bunch of crossover fans, too—was claiming as the new messiah of space music turned out to be a nineteen-year-old kid who had so many rolls of fat around him he would have reminded me of the Michelin Man if the Michelin Man was covered with zits and wore wire rim glasses. He breathed through his mouth, as if he had serious adenoidal problems. When he saw me, he held his arms up across his face as though he was afraid I was going to punch him, but he was such a poor wet puppy not even I could bring myself to hit him, not even if he did steal my song.

"Don't hit me," he whined. "Please."

"Nobody's going to hit anybody, Zak," Hazel said, putting her arm around him in a motherly way, "we're only going to make some iced tea and talk."

We headed for the kitchen. Rahu had disappeared somewhere, I don't know where. He didn't seem to be around the place, but I didn't have time to worry about him right then. Besides, if we needed him, we only had to sniff for french fries. Meanwhile, Violet changed the baby and came into the kitchen with the rest of us. We all sat around the linoleum eating-nook table and had iced tea, all except Zak who sucked at what was left of a Munchee Mart Big Gulp from the fridge.

"You see, we have a problem here, Joey," Dad said.

" 'We' who?" I asked. "It seems to me things are pretty simple. Hazel and this guy somehow stole my song and recorded it and didn't give me any credit or any of the royalties from it."

"We didn't steal anybody's song," Hazel said. "Zak found a tape you left in the guest room. He didn't know it was your song. It was just in a box of stuff you left behind. It didn't have any name, or anything else on it, except the words 'Open Tuning.' "

"Really," Dad said, "Hazel didn't know anything about it. Zak enhanced the tape and asked her what she thought."

Hazel said, "I told him I thought it had commercial potential, so I talked to a couple of guys from an L.A. record company who'd won big at my table. I got them to listen to Zak's tape, and the next thing we know we had a minihit on our hands, a cult thing that crossed over into mainstream. I even heard it on the elevator the other day at the Sahara. The money's been rolling in, Joe, and we're getting calls and trying to put together a concert tour and all that to take advantage, you see, to strike while the CD's hot."

"Only we got one problem," Dad said.

He nodded at Zak and rolled his eyes. I could see what he meant. If this poor kid went on the radio or, God forbid, on television, sales would go down the sewer. Zak seemed unable to string together more than a couple of words at a time unless he was talking about computers. He looked like the sort of computer rodent who'd pop off dweeby jokes about the surface structure of the moon Io or something. He seemed to have difficulty dealing with ordinary reality. In fact, he seemed to have difficulty just keeping his steel rims from sliding down his nose into his Big Gulp. His hair was a mess, too. His head looked like one of those whirling brushes in an automatic car wash, one that had been used too long. It mystified me how he could have put together what I heard on the recording of "Open Tuning."

"Where did you get the money to pay for all the backup musicians, the choir, and all that in the first place?" I asked Hazel. "Did the record company put up the dough?"

Zak giggled for the first time, looking like a kid who's just got caught with his fist in the cookie jar.

"Zak did it all on his MacIntosh," Dad said. "Most amazing thing I've ever seen."

"You mean you're not even a musician?" I asked.

"Not really," Zak admitted. "I mean I don't play any real musical instruments. Who needs to anymore?" He pushed his steel rims back up the bridge of his nose, but they didn't stay there. "Everything's in my computer—the hundred-piece orchestra, the chanting choir, the horns, the other weird sounds. What do you think of that?" Zak sat back in his chair and a big shit-eating grin slowly stole across his face.

"I think it's awful," I said. "Think of all the musicians you're putting out of work."

Zak did a teenage eyeroll, like I was a prehistoric troglodyte which, at least in his terms, I guess I was.

"Join the twentieth century," he said. "*Nobody* plays music on instruments anymore."

"Zak is the wave of the future," Hazel said. "He's the Mozart of the MIDI."

"It's really easy," Zak said, warming into the subject now that he was in familiar territory. "I'll bet even you could do it. And the great thing about it is I don't have to have any other actual people around. I can have, like, a hundred-string orchestra right in my room, and I don't have to deal with other life forms at all." He smiled a big contented smile. "Isn't that neat?"

I had to admit I could see the attraction sometimes, but still, the idea of being able to make that much music without ever touching a musical instrument somehow bothered me. Zak picked at a zit on his chin and giggled. "And it's not only musicians I can create. I can also mix in sounds from humpbacked whales and coyotes howling in the Grand Canyon to get the ecomarket. Then some tabla and heavy breathing for the New Agers."

"You did this on 'Open Tuning'?" I asked. He blushed and nodded.

"I told you he was a genius," Hazel said.

"I also mixed in some ultrasonics, tones above the range of human hearing."

Zak explained that sounds, like light, go beyond the range of human hearing, both above and below the normal sound wave spectrum. Just as ultraviolet light affects us whether we're aware of it or not, Zak said, ultrahigh and ultralow sounds do, too.

"What were you trying to do with that," I asked, "capture the dog market?"

"The real genius was the subliminals," said Dad, shaking his head in disbelief. "I have to confess, Joey, when I heard this stuff I didn't know why I liked it. I usually hate this kind of music. Give me some good old Sigmund Romberg any-day, you know how I am, right? So I hear this 'Open Tuning' and suddenly I want my own copy. I couldn't figure. Go ahead, Zak, tell him how you did it."

Zak blushed and shuffled his foot in an aw-shucks sort of way.

"It was nothing, really," he said. "Eight tracks deep I buried some subliminal suggestions."

"What kind of subliminal suggestions?" I asked.

"Uh, well, I just had a computer-synthesized voice repeat the phrase *Buy this album, Buy this album* over and over again."

"In fourteen languages!" Hazel crowed. "The kid is a marketing genius. When this thing hits the international market in a few months, it's going to go up like a Fourth of July rocket."

"Isn't that subliminal stuff illegal?" I asked.

"Only if you get caught," said Hazel.

"You can't even hear it unless you separate out the tracks," explained Zak. "And nobody's been able to do that yet because of safeguards I put in. If they don't go through the right gates, the whole program scrambles and the subliminals self-destruct."

"Jesus," I said, trying madly to figure out what he'd just told me. "Let me see if I got this straight. You basically hypnotize people with the music track and then give them commands to buy the album?"

"Well, yeah," said Zak. "Basically. I mean, nobody's really proved subliminals work yet, but I figured it was worth a try, sort of like hacking into a person's mental software and reprogramming it a little." He bit his lips and stifled a little nervous giggle.

"That's immoral," I said.

"It's a tough market out there, Joey," Dad said. "You need every angle you can get."

"Besides," said Zak, "I didn't have much to work with. I mean what else did 'Open Tuning' have going for it when I got the original tape? What you wrote was pretty dull until I digitalized it."

I grabbed him by his Star Trek T-shirt and yanked him up out of his seat so hard that his Big Gulp spilled all over the table.

"You said you wouldn't hit me, you said you wouldn't hit me!" he squealed.

"You stole my damned song!" I shouted.

"He didn't know it was your song, Joe. Besides, he's the one who made it what it is," Hazel said, trying to pull me off him. "You only wrote it."

"And *played* it," I said, turning Zak loose. "The only real human being on the album is me playing the original tape. Everything else is Zak's computer."

"Actually," Violet put in, "I personally like what he did with it. I mean it makes it easy to listen to, you know. I mean maybe the two of you ought to think about working together."

"Listen to this girl, Joey," Dad said. "She's making sense."

"This thing's a hit and I haven't seen one penny out of the whole deal," I snapped.

"Oh, all right," said Zak. "Maybe you should get the standard studio musician's fee we would have had to pay somebody to play it for real."

"Standard fee!" I said. "I wrote the damned thing! All you did was run it through your musical Cuisinart and make some kind of hypnotic salad out of it!"

"You're gonna hit me, aren't you?" Zak said. "I know you are."

I probably would have, too, except Dad stood me up and ushered me into the small den off the living room. He used to take me there when I was in high school when he wanted to set me straight on the meaning of life and all that, and I always felt like the Beaver being taken to the den by his dad, only Beaver Cleaver's dad didn't have his den plastered with old circus posters and his knick knacks weren't likely to blow up in your face. In Dad's study, you always had to check for whoopie cushions before you tried to sit down.

As we walked through the living room I noticed the TV was on, as it always was, and a commercial for Munchee Mart was playing starring Munchee Mart Marty, the clown I had almost punched out in Nebraska.

"Do you believe that guy?" Dad said as he sat down in his easy chair. "He must be making millions. He's almost as big as Ronald McDonald."

Then Dad got quiet for a moment as he warmed into his loving-father mode. It was a routine I knew pretty well. Every time I'd get tired of having my head blown off in the dyno-box, he'd take me aside, either alone in the trailer or off to some diner or something, and we'd have a little man-to-man, and he'd always get his way. He was a magician, after all, and he could pull more out of a hat than rabbits—he could also manage to jerk around your insides pretty well, too. But this time, I decided, he wasn't going to get away with it. I had my own life to live, such as it was, and I had to stand up for myself.

"Listen, Joey," he started. "You see our problem, don't you? This Zak is a nice kid and all, but he's not show people like you and me."

He was right, of course. I couldn't deny that. One look at Zak and you could tell he wasn't the kind who could get up and face an audience. Zak, from what I had seen of him, lived in a perpetual state of flop sweat even when he was alone. Only when he was talking about his computer did he seem halfway human. If Zak Bendzi had to go on the air to promote "Open Tuning," sales would go down the toilet fast, especially now that he had gotten a reputation as a mystical holy-man genius.

"The problem is," Dad said, "Hazel jumped way out ahead of herself on this one, Joey. Not only did she get him booked on Miles Kindley's show, but she's even been organizing a concert tour. She started taking bookings at New Age fairs, college campuses, all over the place, and at first Zak went along. He liked the idea of being famous. But when he realized he'd actually have to get up in front of real live people and *do* something like put on a show, he flipped out. She called me to help work him up for a stage show, but it wasn't any use. The kid's hopeless, not a performer."

"So what do you want me to do about it?" I asked. "I've got this chance to get involved in something really big, I mean, I might still have a chance at the big time, Dad."

"What sort of chance?" Dad asked.

I briefly told him about Murray and Sclapped.

"It's already after five in New York, Joey," Dad said. "The day is done, son. I think that gig's history as far as you're concerned. You missed the audition."

I knew he was right, of course, but I couldn't let go.

"I'll call Murray first thing in the morning," I said. "I'll beg. I'll plead. All I want is a chance. Murray will make something happen. He seemed so friendly on the phone. He remembered us and everything."

"Joey," Dad said. "Let me tell you something Fred Allen said about agents—they've got hearts smaller than a flea's navel. If what you've told me is true, Murray had his pick of fourteen hundred guitar players today. By this time, Murray's probably even forgot your name."

"I could have got the gig," I said.

Dad cleared his throat and smiled. He still had his irritating habit of rolling a half dollar from knuckle to knuckle, and now the coin was flashing like a lighthouse.

"You'll just have to kiss that one good-bye, son," he said, the coin shining hypnotically, "but it's not the end of the world. In fact, Hazel and I have a proposition for you. This is what I wanted to talk to you about: we want you to play Zak Bendzi, Joey."

"What?" I asked.

"That's what my phone message was about," he explained. "It's why we hired Lester Thoroughgood to track you down. We want you to pretend to be Zak Bendzi on the radio and on tour, Joey, to impersonate him, you see?"

I jumped up from my chair and started to storm out of the room. "No way," I said. "I want to be a rock and roll star, not some New Age guru."

"Joey, Joey," Dad said, calling me back. "Wait a minute, hear me out, son. Hazel's got it all worked out."

"Hazel!" I shouted and added a choice expletive after that. Dad said he knew she and I were having a little trouble with our relationship, which was like saying General Custer and Sitting Bull didn't see eye-to-eye down at the Little Big Horn, but, he added, business is business. He kept rolling that half dollar over his knuckles until I finally sat back down again.

He reached over to his desk and pulled off a computer sheet. He lowered his voice and leaned toward me in his chair.

"I've been helping Hazel a bit with the business end of this deal, Joey. Look here. 'Open Tuning' is a huge hit," he said. "Check out these numbers."

He showed me some bottom lines that were into six figures. "This thing has gone crossover, son, 'Open Tuning' is bigger than all of us, and it's just starting to peak. This space music stuff is getting bigger shares of the market every week, and lots of people out there are willing to pay big money to hear it. This could be your chance to jump on the gravy train, son. They may even cut a video. MTV. Who knows?"

My head was spinning from the figures.

"So what do you want me to do?" I asked warily.

Between them, Dad and Hazel had cooked up the following plan: since nobody had ever actually seen Zak Bendzi—his picture wasn't on the cassette or CD jacket of Open Tuning—Dad said it would be perfectly easy to put in a ringer for him to do the talk-show circuit and a concert tour, and since I had been the one to play the thing on the guitar in the first place and since they knew they could trust me to keep quiet about it, they thought I was the only logical choice to be Zak Bendzi.

"You mean you want me to go public pretending I'm him talking about a song I wrote myself as if he wrote it?"

"Something like that, Joey," Dad said.

"That's the stupidest idea I ever heard of," I said.

"Joey, you got to do it, son," he said, looking hurt. "If not for you then for me, son."

He put his hand up to his chest and wheezed. He hit his ribs with his fist once or twice as if his heart had already stopped and needed a jump start.

"What stake have you got in it?" I asked, trying to stay as cold as ice through this whole process. It was tough. I mean he was only acting sick, but if the truth be told, even I could see that the Amazing Raymond was not looking too amazing anymore. My father was getting old, and he had no one else but me.

"What am I going to do in my old age, Joey?" he asked. "You know I never made it big, never became a Siegfried and Roy or a Henning or a Copperfield, much less a Houdini or Blackstone. I made a living, Joey, but I never made plans."

"What do you mean?" I asked.

"Retirement, Joey," he said. "It's not that far away. I'm feeling old, son."

"You're not old, Dad," I lied. "You'll never be old."

He waved his hand. "I'm so old I only read abridged novels because I'm afraid I won't live long enough to finish a regular one. You tell me that's not old."

I was trying to hang on to what little connection I had to reality after a week of no sleep and Violet Tansy, but it was a tough battle. I felt like one of those prisoners of war from old movies that they didn't let sleep ever until they finally cracked. I sat up straighter in my chair so I wouldn't say anything stupid. The idea of playing Zak Bendzi on a tour promoting a song I wrote myself didn't appeal to me. In fact, it made me feel sick. I told him so. I stiffened my backbone and told him I wouldn't do it.

"But we're in a bind, Joey," he said. "Miles Kindley has Zak booked tomorrow in L.A. Couldn't you just do the radio show tomorrow, son? Couldn't you do just that much? If you do, we can get somebody else to play Zak on the concert tour. Nobody'll see your face tomorrow, nobody'll know."

"I'll know," I said. "And what if I go on that show and tell the world I, Joe Findlay, really wrote 'Open Tuning' and that Zak is a nineteen-year-old computer nerd? What then, huh?"

"Look, son," Dad said, gesturing around the room at all the posters and signed photos of famous magicians that he had collected over the years. "Look at this. You know what this is? This is show business, Joey. This is all about being somebody else. None of these guys acted under his own real name. You know what Harry Houdini's real name was? Erik Weisz. You can be Zak Bendzi, can't you, for a little while anyway? Hell, son, it'd put you on the map. Zak Bendzi's famous already. If you pretend to be Zak Bendzi, you'll be starting near the top. But who knows Joe Findlay? Nobody. Let's face it, if you go on being yourself, you'll stay at the bottom of the ladder the rest of your life, a nobody."

"Gee, thanks, Dad," I said.

"Face facts, Joey, you're going on thirty in a few years. You've never had a hit. You've spent the last seven years backing up dead people, and the past few months you've been out in Noplace working for drinks and tips. Your career's in a place where the sun don't shine, son."

I hesitated. My mouth was dry, as if I'd been eating chalk dust. I felt on the edge of something totally stupid, but, for the moment, I held on to my sense of self.

"Listen," Dad went on, "Let me tell you about something that happened one time right here in Vegas. I was working the lounge, right? I was doing the old money shredder trick, you know the one where you put a buck in the shredder, chop it up, and it comes out a five, right? Well, this guy comes up after the show, comes right backstage, see, and asks to buy the thing. I tell him he can get one at any magic shop in the country for a couple of bucks, but he's had a few drinks and he wants mine. He thinks you can put a one-dollar bill in there and pull out a five anytime you want. He thinks he's going to get rich. I tell him it's a trick, that in order to make it work you have to have six bucks in the first place because you got to have the five in place before you even do the trick, but this guy is convinced I've been pulling five-dollar bills out of thin air, so he literally jumps at me, Joey, and he starts shouting 'I seen you do it, I seen it right in front of my eyes, give it to me.' I sold it to him for fifty bucks. Crazy, right? But here's the point, Joey, you got to have money to make money, son, and, unless I'm greatly mistaken, you haven't got two nickels to rub together right now, and you've got no place to go."

No argument there, I thought.

"Now Hazel's got money, Joey, tons of it. 'Open Tuning' is a hit and you can climb aboard. A chance like this only comes along once in a career if you're lucky, son. 'Open Tuning' may last only a couple of months. You gotta catch the wave, boy. You've got to patch things up with Hazel and grab the ring right now."

I crossed my arms.

"What's done is done, Joey. Like it or not, she took a tape you threw away, and she made it into a hit, she and Zak. You can have a piece of that pie, or you can piss it away, you take your pick."

I had to think that one over for a minute. Las Vegas was full of good entertainers who had a hit once back in 1958 and then spent the next thirty-five years making money off it. If you hit it really big even once, you could make a career for the rest of your life. At the very worst, you'd end up on *Hollywood Squares* or something, making better than scale. And if you got into big money one time and played it right by making wise investments in real estate and mutual funds, you could be sitting pretty financially for a long time.

"C'mon, son," Dad said. "Play Zak Bendzi. You can do that, can't you?"

I crossed my arms and sat there. I could not make up my mind. If I didn't go with Dad's offer, my career was nowhere. Let's face it, I didn't have a career. I could probably find lounge work in Vegas somewhere, but that was what I had left behind all those months ago. I had blown the Sclapped gig for sure, though I did intend to call Murray the following day and find out. On the other hand, I thought, if I did go on the road as Zak Bendzi, I'd do all the work and he'd get all the credit. It would be different from making up a stage name. If you worked under a stage name, there was no real person with that name standing in the background. But in my case, Zak Bendzi would always be there, and whatever I did he could take credit for. I would be nothing but a face, part of his machine. If I pretended to be Zak Bendzi I'd be nothing more than a part of his program, digitalized bits. And where would Joe Findlay be then?

Dad could see I was getting nowhere arguing with myself, so he finally went for the nuclear option.

He pushed himself up from the chair and went to a cardboard box he had sitting in the corner. He lifted it up, set it on the desk, and opened the top flaps. He reached in and lifted out his old tail coat, the one with the satin lapels he used to wear when we were on the road together. It was faded and dingy, motheaten and smelly, but I recognized it right away.

"I want you to have this, Joey," he said. "I was saving it for you all these years. Here, you're big enough now, put it on."

He handed the thing to me. I held it in my lap looking at the threadbare satin of the lapels. The pull wires for the pigeons were still in place just like they used to be. The tip of the string of magic silks hung out of the vest pocket. I could feel its bulk now, my dad's jacket, stuffed full of his magic, the way it was when, as a kid, I took it off the chair in the trailer and tried it on and looked like a trained chimp.

"Put it on, Joey," he said. "Just like you used to. It's yours now."

I put the coat on. I slipped it over my shoulders and it hung heavily on me, but it fit. The sleeves were now the right length and I could feel the elastics along the forearms for making things disappear.

I looked at Dad. Like most show people, he had spent so much time in makeup that his face was raw and red. He plucked his eyebrows a little and in full makeup he looked great from the third row back, but up close you could see the years all over his face. I remembered how he used to look in the old days when we were on the road, him with his little goatee and all done up in these black tails, this classic magician's outfit. When he'd moved to Vegas, he'd put away the old tux and had himself a bright red sequined dinner jacket made, but I always remembered him as that handsome young magician in his white tie and tails doing his schtick in community centers and high school gyms and at fairs all over the country. He was my hero then when he was wearing this old tail coat, and now he was looking like an old set of tires, and he needed me. He popped a cassette into a boom box he had in the study and it came out real soft. Ethel Merman. *Annie Get Your Gun. There's No Business Like Show Business!*

"Play Zak Bendzi for me, son," Dad whispered as the Merm belted out the performer's credo. "This is show biz, Joey. Be a trouper, son, just like the old days."

I was overcome. Tears came up in my eyes. I caught a glimpse of myself in the mirror that Dad had hanging in the study. There I stood in his tailcoat, a grown man. The song, the coat, it was too much. He had made me what I was. I felt something in my throat as big and hard as an orange. My father put his arms around me.

"This is what you've been waiting for all your life. Finally, after all these years, Joey, you can be a star—sort of."

"I'll do it, Dad, I'll do it for you," I sobbed as he embraced me in a big bear hug.

"Good," said Dad, clicking off the cassette and ushering me back out to the kitchen. "Now let's talk contract."

The Amazing Raymond had worked his magic once again.

*

I slipped the coat off and set it on the couch as we went through the living room. By the time Dad and I got back to the kitchen, Violet and Hazel had become the best of friends. I could tell they had been having a serious talk because of the little wads of damp Kleenex littering the kitchen table and floor. Both of them were red-eyed and teary. They were even holding hands, with Hazel reaching out across the table and resting hers on top of Violet's.

Crying always seems to make women feel better. I wish it worked for me. I had just finished crying a bit myself, but now I felt absolutely awful. Women melt when they cry and then pull themselves back together again and feel better all over, but when I cry I know I'm in for a big letdown afterwards. Like right then I was trying to remember exactly what I had promised my father I would do. I knew I was supposed to be Zak Bendzi the next morning on Miles Kindley's radio show, but beyond that, things were still a little bit vague. Altogether I had the feeling I'd sold myself down the river.

"Dad," Hazel said to my father as we came back into the kitchen. "You've just got to hear this girl's story. It's amazing."

She quickly summarized what Violet had been telling me all the way from Porkville and everything that happened in between, all about her and Billy and high school back in West Virginia, about him upping and joining the Navy and then her finding herself pregnant, and traveling out to Norfolk after the baby was born, and then hitchhiking and the rest of what had happened to us as we made our way across the Midwest and West for the past week.

"That would make a great miniseries," Dad said. He meant it as a compliment, but Violet merely shrugged.

"Except it's not over yet," she said, hugging the baby and dabbing at her eyes again with a Kleenex. Hazel reached over and touched her on top of the hand again. "Thanks, Hazel," Violet said, then, looking at me, she added, "Hazel isn't anything like you described her, Joe. She's real nice. Being a woman and all, she understands."

"Dad," Hazel said. "We've got to help this girl. She's desperate."

Violet let loose again, crying and blubbering and grabbing for the Kleenex.

"I didn't know today was Friday already," she explained. "I got so confused out there. Billy's submarine comes in tomorrow, Saturday, and we just got to be in San Diego to meet it. I want us to be there to see him standing on the deck when they sail in, me and the baby. It'll be the very first time the baby's seen his daddy and I want it all to be so good, but now the time has come I'm so *scared*. I mean I still believe everything will work out fine, but . . ."

"It's all right, Violet," Hazel said, patting Violet's hand in a sisterly way. "You'll be fine. All you need is a little confidence boost. Let Hazel take care of everything."

Hazel picked up the portable phone lying on the table and punched in a number that she knew by heart.

"Sergio," she said, "we've got an emergency. I need a cut and a workover fast." In a couple of clipped sentences she set up an appointment for later that afternoon with her hairdresser. Sergio was not just another haircutter. He billed himself as a "Hair Sculptor," which mostly meant every time you walked in the door it cost fifty bucks plus tip. And that was only for an estimate. Getting done over at Sergio's cost more than getting a new brake job on a car, but the results were usually pretty spectacular.

"Come on, Violet," Hazel said. "Let's get you fixed up for Billy."

"If you don't mind," Violet said, "I'd kind of like a bath first. I've only had one shower this whole week, back at the pagan campground."

Violet handed Dad the baby, and Dad dandled him up and down on his knee as we talked. While Violet took her bath, Hazel and Dad and I were going to sit in the kitchen and try to hammer out a deal. We could hear the sound of water running in the bathroom, and after a few minutes we heard Violet splashing.

"I always thought you and Hazel might have one of these someday," Dad said, tickling Violet's baby and lifting him up like a sack of flour.

Hazel and I just let that remark fall on the table like a dried pea; neither of us touched it.

I looked at her and tried to remember what it was I had liked about her when we got married those seven years before. We were both so young, of course, and being twenty had something to do with it. At the time I was two years out of high school and had been getting pickup guitar jobs around the lounges in town and thought I was hot stuff. She was waitressing at the Lucky Lady. We met there, in fact, when I went into the restaurant after a gig and had bacon and eggs at three o'clock one morning. She had nice eyes, I remember that. I must have drunk fifteen cups of coffee that night waiting around for her to get off her shift, and when she did, I took her out for more coffee. I didn't sleep for the next twenty-four hours and maybe what I thought was love—the restlessness, the excitement—was only the caffeine.

That very first night, I remember, we talked about dreams and plans and all the future you have when you're twenty, and she told me she wasn't going to be a waitress all her life. She had ambition and was going to go to school to become a dealer. Then she hoped to meet some rich guy from New York or California or someplace who would fall in love with her and take her away so she'd never have to work again but could spend her time with movie stars floating around a pool in Beverly Hills or someplace with a piña colada on a raft.

And I told her how I wanted to be a big star someday and have thousands of people coming to my concerts. The more I talked, the more I believed it, until by the end of the night, as dawn was coming up over the desert and the lights along the strip were going pale the way they do in the morning, I had become bigger than the Beatles and Elvis rolled together. I had already got my picture on the cover of *Rolling Stone* and everything. It must have been a pretty good rap because she gave me her number and we went out again, lived together for a while, and eventually got married.

We were sure all our dreams were going to come true. There we were, already in the entertainment capital of the United States. People were coming in by the planefuls. Something big was bound to happen. That was the magic of Vegas. And so we hung on for a few years that way, thinking at any moment the right connection would come along and the great American slot machine called success would deliver big. In the meantime, we told ourselves, we'd pretend we were only a blackjack dealer and a backup musician, but really we were on our way to superstarville.

I don't know when it began to dawn on us that what we had was probably all we'd ever get, but sometime in the past year or two when our slice of the American pie didn't get any bigger and people all around us were hitting it big and we weren't, things began to go bad. We woke up in the afternoon with a sour taste like lemons in our mouths and hauled ourselves off to work again, playing the same songs, listening to the same jokes every night, coming home sometime after midnight smelling like smoke and stale bourbon. We could feel our life together flatten out—like when a plane accelerates for liftoff and then, after a while, the flight path levels out and the exhilaration of takeoff is gone and the tedium of steady flying sets in.

Somewhere in there we began reminding me of my parents. I saw myself becoming Dad, settling down into some mediocre lounge act like the Dead Superstar Revue for the rest of my life. You'd never make it big, but you'd never have to be real good, either. You'd only have to be entertaining enough to divert the losers who'd run out of gambling money and so came to see your show and drink what little they had left in their wallets.

I guess Hazel had more ambition than me that way. In the months since I'd left, she had parlayed that old tape of mine into big money for herself, and, at least for now, I stood a possibility of getting a bit of it for myself. I looked at her again and had to admit I needed her now more than she needed me, and that hurt like hell. I had left Vegas all those miles ago to show her something, and now I was back and she had showed me. I swallowed my pride and began to dicker for a piece of "Open Tuning." Luckily I had this going for me—I could play the guitar and Zak couldn't.

By the time Violet was done with her bath, we had the basics of a deal hammered out. I would impersonate Zak Bendzi in the morning on *New Connections* and we'd go ahead with plans for the concert tour. On Monday, we would call the lawyers and cut a deal on profits from "Open Tuning" and the tour and any spinoffs like T-shirts, videos, and key chains.

That much done, we had to start planning the concert tour.

"What we need is a gimmick," said Dad. "The song itself is good, of course, but we need to package it better, something memorable, something we can build a video around."

"How about the angel?" Violet suggested, coming back into the room and toweling down her hair. She had overheard us talking as she got out of the bath. She looked fresher and younger now than I had ever seen her. In fact, she looked brand new, the way women do sometimes after a bath and a cry.

"What angel?" Dad asked.

Violet came and took the baby back and hugged it.

"Last night," she said, "while we were driving through the desert, this angel came down and flew right beside the van for the longest time."

"What's this, Joey?" Dad asked.

"Some big bird," I said, not wanting to let on that I'd seen him, too. "Probably a condor or something."

"It wasn't any bird," Violet said. "It was a man in a white gown, only he had big white wings, and he sailed along right beside us for a whole fifteen minutes at least. You saw him, too, Joe."

"We were tired," I said.

"Angels?" said Dad. "Like from the Bible?" He put his finger beside his nose, thinking.

"I like it," said Hazel. "Miles would eat it up, too. And we've already got the angel on the CD and cassette liners. Isn't that a coincidence? It might work."

Before I could stop them, Dad started spinning off ideas. We could have backup singers, like the Shirelles or something, all dressed in white, and then they could fly me in with my guitar.

"I know the guy who does costumes over at the Follies," Dad said. "He could probably get us a deal on feathers."

"Wait a minute," I said. "It's bad enough I have to perform under Zak Bendzi's name, but I won't wear feathers. I refuse to do feathers."

"You need a gimmick, Joey," Dad said. "Look at what dying did for Elvis, greatest gimmick in the world, he's made more money since he died than he did while he was alive. Nobody's doing angels as far as I know, are they, Hazel?"

"Can't we just play the music?" I asked.

"Yeah, sure, we'll just play music, Joey," said Dad, "and we'll watch sales sink into the ocean. You got to have an angle these days. I like this angel thing."

"We've got to get Zak Bendzi on the media web, Joe," said Hazel. "It's all tied together. *People* magazine, MTV, movies, record deals, talk shows, the Internet—if you get on one you get on them all. The more outrageous the gimmick, the better. But you've got to get on the web. Zak's already on one strand with *New Connections* tomorrow, but until he climbs out a little more toward center stage, he's nowhere. How many pounds of feathers do you think we'll need, Dad?"

"He wasn't feathers all over," Violet said, "only his wings. He was exactly like the one Grandpa Tolliver told Joe about when he gave him the guitar."

"What guitar?" Dad asked.

I told him about the guitar Violet's grandfather had given me, the one with the roses all over it.

"That one they talked about in *Variety*, you mean? Let's see it," said Dad.

I went out to the van and brought it back in. When I got it out of the case, it looked different again. There didn't seem to be any more flowers on it this time, but the flowers on the front of the sound box were brighter somehow, like they were blooming in the sunlight. Only now, for the first time, I noticed that on the vines growing out of the soundhole there were also tiny thorns sprouting. The thorns weren't very big, but they were there, and I was sure they hadn't been there before.

"Grandpa said it came from an angel who drew the flowers and stuff on it," Violet said.

"It wasn't an angel," I said. "It was a Bird Boy from Iowa."

Dad perked up his ears.

"Bird Boy?" he said. "You don't mean *the* Bird Boy of Iowa, do you?"

"You've heard of him?" I asked, surprised. Dad nodded. I was shocked because I thought the Bird Boy was only something Grandpa Tolliver had cooked up out of his melon-shaped head.

"Yeah, I've heard of him," said Dad. "Remember when we were traveling with that half-ring circus back when you were little, the one where I was bumping the dog lady with the . . . ? Well, never mind that part, but I was having a drink one night with the India Rubber man, and he told me there was this Bird Boy used to travel with the circus out in Iowa with him years back. Great gimmick.

Nobody could figure out how he did the wings, they looked so realistic."

"Wow," said Hazel. "Can you talk that angel stuff on the air tomorrow? Miles will absolutely love it."

"This thing is going to be big," Dad said. "Angels! I love it. What a gimmick!"

"Come on, Violet," Hazel said, "let's go get waxed." She pulled Violet toward the door and they left.

Dad and Zak and I went back into the kitchen while the women went off to see Sergio. Dad had the baby, and it seemed the old man was getting real attached to the kid. As for me, I needed to find out more about what Zak had done with "Open Tuning" so I could fake my way through the interview with Miles Kindley the next day. But there was one problem. Computers made my head hurt worse than math did. After Zak prepped me for a while on the ins and outs of MIDI it felt like somebody was driving an ax into my forehead. I was so confused that I didn't know which end was up. Finally I panicked.

"I don't know if I can fake this well enough, guys," I said. "Miles has been to college and everything. He uses such big words that sometimes I don't know what the hell he's talking about."

"Neither does he," Dad said. "Hazel told me he used to be a sportscaster, but he was too slow on the draw to do play-by-play, so he took a weekend at Esalen or something and picked up some of the vocabulary. You can fake it, Joey. You're not a magician's son for nothing."

I still wasn't convinced. Zak tried to be helpful, in his own way.

"I'll let you borrow my *Star Trek: The Next Generation* tapes tonight," he said. "Captain Picard is always saying good stuff you can use."

"Hey, wait, I got an idea," said Dad. "What about taking along your friend Rocko?"

"Who?"

"That monk guy you showed up with, Rocko. Maybe he could go on the air with you. We could say he's Zak Bendzi's guru or something."

"His name's Rahu," I said.

"Yeah," said Dad. "I wonder what happened to him anyway? He seems to have disappeared."

*

While Hazel and Violet were gone, I stumbled out of the kitchen and fell into a bed in the guest room to try to sleep, but after about six months on the road, I couldn't sleep on a mattress anymore. It was too comfortable, and there wasn't the noise of diesel engines chuffing in the background. I realized that sometime in the past six months, I'd become undomesticated. I tossed and turned on the bed even though I was exhausted. I had closed all the blinds in the room, but it was still too light. Finally, I rolled out onto the floor, and there I fell into a deep sleep. Somewhere in the middle of it I saw the Bird Boy of Iowa riding the thermals way up in the blue sky over Nevada, spreading his arms wide out over the earth, his face beaming with a wide, serene smile. "You've got to find your place on the web," a voice said calmly. A strand of white silk shot out of the Bird Boy's palm, came down from the sky, and wrapped itself around me where I was sleeping on my back on the floor of my dad's house, only suddenly it wasn't his house anymore—it was the desert outside Las Vegas and my body lifted up off the sand in levitation, and the white silk began to wrap itself around me, spinning around my body until it formed a cocoon. I felt peaceful inside the cocoon, as if I were floating in a warm, salty sea, and then "Open Tuning" started playing somewhere, and I was bathed in a soft white light. Everything was blissful, for a moment, but then the dream went weird.

Zak Bendzi came zooming down on his flying computer. "I am the angel Zakeriel," he said, grinning and cackling as the computer hovered above me like a motorcycle at idle, "but in the field of time I am known as Zak Bendzi. It's not happening here, Joe, it's not happening in analog space and time at all, it's all happening out on The Network. You're only real if you're on The Network, Joe. Zak Bendzi is on The Network. You're nowhere. The angel Zakeriel has been digitalized, Joe, you're still analog! Hopelessly out of tune." And then he zoomed away into the sky, laughing like an idiot and trailing the sounds of humpbacked whales behind him. His voice echoed off the dome of the desert sky. "Nyaa-nya. You're still analog."

Next thing I knew, a bunch of dark-skinned women in long purple Buddhist nuns' robes unwrapped me from my cocoon. Their heads were shaved and they were speaking a foreign language. We were in the middle of the desert and the sun burned my eyes as the cocoon came off. The women stood me up—I could not seem to move—and held a full-length mirror before me. Inside the cocoon I had become Zak Bendzi! I looked like the Michelin Man, only I had a pair of big fake wings coming out of my back, old moth-eaten things with raggedy feathers. The women laughed at me, and I felt ashamed.

Zak swooped back in on his flying computer and said, "Well, I suppose we could get *real* musicians to duplicate what I did on my computer. If we had to. As a last resort. Seems kind of stupid, though. Why get human beings involved? Computers are neat. People are messy."

My dad appeared in the desert. "How do you like your new costume?" he asked.

"I want my own face back at least," I said.

Dad was wearing his bright red sequined magician's coat and he pointed at the purple nuns. I turned, only now the nuns' outfits had huge shoulder pads on them, and you could see their skin through them because the purple panels of the robes were only tied together with strings. They looked like Cher would look if she became a Buddhist nun.

"This is how they'll look on the video," Dad said.

"But I don't want to be Zak Bendzi!" I screamed.

"You *are* Zak Bendzi," Hazel said, appearing from behind a saguaro cactus. Her shoulder pads were like off a Stealth bomber.

"I'm not Zak Bendzi," I shouted again, but all the nuns in their Bob Mackey nun outfits started bowing down to me and chanting, "zzzzzzzzzzzzzaaaaaaaaaak."

"Let me out of here," I screamed.

Zak buzzed over us again in his flying computer, strafing the ground with logarithms, and I started to sweat. "You're on The Network now, Joe," he said. "If they pull the plug you're dead." And he flew off over a range of mountains.

Then Munchee Mart Marty showed up in full costume, holding a bag of blue corn chips. "This dream is being brought to you by Maya Corn Chips and Munchee Mart. You can buy real Maya Corn Chips at any Munchee Mart in America. Yes, Maya Blues, just like your Maya Mama used to make, only at Munchee Mart." My dream had commercials in it! Wasn't there anywhere you could go to get away from advertising?

I fell on my back, immobilized, and found myself looking up. The Bird Boy hung there in the sky above me, his arms outstretched like Jesus on the cross. He shook his head No. "That's not it," a voice said. "That's not it at all." And as I watched, drops of blood started flowing from his palms and came raining down out of the sky. Soon, the sand around me turned red with the Bird Boy's blood, and I woke up groaning.

*

"Well, what do you think?" Violet asked. I didn't even recognize her at first. I felt like snake guts, and my head was still reeling from the weird dream I'd had. I couldn't even remember for sure where I was. It was almost dark outside, the sky red over the desert, and Violet stood in the bathroom in front of the mirror staring at herself. When she turned from the mirror, she looked like a different person to me.

Her hair that had been all different colors when I picked her up in Porkville was now all dark and trim, not cut hard like Hazel's but soft, framing her face in a way that made her thin nose and cheeks stand out. Violet seemed a little amazed by the transformation herself. She kept touching her face and her hair as if she didn't believe it was really her. I had to give Sergio credit. He was an artist in his own way.

I'm not saying he made Violet actually look beautiful or even pretty, for that matter, but she sure looked a whole lot better than she had any time since Porkville. After you've been with somebody twenty-four hours a day for a week or so, you start to take their looks for granted and don't even really see them anymore. I guess that had happened with me and Violet.

Hazel had given Violet some money and she had gone to Penney's and bought herself a nice skirt and blouse and some new shoes, too, nothing real stylish like what Hazel would have bought for herself, but simple clothes, things a girl like Violet would think made her look good. And as I looked at her standing there in the bathroom, something weird happened. For the very first time in the week or so I had been with her, I found myself thinking of Violet Tansy as a woman instead of an unwanted growth clinging to me. I could even understand what a jughead sailor like Billy would see in her. And, I hate to admit it, I even felt a little jealous of him.

"Well, what do you think?" she asked again.

"I figure after eleven months in a Thermos bottle beneath the ocean, Billy is going to consider himself a very lucky man tomorrow." And, the odd thing is, I meant it.

She blushed and looked at herself in the mirror again.

"That's the nicest thing you've said to me since we met," she said. There was a little minute of awkward silence, and I realized she was right. All the time she was dragging me west, my mind had been heading east, and I hadn't exactly been on my best behavior with her.

She looked at herself in the mirror some more, admiring herself the way women do, standing on her toes and feeling all full of her femininity. I hadn't really thought about it much before, I guess, but only then did I stop to think about what Violet must have been through in the past year. Barely out of high school, she had gotten pregnant by a local boy who was about to go off and join the Navy and leave her alone to have the baby all by herself in that little West Virginia town they grew up in. Maybe they didn't even have a hospital there, and from what I'd seen of her family, they wouldn't have been much help. So the baby got born some-how, and a few months later, desperate, she had hit the road with him and headed to Norfolk, which was where Billy had been the last time she'd heard from him, but she didn't find him there, so she took off into the map not really knowing where San Diego was except that it must be near an ocean because her sailor boy was going to land there in ten days. And then she had the luck to run into me and climb into my van, and I had to admit as I looked at her that I hadn't been real easy on her the past week. And yet, in spite of it all, she was still a virgin, as innocent and simple, in some ways, as the day she was born, still believing everything would work out.

"I never had my legs waxed before," she said. "It kind of stung. Do you really think he'll like me?"

"You look fine," I said.

She turned to herself in the mirror again and laughed lightly.

"I can't believe all this is happening. Tomorrow all my dreams come true. And it's all because of you bringing me west. I can't thank you enough, ever, Joe."

"Yeah," I said, feeling guilty as hell about all the things I'd thought and said. It made me feel smelly and scruffy to see her looking good, and I realized that things had been so crazy since we'd gotten to Dad's that I hadn't bothered to clean myself up or shave or anything yet. I felt dirty in a lot of ways. "Hey, you wouldn't mind giving up the bathroom now, would you?"

Hazel went back to our old house and Dad had gone to work. He left a couple of comp tickets for his show, saying Violet and I should come on down later to the lounge and catch his act. I had seen it already—twenty years worth—but Violet thought it was a great idea and was aflutter with the idea of actually knowing somebody in Show Business. Seeing as how she was all dressed up, and since I had no place to go that night myself, I agreed to take her and the baby downtown later.

While I showered and shaved and changed, Violet cooked up a supper out of stuff she found in Dad's refrigerator, not that he kept much there. As a rule, he ate at one of the clubs and only kept cereal and odds and ends around the house, but Violet managed to find rice someplace and some beans and other vegetables in cans, and out of it she made a nice dinner that she cooked in a casserole dish. We sat there in the nook and ate it, just the two of us. It was the first time we had actually sat down together and eaten a real meal since breakfast back in that Indiana tollway oasis.

"This is a nice house," she said, looking around at the little ranch house. "I'd like to have a house this nice some day."

I looked around too. Dad's house was nothing special as far as I was concerned. It was a typical fifties-style ranch with low ceilings and high windows like rifle slits. Dad's taste in wall decorations leaned toward funeral home calendars, and the kitchen still had the pink stove and Kelvinator fridge that were there when we moved in.

"You might get your dream house after all," I said, taking a bite of the bean and rice mix she had put together. It was hot and tasted good in a down-home sort of way.

"All I need is that swimming pool ticket," she said. "When I get that, I'll have my dream house, and Billy and I will live in it and I'll be happy."

"You think that'll be enough?" I asked.

"What more is there?" she asked, peering at me so innocently I had to turn away and look down at the beans and rice. "Me and Billy and the baby, on a base somewhere, and I'll go with all the wives down to the laundromat every week, and we'll talk about how we're waiting for our men to come home. That's all I want. It's what's kept me going these past months. If I could get that, I'd be happy."

I looked at her sitting across from me at the table and realized that, for her, that probably was enough. And, for a moment anyway, sitting with her in the quiet kitchen, I almost thought it would be enough for me, too. But then I remembered that Hazel and I had had all that stuff for seven years, the house, the jobs, the life, all of it—even a dog—but it was never enough for us. Maybe nothing would have been.

After supper I took Violet and the baby down to the Strip. Hazel had bought the baby a regular baby carrier that afternoon, which was a good thing because the laundry basket we bought in Denver wasn't really the best thing for a kid to start out in.

The lights were bright as day along the Strip, and a steady stream of people moved along the street like a river flowing from one casino to the next, all in search of the big score. We could feel the heat from the filaments in the millions of bulbs above us on the marquees that were near to busting as they flashed on and off. From inside the casinos came the sounds of bells and sirens, the screams and whoops and cheers of the winners, the music and the rattle of dice and the whirr of the big wheels. I suppose if you stopped any one of those people walking along the Strip and asked them, they'd agree that money never bought happiness for anybody in the whole history of the world, but I'd also be willing to bet that each one of them along the Strip thought he was a special case, that money would do for him what it never did for anybody else ever.

My big dream never centered on winning at the slots, but I had dreamt of the big score, too. For me, it was to have a monster hit record and now, in a way, I had one—but it sure didn't feel like what I had expected. In fact, now that I had, in a way, gotten what I always wanted, I wasn't so sure I even wanted it anymore.

We stopped in front of the Golden Nugget, the place where the lights are the brightest and the noise is the loudest. I looked around and saw only the losers and the litter, the cigarette butts and old Keno cards blowing along the street, but Violet turned her face up into the bright blinking lights and was bathed in all the colors of the neon rainbow. Her eyes were full of it all, and she said, "This must be the most exciting, beautiful place in the whole world. I'll bet in this place anything can happen." She hugged her baby, which was wrapped in a light blanket.

Just then, we noticed a ruckus going on up the street at the Lucky Lady. A mob of people was trying to press its way through the double glass doors of the casino. They were screaming and cramming themselves through the opening like riders in the Tokyo subway at rush hour, falling all over each other and jamming any part of their bodies that they could through the door. Guards tried to keep people from trampling each other as they pressed in. Violet and I drifted over with the rest of the crowd. I recognized one of the guards from the days when I used to play back up in the Dead Superstar show.

"Damndest thing I've ever seen, Joe," he said, linking arms with another cop to form a human chain after he let us slip in. "The slot machines are going nuts inside here. People can't lose on 'em. They're all hitting at once! The crowd is going ape shit."

The inside of a Vegas casino is usually pretty wild anyway, but the Lucky Lady was absolute pandemonium. Sirens wailed. Strobe lights flashed. Twinkle lights blinked on and off. Bells rang and people screamed as coins tumbled out of the mouths of the machines like Niagara. Every single slot machine was lit up and flashing like Christmas. The coins cascaded out like rivers, so fast that people couldn't catch them. They tried to scoop them in buckets, in bags, in their bare hands, but the flow was too fast. Human beings crawled all over the floor like crazed cockroaches, trying to pick up the coins other people dropped, and sometimes those who dropped them didn't bother to bend over and pick them up because there were plenty more coming out of the machines.

"I'm going to win money for my honeymoon," Violet said, handing me the baby as she pulled a quarter out of her purse and elbowed her way up to a machine. She hit three cherries and out came two handsful of coins. I had to help her catch them all. She took another quarter, and fed it in, and she hit again. Coins came spilling out like a waterfall. She unwrapped the baby and let the quarters fall on the blanket on the floor.

Everywhere we looked, people were having trouble keeping up with all the money flowing out of the machines. If it went on much longer, we'd be ankle-deep in change, and I had visions of the coins flowing out of the machines and filling the whole room, spilling out the doors into the street, where people could shovel them right into pickup trucks. Those who couldn't get to the machines were on their hands and knees on the carpet, trying to pick up what the winners couldn't carry.

"You see?" said Violet, pumping quarter after quarter into the machine she'd cornered. "Dreams do come true, Joe Findlay. I told you so. You've only got to believe!"

It was the most bizarre scene I had ever witnessed in Las Vegas. The house staff were madly trying to rope off the slot room to keep any more people from jamming in, but the mob pushed against the rope and was getting ready to riot. Finally the security men realized there was no way they were going to keep the crowd out, and they let the rope down. People came in like locusts going for a fresh cornfield. I even got a little afraid we might get crushed to death like down in a South American soccer stadium, but somehow we didn't, and when people had won so much they couldn't carry any more, other people came up to the machines and won again.

Nobody could figure out what the hell was going on.

And then, from the middle of that swirling mass of people, I heard high-pitched laughter, the laugh of a very crazy person, I thought for a moment, the gleeful laugh of somebody who'd won so much money it drove him insane. But then I realized that I had heard that same laughter the night before, in the van, back there in the desert when the Bird Boy was flying all around us. It was Rahu!

I grabbed Violet's hand and pulled her toward the sound. There in the middle of the room, like a queen bee in the middle of a buzzing hive, stood Rahu in his purple robes and sandals, with his hands palms up in front of him, his eyes closed. He was turning in a three-hundred-and-sixty degree circle, humming, chanting, and bowing like a Tibetan prayer wheel. At his feet he had two big buckets, the kind you get with the full dinner for twelve at Kentucky Fried Chicken, and they were full to overflowing with coins from slots.

"Aummmmmmmmmmmmmmmm," he sang to the machines as he held his palms upward and bowed. No matter what direction he turned, the machines hit whenever he faced them. Lucky winners tossed more and more coins into his buckets until his feet were buried in money. And he simply stood there looking like a Buddha humming and turning, though every once in a while he looked up at what was happening, and his eyes got as big around as twin moons, and he'd let out big peals of laughter as if it was the greatest joke in the whole world.

I grabbed a Susan B. Anthony dollar off the floor and put it into a machine. I waited until Rahu was facing my direction and pulled the handle. I heard his deep guttural chant as the tumblers whirled round and round. "Aummmmmm," then, bing, bing, bing! My machine came up a winner and out poured more coins than I could catch. Then I noticed that between all the screaming and shoving and shouting, people all over the place were starting to chant and bow to the slot machines like Rahu was doing, and they kept on hitting like mad, every one. And then they laughed and Rahu laughed with them until the casino was filled with laughing, crying, happy people.

Not everyone thought it was so funny, of course.

Two guards finally shouldered their way through the crowd and grabbed Rahu, one under each arm, and started to escort him away. The crowd got ugly and started heading for the guards. That's when I stepped in because one of the guards used to do security backstage at the Dead Superstar Revue.

"You know this guy?" the guard, whose name was Dave, asked me.

"Sort of," I said.

"Well how's he doin' what he's doing?"

"All you must do is be attuned to dharma," Rahu said.

"Who's this dharma guy?" Dave asked. "What do you mean tuned? Have you got some kind of radio device here, buddy?"

I explained Rahu was a holy man who'd grown up in Tibet, too naive, in other words, to jimmy the machines, but just to make sure, the guards took him away and searched him. It didn't take long, since all he was wearing was a purple robe that didn't even cover him all the way. They were back in a minute. Meanwhile, the machines went back to normal and the crowd began to thin out.

"Nothin'," Dave said. "We couldn't find any wires or magnets or anything else on him, nothing that would affect the machines anyway."

"All you must do is be attuned to dharma," Rahu said.

"Well, we can't have that," the guard replied. "If we did, pretty soon Las Vegas would be out of business and we'd all be out of work."

"Ah," said Rahu looking down at the buckets of coins people had given him. "Rahu is most terribly sorry. You like some coins, yes? Thank you very much."

He reached down and scooped up two handfuls of coins and gave them to Dave and the other guard. Then, picking up the buckets, one under each arm, he said, "We go get some french fries now, yes, Joseph?"

We took Violet and the baby and headed for McDonalds.

"Why did you do it, Rahu?" I asked as we picked up an order of fries at the drive-thru for the trip home. "Why did you make all those machines hit at once?"

Rahu shrugged and placed a fry thoughtfully in his mouth. "How to explain? When I see all these people in casino, I see only suffering, no joy, only suffering, all caught in the net of Maya, on fire with desire, you see? The wheel that spins in casino is wheel of samsara, not wheel of dharma, and all is suffering, so I follow compassionate Buddha and for one moment only, I relieve suffering. Nothing is changed, only people think they are happy now."

The lights along the Strip lit up the night with their unreal colors. Violet was in the back counting her winnings.

Rahu dipped another fry in ketchup. His freshly shaved head reflected the lights from the Strip like a bright bowling ball. He reached over and popped "Open Tuning" into the tape deck. The sound of me playing the opening bars filled the van.

"The Dhammapadda says all life is illusion, Joseph, but somehow we must live anyway. Strange business, is it not?"

I later heard that by the end of the night, everybody in the Lucky Lady casino was chanting "Aum." No more "Seven come eleven." No more "C'mon, baby, c'mon." At the roulette wheel, the craps table, at the blackjack tables, everywhere in the place, everybody and his brother was singing "Aum." Of course, once Rahu left, the odds fell back to normal, but that didn't keep anybody from trying the chant for a couple of hours before stopping and going back to their old mantras and charms. The bosses at the Lucky Lady closed down the slot room early. They hung a sign outside that said "Technical Difficulties."

By dawn Rahu's description and picture had been faxed to every casino and hotel in Nevada.

CHAPTER SEVEN

Rahu, Violet, and the baby spent the night at my dad's, and I drove the few blocks over to Hazel's and my house. I knew it was finally time to pick up the pieces of the conversation Hazel and I had dropped when I left six months before. We had been so busy getting the business of this *New Connections* radio appearance together that we hadn't yet said one word about us and where we stood with each other. In the eyes of the law, of course, we were still married, but that tenuous connection was about all we had holding us together—that and the as-yet only verbal agreement we had made about my being Zak Bendzi the following day.

The house had a strange feel to it. At first, stepping through the door was like going back in time, as if the past six months had not happened. Every house has its own smell—its own mix of cooking odors, the smell of old clothes and perfumes—and that smell came back to me immediately and made me question if I had ever left. The furniture had not been changed, either, and for a moment, I half-convinced myself Hazel and I would not even have to have the conversation we had both been avoiding all day. But it was the middle of the night, about three A.M., the time when the minds of those who are still awake get tracked into the dark corners they've managed to stay out of during daylight.

Hazel sat up alone in the living room with her legs making a bridge between the sofa and the coffee table. She had been waiting for me, unable to sleep. Zak was in the guest room, and I could hear him tapping away at his computer. Hazel said he spent the whole night on Internet sometimes.

We attempted to chitchat for a few minutes. I told her about Rahu and the Lucky Lady's slot machines and how Violet won enough money to pay for her honeymoon. But the conversation kept collapsing back on itself until Hazel finally said, "It hurt like hell the night you left, Joe. You don't think you can simply walk back in here after six months and start over, do you?"

"I'm not that stupid," I said.

"Good, there's coffee in the kitchen. We need to talk."

As it turned out, I was not the only one who had felt in a rut that past year or so. Hazel, too, had grown tired of the Lucky Lady, tired of dealing out blackjack hands to drunks every night, tired of the same jokes and half-witted passes. As long as she stayed at the Lucky Lady dealing cards, she'd have a steady income, but that life had started to look to her like a long, dark tunnel. She had endured her boredom and desperation a little better than I had, but my leaving forced her to take a good look at where her life was headed.

When Zak came to her with the *Open Tuning* tape, she saw a chance to get ahead of the game a little. She had done some Zen once years before, and after I left she got into a women's support group. That, along with a trip to a New Age bookstore, allowed her to fake her way through interviews like the one she'd had with Miles Kindley on *New Connections*.

By an hour before dawn, we were both totally wired with caffeine and not much closer to figuring out where we stood, except we both knew things couldn't ever go back to the way they were before I left. We agreed that even if we couldn't stay married to each other, we could at least work together long enough to make *Open Tuning* an even bigger hit than it already was.

About four-thirty, we unplugged Zak from the Internet, picked up Rahu and Violet, and said goodbye to Dad. He handed me the black tail coat from his act, and I tucked it under the van's backseat.

Among the other things Hazel had discovered in the six months since I'd left was a love for motorcycles. Now she led the way to L.A. on her Yamaha with Zak holding on for dear life behind her. She roared across the desert flats like a thunderbird, scaring off every lizard within a hundred miles of 1-15. Violet, the baby, Rahu, and I followed in the van, trying to keep Hazel's red taillight in sight since the old van couldn't hope to keep pace with her. Not that there was much of any place to go out there except straight ahead. As light broke, we had already driven between Death Valley and the Devil's Playground, past the Soda Mountains and through the landscape of dry lakes out in the desert. We may as well have been on the dark side of the moon. No angels flew beside us in the desert dawn.

We had to be at the radio studio at UCLA by eleven in the morning for the *New Connections* interview with Miles Kindley. The station would have a satellite uplink to the crucial Saturday morning National Public Radio audience. After that, I was going to drive Violet down to San Diego and deliver her and the baby to Billy. We could have bought her a bus ticket, I suppose, but having gone over two thousand miles with her already, a couple hundred more didn't seem like much trouble. Besides, I couldn't resist seeing this Billy who was such an incredible guy that a girl would take off across a whole continent for him.

We actually got to the studio before Miles, who showed up about five minutes late, panting and sweating and carrying a conga drum with a goatskin head. He had a pony tail, of course, but other than that, he didn't look anything like I expected him to. It's that way with radio people.

On the air, Miles had a deep radio voice, the sort that sounds like it's coming out of the middle of Carlsbad cavern. I expected some huge guy with a big head of hair and half-closed eyelids, but, in reality, Miles was a short and nervous guy with a close-cropped red beard. He was scrawny, like a plucked starved chicken or one of those marathon runners who run so much they don't have anything but a thin layer of muscle over their bones, and their skin flaps on them when they move. He was the sort of guy who never stops jiggling, like he was wired on coffee or something. He wore a red bandana around his neck and he took it off and wiped the sweat from his forehead.

"Zak Bendzi?" he asked, reaching out to shake my hand.

"*The* Zak Bendzi?" It was weird to hear that radio voice coming out of such a small, thin body.

Behind me the real Zak started to jump ahead, but Hazel held him back.

"Yeah," I said, reaching out and grabbing Miles's hand.

"You have *no* idea," he said pumping my hand with both his hands, as if I had been a long-lost relative at a funeral or something. Then he dropped it and swept his arm at Rahu, Violet, and the others. "And this is your *entourage?*" he asked. Before I could set him straight, he suddenly put his palms together and bowed to Rahu and mumbled a few words in Tibetan. It seemed Miles recognized Rahu from someplace, maybe from the time he interviewed the Dalai Lama on *New Connections*. Rahu rattled something back in his native language, and I could see Miles didn't have a clue as to what he was talking about. Probably Rahu was asking if there were any french fries nearby.

"I've just been drumming," Miles announced. "They have several powerful men's tribal groups here in L.A. Do you drum, Zak?"

"No," I said. "I play guitar."

"Oh, right, you leave the drumming up to the Samsara Consort, eh? Well, as for me, I've been getting in touch with my deep masculinity lately. The shamanistic impulse lies dormant in every male, don't you think? A man who doesn't drum can't be in touch with the dance of the universe, can he?"

I mumbled "I guess not" or something equally bright as Miles put his arm around me and ushered me into the studio. We only had a few minutes until air time, and the technicians quickly sat us down at a low table with boom mikes hanging over it, did a few sound checks, and got ready to start. The live-link telephone lines were wired direct into the headphones, and through the glass wall of the studio I could see Hazel, Rahu, Violet, the baby, and Zak listening on the studio monitors. It looked like they were in a fish tank.

"Right after the signature, we're going to go into about a minute of 'Open Tuning,' and then we'll segue into the live discussion. I want to talk about the song first and hold off on the authorship question until we get the phone lines lit, okay, Zak?" Miles asked. He had to repeat "Okay, Zak" two or three times before I remembered *I* was supposed to be Zak Bendzi now.

"Yeah, sure," I mumbled.

In the tech booth, the director was counting down. Five, four, three. Two seconds of silence and then the mellow New Age signature tune of *New Connections* started. A pre-recorded tape of Miles's velvety voice announced the title of the show and then we were on.

"Our guest today is Zak Bendzi, composer of 'Open Tuning,'" said Miles in his New Age voice, something like the way you might talk if you'd been drugged for about three days. All trace of the usual nervous Miles was gone. "Welcome, Zak."

I made some sort of grunt. "Hi."

"We're going to take a listen to 'Open Tuning' right now, Zak, though I'm sure to our listening audience it needs no introduction, but it should set the tone for our discussion this hour, all right?"

I nodded.

Suddenly I heard a sharp click in my left ear and Hazel's voice cut into my headphone. Apparently there was a studio interlink so she could talk to me without going on the air herself.

"You're on the radio, Joseph, you can't just nod, say something."

"Oh, yeah," I mumbled as the guy in the tech booth put on the *Open Tuning* CD.

There it was again, me in the bathroom playing the opening bars and then, after a minute or so, Zak's digitalized humpbacked whale calls and wolf yelps, tabla music and chanting.

After about a minute, the song faded out and we were back on the air.

"Tell us about 'Open Tuning,' Zak," Miles said. "So many of our listeners, myself included, have been inspired by this song. It's reminded people of mountains, of the temple at Angkor Wat, of zen gardens, of the architecture of Chartres. What inspired *you*? Where were you when the idea first came to you?"

"In the bathroom," I said.

Miles fumbled. His eyelids went up for a moment. "The bathroom, surely you're joking."

"No," I said. "I used to sit in my bathroom back in Las Vegas and write. I liked the acoustics."

Hazel cut in again. I looked out through the studio window. Her face was as sharp as a hatchet.

"Get serious, Joseph," she snapped. "People out there think 'Open Tuning' is mystical. Get cosmic or sales will go down the sewer."

"Um, well, to tell the truth," I said, "I woke up from this dream. I heard it in a dream first."

"Aha!" said Miles.

"I only worked it out in the bathroom for the echo effect. I wanted to get it on tape before the idea disappeared."

"Before consciousness, as it always does, eats the contents of our dream life."

"Uh, right."

The phone beside us lit up.

"We have a caller from Minnesota," said Miles, opening the line. "Welcome, Minnesota, you're New Connected."

"Yeah," came the voice. "Listen, like I was listening to that section of 'Open Tuning' and I was like wondering if the Neoplatonic Christic analog I sense in the underlying harmonic is intentional, or do you think it arose from the collective unconscious?"

"Huh?" I said.

"Would you mind repeating the question?" Miles asked.

"Well, it's basically simple," said the guy. "I sense the coming of the cosmic Christ here and was wondering if you, Zak Bendzi, like ever saw God."

"I've seen pictures of him," I said, still trying to figure out the question. "Old guy with a beard, right?"

"Joseph!" Hazel snapped.

I looked up in panic. What was I supposed to say anyway?

"We have a caller from Des Moines," Miles said, flicking a button. "Greetings, Des Moines, you're New Connected."

"Yeah," said Des Moines. "The heavy breathing that occurs at the end of the track, right after the songs of the humpbacked whales, it reminded me of the union with the shakti, you know the Hindu concept of the inner lover, the *lingam* and *yoni* coming together to form the whole cosmic consciousness, am I on to something here or what?"

"I don't know," I said. Hazel rolled her eyes, and Miles frowned at me. Suddenly I started breaking out in flop sweat. I mean it suddenly occurred to me that what people liked about "Open Tuning" wasn't the part I had written, after all. It was all Zak's computerized stuff that they were raving about. And so there I was, on the air, live on national radio, thinking I was going to talk about *my* song, and all people wanted to talk about was what Zak Bendzi had done to it. As I listened to my own voice over the headphones, I realized I was sounding like an idiot. My mouth started going dry and my lips began to feel like they were made of old Goodyear tires. I felt like I was getting dropped in the old velvet bag again, sucked up the old black tube into the dizzy place of the arrowhead trick.

Call after call came in with people gushing all over "Open Tuning," telling how it made them cry or laugh or made them feel in touch with things they usually didn't feel, and as they talked, I started to feel more and more out of it, like I had missed something on the album they all heard. Maybe there was something to this after all.

And I realized even though I had written this song everyone said was so spiritual, I didn't really seem to know what it was all about. I must have been turning seasick green because Hazel came on the headset and talked to me in an almost motherly way.

"Don't panic, Joe," she said. "We'll talk you through this."

I was now in one of those old movies where the passenger has to land the plane after the pilot dies. Hazel and Rahu were like the ground crew in the tower calling in instructions. Whenever I got fumblemouth, Hazel or Rahu fed me something mystical to say. Zak filled in the technical details.

One caller said, "Did you purposely attune the rhythm track to alpha wave patterns?"

"The mind is like a river," Rahu said to me over the headphones.

"Uh, the mind is like a river," I repeated. "It, uh, flows, sometimes fast and sometimes slow, there are rapids and deep holes, and each has its own rhythm."

"Oh," said the guy. "Now I get it."

That was good, I thought, because I didn't, even though by the end of the hour I was sounding like a switched-on swami. Between Miles calling me Zak all the time and my trying to repeat what Hazel, Zak, and Rahu were telling me through the headphones, I was feeling like a wooden head yakking away about stuff I didn't know anything about. What I *did* know about was playing the guitar, and I wished I had one in my hand right then so that I wouldn't have to go on talking of things I didn't really have a clue about. By the end of the hour with Miles, I knew there was no way I could do this in town after town on the *Open Tuning* tour. Hazel had it all planned out, but all I wanted to do was get the hell out of the studio because the little glass booth had started to feel like a gas chamber. There was only one big question left, and Miles finally asked it.

"So now," said Miles, with only about ten minutes left in the program, "now we come to the question that prompted this special broadcast of *New Connections*. As you know, Zak, there have been reports in newspapers over the past few days saying that an unknown musician named Joe Findlay really wrote 'Open Tuning.' Some people have grown concerned. 'Open Tuning' is, after all, a very spiritual piece of work, it has opened inner gateways for people, and it would be very crushing to them to think that even a breath of scandal or impropriety was involved with this song. So now, Zak Bendzi, the question. Who wrote 'Open Tuning'?"

I looked through the studio wall and saw Hazel standing there. I geared myself up to tell the truth. I wanted the world to know I wrote the song and that I was Joe Findlay. Then, looking through the smoky glass of the studio wall, I seemed to see, standing behind Hazel and Rahu and the others, the angel of Iowa. Him again! He was there but not there, a ghostly image behind the glass, hovering in the dim light, looking at me from where nobody else could see him. My mouth opened, I wanted to speak, but suddenly it was like my lips weren't connected to my brain anymore. I was seeing an angel, a being from another realm! I did a Ralph Kramden for a couple of seconds, "Hamada, hamada, hamada."

"Pardon me?" said Miles.

I blinked my eyes shut and looked again. The Bird Boy was gone. I licked the inside of my mouth, trying to get some moisture back and to make sure that my tongue could still move.

"I wrote it," I said.

"And you are?"

"I am . . ."

I looked again at the window. I couldn't really tell if the Bird Boy was there or not, but I got to thinking: *What difference did it make, after all, who really wrote the song?* I knew I wrote it and so what if it went out over Zak Bendzi's name? It was still me playing it there on the album and somebody out there in Ohio or Pennsylvania or someplace couldn't care less whether Zak Bendzi was himself or was me. What was important was the song itself and what it was doing to people. I mean, people had never come at me with questions about the meaning of life like they were doing now, as if I was expected to know something about it because I'd written a few notes and chords. And after that burst of angelic logic, I blurted out the following:

"I am Bak Zendzi."

"What?" asked Miles.

"I mean, I am Zak Bendzi."

My hands flew up to my lips. What had I done? I had sold myself up the river. I, Joe Findlay, had become Zak Bendzi, live, over National Public Radio.

"And this Joe Findlay we've read about, the one who claims to have written 'Open Tuning,' who is he?" asked Miles.

"Joe Findlay," I said, "is a liar and a maniac."

"Thank you, Zak," Miles said. "Thank you so much. We have a call from Santa Fe. Hello, Santa Fe, you're New Connected."

*

"That's it," I said, charging out of the studio after *New Connections* was off the air. "I'm through with this Zak Bendzi routine. I'm done lying, Hazel, you hear me? No

more. That was the worst hour of my life. If you want a
dummy, hire Charlie McCarthy."

"You did fine," Hazel said. "This is only the beginning,
Joe. Besides, from now on it's mostly performing. Zak is
almost done programming the act for you."

"I don't want to be programmed," I said. "I want to be a
musician, not a piece of computer software."

The word *software* must have caught Zak's attention
because he said, "I'm almost done digitalizing 'Open Tuning'
and reconfiguring the old album. By the time I'm done with
it, we'll have enough material for a whole concert and two
more CDs, and you won't have to play a note."

"I hope lightning strikes your fucking computer," I
hissed.

"It's on a hard disk," he said. "Lightning won't affect it."

We spent a few more minutes arguing there in the studio,
and finally I said, "Look, I need time to think about this,
Hazel, I don't know if I can be Zak Bendzi. I think I'd rather
just be me."

"Well, fine," Hazel said. "Go on being Joe Findlay for the
rest of your life, see if I care, but if you walk out on this,
you're walking out on a once-in-a-lifetime opportunity."

I knew she was right, of course, but somehow I simply
couldn't bring myself to admit it.

There was a moment of silence as we all realized there was
nothing more to say on the subject right then. I wanted to be
done with it all and be on the road again with no obligations,
no people, no nothing. I was ready to go, all right, all the way
to the moon if I had to, in order to get someplace where
nobody had ever heard of Zak Bendzi or Hazel or Joe Findlay
or "Open Tuning."

"Does this mean we can go look for Billy now?" Violet
asked softly.

"Yeah," I said. "Let's go look for Billy."

And Rahu said, "I can come, too, yes?"

*

The freeways out of Los Angeles gradually narrowed from a hundred lanes down to only about fifty with traffic flying by us faster than the Tokyo-to-Kyoto bullet train. Rahu, Violet, the baby, and I joined the flow of chrome and paint as best we could and went south on I-5 toward San Diego.

As soon as we left the parking lot of the radio station, Violet dug out her travel bag and pulled out all the amulets and scapulars and good-luck charms she had brought and began to rub them between her fingers with her eyes closed. She checked to make sure she had her unicorn powder, and she kept fiddling with the charm around her neck.

Before we left Vegas, she had dressed up in the outfit from Penney's that she and Hazel had bought the day before. Now—in between prayers—she kept flipping down the front visor and looking at herself in the little mirror there, fussing with her hair and combing it this way and then that and not having much luck, it seemed, getting herself to look exactly the way she wanted for Billy. Once the baby cried and she had to feed it, and she was very very careful to make sure no milk or baby puke got on her new blouse. She wanted everything to be perfect, but the closer we got to San Diego, the more nervous she was getting, it seemed, until she couldn't stand it any more.

To tell the truth, I hated to see her this way. Her optimism about Billy and her faith in what would happen once she got to San Diego had carried us over two thousand miles against stupid odds. Maybe seeing how far my own reality, with "Open Tuning," was falling short of my dreams made her more skeptical of her own success.

Finally I asked what the matter was, even though I figured I already knew the answer.

She sighed and bunched up her fists in her lap.

"I'm scared," she said simply.

"Of what?"

"I'm scared Billy won't like me any more."

She bit her lips for a minute, then looked out the side window at the flow of traffic to hide the fact she was almost crying.

"Hey," I said, trying to cheer her up as best I could. "You look great, Violet, you look beautiful."

She shook her head.

"No, really," I said. "You're ready for anything. Hey, you got your legs waxed and your hair looks great. Billy will be all over you in a minute."

She turned to me and tried to smile, but I could see her face was bunched up and scared, and the only thing that was keeping her from crying was that she didn't want to ruin the mascara job Hazel did on her.

"I haven't seen Billy for over a year now and people change," she said, "especially when they're down in a submarine for eleven months. I'm scared to death that Billy went and changed on me. He wrote me a letter right before he left and said he'd always love me no matter what, but what if he sees me and he *doesn't* like me anymore, and what if he says he won't marry me? Then what have I got, huh? I'm just stuck out here with a baby and no life."

"There's always the dream house," I said.

"I haven't got the swimming pool yet," she said.

I was about tell her not to give up hope—imagine *me* saying that—when Rahu, who had been sleeping in the back with the baby, woke up and crawled up to the front of the van like a big dog.

"I think we get off here, yes?" he said, nodding and smiling his big all-purpose smile that made up for all the demands he put on you because he didn't speak English very well.

"No," I said. "We've got a couple more hours yet. We aren't anywhere near San Diego."

"Excusing to pardon," Rahu said, smiling his idiot grin, "but here is fooding exit." He pointed up to an exit sign that showed the crossed knife and fork symbols for food. "Rahu's body is like donkey, must eat, yes?"

"Is this for dharma again?" I asked.

"No," he said, "It is for french fries."

I realized none of us had eaten since we left Vegas eleven hours before, so I pulled off. I didn't even notice what exit it was, but it turned out to be San Juan Capistrano. Not that it made any difference to Rahu. His eyes lit on the first restaurant that was likely to have his favorite food, and he told me to make a beeline for it, not in those exact words, but I got the message clearly enough. It didn't matter to me where we ate, so we pulled into a place right across from the old mission and grabbed some lunch.

Violet pecked away at her food, but she was too nervous to eat. I told her to try because she needed to keep her strength up for Billy, so she dipped a couple of french fries in ketchup, but from the way she chewed them I could tell they probably tasted like cardboard to her.

The old mission stood across the street, tan and beautiful. It was half broken down with the walls tumbling all over the place, which only made it look more intriguing. There was a cactus garden in the front, and the tourists stood around taking pictures of the doves pecking at the seeds and stones on the hot pathways. The swallows flitted, twittering, from the holes in the adobe wall where they nested.

After lunch, which she didn't finish, Violet said she wanted to visit the mission, and I went with her while Rahu said he was going for a walk. He said he had been to the mission once before when the Dalai Lama passed through and didn't feel the need to go again. I wondered why Violet wanted to visit a tourist spot when Billy was only a couple of hours away, but it turned out she didn't want to go there for the gift shop.

Instead, she carted the baby and her bag to the mission church and went inside the sanctuary through the heavy wooden door. She wanted to pray.

The church was cool and dark inside. The light filtered in from little slit windows up high, and it seemed at first like we were all alone in a big cave, and then our eyes got used to the dimness and we could see other people shuffling around in the near-deserted church.

Hanging up in front at the holy end was a Spanish-style Jesus, his body all distended, with red blood flowing down his limbs. Mexican churches are full of that kind of Spanish-style suffering. It all seemed dark and frightening to me. But Violet didn't go up to the main altar end. Instead, she carried the baby over to a side altar where there were about a thousand candles in colored jars burning in front of a statue of Mary and the baby Jesus. Violet set her travel bag down on the floor and rooted around in it for change. She came up with some coins and slipped them into the slot of a tin box on the rail in front of the statue. The money made a loud clanking noise that echoed through the whole inside of the old church.

There were big candles that looked like they would burn for a week and then there were smaller ones that would burn perhaps for a day. She picked up a box of matches and reached for a short candle. I guess she figured she only needed luck until she got through her meeting with Billy that afternoon. If I were her, I would have taken the big one, but I didn't say anything.

She didn't make the sign of the cross or do anything Catholic, and she didn't kneel down or pray or anything, as far as I could tell. She just stood with her baby and stared at the statue of Mary and her baby for a few minutes without saying a word. That appeared to be enough because she turned to me and nodded and said she was ready to go.

"I didn't think you were Catholic," I said when we got outside. It was bright and I had to squint in the sunlight.

"I'm not," she said, "but I need some big magic today. They got big magic in those old churches. While I stood there looking at Mary and her baby, I realized everything's going to be all right."

Violet glowed after we left the church, as though simply lighting a candle and looking at the statue had taken away all her fear. When she got in the van, she held the baby in her lap and looked straight ahead now, sure everything was going to work out fine. She was ready for Billy, and she was certain once again that everything was going to work out the way she had planned it.

From her travel bag, she pulled a piece of paper that had been folded so many times it was like cloth. She showed it to me. It listed the naval base and the dock where Billy's submarine was due to come into that afternoon. If we pushed, we might make it in time to see his ship come in.

Meanwhile, Rahu came waddling back down the street. He had brought his buckets of coins from the casino and was carrying one of them under his arm. When he needed money, he scooped into it and asked whoever was taking the money to take what he needed. He paid for lunch that way and then told the waitress to tip herself by grabbing a fistful of change. Now he had the bucket in one hand and a Munchee Mart Big Gulp in the other as he came down the street towards us. I honked the horn to get his attention, but he was in no hurry. He paused once to put a nickel into an expired parking meter. Some tourists stopped him to take his picture. They probably thought he was a monk from the mission or something, and he obliged them by standing in his mirrored shades with his big bucket of money from the Lucky Lady under his arm.

Finally he reached the van and slid open the side door.

"You may be wanting such a thing," he said, handing Violet a Munchee Mart Dream House ticket he had picked up with his Big Gulp. It was one of those silvered over kind where you have to rub away the coating with a quarter to see what you won. Rahu gave her a quarter from his bucket and she went to rub off the silver but then she stopped and said, "Not yet. I just *know* it's the swimming pool, but I'm not going to rub it off until I see Billy," and all the rest of the way to San Diego she sat there with that ticket in her hand, holding it tight and looking straight ahead with a special light in her eyes.

*

Of course, finding Billy wasn't as easy as we thought. First we went to the place where Violet's note said he would be, but his sub wasn't there. The Navy being what it was, it had rerouted him, and his submarine was actually docked a couple of miles away. It had come in that morning already, and the guard at the gate said everybody who was going ashore had already gone ashore, and that included Billy.

Now, looking for Billy in a small town in West Virginia would probably not have been too difficult, but looking for one particular sailor in a city that has maybe fifty thousand of them crawling around in various stages of inebriation was almost impossible.

After twenty thousand leagues under the sea, the sailors of the u.s.s. *Trident* had hit the shore and scattered like roaches when you turn on the light in the kitchen, and I didn't see any way we were going to find Billy, especially since none of us knew our way around San Diego.

"We *will* find him," Violet said about five hundred times as we spent a couple of hours driving around aimlessly through the town and suburbs. "I know we will. Everything will work out right."

As for me, I was about to give up hope altogether when I happened to look up and see a billboard for aluminum siding.

"Swami Jody!" I said.

"What?" said Violet.

"Remember Fagan said that he was going to work with Swami Jody, the guy who was the Billy Graham of aluminum siding out here? That's his ad up there."

"So what?" asked Violet.

"So we're looking for somebody who knows where to get cheap beer in San Diego, right?"

"So?"

"So who would know better than our old friend Fagan, eh?"

We phoned Swami Jody's ashram in Chula Vista and, sure enough, Fagan the Pagan was in residence. He had just come back from a day of siding a house in La Jolla ("Big house, good vibrations, man") and said he would be more than happy to help us find Billy. Actually, what he said when I explained what we were up to was, "Outrageous, man! I put myself at the service of the great god Eros. I will be like an arrow from Kama's bow, man, and then when we've found the dude, let's you and me go get majorly blasted and talk about old times, eh?"

Swami Jody's ashram looked pretty much like all the other aluminum-sided ranch houses around it in the subdivision. The Pagan hadn't changed a bit since we left him on I-80 back there in Nebraska, except that, like all of Swami Jody's followers, he had shaved his head. The state police had picked him up for being sky-clad on the roadside, but after half an hour of questioning he drove them so crazy that the cops all chipped in and gave him some old clothes and a bus ticket to Omaha. From there he flew direct to San Diego and Swami Jody's.

"So where is this lost son of Neptune?" Fagan asked as he climbed into the van. He was wearing a saffron-colored mechanic's jumpsuit with "Swami Jody's Siding" written on the back. Sitting in the van, with his newly shaved head, he looked like Rahu's long-lost twin brother, and the two of them bowed to each other with palms together.

"That's what we were hoping you might tell us," I said. "Where would a sailor go on his first day ashore?"

Fagan rubbed his hand over the stubble on his scalp.

"What you're looking for," he said, thoughtfully, "is the sort of place filled with a wild-eyed desperation, you know? You've got to tune into the aspect that these poor pilgrims have been at sea for a long time without women. You got a picture of the dude?"

Violet pulled out Billy's service picture, the one she'd showed me back in Ohio, and Fagan sniffed it like a dog would do.

"I think we can do it," he said. "I'm getting vibes."

"I don't want vibes," I said. "I want to know where a horny sailor goes as soon as he gets off a ship."

"Whoa up," said Fagan, "This psychic search stuff can't be rushed." He turned to Violet. "Now is Billy A.M. or F.M.?" he asked.

"What?" she said.

"His vibes. A.M. or F.M.?"

Violet didn't understand.

"Definitely A.M.," I said.

"Good," said Fagan. He licked the back of Billy's picture with his long red tongue and stuck it to the middle of his forehead. He sat down on the foam mattress in the back in a lotus position and closed his eyes. After a minute, Fagan said, "Stand by, folks, something coming in here." He tapped the side of his bald head as if he were fine-tuning the frequency. "Whoa," he said suddenly. "Wild vibes. We'd better hurry."

"You have an idea where he might be?" I asked.

"I do indeed, pilgrim," he replied. "Put up your shields, brothers and sister, we're headed for Rosecrans Avenue!"

He made a noise like the sound of automatic car windows going up—"neep"—and raised his hands alongside his head. "Don't worry, little lady," Fagan said to Violet. "We'll get you to your man in no time." He reached out and patted her on the shoulder, then said to Rahu, "A little traveling music, Rama," and the two of them began to chant. "Turn right at the light, James," he said to me, and I did.

*

Rosecrans Avenue had everything a sailor needed to make him feel right at home after a long tour at sea. There were pizza joints, tattoo parlors, bars, and more working girls in tight micromini skirts and high-heeled boots than you could shake a dozen sticks at.

"My Billy wouldn't be down here," Violet said in a shocked voice as we cruised up and down the street, looking at every sailor in a white suit staggering along the pavement.

Fagan shushed her from the back seat and kept on chanting. He still had Billy's picture stuck over his third eye and was moving his head back and forth like a radar dish.

"We're getting close," he said. "I figured he'd be down here or over at Midway. Now I'm sure he's in the neighborhood."

Rahu had given up chanting with Fagan and was staring goggle-eyed out the back window.

"We stop here, yes?" he said, pressing his nose against the glass.

I doubted whether he had ever been down in this part of town with the Dalai Lama's entourage.

We drove past a topless bar called Lady G's, and suddenly Fagan started beeping like a smoke detector.

"Neep-neep-neep! Park the van," he said. "We're right on top of him. I can feel it."

Two or three sailors spilled out of the door of Lady G's with some brightly colored girls twined around their arms like sweet pea vines. The blinking neon sign above the door showed a naked woman—Lady Godiva herself—riding on the back of a white horse, and photos in a showcase under the marquee showed Lady G—or someone dressed up exactly like her—doing amazing things with a stuffed horse on stage.

"My Billy wouldn't never be in a place like that," Violet said. "Let's get out of here right now."

But Fagan merely tapped the picture on his forehead and said calmly, "The third eye does not lie, little lady. He's in there."

Believe it or not, I was able to find a parking spot less than a block away, and I volunteered to do some preliminary scouting. Rahu was right behind me all the way.

"I see America is most amazing country," he said as we arrived at the door of Lady G's. He looked at the grainy black-and-white photos of the topless dancers inside and said, "I think we go see show, yes?"

But when we got to the door, a big burly doorman in a black T-shirt stopped him.

"Can't you read, buddy?" the doorman asked, jerking his thumb at a sign on the door. "No shirt, no shoes, no service." Rahu was wearing sandals, but his purple monk's robes only covered one shoulder and so half of his chest was bare. I figured his monk's robe could count for a shirt, but the bouncer had his own definition of what a shirt was, so we got nowhere.

"He's a visiting foreign dignitary," I said. "He's a lama, like the Dalai Lama."

"I don't care if he's a rama-lama-ding-dong," the bouncer said. "No shirt, no service. It's bad enough he's wearing a dress—this ain't that kind of place. In fact, dressed the way he is, he might get himself beat up in there, so consider I'm doing you a favor."

"We merely wish to buy french fries," Rahu said, peeking in the door every time it opened. The air was blue with smoke and the purple lights they used for the stage show.

Every time the door opened, a wave of sound washed over us like a six-foot curl on Malibu beach, and you could catch glimpses of the topless waitresses carrying their trays of beer from table to table. I doubted the first thing on Rahu's mind was really french fries this time.

As best I could, I tried to explain to Rahu why men going into Lady G's had to wear T-shirts while the women working there didn't have to wear anything at all except G-strings, but I don't think he fully understood the message. I sent him back to the van while I plunked down the cover charge and went in to look for Billy.

I didn't for a minute believe in Fagan's psychic radar, but Lady G's did look like the sort of place a sailor coming up from a deep dive might gravitate toward. Nude dancers stood on nearly every table top, their G-strings full of bills the sailors stuffed in. Over in the corner was Lady G's version of a salad bar, with a near-naked girl sitting in a bathtub full of salad fixings under a plexiglass top. She sat with her breasts in the lettuce and made you up a salad to go with your burger and beer. Everything else was wall-to-wall sailors, whooping, shouting, drinking, and grabbing, a sea of white uniforms inhaling beer as fast as they could.

It would be tough trying to sort Billy out of the crowd, but finally I saw him, sitting way in the back, in a booth with a couple of other submariners who were deeper into their beer mugs than they had ever been in the ocean.

All the way from Porkville, Violet had been building Billy up, staring at his picture and telling me about how smart and brave he was, about how sensitive and handsome he was. Of course, the reality was less than the dream.

The Billy I saw in Lady G's had big buck teeth, and his hair had been cut in a fade with white sidewalls up the side, which made his ears stand out like loving-cup handles. He had red zits on his forehead, and his large Adam's apple was scratched from where he'd almost shaved it off. He was far

from handsome, but he wasn't so ugly that a hundred dollar
hooker wasn't hanging on his arm and laughing at his every
joke as if he was the funniest thing since David Letterman.
There was a forest of beer bottles in front of them, and Billy
was showing the girls and his friends how he could roll up a
paper napkin, start it on fire, and send it off like a rocket
right up to the ceiling. I didn't think Violet would like to
find him that way, but I didn't go up to Billy and say anything right then because it wasn't my life and it really wasn't
my business. I had only agreed to help Violet find Billy and
we had found him, such as he was.

I got my hand stamped at the door so I could get back
into Lady G's, and I made my way back to the van through
the gauntlet of retching sailors and street walkers. Fagan,
Violet, and the baby were all out on the sidewalk waiting for
me, but Rahu was nowhere to be seen. I hoped he wasn't out
on the street somewhere walking alone.

"Is my Billy in there?" she asked.

I nodded. "He's in there with two other sailors and . . ."

"It's probably his friends who made him go in there," she
said, trying to reassure herself.

"Yeah," I said. I didn't see any point in adding anything
because I figured it was something she needed to see for herself. If I said anything at all, she'd only get mad at me again
for downgrading Billy, but I also figured it would be better if
I went in with her. Any woman walking alone into Lady
G's—even if she had a baby in her arms—could be in for a
lot of hassle.

Just then Rahu stepped out of the van. "We go now in,
yes?" he asked. I had to do a double take. Over his purple
monk's robes, Rahu had put on the old tail coat my dad
had given me the day before. Under his arm, Rahu held a
bucket of money from the Lucky Lady. He looked like a
cross between Mahatma Ghandi, Fred Astaire, and
Colonel Sanders.

"Wild threads, man," said Fagan.

"This will be okay, yes?" asked Rahu. "I have shirt, I have shoes, I get service, yes?"

There were already three or four hookers surrounding us, drawn to Rahu's money bucket the way flies go after cinnamon buns.

"You may get more than you bargained for, Rahu," I said, and we headed for the door with the hookers trailing.

Rahu got in with no trouble this time. One look at his bucket of money was all the bouncer needed. Fagan grabbed a handful of coins from the bucket, paid the cover for us all, and dove through the door with Rahu in tow. Violet, being an escorted lady, got in free, but before we went in to Lady G's, she held me back a minute.

"I guess this is good-bye, Joe," she said.

"I hadn't thought about it," I said. "But I guess it is. After this, it's you and Billy."

In her J.C. Penney outfit, she looked all out of place there on the Avenue. Compared to the girls in miniskirts and hot-colored tube tops, she looked as plain as the countryside. Even with the makeup Hazel had put on her that morning, she looked as fresh as a sunrise in Iowa, and all of a sudden I had this weird feeling right down in the middle of my chest. If I'd been a few years older, I would have thought I was having a heart attack, but I knew it couldn't be that. It hurt about the same, though.

"I want to thank you for bringing me and the baby this far," Violet said.

"Don't mention it," I mumbled. I wanted to tell her she was too good for Billy, but it wasn't my place. She started toward the door, but then turned back.

"One more thing I want to ask," she said. "I know I asked a lot of you in the past ten days, and you've been real kind, but there's one more thing." She hesitated and then said, "If you're in Las Vegas, will you play for me and Billy's wedding?"

She started to cry then, and the mascara was running down her face, and I took out a hankie that was pretty clean and let her use it to wipe off all the stuff she could, and then I wiped off the rest. She looked like herself again without the makeup on.

"Could you play that song?" she asked, sniffing back a couple of times and trying to pull herself together.

"What song?" I asked. " 'Open Tuning'?"

She shook her head. "Uh-huh. I really kind of got to like it."

"Sure," I said. "For you, I'll do it. Now, come on. We better get in there and get you your Billy."

"Do I look all right?" she asked, patting her hair all over.

"You look wonderful," I said.

She hugged the baby and kissed it on the head for luck, and in we went.

*

Of course, by the time we got in there, Billy was long gone. He had seen Fagan come in first with his picture stuck on his forehead and asked him what the hell was going on. Fagan blurted out he didn't know, but there was some girl named Violet and a baby outside looking for him, and didn't he remember meeting him when they did that astral projection down to the submarine the week before? Before you could say *matrimony*, Billy and his sailor pals high-stepped it out the back door of Lady G's, leaving Rahu and Fagan with the call girls. By the time we got back to the table where Billy had been, Fagan was drinking what was left of Billy's beer and Rahu was sitting there laughing his head off as he pulled a thirty-foot string of magic silks out of Dad's tuxedo pocket. As for the girls Billy and the sailors had ditched, they already had their hands in Rahu's money bucket, so they were satisfied.

Violet and I ran back to the van as fast as we could, leaving Rahu and Fagan to find their own way home. We cruised all the side streets off Rosecrans Avenue but, of course, we couldn't find him anywhere. He and his buddies disappeared like water into sand. We even went back to the base where his submarine was, but as I could have predicted, nobody on duty had seen hide nor hair of him since he had gone ashore. Even though it was after hours, we bounced around from office to office on the base, trying to find a way to get to him, but every which way we turned, we got stonewalled. One thing about the Navy, they stick together, and when one sailor sees a girl with a baby come looking for another sailor, all of a sudden that sailor gets real stupid and doesn't know anything about anything. We parked the van outside the gate and saw lots of dead-drunk sailors stumble in, but Billy wasn't one of them. We hung around the whole next day and into the next night, but no sign of Billy. We got to be such a nuisance that the shore patrol finally came over and threatened to have us ticketed. So we drove away for a while and got cleaned up and got something to eat, and when we came back, Billy's sub was gone.

"Called up for emergency service," was all we got out of the duty officer.

"When will they be back?"

"No way to know."

So Violet cried all the way out to near Needles, which was where her brother Arzo lived.

"I had such plans!" Violet cried all the way through the desert. "Billy said he was gonna marry me and then I could have lived on base and talked with other service wives, and now all that's gone. I haven't got anything left, nothing at all."

I couldn't do much but watch her cry because she was right. Every few miles she'd pull herself together, but then, after a while, she'd hang her head down and her hair would fall over her face like a tent and tears would flow again and quickly evaporate in the dry heat of the desert.

To get to Arzo's was a day and a half's drive from San Diego, up Route 15 to 215, and then to Barstow, where we turned east and headed out Route 40. We asked some local police about where Arzo lived, and they rolled their eyes like they knew him pretty well and told us which dirt road to turn off to get to his shack. About the only way we could tell it was a road at all was that the sand was packed down into a two-track rut. By the time we passed between the black lava beds and the dried lakes and the craters and everything else that makes folks say the West is so beautiful, we were almost there. Then you passed an army base where they practiced for desert wars by using cruise missiles to blow up lizards. We saw a faded NAPA sign bleached by the sun and beyond that, out on the desert horizon, we saw a tarpaper shack with a little curl of woodsmoke coming up from it, and that was where Violet's brother Arzo lived.

Arzo Tansy was all I expected him to be—a stinking, greasy, scrawny little runt of a man about thirty years old who hadn't washed his stringy black hair since the last time it rained in the desert, which was about a thousand years ago to look at the land around his shack. He apparently didn't do much but drink, and when we got there at eleven in the morning, he already reeked of liquor. Outside the shack, he kept the rusted remains of an old pickup truck that looked like a carcass picked over by the buzzards.

"Where'd you get that?" Arzo asked, jerking his finger at the baby as we got out of the van. He was waiting for us at the door with a .357 Magnum hanging from his hand as if it was attached there. He must have been able to see us coming from a long way off, and since he probably didn't get much company out there in the desert, he was naturally suspicious.

"He's mine," Violet said.

"Figures," said Arzo.

Arzo flung open the door, which almost fell off the dry-rotted hinges, and let us into the shack where his wife was leaning over the woodstove, cooking. It was a hot day, hot enough to where you could feel your brains sizzling and popping inside your skull, but she had a wood fire going all the same because Arzo was the type of guy who would insist on a hot meal.

On the table sat a half-empty bottle of High Times Kentucky Bourbon, and Arzo set his gun down next to it. The pistol lay there on its side like a dog panting in the heat of the cabin. Arzo took a swig from the bottle and then picked up the gun again.

"Like that?" he asked me, stroking the barrel. His voice was slurred, his tongue thick as shoe leather. "I got me that gun up in Barstow a couple of weeks ago. Already killed me three snakes wif it."

He lifted it up over his head a while, pretending to squeeze off shots into the ceiling. "K-poo. K-poo." Then he let out a whoop as he knocked back another swallow of the liquor right from the bottle. His hairy Adam's apple bobbed as he gulped it.

"I'm Arzo fuckin' Tansy, last of the American cowboys!" he shouted, eyeing me suspiciously. "Who're you?"

"I'm Joe Findlay," I said. "And I brought you your sister and her baby because she said she didn't have anyplace else to go."

"Well, wha-hoo," said Arzo.

Then he pumped a single shot up through the roof of the place, and you could see the blue smoke swirling in the light the hole let in. In fact, you could see sky in five or six places up there, but it never rained in the desert, so it didn't make any difference. The baby started wailing when the gun went off, and that seemed to make the shack even smaller and hotter than it already was.

Arzo's wife served up some lunch. It was carrot mush, and I figured she got the recipe from Verna Mae or somebody else in the family. I never did find out the wife's name.

She hovered around the edges of the shack, clinging to the walls like a scared rat. At first I thought she was a deaf-mute, but then she mumbled something while she was serving up the carrot mush, and Arzo unleashed his arm quick as a rattlesnake. The flat of his hand hit her on the cheek, just enough to sting her bad. After that, she didn't say anything else. She held her cheek with her fingertips for a while and pouted until he asked her if she'd ever say it again, whatever it was she had said, and she silently shook her head.

I didn't see any tears in her eyes, though, and I figured it was only a matter of time before Arzo Tansy, last of the American cowboys, caught himself a faceful of hot grease from her frying pan or a head full of bullets from his prize Magnum one night while he slept.

It didn't seem like the kind of place to leave Violet, much less the baby.

"You want to keep your baby here?" I asked her as I climbed back into my van and got ready to go.

"They're kin," she shrugged.

"That good enough for you?"

She shrugged again.

I don't know why, but I thought then of the Munchee Mart ticket Rahu had given her back in Capistrano.

"You never did scratch that last ticket," I said. "It might be the swimming pool, you know. You may have won your dream house after all."

"A dream house doesn't mean anything if you haven't got somebody to share it with," she said.

I'd already sat down in the driver's seat and was looking at her out the window. It was hot as an oven inside the van.

"Well, I'm going now," I said.

"So go," she said.

"Right," I said and started up the engine. But I didn't pull away. I just let it idle there. "Well, I guess this is good-bye."

"Good-bye," she said.

"I'm gone."

"So go," she said, her face turning all red and angry, "Go. I don't want to see you any more. Get."

So I got.

Violet Tansy and her baby got smaller and smaller in the rearview mirror like they had that time before, back in Ohio when I had left them on the turnpike. Only this time I didn't turn around. I'd only known her for about two weeks, and I knew I'd forget about her sooner or later. She had her life to live out and I had mine. I was ready to hit the open road again, with no Violet and no baby. And no Hazel or Zak Bendzi, either. I wasn't going to puppet for any computer nerd. That much was clear.

About two hours of desert driving later, however, I saw a glint up ahead of me in the white-hot desert. I couldn't make out what it was for sure, but the light from it kept shining in my eyes and blinding me like arrows shot into my face. I held up my forearm in front of my eyes to try to block the light out, but it wasn't any use. The flashes kept coming right into me like sharp pieces of glass.

I couldn't imagine what it could be, but it wasn't moving, and when I was about half a mile away I thought I could see the figure of a man standing in the rippling road mirage where the light was coming from. Most likely a breakdown, I thought, a guy signaling with a mirror. I figured he probably wanted a lift to the nearest town, but I decided right there and then I wasn't picking up any more hitchhikers.

But as I got closer, I could see that there wasn't any car anywhere around. There was nothing but desert for miles and miles, as far as you could see, and the glinting light got brighter as I approached, until it almost seemed to outshine the desert sun, and I had to put down my visor and reach for a second pair of sunglasses because I was getting blinded by the shafts of light.

Pretty soon I couldn't see anything at all but this great big ball of light glowing right in the middle of the road, all white and red and yellow at once. It burned with an intense heat, like an oil well that's caught on fire, only there wasn't any smoke rising up, only rolling brightness and a savage incandescence.

Blinded, I slammed on my brakes and started to skid. I could feel the heat through the windshield and was afraid my tires would begin to melt.

As the van careened to a stop, I panicked and wondered if I had taken a wrong turn and ended up on the firing range. The military tests nuclear missiles out here, I thought. Maybe this is ground zero! And no more had I thought that than the white light seemed to engulf everything in front of me. In a screaming panic, I threw my arms over my head and dove beneath the dash, trying hard to curl up into a tiny ball like an armadillo. I lay there on the floor of the van with my eyes squeezed shut, expecting to hear a roar that would take me out in one flash, but there was nothing. I opened my eyes, and the light seemed less intense somehow, and, after what seemed like about four hours, I got up the courage to poke my head up and peek over the dashboard to see what was out there.

I almost wished it had been a nuclear bomb, but it wasn't. There in front of me, his white gown glowing in the hot desert sun, stood the angel of Iowa, as big as life. Gripped in both hands, he held a six-foot-long double-edged broadsword with flames flashing out at both sides like wild coyote tongues.

"Holy crapping shit," I whispered. He was like nothing I had ever seen before, an apparition right out of some terrible book. His blazing hair rose up on its ends, and his hands glowed around the hilt of that flaming sword. I remembered the visions my mother read to me from the Book of Revelations: *And in the midst of the seven candlesticks, one like unto the Son of man, clothed with a garment down to the foot, and girt about the paps with a golden girdle. His head and his hairs were white like wool, as white as snow; and his eyes were as a flame of fire; And his feet like unto fine brass, as if they burned in a furnace; and his voice as the sound of many waters. And he had in his right hand seven stars: and out of his mouth went a sharp two edged sword: and his countenance was as the sun shineth in his strength.*

I waited for something to happen. I pictured a fireball coming and exploding my van. I waited for the hot tongs and pincers, the devils and monsters and gargoyles to carry me away for all my sins. I half-expected my head to blow up like an exploded melon. But the Bird Boy didn't move or say one word. He glared at me with his fiery eyes.

I could hear my heart pounding. My hand shook as I opened the door of the van, and my legs felt like jelly beneath me as I stepped out on the skittle-hot roadway. The desert wind raised up swirls of golden dust around the Bird Boy's bare feet, and I saw they were not touching the earth. They floated about half an inch above the pavement without touching it at all. I pinched myself. This was no dream.

My mouth was as dry as the sand around us, but finally I found my voice.

"Um, is there something you want?" I croaked.

But the only sound that came back in reply was the luff of the flames from his burning sword. His eyes blazed holes in me until finally I had to turn away. Then he lifted up his sword, and the desert around us burst into bright orange flames.

CHAPTER EIGHT

About a month later, the moon hung bright above the desert like a pockmarked pearl, and the flatlands around glowed blue in the night and looked almost like the moon itself, with nothing for miles around in any direction but strange mesas and the shapes of hardened lava. Violet slept beside me as we drove, and the baby rested in a car seat in the back.

The moonlight played on Violet's face and painted a blue triangle on it through the window. Her head rocked back and forth a little as the van swayed in a crosswind, but she didn't wake up. There was nothing at all on the radio band, and it was as though she and I and the baby were the only ones left on the whole entire planet, as if the world had been blasted apart in a nuclear war, because all around us in the desert there were only the sorts of plants that might survive the bomb. Once in a while a chuckwalla darted out to the roadside, appeared in the headlights for a second, looked right and left, and then darted back into the sand. Other than that and us, there was no life anywhere else out there, and we were going a mile a minute through all of it, following that dotted white line in the middle of a road without any beginning or end.

And I got to thinking that would be okay, I mean if nothing else existed but just the three of us. That would be all right; it would be enough somehow. I had learned that, I guess, the day the angel stood in front of me in the desert with his flaming sword.

There we were, face to face, and I could feel the heat from the flames bursting up all around us. I thought he had come to kill me. I mean, what was I supposed to think, surrounded as we were by a ring of fire and him standing there right out of the end of days and looking at me as fierce as a burning tiger?

I didn't know what to say. I mean, what do you say to a six-foot angel with flaming wings standing in front of you with a fiery sword cocked back to slice your head off? I choked and groveled there on the roadbed for a while, trying to think of something to make him back off a little.

"Is it the guitar?" I finally stammered. "Do you want your guitar back?"

But he only stood with the desert wind blowing through his burning hair like I was supposed to know what to do without him telling me. So I smiled like a grinning idiot and very slowly moved toward the door of van, inching my way back the way you might if you were out in the woods and got confronted by a grizzly bear. When I got to the door, I reached back carefully and felt for the handle of the slider and pulled it open. The guitar case was right inside the door, and my plan was to get it out as gently as I could and set it on the road in front of him, as a kind of peace offering.

"I'm getting your guitar now," I said, keeping both eyes on the avenging angel's grim face and groping around with my hand. "It's a real nice guitar, and I'm glad you let me play on it and all. It was a real privilege, uh, sir or whatever, to play on it."

I took a deep breath, closed my eyes, and prayed he wouldn't slice my head off as I turned my back on him for the second or two it took to get the guitar case out of the van. He must have heard my prayer because my head was still on when I took the case out and lifted it up in both my hands, holding it out to him like a votive offering. Instead of taking the guitar, however, he pointed down at the highway with the tip of his flaming sword like he wanted me to lay it down there, so that's exactly what I did.

After I set the case down on the blacktop, I backed away a few feet so the guitar was between us, but the Bird Boy didn't move at all. He still stared at me as if he was waiting for me to make the next move, but how was I supposed to know what to do next? How was I supposed to know *anything* at that point? I hadn't ever run into an avenging angel before. For a minute I even wished I had been brought up Catholic or something because I'd heard somewhere they learned how to deal with this stuff in their catechism classes. But I never was brought up with any religion other than my mom's readings from the Gideon Bible, and nothing useful was coming back to me, so I guessed I would have to do the best I could in the way of improvising something right there on the spot.

I knelt down in the road and started to undo the latches on the guitar case. I intended to open it up and show him that the guitar was still in good shape, that I hadn't wrecked it or anything, but when I lifted up the lid of the case, I saw the guitar had changed.

Instead of the beautiful rose-covered instrument I was used to, there was now an old cracked wooden guitar inside with not one single flower anywhere on it. The face had gone totally blank. The wood was cracked and rotting. Wormholes peppered the sound board. The strings were rusted, and it looked like the glue holding the body together was about to give way. The thing just lay there, inert, broken, totally useless.

I started trembling uncontrollably on the roadway. This was deeper stuff than I had ever been in before, and I didn't dare look up to see the expression on the Bird Boy's face. My heart jumped up into my mouth, and I knew then that my life was over. All I could manage was to kneel there quivering, staring down at the bare wood of the guitar, and finally even that was too much, and I closed my eyes and lowered my head so that my neck was stretched out long enough for the Bird Boy to have a clear shot at it. I wanted it all to be over fast, with one clean swipe of the flaming sword, because it was only then that I finally realized the flowers on the old guitar didn't have anything at all to do with my playing music on it.

You see, when all those new flowers kept appearing on the sound board, I was thinking it had to do with "Open Tuning" being played on it again after the guitar had languished all those years in Grandpa Tolliver's closet, but as I knelt in front of the avenging angel, waiting for his flaming sword to come down, I realized the flowers bloomed only when I was with Violet Tansy, and when she was away, like when I tried to leave her at the bus station in Denver, the thorns began to grow, and now that she was at Arzo's and I had made up my mind that I would never see her again, they had all disappeared. It was Violet who had everything to do with the flowers on the guitar, and now that I had left her in the desert, the Bird Boy showed up looking to take my name.

With tears in my eyes, I looked up to beg some mercy, but the road in front of me was empty. There was nothing around me but heat waves, sand, the wind, and, above me, the hard blue shell of the sky. The Bird Boy was gone, and so was the ring of fire. They had vanished, disappeared when I wasn't looking, evaporated like rain in the desert.

Well, I wasn't so dumb that I didn't get the point, so I closed up the guitar case and turned my van around.

I won't say Violet wasn't happy to see me when I got back to Arzo's a couple of hours later. While I was gone, she had scratched off that last Munchee Mart Dream House ticket, the one Rahu had given her back at the mission, and, sure enough, it was the swimming pool. She had won her dream house. That was the good news. The bad news was that the contest date had expired the day before and it was too late to claim the prize. But that didn't really seem to bother her much as she loaded the baby and her stuff back into the van. In fact, she dumped all of her religious medals and lucky charms and even the unicorn powder in the desert behind Arzo's shack. She didn't believe in any of that anymore, she said, she only believed you had to find somebody to share your troubles with and if you could, you were about lucky enough.

I guess I had to agree.

One night when I was alone, a long time before I met Violet, I was riding through the high desert toward Albuquerque, the way we were doing that night. I was feeling lost and lonely when all of a sudden a Santa Fe freight train appeared right alongside me out of nowhere. My heart started racing because that train shocked the hell out of me when it pulled up way out of the darkness. One minute it wasn't there and the next minute it was. Out of nowhere it appeared, a long train, a five-engine jobber hooked up to a mile of cars and flying like thunder on the tracks beside the road, a long slithering snake of boxcars and flatcars and oilers burning through the dark desert night at about eighty miles an hour or more, clickety-clack.

And I said to myself, "Well, you're not alone anymore. Keep up with that train, see if you can." It was only me and the train in the whole night, and so I pushed down on the gas and kept up with it. Pretty soon we were flying along side by side, but there was no sense of moving at all because of the dark. It was like the train and I were the only two things out in space, keeping each other company in the emptiness between two galaxies.

The cab where the engineer sat was a lonely yellow square and I could see him staring ahead, all alone, into the thick black of the desert night along the endless track, traveling through the dark. The giant engines ate up the rail by the mile and spat it out the train's tail end. I opened up my window to hear the train better. The dull roar of the diesel motors was broken by the clacks of the wheels against the steel rail lines, clickety-clack, like tambourines, and, when I fell behind the engine once or twice, I saw sparks flying from the rails like a thousand million stars in space. God, it felt good for a minute to be flying into the night with the train, like we were the only two things left on earth, in the whole universe maybe, so I lay on my horn to let him know I was still with him, and it blew loud. Pretty soon the engineer heard me or saw me or something because he lay on his own horn, and there the two of us went down our two straight lines through the desert, our horns howling away into the night and spreading music all over the sky and all over the dark flat land around us like honey of some kind made of thistle flowers, tart and sweet and sharp and needly like a cactus, but warm as flannel at the same time. And we rode like that, laying on our horns and laughing until it seemed like our music filled the whole round sky above us and made the stars dance.

But then the Santa Fe tracks, for no particular reason, veered away from the road off into the desert just as quick as they had come up on it. The train disappeared into the night, and I was alone again.

Then I knew, maybe for the first time, most people run exactly like the train and me, on two tracks that never meet, and they make music together for a while before they split off and never see each other again, and it's all very sad.

Now Violet, the baby, and I were on our way to Albuquerque for an *Open Tuning* concert. The road crew and the band were in front of us and by the time we got there, the stage would be set up for sound checks.

After I had picked up Violet at Arzo's, we didn't have any place to go or anything to do, so I drove back to Las Vegas and ate crow. Hazel was more than willing to feed me. I agreed to be Zak Bendzi on the concert tour. During the month of rehearsals, Hazel and I realized that even though we needed each other for business purposes, we had grown too far apart to stay married anymore. Luckily we were in Las Vegas and, after letting our lawyers fight for a while so they'd feel they'd earned their fee, we signed the divorce papers and the *Open Tuning* contract on the same day. Violet and the baby and I bought a new van with my advance money and the back royalties from the CD and tape sales, and we lived in the van outside the old warehouse we'd rented for the concert rehearsals.

Dad was doing the special effects for the show. He was able to get his friend from the Follies to design me a set of wings with brilliant white feathers, just like the Bird Boy's, and after the band got the audience warmed up, the lights would go out and I'd start playing the guitar part of "Open Tuning" in the dark from up on a platform about forty feet above the stage. Then a single spot would shoot upon me playing alone, and after a few bars of "Open Tuning" I'd be lifted off with a flying harness attached to aircraft cable and the techies would lower me down to stage. The lasers would come up, and the band and I would go into a concert-length version of "Open Tuning" guaranteed to take the audience halfway to nirvana. Everyone chanted "Zak! Zak! Zak!" when I appeared, but that didn't bother me anymore. I knew who I was and that was all that mattered. Meanwhile, the *real* Zak Bendzi was underneath the stage, orchestrating all the heavy breathing and the whale noises on his computer, so he was happy, too.

For a backup band—I insisted on having some human beings on stage with me—we had hired some of the guys from the Dead Superstar Revue. It seemed the Revue was about to go belly up because there was so much competition from other dead-star revues around town. It was a question of supply and demand. I mean, how many dead Elvises does one city need, right? We also called up Rahu and Fagan and hired them to lead the chanting part of "Open Tuning," so they kept things lively on the road. The music Zak Bendzi digitalized wasn't that hard to learn, and the audiences ate it up when we road-tested the show. We even got Violet and the baby new T-shirts that said "*Open Tuning* World Tour." On the back they read, "I'm with the Band."

By the time we were ready to tour, Grandpa Tolliver's old guitar had vines and flowers and buds and blossoms bursting out all over it, and when we opened at a small outdoor concert in Flagstaff, it was covered with more roses than it had ever had. The thing positively glowed, and that night in Flagstaff as I got ready to play "Open Tuning" to a small audience of about two thousand at an outdoor stadium where they were having a New Age convention, I knew I had done the right thing because as I stood there on the platform in the dark ready to start the opening chords and fly down to the stage, I looked up at the sky and saw the Bird Boy again. The full moon was rising above the stadium and there, across the face of the big silver disk, I saw his silhouette hovering above the crowd where they couldn't see. No avenging angel now, he hovered there as a sign of peace and love, like the angels who sang "Goodwill to men" two thousand years ago. I reached up my hand and waved, and he waved back, and then he was gone.

I don't know why I was the one chosen to play "Open Tuning"—if you can call it being chosen—or why any of this stuff even happened to me, but it did, and I guess when you count it all together, I'm not really sorry any of it happened.

Sclapped and Snidely Whiplash were a smash success, of course, and even hit the front pages when their new guitarist, the one who got the gig I never got to audition for, had his hair burned off in a flashpot accident. Their sales went through the roof, but I wasn't jealous.

I had learned something along the way. I discovered there is real magic in the world, and it doesn't come from lucky charms or amulets or mantras, and it's not the kind that depends on a few wires or false bottoms or velvet bags. Real magic is what happens inside, between a man and a woman when the Fates step in and make them fall in love, and nobody can explain it. Nobody knows where this magic comes from when it arrives, and nobody knows where it went when it's gone, but while you've got it, it's nice to enjoy, it's nice to have, to hold it and to try to keep it from flying away.

Maybe that's what angels are for, I thought, to make sure we keep doing the right things. They're out there. You never know when they're going to show up, and you may go your whole life without seeing one, but it's good to know they're looking after things, playing their guitars. (You didn't think angels played harps anymore, did you?)

I'm not so sure these days that I was right about a lot of things I used to know were so. I've seen angels make the desert burn, and I've seen roses grow on an old guitar. I even got to like what Zak had done to "Open Tuning"—sort of. I could see how it changed people. As soon as I started to play it, I noticed people in the audience getting real mellowed out, and as I flew down from the rafters, I could see I was making people forget about their troubles for a while and I guess that was all right.

The tour was passing through Albuquerque, and then we would visit fifteen more cities in twenty days. It was like being a kid again, on the road nearly every day, coming into town, setting up the show, doing the show, striking the show, hitting the road, moving on. Once again, there was no place to call home. This was the only life I knew, after all. And the only one I loved.

Only this time it was different. I wasn't traveling alone anymore.

Violet turned in her sleep and mumbled something I couldn't understand. I was hurrying because I wanted to get to Albuquerque before dawn so she could see the city lying below us, glittering in the night.

Hitting Albuquerque at night was always one of my favorite things. You dropped down toward it from the high plateau you'd been riding on, and the lights of the city sparkled like a zillion stars below you, and I wanted to take her and the baby and me down into it like a plane landing, coming in from some far-off place. I thought she'd like that. I wanted her to be happy, her and the baby, too.

Oh yeah, about the baby: she finally decided what to call him. She named him Joe.

* * *

COLOPHON

The text of this book was set in Garamond. It was printed on acid-free paper, and smyth sewn for durability and reading comfort.